HATE TO
FAKE
IT
TO YOU

HATE TO FAKE IT TO YOU

Amanda Sellet

ST. MARTIN'S
GRIFFIN
NEW YORK

First published in the United States by St. Martin's Griffin,
an imprint of St. Martin's Publishing Group

HATE TO FAKE IT TO YOU. Copyright © 2024 by Amanda Sellet. All rights reserved.
Printed in the United States of America. For information, address St. Martin's
Publishing Group, 120 Broadway, New York, NY 10271.

www.stmartins.com

Design by Meryl Sussman Levavi

The Library of Congress Cataloging-in-Publication Data
is available upon request.

ISBN 978-1-250-90624-3 (trade paperback)
ISBN 978-1-250-90625-0 (ebook)

Our books may be purchased in bulk for promotional, educational, or business
use. Please contact your local bookseller or the Macmillan Corporate and
Premium Sales Department at 1-800-221-7945, extension 5442, or by email at
MacmillanSpecialMarkets@macmillan.com.

First Edition: 2024

1   3   5   7   9   10   8   6   4   2

For all the branches of the Howlett tree,
island and mainland.
Especially Aunt Kathy the Great: traveling
companion, lifestyle icon, and goat consultant.

Author's Note

Dear Readers,

This book is a comedy, and a romance, but it is also a love letter to a place—specifically, a stretch of land (and sea) on the North Shore of Oahu. My mother was born and raised there, and part of my family still lives on the island. Instead of high-rise hotels and tourist hot spots, childhood trips meant fresh papaya with a squeeze of lime, Pass-O-Guava juice, body surfing while dodging "blue bubble" stings, and cracking up over vintage Poi Dog sketch comedy.

Most of the locations in Hate to Fake It to You are real, though I changed a few identifying details to allow room for slapstick shenanigans. Those who know the area between Laie and Haleiwa will likely recognize the settings despite these fictional liberties. Other details are taken straight from life. Shout-out to my cousins Pohai and Kalanikau, fellow foodies and adventure guides whose expertise is woven into the story; Tutu Lua gets both her surname and skill at talking story from their mom, my auntie Margo.

Personal ties aside, this book is not intended as a definitive account of the history and culture of the islands. My hope was to conjure a sense of this incredible place I've been privileged to visit, and in doing so to share a taste of paradise with you.

Your fellow armchair traveler,

—Amanda Sellet

Chapter 1

lovelillibet I love holidays as much as the next gal, but here's my truth: it can be a struggle to put my personal stamp on a day defined by the expectations of others. Yes, I plan the menu, curate the tablescape, select the guests, and choose what to wear, but it's never entirely about me.

Instead of constantly stifling my need for self-expression, I started to wonder what it would look like if I had a celebration that was a true reflection of me and my tastes, down to the smallest detail.

Don't we all deserve a Me-mas once in a while?

This year, I invite you to join me in breaking free of the calendar and creating a new tradition. Pick your favorite season, a meaningful place, your best people. Or fly solo! You get to decide, because this is Me-mas, a tribute to the sacred *me* in each of us.

Own your joy. Honor yourself. Make it a Me-mas to remember.

Love, Lillibet

Image: Flickering votive candles and white orchids arranged in the shape of a heart on an antique mirror.

#songofmyself #memasmyselfandl #alwaysinseason #cultivatebliss

"My Me-mas morning," Libby narrated as she typed. Her fingers froze before frantically hitting the backspace key. "Maximizing my Me-mas." More deleting. "What Me-mas will mean for me is a time to Me-mas the crap out of—" she broke off with a groan.

If you repeated a word too many times, it started to sound fake. Not just odd ones like toboggan but the normal, everyday kind. Say "coffee" often enough and it turned into nonsense. Never mind something as inane as *Me-mas*.

It was too late to choose a different name for her made-up influencer's fake holiday. Anyway, that was part of the joke. Why stop at self-esteem when you could catapult all the way to self-worship? A one-woman cult of personality. Also Me-day sounded too much like a distress signal, and (despite her roommate's intense lobbying) My-ween was an obvious non-starter. Which left freaking Me-mas.

This was not the right headspace for what she needed to write. *Think serenity. Unlimited free time. Smugness.*

"Making the most of my Me-mas means starting the day with sunrise yoga, followed by a salt stone massage while Mr. L prepares a brunch of hibiscus Me-mosas and Crepes Lillibet. We'll eat on the lanai, lulled by the gentle sound of waves, and— Are you kidding me, dickheads?"

Forget wind chimes and murmuring surf. The only thing Libby could hear was the Pukui brothers blasting Adele on repeat while they worked on their car. This was hour five. "Rolling in the Deep" had shaken her out of bed; she'd lost count of the number of times she'd been *Hello*-ed since then. Emoting and power tools: the soundtrack of her life.

The bathroom door cracked open, revealing a sliver of her roommate's face: one dark eye and crimped black hair that skimmed her chin.

"Trouble in paradise?" Jean called over the sound of the faucet.

"I'm trying to finish this My Me-mas Is Better Than Yours caption." Libby stood, arching her stiff back. Finding like-new kitchen chairs on the curb had seemed like a major score until they tried sitting in them, at which point they understood the previous owners' decision to put them out with the trash.

Crossing to the window, she squinted at the grid of fences, clotheslines, and slivers of backyard. In her mind's eye, she tried to replace the actual scene with an idealized version. What would Lillibet see? An ocean view, obviously. A lush yet manicured garden. The fleet of employees to take care of it all so she didn't have to chip her perfect nails. She probably had a chef, too.

Maybe food would jump-start Libby's brain. She yanked open the fridge. "Did you eat all the Spam musubi?"

There was a garbled affirmative from the bathroom. Frowning, Libby shoved aside a jar of olives, sending a lone pimiento bobbing to the surface. If she wanted to do mustard shots, she was set. Otherwise, she was looking at a foil-wrapped pita— probably old enough to use as a shiv—and whatever was in this white box. She closed the door with her hip as she peeled back the lid.

"Hey, can I finish your sandwich?"

The water turned off as Jean opened the door. "It's not mine."

"Do I want to know?"

"Somebody ordered bar service, but they left most of it."

Libby stared at the teeth marks. Neither she nor Jean had ever been shy about bringing home free food from a job, but they usually drew the line at finishing things that had been inside a stranger's mouth.

"I was going to use it in a still life," Jean explained, joining Libby in the kitchen. Two narrow pink foam curlers wrapped her bangs to the hairline. "Old Master vibes but also kitsch."

"What is Lillibet supposed to say about a half-eaten sandwich?"

"That's the challenge, isn't it? But I'll find something else, if you're starving."

Libby hesitated. Desperate times and all. "Is it from last night?"

"No, but definitely this week." Jean's dark eyes fixed on a spot near the ceiling. "I think. Did you smell it?"

"Exactly what you want to hear about a cheese sandwich." Libby took a cautious sniff, immediately jerking her head away. She slapped the lid on and buried the box at the back of the refrigerator, closing the door to keep the stench from escaping.

The cherry on top of that moment of glam was the tickle of sensation that brushed Libby's toes. Grabbing the rubber sandal next to the trash can, Libby pounded the linoleum. She was pretty sure the massive roach laughed at her as it slipped under the door to safety.

"Did you get it?" Jean yelled.

Libby grunted. The splat would have been worse than the skittering. "How do we still have bugs when there's nothing to eat?"

"Maybe that's why it ran away?" Jean strolled back into the kitchen with her brows filled in and her lips lacquered a deep red. That level of eye-hand coordination was a source of endless amazement to Libby, who struggled to draw a recognizable smiley face.

"We should leave the sandwich out. See what happens."

"That would be cruel."

"You were going to let me eat it," Libby reminded her.

"It's good to give your immune system a workout. Didn't Lillibet say something about that once?"

It wasn't impossible. Lillibet was fluent in the language of dubious health advice.

Jean yanked open the warped silverware drawer, digging under the plastic-wrapped bundles of take-out utensils. "Here."

Libby accepted the generic granola bar with a defeated sigh, noting that the label didn't say anything about chocolate. Which was probably why it was still hanging around.

"What do you have so far?" Jean was already waking up the laptop, *hmm*ing as she read. "This is impressive." She looked up at Libby, whose entire body had gone on alert at the prospect of praise. "For a person who hates to be perceived three hundred and sixty days of the year, you are channeling some next-level narcissism." Jean scrolled down. "And the product placement is totally on point. Love the casual mention of your bespoke silk nap dress."

"I'm not sure that's something to be proud of."

"It shows range. You don't even own night pajamas, much less special daytime ones."

"More like *derangement.* Can you imagine if someone was like that in real life? What a nightmare." Libby winced as she took another bite of granola bar, feeling a molar with her tongue afterward to make sure she hadn't chipped the tooth. "Am I eating plywood?"

"Questions Lillibet never has to ask herself."

"Since her kitchen isn't a wasteland." Libby shuddered as she reached for the computer. "I need to wrap it up. A few words of wisdom."

Jean must have seen the struggle on Libby's face and decided to step in, as she sometimes did if Libby was taking too long to figure out what to order at a bar. *A gin and tonic for my tall friend.* It was possible Libby relied too much on Jean's bottomless well of decisiveness. "Talk about skin care. Lillibet is a slippery bitch."

"I kind of wanted to go deeper this time."

"That's what she said."

Libby ignored the rim shot Jean was tapping out on an invisible drum kit. Maybe it was the Adele marathon, but she was feeling a little maudlin about the state of her life. Taking pictures for *Love, Lillibet* was a side gig for Jean, part of the smorgasbord of art projects she collected like refrigerator magnets. A commission here, a random installation there, pop-up shows at bars and bookstores when she was in the mood. Chaos and uncertainty seemed to feed her creative energy, whereas they left Libby feeling . . . uncertain.

"It's pretty sad when the only thing you're good at is being a garbage person." She glanced at her roommate, not sure whether she wanted her to sympathize or disagree.

"You need to get some real food in you, Bitter Betty." Jean jerked her head at the door. "Come on. Let's go to Foodland."

"Did you get paid?"

"The check is allegedly in the mail. The logo I did for that kayak place."

"I should stay and finish this." Even if it wasn't her real name on the account, Libby wanted it to be good. Ridiculous, maybe, but still well written.

Jean handed Libby a reusable shopping bag. "Why deny yourself nice things? Channel your inner Lillibet."

"No thanks," Libby said, following her out the door.

The shortest route to the grocery store ran along Kamehameha Highway. The breeze that usually relieved the sticky warmth on this side of the island was no match for the asphalt and passing cars.

"It's hot," Libby complained, raising her voice so Jean could hear her above the hum of traffic.

"You gotta want it."

Easy for her to say. Libby suspected Jean had ice water in her veins. That was the only logical explanation for her lack of pit sweat.

"Remember when we had a car?"

"Do you remember what it smelled like?" Jean yelled without turning. "Everyone thought we were high, even when we weren't. Besides, it's not like White Lightning had AC. You'd still be sweating balls."

However much their car had sucked, not having one felt like a message from the universe. *You're going down!* Saying no to gigs that weren't on the bus line had quickly translated into fewer calls from the catering company, shrinking their paychecks even more.

Her thoughts full of tumbling dominoes and slippery slopes, Libby ignored the car pulling up alongside them until the familiar whine of the brakes tipped her off.

"What's going on?" Keoki yelled over the soft rock blasting from the radio.

Libby held up the shopping bag. "Foodland."

"You two are cooking?"

"Sure." Jean poked at the air. "Beep, beep, ding."

"Microwave," Libby translated.

Keoki reached across the seat to open the door. "Get in. I'm going to Tutu's house."

Libby's eyes met Jean's for an instant before they lunged toward the car, shoving each other out of the way.

"Shotgun," Jean grunted, throwing an elbow. Libby had the advantage of height, but her pocket-sized roommate wasn't afraid to fight dirty.

"It's my turn," she reminded Jean.

"Snooze, you lose, loser."

Behind them, someone honked. Libby gave in and climbed into the back.

"Careful," Keoki warned, sliding a small red-and-white cooler out of the way.

Libby tracked it like a dog watching a squirrel. "What's in there?"

"Profiteroles," he said, pulling onto the road with a one-handed spin of the steering wheel.

Jean waited until he glanced at her to work the big eyes and pouty lips.

"Forget it. You're not getting Tutu's profiteroles."

"You should be nice to us!" Jean folded her hands under her chin like a ceramic cherub. "We're having a bad day."

"Yeah, big bummer about Kalanikau's."

Libby leaned forward to poke Keoki in the shoulder. "What is?"

"You didn't hear? Bought out. A mainland company. They're going to make it a fancy place. Condos and all that."

That was . . . not good. The old family-run hotel was the main venue for the banquets and business lunches that accounted for half the shifts she and Jean picked up in an average month. Libby fell back against the seat.

Keoki sent her a worried look in the rearview mirror. "Why? What else happened?"

"Our rent's going up," Jean said.

This was also news to Libby. "Uh, since when?"

"Today. I saw Mr. Akina by the mailboxes. He needs to fix the roof, so." She pointed a finger upward.

"Dang," Keoki said. "That's rough."

"Why didn't you tell me?" Libby shoved the back of her roommate's seat. "We can't afford mini-quiches!"

"It's like a last hurrah. At least we can eat something good while we're looking for jobs. And probably a new place to live. Unless somebody wanted to *give* us something tasty. So we don't starve to death. On the streets. Like trash pandas. Who also have rabies."

"Okay." Keoki sighed, defeated. "You can have profiteroles."

"Can I also have some of your water?" Jean was already tipping the insulated bottle to her lips.

He held out his hand to make sure she didn't drink it all.

"Do you know about peecycling?" Jean asked when he had a mouthful of water.

Keoki choked. Liquid sloshed down the front of his shirt as he slammed the bottle back in the cup holder. "Why?"

"Because of the fertilizer shortage, people are collecting their piss and pouring it on fields. It has all the right nutrients."

"No," Keoki said. Libby understood that he meant it as a blanket denial: *No, we're not doing that. No, I don't want to hear more about it.*

"I'm not saying *we* should pee in jugs." Jean shook Keoki's water bottle as a visual aid. "It's for Lillibet. Doesn't that seem like something she'd get into? My body, my garden, I'm so green, la la la."

Libby needed to nip this in the bud. "I don't think urine fits Lillibet's brand."

"That's the genius of it." Jean twisted sideways, going into full sales mode. "We keep pushing the line farther out there until people are, like, *I guess it's time to shove this polished rock up my vajayjay and call it self-care.* Aren't you curious to see how far we can go?"

"Not in a gynecological direction." Libby paused. It was like wording wishes with a genie; you had to cut off all the loopholes. "Or anything pee-related."

"And no poop," Keoki added.

"You don't understand what it means to be avant-garde," Jean complained. "We're doing something punk rock. In your face."

"That's not actually what avant-garde means." Keoki had picked up a smattering of French phrases from his job at a fancy bistro in Waikiki, always delivered with zero attempt at an accent in his impossibly deep voice. *Beurre blanc. Croque monsieur. Amuse-bouche.* It sounded like he was talking about car parts. "And please don't mention your lady parts in front of my grandmother."

"Better get used to it, daddy-o. A couple months from now you're going to be pulling a slimy baby out of Cici's hoohah. It's going to be vagina this, vagina that, all the livelong day."

Keoki shook his head, but he couldn't suppress a smile. To say that he was excited about being a father was like calling the waves at Pounders a little rough. Five minutes after his girlfriend Cici found out she was pregnant, Keoki signed up for a class on prenatal massage and started researching car seats. He'd always given off major dad vibes, but until now it had largely been directed at keeping Libby and Jean out of trouble.

Libby figured she had a few more months to stamp out the tiny part of her that worried they were going to lose him completely to his new life. People grew up and had families. It was healthy and normal! Unless their development was stunted, and they wound up living like college students forever.

"I like *hoohah*." Keoki's deep voice made it sound like a cheer. "Think I can say that at Lamaze?"

"I will pay you money if you do."

"You have money? Thought you two lolos were broke." Keoki rubbed his fingers together. "Show me."

"She might have money later," Libby told him.

"Why are you both so literal?" Jean faced the window, as if she couldn't bear to look at their annoying faces. "I'm surrounded by doubters."

Gravel crunched under the tires as they turned onto Tutu Lua's driveway. The house in which Libby had spent a sizable chunk of her childhood was solid and square. Whitewashed cement block walls surrounded the lanai, where a rotating array of half-wild cats could be found napping in patches of sun. Tutu Lua relied on them to keep the rodents away from her prize mango tree.

Before they'd taken more than a handful of steps, the screen door slammed.

"My baby," Tutu Lua sang, holding her arms out to all six feet five inches and 350 pounds of Keoki. He and Libby were the tallest kids in their class all through elementary school, but where Libby was known as String Bean, Keoki had always been solid, like his Tongan and Samoan ancestors.

She stepped back, poking him in the belly. "Which one's hapai, you or Cici?"

"Seriously, Tutu?" Keoki rubbed his stomach as his grandmother cackled.

"Can I have her cream puffs?" Jean whispered.

Tutu Lua grabbed the handle of the cooler, waving an admonishing finger as she headed back into the shade of the breezeway.

Libby detoured into the house to grab plates and forks. She could walk into this kitchen after twenty years away and still know where everything was stored. Not that she was likely to be going anywhere, if her current lack of momentum was any indication.

When everyone was seated around the outdoor table with a profiterole in front of them, Tutu Lua turned to Libby. "Still no boyfriend?"

"Since last weekend? No." Unless you counted the guy who tried to tip her with his phone number while she was passing out sandwiches at a business lunch.

"You need a man to cook for you." Tutu made it sound like a basic necessity, up there with a roof over your head.

"Hashtag goals," Jean agreed, nudging her plate in Tutu's direction. "How come you never ask me if I have a boyfriend?"

"Because I know you, Trouble. And Trouble makes its own bed."

"See? Tutu understands me," Jean told the other two.

"How's the writing?" Tutu asked Libby, as Keoki got up to make coffee. "Almost done with my story?"

"I'm working on it." She waved a fly away from her face. Maybe they were attracted to the scent of lies.

In some nebulous future when she wasn't busing tables and inventing skin-care regimens, Libby aspired to be a serious journalist, the kind who crafted deep, incisive profiles that captured the story of a life in paper and ink. Tutu had volunteered to be a test subject, sitting for hours of "interviews" that bore a strong resemblance to her usual post-meal storytelling sessions.

It seemed like a good idea at the time—Tutu was a colorful character, and Libby had unlimited access—but the pressure of getting it right was even heavier when you knew and loved the person you were writing about.

"She's working it to death," Jean corrected. "It's already great."

Libby frowned at her. "You read it?"

"I figured you'd freak out if you knew, so I waited until you were in the shower."

"Uh, thanks?" By Jean's standards, that was surprisingly sensitive.

"You're welcome. Now quit screwing around and send it off."

Tutu nodded. "You need a push, baby girl. Can't stand on the edge forever. Going to have to take that jump."

Libby mentally supplied the crash-and-burn sound effects.

"It has to be perfect. I don't want to blow it." That probably sounded like an excuse, but trying to break into the industry as a freelancer with no connections and a résumé heavy on food service had made Libby an expert on rejection. "I want people to see the real you, Tutu."

"Eh." Tutu fanned herself. The breeze had died down, and the heat was clinging. "I know you'll make me look good. Sunday version, with my lipstick on."

"You always look good," Keoki said, dodging the fly swatter Jean aimed at his head.

"Thank you, baby." His grandmother patted his cheek, frowning as she pulled her hand away. "You're sweating."

"I had two fans on last night and I still couldn't sleep. Me and Cici had to get up and eat ice cream."

"Ew." Jean stuck her tongue out at him. "TMI."

Keoki shook his head while his grandmother belly-laughed.

"Don't worry," Tutu Lua told him, wiping her eyes. "Cold front's coming. They got a big blizzard on the mainland. I saw it on the Weather Channel."

That probably meant the daily high would drop from eighty-two to seventy-eight. Still, it was strange to think that a phenomenon as foreign as a snowstorm—in May!—could touch Libby's life.

Jean stacked the plates with the efficiency of a person who'd started waiting tables before she could drive, toeing the door open on her way into the house. Libby shifted to peel her thighs off the seat, angling her arms away from her body to reduce the sweat. Maybe they could walk over to the beach after this, to wash away the funk of the day.

"Uh, Libby," Jean called from inside. "Can you come here a second?"

In the living room, her roommate was staring at the television, where a reporter in a fur-lined parka strained to make himself heard over howling winds, against a backdrop of pure white.

"The girl they're talking about." Jean's voice was tight. "What did they say her name is?"

Libby squinted at the headlines crawling across the bottom of the screen. ROAD TO NOWHERE: EYEWITNESS DESCRIBES "TERRIFYING" WHITEOUT. SORORITY CAR WASH SUPPORTS MISSING COED: PICTURES AT 11. HAVE YOU SEEN HILDY? CALL THE 24-HOUR TIPLINE!

And finally: MEDIA HEIRESS HILDY JOHNSON MISSING IN WYOMING SNOWSTORM.

"Hildy Johnson," Libby said. "I take it she's one of *the* Johnsons?"

"You've heard of them?"

"Johnson Media? Yeah. I live on a rock, not under one."

"So they're a big deal?"

"One of the biggest." Maybe not a household name unless you were an aspiring journalist, in which case their presence was inescapable. The parent company owned outlets in hundreds of markets: print, TV, online, probably soon-to-be beaming directly into people's brains.

Jean grabbed the remote, turning up the volume as a series of still photos filled the screen: a young woman with corkscrew curls in a strapless velvet gown; wearing sunglasses on the deck of a yacht; standing on a trail with crumbling stone ruins in the background. The broadcast cut back to the guy in the heavy coat, who was waving his arms as he described how very terribly horrible the conditions were. Zero visibility, horizontal winds, a rate of accumulation that meant nothing to Libby until she imagined it as the kind of rain that would flood the low-lying streets.

"I have chills." Jean stuck out her arm as evidence. "Hildy Johnson is a real person."

"Yes," Libby said slowly. "She's a human being, like you and me." She and Keoki did their best to encourage Jean's occasional twinges of empathy.

Jean blew out a long breath. "I think I might have messed up."

"Unless you have some power over the weather I don't know about, I'm pretty sure this isn't your fault?"

On-screen, News Man was going full apocalyptic. *Darkness! Falling temperatures! Hypothermia!* That was the problem with breaking news: the pressure to sensationalize. How else were you supposed to churn out headlines when there was nothing new to tell? At least with Lillibet, there was a bottomless pit of self-obsessed-but-pretending-not-to-be babble to be mined.

Jean grimaced. "I hope she didn't lose her phone."

"Probably not the worst-case scenario here." Libby watched her roommate frantically tap out a text. "What are you doing?"

"Might have something cooking."

"Food?"

"No, one-track mind. A job."

"Really? What is it?"

"I'll let you know if it pans out." Jean shoved the phone back in her pocket. "Let's ask K if he'll drive us to the Laundromat. If this comes together, you're going to need clean undies."

"How did you know I'm out of underwear?"

"Because you're wearing them inside out."

"Maybe I put them on wrong."

"Yeah. Two days ago."

Rude, but sadly not untrue. "I wonder what it would be like to have actual privacy."

"You can ask Blizzard Girl. If she survives her alone time."

"Okay, Grim Reaper. I'll give her a call. I'm sure she'll be thrilled to hear from me."

Jean elbowed her, hard. "You could interview her!"

"Because they'll definitely give that story to a rando from Oahu whose biggest byline is from a free community newspaper."

"Want to bet?"

Libby ignored her roommate's outstretched hand. "No way, no how."

And not only because Jean was a notorious cheat. Why gamble when you had zero chance of winning?

Chapter 2

> **lovelillibet** There are so many areas in life where we can either accept the average or seek our own extraordinary. Take ice, for example. Are you settling for the same square edges as everyone else, or do you challenge yourself to explore the full spectrum of frozen expression? Crushed, shaved, craft, etched, infused: there's an entire world of cold waiting if you're willing to push beyond the basic.
>
> Love, Lillibet
>
> Image: An ice sculpture depicting a swan embracing a naked woman.
>
> #neversettle #chillvibes #amateurmixologist #bemoreseemore

The scene was a Christmas card come to life: vanilla-frosted slopes and inky fir trees as far as the eye could see. Stick it in a frame and every gallery-crawling tourist would get a whiff of pine boughs and crisp mountain air. No need to tell them it had been taken in May.

A splash of auburn trotted into the picture. Jefferson's four-hundred-millimeter lens picked up every glint of copper and rust threaded through the vixen's fur.

"What's a high-class dame like you doing in a joint like this?" The words emerged as frosty puffs, a reminder that he was talking to himself.

Like an antisocial loner, said the memory of Genevieve's voice. As if there were another type of loner who loved crowds.

And yes, sometimes Jefferson spoke to animals, but it didn't mean he preferred them to people (another of Gen's accusations) or had forgotten how to be civilized (because he never posted pictures of her on Instagram). He happened to like the quiet of open spaces, and the what-you-see-is-what-you-get behavior of wild animals. It was a lot harder to lie when your actions did the talking.

Speaking of which: A male fox was creeping into view. It looked like he was psyching himself up to shoot his shot, which meant Jefferson needed to be ready to do the same. He adjusted the exposure to compensate for the bleached brightness of the snow as Mr. Fox circled the vixen, hopping and kicking like a rodeo bronco.

The female settled onto her belly, head resting on her paws in an attitude of deep boredom.

"Could be worse," Jefferson murmured into the fleece bala-clava he'd pulled over the lower half of his face. "At least he doesn't wear purple leggings." And strut around behind a plate-glass window all day waving his oversized knives while his Edgelord 101 playlist shook the walls. To choose an example at random.

"Is that supposed to be a martial art?" Jefferson had asked Genevieve the first time she insisted on stopping to watch Crispin the Artisan do his thing. If that was even his real name. It sounded as made-up as his job title. What the hell was an ex-periential butcher?

"He's doing capoeira," she'd hissed, as if Jefferson was eating his soup with the butter knife. It didn't occur to him to ask how she knew, any more than he'd questioned Gen suddenly sprin-kling words like bavette into casual conversation.

Lesson learned: Some females preferred a flashy mate. Which was why Jefferson was out here in the cold, trying to capital-ize on the soft shadows of an overcast sky instead of hunker-ing down ahead of the storm. The weather had started off mild enough by Mountain West standards, but the temperature was dropping fast.

A dozen yards away, the foxes were stalking something, a silent glide across the surface of the snow. Not a new romance, then, but an established pair, probably with a den nearby. No sad bachelor pad for Mr. Fox. They must be hunting to feed a litter of kits. Jefferson felt the buzz in his blood that told him he was on to something. Fat white flakes sifted down from the sky. If he could get a shot of one of them mid-leap, it would be worth the chill in his fingers.

Almost.

Wait for it . . .

A squawk of static pierced the silence. Jefferson lunged for his backpack, but it was too late. With a last look at the paw prints that were all that remained of the foxes, he radioed back.

"Jefferson Jones."

"It's Nate, at Jenny Lake station. We have a problem."

The snow fell hard and fast, like someone had gotten tired of shaking out a few sprinkles at a time and decided to take the lid off the jar and dump the whole thing. The spring storm didn't care that it wasn't supposed to arrive until after midnight, or that the worst of the weather had been forecast to hit a hundred miles to the north. Jefferson was no meteorologist, but he had eyes— even though he could barely see his gloved hand at the end of his arm. The blizzard was here in full force.

He should have been in his truck by now, inching back to town, but an out-of-towner with more vacation time than brains had chosen today to head for one of the backcountry yurts. Which meant they were hiking across miles of snow-packed terrain alone—and not responding to calls on the number they'd left with the rental agency.

It wasn't unusual for a few yahoos to hear "major storm" and think "fresh powder," but that type usually traveled in groups. Jefferson wasn't sure what kind of person shelled out hundreds of bucks to sleep in a glorified tent with a pit toilet in the middle of a whiteout. All the ranger station had been able to pass on was that their missing person was from California (always a bad sign) and had given their name as H. Johnson.

If H. Johnson wasn't in trouble now, they would be soon, with the windchill well below zero and snow piling up fast. It was the kind of thoughtless stunt that put the lives of search-and-rescue teams at risk every year. Only this time every available park employee was scrambling to divert traffic back to Jackson, and Nate's team had been about to head out in search of a party of lost snowmobilers, leaving Jefferson closest to the missing party's probable location.

On minute ten of the final fifteen he'd allotted before turning back, he spotted a patch of neon-yellow on the slope ahead. As he waded uphill, forcing himself not to run, Jefferson was relieved to discover it wasn't a body. H. Johnson (he presumed) had tucked a sleeping bag under a fallen tree. The trunk was spindly and cracked, probably the result of tumbling down the mountain from wherever it had sprouted from the ground. Nothing was growing here.

The lack of vegetation, the steep angle, the weather pattern over the last twenty-four hours: Jefferson tallied it all up and didn't like the result. A rapid melt followed by a sudden drop in temperature and major accumulation was the classic recipe for avalanche conditions. Maybe his nerves were shot from worrying he wouldn't find H. Johnson in time, but the closer Jefferson got, the louder his instincts screamed, *Danger*.

"Hello," he called out. "Can you hear me?" The wind swelled, carrying the words away. Jefferson reached for the edge of the sleeping bag.

He felt the sting before he registered the canister aimed at his face. Jefferson was already twisting sideways when the force of a full-body collision sent him flying backward into the snow. They rolled a few times before he managed to throw off his attacker, mostly so the stranger would stop screaming in his face. Slipping off his backpack, he sat up, raising both hands to show he meant no harm.

"Are you H. Johnson?"

"Maybe." She tested her weight, like she was getting ready to bolt. *Good luck with that,* Jefferson thought. It would be like running through waist-deep oatmeal. "Who are you?"

He brushed the snow off the top of his head. "Jefferson Jones. Search-and-rescue."

"Oh." She relaxed her stance. "Sorry about the bear spray."

"It wasn't a direct hit." Though his eyes were still burning. Jefferson used a handful of snow to try to clean off the residue.

"You scared the bejeezus out of me."

He held up a hand for silence. The wind had died down, and he wanted to make sure the yelling and crashing around hadn't destabilized the snowpack.

A beat of silence, and then another. Maybe they were okay. He willed his heart rate to slow, but his body was still keyed up, almost as if . . .

Whomp.

Faster than thought, he was up and grabbing the woman by the sleeve. "Go," he yelled, shoving her ahead of him.

Chapter 3

"Stop it," Libby groaned, dodging the bony finger poking her in the ribs.

"No," said Jean's voice, because no one else could possibly be this annoying. "Time to wake up. We have places to go and people to see."

"We do not. No jobs, no money." At least sleep was free. Libby rolled to face the wall. She might have drifted off again if her roommate hadn't started slamming the drawers of Libby's dresser. "Unless we got called in?"

"You could say that."

It was the tone that tipped Libby off more than the words. There was a lot of intent there—or rather, portent. Ice trickled under her skin, snapping her to full alertness. Shoving the sheet aside, Libby struggled upright. "What did you do?"

Jean made a show of checking over both shoulders. "*Moi?*"

Oh yeah. Something was up. Jean's MO had always been, *When in doubt, double down.* They stared at each other, locked in a telepathic battle of wills.

You know I don't like surprises, Libby thought at Jean.

But if I tell you ahead of time, you'll say no, her roommate frowned back at her.

A knock sounded on the front door.

"Everybody ready?" Keoki called from the living room.

"Slugworth is still in bed," Jean yelled back. She clapped her hands at Libby. "Time is money."

"Am I having a nightmare?" Libby asked the ceiling of her room. She staggered to her feet, rubbing the sleep from her eyes as she walked into the kitchen.

Keoki greeted her with a hug. "Big day."

"Is it?" Libby got a glass from the cupboard.

"You didn't tell her?"

"I was just about to," Jean hissed. "Hey, Libs."

"Hey," she replied warily, sipping lukewarm water while her roommate unleashed a grin worthy of the cheap cosmetics "brand ambassador" Libby's mother had once invited to a "party" that involved shaking down your "friends" so you could get a free lipstick.

"You remember that freak blizzard in Utah or Idaho or whatever?"

"I guess."

"And that girl who got lost in the mountains?"

"My short-term memory isn't that bad."

"Well, it turns out she didn't freeze to death!"

"Oh." That was a twist. Most of Jean's anecdotes tended toward the macabre. "Good."

Keoki nodded agreement.

"And do you want to know *why* it's good?" Jean continued, like she was hosting a children's TV show.

"Um, because she's a human being and we're not sociopaths?" Libby guessed.

"Nope." Jean rummaged through the piles of stuff on the kitchen counter they were absolutely going to put away any day now, once they got some of those cute canvas baskets. Or fancy plastic tubs. Whatever adults used to organize their junk.

"Check this out." She held up her phone. The video on the screen cut from a worried newscaster in a painted-on purple dress to grainy footage of a man in heavy winter gear trudging toward the camera through hip-deep snow. In his arms he cradled a smaller person, face tucked protectively against his chest. On the choppy audio a voice shouted until the one being carried lifted her head. Her hood fell back, revealing a riot of dark curls that gleamed in the beam of sunlight that broke through the clouds at that precise moment, making the snow sparkle like a blanket of crushed diamonds.

It was like a scene from a movie. Even the weather was perfectly choreographed. "Wow," Libby said, inadequately.

"I know." Jean started to set her phone down, but Libby held on, rewinding the video.

"Who's that? The guy, I mean."

"Some dude. He found her out there in Butt Lick, Nowhere. They survived a freaking avalanche *and* a night in the wilderness. Hashtag Iceman Cometh."

Libby tore her eyes from the screen in time to catch her friend's suggestive brow wiggle. "What?"

"More like *strip* search and rescue. A little ice planet action, if you know what I mean."

Keoki stuck his fingers in his ears, humming under his breath. Bedroom talk was where he generally checked out of the conversation. *It would be like finding your little sister's sex toys,* he'd once explained. *Instant brain bleed.*

"That is not what I was thinking." Libby replayed the part where the Iceman, for lack of a better name, hoisted the girl above the sea of white. "She got lucky."

"I'll say."

"That he *found* her. And they didn't die."

Jean waved this off, as if their survival were a footnote. "Guess who the really lucky one is."

"Um," Libby said, after a prolonged silence. "I got nothing."

Jean stuck the phone in Libby's face. "Say hello to your new best friend."

"Are you breaking up with me?"

"Fun fact about the errant heiress. She *loves* Lillibet."

Keoki gave a double thumbs-up, which Libby took to mean either *congrats* or *true story.* Sometimes when Jean built up a head of steam, the line between fact and sales pitch blurred.

"There's no way." Clearly it was up to Libby to be the voice of reason. "How does she even know we exist?"

"For your information, we're up to like quadruple digits. Followers," Jean clarified, though what Libby had really been puzzling over was the math.

Were there seriously more than a thousand people reading *Love, Lillibet*? Or at least scrolling past the pictures and maybe the first sentence of her captions? Jean had pointed out before that more followers would mean the potential for profit, or at least some free merch, but the last thing Libby wanted was to monetize that stupid account. You couldn't call yourself a fake influencer if you were making real money. Her squeamishness on that front was the number one reason Jean handled all the admin, leaving Libby free to focus on making up words. A close second was Libby's inability to remember passwords (or find the scraps of paper on which she'd jotted them down).

"We had a moment with that post about our day in Waimānalo," Jean continued, mistaking Libby's continued silence for disbelief.

"You mean the petting zoo? Where I allegedly donated four dozen imported boar-bristle brushes to groom the animals?"

"What can I say? There's a sucker born every minute. Also, the algorithm loves baby goats."

"Because they're the GOAT." Keoki held up both palms, a high one for Libby and a low one for Jean.

"To be fair, I also assumed we were being catfished the first time she reached out," Jean admitted, shaking off the impact of Keoki's high five. "She was all, *Hey, great post, I might have an opportunity for you,* and I was like, *Sure, bottom feeder, here's my bank account number.* But then all that winter wonderland business went down, and I realized she wasn't a spammer."

"Which post was it?" It was a ridiculous thing to care about, but Libby couldn't help herself.

"The one about foraging for pumice stones and how we should also be conscious of our 'soul calluses.' Classic Lillibet. 'I'm more evolved than you and I never forget to exfoliate.' "

It *was* vintage Lillibet. Pretending to care about deeper things but mostly talking about her beauty routine.

"The important part of this story is that Lillibet's number one fan did not freeze to death after all, so I was able to reach out."

"Why?"

"Um, she's majorly connected and could make all your dreams come true? And we're not exactly setting the world on fire, career-wise?"

Libby shook her head. "I mean, why is she a fan?"

"Because Lillibet is totally of the moment, aesthetically *and* spiritually. Finger on the pulse of the zeitgeist. Those are exact quotes, by the way. More or less."

"You mean the Lillibet we invented?"

"Yes!" Jean had either willfully misunderstood Libby's sarcasm or was too caught up in her own spin cycle to care. "I told you it was destiny."

"More like drunkenness." All because a particularly rollicking retirement party had tipped them in leftover wine. There should be a sobriety test before they let you use social media.

Not that the wine was entirely to blame. The prospect of a more creative side hustle than selling ice-cold coconuts to tourists had short-circuited Libby's sense of caution. Being "Lillibet" let her pretend that waiting tables was a temporary state. Even if the persona was only one-third her, since Keoki came up with the food content and Jean handled the visuals. Still, churning out insufferable captions was a kind of writing.

Jean punched her in the arm. "This is your big break."

It was like biting into a poisoned cookie: the mindless rush of excitement, with an aftertaste of horror. "How do you figure?"

"Why else would she be coming here?"

"Here as in *here*?" Libby looked around their dingy apartment. Surely the poor girl had suffered enough.

Jean pulled up another video clip. A radiant Hildy Johnson (helpfully captioned "Snowbound So-Cal Socialite," as if she were a contestant on *The Bachelor* and that was an actual job) addressed a room full of reporters. She was pretty enough for TV, with a halo of dark curls and sparkling brown eyes.

"Is that him?" Libby asked Jean, pointing at a man in a suit seated next to Hildy.

"Who?"

"The one who saved her."

"Yeah, no. That'll be some kind of handler. Lawyer, maybe. I don't think this dude has ever walked on anything that wasn't paved."

The phantom weight of disappointment lifted. The real hero

could still be closer to Libby's imaginary version. Younger. A little raw—or at least less slick. Especially in the hair department.

On the tiny screen, reporters shouted questions. Had Hildy heard there were two different TV movies in the works about her ordeal? What really happened in that snow fort? Did the power of love keep them warm? Where was her rescuer now? Was it true he'd lost a toe to frostbite?

Hildy handled them like a pro, deflecting with a coyness that stopped shy of being cutesy. "He saved my life," she reminded them. "I'm not going to throw him to the wolves. If you want the inside scoop, you can read all about it—in a Johnson Media exclusive." A pause, while she flicked her hair over her shoulder, flashing a perfect dimple. "But I can assure you all of his *appendages* are fine."

Laughter and a volley of camera flashes rippled across the press corps.

"Saucy," Keoki rumbled.

"I guess she didn't need the handler after all." Libby watched the suit sitting next to the rescued girl try to interject something about the sizable donation her uncle's company had made to local search-and-rescue groups.

"Yeah, well." Jean sniffed. "She probably went to a fancy Swiss boarding school."

"I thought that was about walking with a book on your head. Never crossing your legs in a skirt."

"You're thinking of *The Princess Diaries*. The spawn of oligarchs all get media training nowadays."

"Ah." Libby accepted this as gospel, though she wasn't sure thinly veiled dick jokes would have been on the finishing school curriculum. Jean had always been far more conversant with the quirks of the one percent.

On-screen, things were wrapping up. "What's next for you, Hildy?" a reporter called out as she started to rise.

"Let's just say I'm going someplace nice and warm. With a special someone."

"No more questions," her companion announced.

"Is she talking about the guy who saved her?" Libby asked as a new video started playing.

"Backcountry Beefcake? Probably. But that's not the main takeaway here." Setting down her phone, Jean wrapped her hands around Libby's upper arms, punctuating each word with a shake. "This. Is. It. Opportunity with a capital *O*. The fact that she almost bit it the week before Me-mas is like the universe sliding into your DMs. *Hey, girl, ready to say hello to your destiny? Because she is on her way to meet you.*"

"You mean Lillibet. Who I am not."

"You know that and I know that, but *she* doesn't."

"Pretty sure it's going to come up."

"Not if we play our cards right."

Uh-oh. Libby had seen that demented gleam in her roommate's eyes before. "What does that mean?"

"All we need to do is pretend. It's a couple of days, totally manageable. Fake it till we make it."

"You mean all we have to do is lie."

"Potato, potahto. I'm not going to cry for the poor little rich girl. She probably wears fur."

"Jean. It'll never work. I'm like the anti-Lillibet. I can't cook, I know diddly about yoga, and I don't speak in inspirational slogans. Also, in case you haven't noticed, we live in squalor."

"It's taken care of."

Libby froze as if a brick wall had materialized inches from her face. "What is?"

"We found the perfect spot." Jean linked her arm through Keoki's. "Some guy K knows from the restaurant. The most incredible house. It's so Lillibet. You're going to wet yourself when you see it. Although I guess not, since Lillibet is the queen of Kegels."

"Please never say that out loud again." Libby might as well have waved a red flag in front of a bull.

"She works that pelvic floor like ... a loaf of homemade rye. Something-something sauerkraut fermenting, harness the power of your gut biome?"

Keoki was too traumatized to protest, so Libby spoke for both of them. "Step away from the metaphor."

"Fine. The point is that the stage is set. Still working on the goats, but how hard can it be?"

"One of our suppliers makes his own chèvre," Keoki volunteered, earning a slap on the back from Jean.

"See? It's all happening."

"Slow down. Rewind. What's this about a house? I thought this was supposed to be a work thing."

"That girl almost *died,* Libby. But through the darkest hours of the night, she held on to a dream." Jean pressed her hands to her heart. "A dream of meeting a hot yoga wife with money to burn who isn't afraid to tell other people how to live."

"Seriously?"

"Wouldn't you want a tropical vacay after almost freezing your nads off? Besides, it's like they say. The end justifies the means."

"You do realize that's not a motivational quote?" Libby summoned her best for-real-this-time expression. "Give it to me straight. Is she coming here for Lillibet or mai tais by the pool?"

"It's a package deal," Jean said with the pseudo-casual air of someone who didn't want to discuss the fine print. "Enjoy some sun and surf, stage a bunch of photo ops with the guy who saved your life—"

"So that is who she's bringing?"

"Who cares? The important part is your future boss."

Libby wouldn't have minded talking about Mr. Wilderness a little more if her world wasn't on fire. "But they don't even know me. I mean *her.*"

"You did say you prided yourself on always being ready to welcome unexpected guests. And with the way you talked up Me-mas, who could resist?"

"I guess I should have been more careful about our *imaginary character* talking out her ass about her hostessing mojo. Or her nonexistent holiday!"

"I told you. It's all good. K has a whole menu planned."

"He gave me carte blanche," Keoki said.

Usually Libby appreciated his mellow vibe as a counterweight to Jean's manic energy, but right now it grated on her nerves. "Who?"

"Mr. L. One of our regulars. I talked to him about Keoki's Kitchen. He might be willing to invest."

"Really?" For a second Libby forgot about the rest of the mess. "Tutu will be so pumped." Especially since she was the one who'd taught Keoki to cook. And unironically love cheesy pop music, but that was more of a mixed blessing.

"It's not a done deal. That's part of why he's letting us use his house. This is like an audition. A chance to show him what I can do."

"This?" Libby asked, hoping the answer wasn't, *This disaster waiting to happen. The Lillibet fiasco. Impending doom, on a silver platter.* "What about work?"

"I had some time off coming."

Libby might have been taken in by Keoki's breezy delivery if she didn't know what a hard-ass Jacques was about vacation. "Please tell me you're not using your paternity leave."

"It's okay, because I'll be my own boss by then." He smiled like this was the most logical plan ever, instead of a horrifying new layer of catastrophe.

"What about my make-believe husband?" Libby demanded, trying to slow this runaway train. "Is that also magically falling into place?"

Jean waved this off. "Worst-case scenario, we say he's away on business."

"Lillibet's husband is skipping out on Me-mas? What kind of douche do you think I fake-married?"

"I might have a line on that, actually."

Libby rounded on Keoki. "What, you went to the Husbands-4-Less sale at Longs Drugs?"

"Whoa, there." Jean tugged her by the belt loop. "You need to keep your eyes on the prize."

"Humiliating ourselves in front of strangers?" One of whom happened to be a real-life hero. Libby couldn't imagine the kind of guy who stoically rescued people from a snowy death ever doing something this shady.

"If we pull this off, you could have *one* job. Just one." Jean narrowed her eyes at Libby, making sure she appreciated the enormity of the stakes. "That pays all the bills. And doesn't involve touching other people's food." She glanced at Keoki. "No offense."

"You have your art, I have mine," he said philosophically.

"And Libby has hers," Jean concluded, as if that tied a bow on the whole conversation.

"I hope you're not talking about Lillibet. Because I don't think pretending to be the world's biggest phony counts."

"You're a great writer, Libs. They'd be lucky to have you. If this is how you get a foot in the door, so be it."

"Except the number one job qualification for a journalist is *telling the truth*. Which this is not."

"It's satire. Performance art. That's a totally separate category. I'm sure she'll understand. Eventually. Besides, that ship has sailed. Although it's more like 'that plane is about to take off.' " Jean squinted at the clock on the stove, which only ever showed the time as noon—or midnight, depending on your perspective. "We have less than twenty-four hours to get our Lillibet on."

"You're kidding."

"Come on, Libs. Buck up. This is going to be our most amazing adventure yet! It's too late for second thoughts."

"These are my first thoughts, though."

"What I'm saying is we don't have time for regrets, *Lillibet.* What's the one thing you never want to do on a waterslide?"

"Oh, so we do have time for rhetorical questions?"

Jean pinched Libby's love handle. "Focus."

"I don't know." Libby sighed. "Lose your bathing suit?"

"Nope."

"Drown?"

"Stand up." Jean lifted a hand toward the ceiling. "Once you're in the chute, you have to ride that puppy all the way to the end. Otherwise, the next person who comes along will mow you down and suddenly you're doing the horizontal tango with a hairy insurance salesman. Assuming you don't get lodged in the pipe like a massive turd."

"Is that . . . supposed to make me feel better?"

"It's funny you brought up plumbing." Keoki huffed a laugh.

Libby was afraid to ask. She was still imagining herself watersliding through a sewer.

"Come on." Jean pulled her keys out of the junk drawer. "Let's get ready to dazzle your fairy godmother with a warm island Me-mas."

She swiveled her hips in a terrible approximation of the hula. Keoki did a step-slide to Jean's side, dipping one shoulder and then raising it again in time with his chin thrusts. He beckoned for Libby to join them.

She shook her head, gripping her stomach instead.

"Keoki will feed us when we get there," Jean promised. "Right, K?"

"I could throw together a smoked marlin Caesar. Made a big

batch of croutons with leftover baguette. And the fish is from my cousin Jimmy. So ono."

"I'm not hungry anymore," Libby lied. "I feel too sick."

"You'll get over it when you see the house. Did I mention the hot tub? This is going to be the best week of our lives."

Libby had her doubts. In fact, her doubts had doubts of their own, tucked away like baggies of worry inside a doubt drug mule—who had just been pulled aside by airport security.

Keoki pulled her into a one-armed hug. "Cheer up, Li'l Bit." It was a funny nickname for a six-foot tall woman. Or at least it used to be, until it got twisted into that other name. *Lillibet.* "You know what you need?"

"Don't," she warned, but he was already hoisting Libby off the floor, squeezing her like a chew toy he wanted to hear squeak. Her teeth rattled as he set her down.

"Feel better?" he asked. "Or do you need me to sing?"

"No!"

Keoki actually had a nice voice, but it was hard to notice when he *always* sang the kind of song you least wanted to hear. Pure Top 40 earworms that would get stuck in your head for the rest of day, with a side of Disney ballads. The mainland kids in college all expected him to show up to parties with his ukulele and strum something mellow and beachy, only to get hit with the acoustic version of "My Humps."

"I was trying to shake out the bad feelings."

"You almost shook out my breakfast."

"Ginger tea. That's what I make for Cici. Did I tell you I felt the baby? Little KeCi kicks up a storm if Mama eats something sour."

"Nothing but black coffee and regret kicking around in this one." Jean thumped Libby's midsection like Libby was a vending machine that wasn't giving up her Oreos.

"Don't forget the rice crackers," Keoki said. "She's more snacks than blood."

Jean held up a finger as inspiration struck. "You should think of this as a mini-retreat. Our own little spa vacation, complete with healthy meals."

"I feel so relaxed already." Libby added two thumbs way up in case the sarcasm wasn't coming through.

"Come on, Libs. What's the worst that could happen?"

Examples flooded Libby's memory of other "foolproof" plans Jean had presented with equal certainty. *They won't even check the guest list. I'm sure those are complimentary. Why would there be a gate if they didn't want people to use it?* "Do you really want me to answer that?"

"No," Keoki and Jean said in unison, pushing her out the door.

Chapter 4

A highway was a highway, in Jefferson's experience. Asphalt, concrete, and cars set the scene, whether you were in Wyoming or West Virginia. That wasn't the case here. The signs were the same Astroturf-emerald but the place names were so long and full of vowels you needed a deep breath before diving in.

As their route led them farther from the airport, more details crept into the frame. Trees that looked like something from Dr. Seuss. Mountains that were too close and the wrong color, an electric-green instead of the rocky gray and brown of the Tetons. The vertical ridges were rounded and undulating, with peaks that disappeared into a blanket of low-hanging clouds.

And then there was the ocean, flashes of crystalline blue that became more frequent after their town car turned onto a two-lane road that wound along the coast, playing peekaboo with the Pacific. Fruit stands and shrimp shacks with hand-lettered signs dotted the shoulder.

"Amazing, isn't it?" Hildy's voice said from the seat beside him. "You're so grateful you came. This is exactly what you needed. Thank goodness I let Hildy talk me into this," she prompted, when he turned his gaze from the window. "I totally forgive her for the bear spray."

Jefferson patted the back of his head.

"What are you doing?"

"Checking for strings."

"Very funny. Obviously you're free to be yourself. Within certain parameters."

One of the things Jefferson appreciated about Hildy was her directness. You always knew where you stood with her, because she'd told you where to go and how to act once you got there. Hildy wasn't the type to say, *Can we eat at that new steakhouse tonight? I have a craving for red meat,* when what she really meant was, *The guy I'm sleeping with behind your back will be there and I enjoy the drama of lying to your face.*

"I was planning to hang back and let you do your thing. Carry heavy bags as needed. Is that about right?"

"Don't sell yourself short, JJ. You're not my golf caddie. This is a time for you to relax. And take plenty of pictures. Did you know I've always wanted to have my own photographer?"

"I shoot pictures of wildlife, Hildegarde. It's not exactly covers for *Vogue.*"

"Yes, but if you can make bighorn sheep look hot, imagine what you'll do with all this." She fluffed her hair, waiting a beat before elbowing him in the side. "Joking aside, I super-appreciate you being here. I know this is a big step outside your comfort zone."

He gave a stiff nod. A certain amount of steamrolling had been involved, but they both knew he was letting her get away with it. Despite being an only child, she'd taken a page straight from the little-sister playbook, a deadly combination of sad eyes and badgering. *Come to Hawaii with me! We'll have a super-fun time! And stick it to your ex-girlfriend! Did I mention that I'm an orphan?*

Maybe Hildy was the one who needed a vacation, and didn't want to go alone. She put on a good front, but there was a ticking intensity underneath the smiles—not surprising after a near-death experience.

"Try not to get all choked up," she teased. "The optics are also on point."

"That's a relief." Whatever it meant.

"Having you in the picture gives me gravitas." She stroked her jawline with freshly painted nails. He had no idea when she'd had them done, especially considering they were a different color than last night. "I think that's the real reason young women on the rise take up with old dudes. People assume it's about the money, but I already have that, you know?"

He did know. Even by the standards of the wealthy winter sports enthusiasts who flocked to Jackson Hole, Hildy was in a class of her own.

"What I need is some of that craggy, old school, you-can-trust-me aura. Which you bring to the table in spades. People look at me and they see hot, young, steal-your-girlfriend-*and*-your-boyfriend energy. Maybe I frighten them a little, so they make assumptions about my messy personal life and lack of am-bition. But then they get a load of you and it's like, *So silent! So scowly! So male! He seems solid.*"

Jefferson had never thought of thirty-two as particularly ancient until he met Hildy. "Glad my geriatric self could be of service."

"Same. Honestly, I should have thought of doing this a long

time ago. Maybe not the lost-in-the-woods part but the aftermath. Our quote-unquote journey. Even my freaking uncle is giving me space. It's like, wow, is this what it takes to get you to respect my independence?"

Hildy mentioned her uncle so often that at first Jefferson had assumed she was starved for his attention, in the same way the younger of his nieces would collapse in a heap, exaggerating the smallest injury, when she needed a cuddle. The image of an absentee billionaire too busy running his business to worry about family was less surprising than the apparent reality: a helicopter uncle who smothered Hildy with affection.

"I don't know if it's the ratings bonanza or being with an old guy, but I think he's finally starting to see me as an adult woman instead of his frilly little princess. Which obviously I'm not saying you're Viagra-ad old, because that would be creepy. You're just different from guys my age. Not all waxed and cut with that generic gym body." Hildy ran a hand in front of her abdomen, indicating the six-pack he didn't have.

"I'll put that on my tombstone."

"Relax, Mr. Sensitive. You know you're at least a seven, maybe a seven-point-five if you'd let me take you shopping." She squeezed his forearm. "What I'm saying is, I'm glad you're here."

"I'm sure you would have managed just fine without me." His mind supplied a picture of white-out winds strong enough to strip flesh from bone. "Once we got you off the mountain."

"But it's more fun this way. For both of us."

Fun wasn't the first word that came to mind for Jefferson, and not only because it wasn't part of his standard vocabulary. The chaos of the last few days had left him feeling as though the avalanche had caught them after all and they were churning down the rocky slope at bone-crushing speed. "I appreciate the vacation," he said politely.

"Don't thank me. We're on the corporate dime. Anyway, this is nothing. You should see how my uncle travels. Plus, he totally owes you for saving my life. Not to mention the part where this is a legitimate business expense. *And* a wonderful opportunity for personal growth."

That last bit had the distinct aroma of something Hildy's hero, the legendary Lillibet, would say. Indulgence as a spiritual pursuit. Hallmark for millionaires. Jefferson's reasons for agreeing to this trip might be a little hazy, but he knew one thing: It wasn't due to a burning desire to meet Lillibet. Thanks to Genevieve, he'd been inoculated against the charms of self-obsessed attention seekers.

"I didn't have much else going on. As you helpfully pointed out." The timing had swayed him almost as much as Hildy's full-court press. A perfect blank on his calendar, in a week that happened to include his birthday. A change of scenery didn't sound like the worst idea, to bridge the gap between his old life and the next chapter.

"Honestly? Kind of an understatement. No offense, but you majorly needed to get out of town. You were in a dark and lonely place there, JJ."

"Wyoming is an acquired taste."

"I'm talking emotionally. Because of your cheating ex dumping you for that meat gigolo."

"Ah." A strange type of intimacy developed when you nearly died with someone yet had also known them less than a week. Hildy knew things Jefferson would never have shared under ordinary circumstances, but there were Swiss-cheese-style gaps in their awareness of each other's pasts. Which was probably why she brought up his breakup so often. Jefferson generally preferred to downplay that chapter of his existence—to the point of total silence.

Though he didn't hate the idea of Genevieve hearing about the happenings of the last week, or finding out where he was now. How was that for trying new things? Putting himself out there? Caring more about people than his "precious animals"?

Hildy nudged him with her shoulder. "Don't man-panic. I'm not going to make you talk about your feelings."

"Thank you."

"I'm glad I could repay the favor. You saved my life, and I'm helping you get a life." She raised and lowered her cupped palms. "We're balancing the scales."

Jefferson refrained from telling her that he would have left town on his own soon enough. Two days after getting back from this little adventure, he'd be on a plane to Alaska, where he'd signed on to take pictures for an environmental watchdog group. But he didn't want to rain on Hildy's parade, and she probably wouldn't think three weeks off the grid in the arctic wilderness counted as a change of pace. Besides, she wasn't wrong. He'd been stagnant too long. It was past time for a spring thaw.

He turned his attention back to the passing scenery. There were still patches of undeveloped land on this side of the island, instead of hotels and condos crammed together like the slats of a wooden fence. Tourism was a presence, in the scattered T-shirt stands and souvenir shops, but you could tell real people lived here, too. They passed a school and a small white church, a hardware store and hole-in-the-wall restaurants that clearly catered to locals.

"There's a resort behind those trees." Hildy pointed at a winding road that disappeared over a suspiciously manicured rise. "My uncle stayed there on his honeymoon. One of his honeymoons," she amended. "Amazing private beach."

What could be worse than sharing sand with people who hadn't paid through the nose for that privilege?

"I'm glad we're going to have an authentic island experience. One of the best things about Lillibet is how real and grounded she manages to stay in the midst of so much privilege."

Of all Hildy's claims regarding Lillibet—that you could tell she was hot *because* she never posted pictures of her face, that she had the ideal marriage, that she made all those meals herself—this was possibly the most far-fetched. Jefferson suspected Lillibet would turn out to be as "real" as the nonsense that had been printed about him.

"Does she know you want to recruit her?"

"It was pretty strongly implied." She smoothed her lip gloss with the tip of a pinkie, a nervous gesture at odds with her confident tone.

"How's that going to work with her perfect life out here harvesting her own salt?"

"First off, she doesn't do everything herself. Lillibet is all about supporting local artisans. Yes, she makes her own cheese, but that's because of the goats. And second, if anyone can balance career and private life, it's Lillibet."

Jefferson grunted.

"Use your words, Grizzly Adams."

"Seems like poisoning the well."

She fanned her lashes at him. "I don't speak rural."

"What if it changes her? Different life, different person."

"People evolve. It's called progress. Just because you've had the same haircut since second grade doesn't mean change is bad."

His hair was actually a bit longer than the buzz cut he'd sported in those days, mostly because he hadn't had time for a trim in the rush of their departure. Or at least it had seemed frantic to Jefferson, especially after the emptiness of the past few months. Getting a temporary phone so reporters would stop hassling him, letting his sister know he was leaving town, turning down the heat in his half-furnished apartment . . . the list was depressingly short, now that he thought about it. Maybe he should get a plant. He pictured a runt of a cactus, sitting on a lonely shelf in a plain little pot.

"I think this trip is a chance for all of us to embrace the new." She wrapped one of her curls around a finger before smoothing it back into place. "You, me, *and* Lillibet."

"Like when tourists come back from Santa Fe with a suitcase full of turquoise jewelry?"

"Or maybe it's like a bunch of forward thinkers gathering on the slopes at Davos before saving the world over drinks at the lodge." The corner of her mouth twitched. "Okay, fine, it's not on that level."

At least she had a sense of humor about her delusions of grandeur.

"But we are at a crossroads. Major potential energy. Remember what you told me about starting a fire in the woods?"

Although Jefferson was gradually acclimating to his companion's lightning-fast subject changes, it still took him a few beats to catch up. "Uh, don't do it?"

"The other stuff. Like when we were in the snow fort, and you were being super-survival-y."

"Keep your matches dry and carry a flint steel for backup?"

Hildy's nose wrinkled. "Doesn't ring a bell. I'm talking about the control part. How you choose the place and find the materials, and once you light the spark it has to be nurtured like a tender, defenseless infant so it's there when you need it. The primal power of fire at your command."

"I said that?"

"I zhuzhed it up a little."

"And in plain language?"

"I'm gathering sticks."

"Uh-huh." Jefferson had learned that if he held on long

enough, he'd find the nugget of meaning in the maelstrom of words.

"Talent-spotting is a crucial skill for an editor. Lillibet is my discovery. If she hits big—and she will—I get the credit. Corner-office time."

"What about college?"

Hildy bristled. "What about it?"

"Don't you have a year left?"

"Who cares? If I already have the job I want, the degree is meaningless."

"You might feel differently about it later on."

"I'm an attractive young woman with a trust fund who happens to be in a *sorority,* Jefferson. People are going to judge me no matter what piece of paper I have hanging on the wall. I could rack up a dozen Pulitzers and they'd still be like, *You know she only got that job because of her family.* So spare me the lecture about making good choices. Sometimes the unconventional path is a shortcut to fulfillment, even if it looks like a rockier road."

"Lillibet?" he guessed.

"She speaks to me. It's like she knows exactly what I need to hear. Lillibet would understand that this is my moment. I have the taste, I have the talent, it's my time. You know what that means?"

Jefferson was still imagining Hildy's affirmations shellacked to a plank in one of the tourist gift shops, with a watercolor sunset in the background. "Unlikely."

"I'm ready to pour on the gasoline, and then boom!" She sketched an explosion with her hands. "Fire."

"Just to clarify," he said, after a troubled silence, "you would never do that under real-world conditions. Especially in the backcountry."

"Totes metaphorical, babe." She patted him on the knee. "We're learning so much from each other. Although this is nothing compared to the wisdom Lillibet is going to drop. You better get ready to have your mind blown."

That seemed about as likely as a polar bear attack, but Jefferson kept that to himself. "I'll try not to swoon."

Chapter 5

> **lovelillibet** Even if your home is a literal castle, it should still be cozy. Small luxuries make such a difference: cashmere throws, an heirloom rug, linen and leather. Your space should speak to you, but it can also speak for you, telling the world, "This is who I am. A person who values her own comfort. And has great taste."
>
> Love, Lillibet
>
> Image: Pastel balls of yarn stacked in a hand-carved wooden bowl.
>
> #homeiswheretheartis #comfortmewithcashmere #irishlinen #organicfibers

Libby tried to lower the lid of the toilet so she could sit. It resisted the pressure of her hand, closing at its own stately pace, because nothing in her life was simple anymore. There must be a magical wealthy-person mechanism to keep the commodes in this house from clanging shut like tacky peasant toilets. Most likely this had been explained to her during the tour, but there was only so much information about plumbing fixtures her brain could retain.

With a final whisper-soft sigh, the lid settled into place. Libby's descent was less graceful. Her legs had gone wobbly from standing at attention all morning as Mr. L showed them around his beach house. Not to be confused with his other homes scattered across the globe. Designing bathrooms for the filthy rich was apparently big business. Libby probably shouldn't even be sitting on something that cost more than a used car, but there was nowhere else to hide, and she needed a break. A few quiet minutes to let the smile slip off her face and her shoulders droop while she escaped her present "reality."

The entire situation still felt like a waking dream, with a slightly warped storyline. Although Libby mostly tried to deny it, buried underneath the other reasons she'd gone along with *Love, Lillibet*—boredom, to make Jean laugh, annoyance with the sort of people whose tunnel vision led straight to a mirror (hi, mom!)—there was a kernel of "what if?" A ridiculous flicker of hope that someone would see these posts and say, *I can tell there's a promising writer behind that steaming pile of excrement.*

It was the same wishful thinking that made her dress up to go out, on the off chance she was about to meet her soulmate in a crowded bar, even though Libby's rational mind knew she was headed for another guy with more hair gel than manners who would grit his teeth through ten minutes of awkward conversation before making a move, despite the total absence of chemistry or connection. At which point Libby generally fled to the bathroom . . . kind of like now, though obviously this was a much nicer setup than the back of a club. Her feet weren't sticking to the floor, for one thing. Progress?

Libby pulled out her phone. Super-casual, checking the old email . . . or whatever. The link to the video was right there at the top of her Frequently Visited page. Go figure. Libby hit play, then levitated off the toilet when someone knocked on the door.

"One second." Lunging for the sink, Libby tried to turn on the tap. *Just in here splashing a little cool water on my temples, as one does!* The faucet did not appear to have any moving parts.

"Crap." She poked at the bronze lump that filled the space where you'd expect running water to emerge.

The door flew open. Jean scowled at her. "What are you doing?"

"What does it look like?"

Her gaze snagged on the phone in Libby's left hand. "Hiding in the bathroom to watch a grainy video you've seen a bajillion times?"

That was an exaggeration. At most Libby had watched it a dozen times. Thirty, tops. "At least I don't barge in on people who could have been going to the bathroom!"

Jean shook her head. "You're too scared to pee here. You said so yourself."

"That was a joke." Mostly.

"Sure." Jean stepped from the wide bamboo planks of the living area onto the textured slate floor of the bathroom. This one was done in shades of green, from lichen to forest. Libby had forgotten the details: something-something wood and a slab of pure blah-blah-blah for the counter. She really should have taken notes.

"Not bad for the guests' guest's guest restroom," she quipped as Jean bent to sniff the impossibly fluffy white towels. It looked like Libby wasn't the only one afraid to touch anything with her grubby lower-class hands.

Striking like a cobra, Jean grabbed Libby's phone. "I knew it!" she said as the video started playing. "I think you have a problem, Libs."

"Uh, yeah. So do you. We're up to our eyeballs in it."

"I'm not talking about our genius plan. The issue is your little obsession." Jean waved the phone in Libby's face.

"It's research."

"You don't even know what this guy looks like. He could be somebody's grandpa under that snowsuit."

That was demonstrably false, given the way he'd carried the Naughty Niece (as the headlines styled her now that she was officially not dead) through the snow. For Libby, the message was clear. *Here was a person you could count on in a crisis.* The man version of a St. Bernard. Unlike the last guy she dated, who wouldn't go five minutes out of his way to drop her off because it was "just as easy" for Libby to catch the bus from his apartment.

"He's like a fireman," she told Jean. "Except with snow."

Jean pressed a hand to Libby's forehead. "The only fire is in your brain. Or possibly your pants."

"I'm just stressed. I need something to take my mind off all this."

"Maybe you should try yoga?" Jean suggested. "For real."

"Is it so wrong to want to meet someone decent for a change? When is it going to be our turn to get lucky?"

"*After* you get a job. Once you're a star reporter, you can sleep with whoever you want."

"That is not what I meant."

"Yeah, but think about it. You'll be meeting new people constantly. Perfect time to play the field."

"I can't have sex with someone I'm interviewing."

"Well, not while you're asking them questions. But after—"

"No." Although Libby wasn't really in a position to lecture anyone about journalistic ethics. "I want to meet someone the normal way. You're going about your business, and boom! There he is. Like it happened for them." She took her phone back from Jean, tapping the dark screen. "I know it was a near-death experience, but it still seems like she won the lottery."

"The system is rigged, Libs. The rich get richer *and* they steal your imaginary boyfriends. The real luck is being born into money. But it's okay, because we're scrappers. We'll make our own fortunes."

Libby wasn't quite ready to change the subject. "How many guys do we know that you can count on when shit gets real? Besides Keoki." Who they needed to stop depending on for everything, because soon he'd have his own family to worry about.

"Um, how about a certain plumbing magnate with a super-sweet house?"

"Well, yeah—"

"But me no buts. I know you're hard up, but we can't afford distractions right now. Rudy is doing us a solid and a half. The least we can do is listen."

"I have been." All yesterday afternoon and again this morning, as Rudolf Lamers, founder and CEO of Lamers, Inc., described the provenance, price point, and shipping history of every object in his "villa." It was an incredible place, and extremely generous of him to let them pretend Lillibet lived there. *Weirdly* generous. But it also felt like she was trapped inside a high-end home shopping network.

"So you're good on the floor plan? Not going to get lost on the way to the front door?"

"It's a big house," Libby hedged, though the real issue was that she'd started dissociating a few minutes into Mr. L's extended monologue. "Also, I'm going to feel like a jerk acting like all this is mine."

The futuristic plumbing was surrounded by a smorgasbord of imposing antiques, many of them sourced from a Balinese palace. Libby had taken one look at the massive front doors with their gold inlay and intricate carvings and tried to turn around and leave.

"It's a show home. Hence the showiness." As usual, Jean found the trappings of wealth more aspirational than intimidating, though there was an edge of hate-to-love in her attitude. Libby suspected it had something to do with her friend's less-than-privileged childhood, a subject Jean preferred not to discuss. Keoki said it was because she was like a shark, constantly moving forward—even when it meant leaving a cloud of blood and body parts in her wake. Whereas Libby was more of a turtle: slow, guarded, always chewing. Not the most flattering picture, but also not wrong.

"This place is perfect for our purposes," Jean reminded her. "Lillibet is exactly the kind of ho who pays someone to rake the crushed shells in her Zen garden while she sits on the deck with a cocktail and lets people think she's deep. The house sells the story."

"As long as they don't ask me too many questions about it."

"When in doubt, defer to Mr. L. You just need to be able to point them to a bathroom."

"Yeah, but which? There are like nine." One featured a sauna, another had a soaking tub the size of a pond set into the floor next to a living wall of moss, and then there was the walk-in shower with the floor-to-ceiling mosaic copied from a villa in Pompeii . . . Libby had never understood why a house would have more bathrooms than bedrooms. It wasn't like you could relieve yourself in two places at once. "You don't find it a little strange?"

"He's a bathroom man. To each their own."

"I'm talking about the whole thing. Why would this ultra-successful businessman let us use his house? Besides wanting Keoki to cook for him."

"Out of the goodness of his heart?"

She was obviously being facetious, because no one had a more jaded view of humanity than Jean. "It's not just the house. I can't figure out what's going on with him." Because Mr. L wasn't only lending them his palatial home. He'd also agreed to play the part of Lillibet's husband.

Jean frowned. "You think he wants to get in your pants?"

"No, I don't get those vibes." If anything, he was physically standoffish. When Libby tried to shake his hand, he'd winced and taken a step back, like she was holding out a dead fish. "Do you?"

"He's hotter for this faucet than he is for either of us," Jean confirmed.

And yet. There was something there, under the surface. Not sex or money, but *something*. "Maybe he needs a kidney?"

"Or maybe he's lonely. Not everyone is as blessed in the companionship department as you are. It's probably hard for billionaire plumbing magnates to make friends."

"Yeah, because he's always talking about his drains."

Jean's cackle turned into a yelp as the door swung open behind her, knocking her into Libby. When Mr. L stuck his head through the gap, Libby tried very hard not to think of Jack Nicholson in *The Shining*. Their host's grin wasn't murdery, exactly. Just a touch overeager, like a puppy at a bacon factory. The expression sat oddly on his face. Mr. L's large deep-set eyes and droopy lids, plus the vertical lines bracketing his mouth like parentheses, gave him a perpetually mournful look. Add to that the neatly slicked-back hair and impeccably tailored silver-gray suit (likely custom-made, unless men's business clothing came in juniors sizes), and there was a distinct air of funeral director about him.

"There's my lovely bride," he said, squeezing between Jean and Libby.

"Lose the wink," Jean told him, pointing at her face. "In gambling circles, we call that a tell."

"Of course," he agreed, apparently unbothered that one of the strangers staying in his house liked to play the odds. "Are you well, *wife*?"

"You can just call me Libby. It's probably simpler."

"She means Lillibet," Jean corrected.

"Ah yes! Code names." His eye spasmed like he'd stopped himself on the verge of another wink. "And I am your husband. Mr. L."

"Sounds super-cool, right?" Jean flashed him a thumbs-up. "Like an international assassin."

"As opposed to a local assassin?" Libby asked, mostly under her breath. "Contract killing at the county level?"

Frowning, Mr. L pulled a handkerchief from his breast pocket and snapped it open. "Were you admiring the Golden Lotus?" he asked, edging around Libby.

"I—yes?" She wasn't sure it was the right answer, especially since he appeared to be wiping off her fingerprints with the square of white silk. Maybe she should have denied everything.

"Who wouldn't?" Jean elbowed Libby in the side, giving her a try-harder glare.

"Totally. Since it's so elegant."

Jean nodded like she'd said something profound. "Yet strong."

"Two-point-oh GPM," Mr. L informed them. He flicked a finger under one of the bronzed leaves, and a spurt of water hit the sink. "It doesn't get more powerful than that. At least not *legally*."

"Wow." Jean looked expectantly at Libby, who was still wondering whether Mr. L was part of an underground fight club of faucet designers, illegally souping up their plumbing.

"That's . . . a real gusher."

Mr. L inclined his head. "Do you know what I dreamed of as a young man, before I found my true calling?"

"No." Libby wasn't sure she wanted to find out. Was this it, the dark secret?

"The stage." A swish of the handkerchief for emphasis. "But my academy only had chess club and engineering team. No shows for Rudy."

"I'm sorry." Libby could sort of imagine him doing magic tricks.

"But now at last I get my chance!" He carefully refolded his handkerchief and tucked it into his pocket. "To test my dramatic skills for an audience."

Was that why he'd signed up for this charade? Somebody should really tell him about community theater.

"Do you know *Mamma Mia*?" he asked.

Libby imagined a vise holding her head in place. Even the slightest eye contact with Jean would spell the end for both of them. "I do, yes. Well, the movie."

"I'm afraid this is going to be a little less . . . Broadway than that." Jean managed to sound sad about it.

"Fewer musical numbers," Libby added.

"Very tasteful," Mr. L agreed. "Top-quality." He glanced at Libby, and she felt another prickle of suspicion. What was this guy's deal? And if it did involve internal organs, did she really owe him that much? If she somehow wound up with a staff writing job at a legit media outlet, maybe a kidney wasn't an unreasonable price to pay.

"Before our guests arrive, I have a little surprise for you." He pressed his palms together like he could barely contain his excitement.

"Here?" Libby pointed at the floor. "In this bathroom?" *Please let it be a showerhead,* she silently prayed, despite having wished the opposite many times that day. As opposed to his personal plumbing.

"You are funny. Another reason to marry you, *Lillibet*!"

"Plus she's hot," Jean prompted. "And a really good cook."

"Very all-American," Mr. L agreed. "Do you play volleyball?"

"No." She didn't cook, either, but hopefully he understood they were talking about Lillibet, not Libby.

Jean looked thoughtful. "She could be sporty."

"No," Libby said again, imagining a tetherball smacking her in the face. "I don't think we need to introduce any more props."

"Ah-ah, not so fast." Their host held up a finger. "Come. This way, please. I have something to show you."

"Does it involve goats?" Jean asked hopefully as they followed him down the hall.

They were still working on that detail of Lillibet's so-called life. Like many things about this charade, it had seemed like a clever idea at the time. When Jean suggested Lillibet have fictional offspring (so she could also flaunt her superior skills in the parenting arena), Libby had proposed four-legged kids instead, never guessing she would one day be required to source actual farm animals. She supposed it was preferable to Jean "borrowing" someone's human children.

"Patience," Mr. L chided, skipping up the floating staircase ahead of them. He stopped outside a room Libby was fairly certain they hadn't visited earlier, unless she'd been having an out-of-body experience at the time. Curling his hand into a fist, he pretended to blow a fanfare on his air trumpet before throwing open the door.

Libby took in the velvet lounge and massive gilt-framed mirror before registering the closet that filled an entire wall. Sliding screens had been pulled back to reveal a candy box of shimmery pastel fabrics.

"Holy glitter bomb." Jean crossed the room like she was on skates. "Did a fairy princess explode in here?" She glanced over her shoulder at Mr. L. "What are we looking at, secret wife or your personal playroom?"

"No wife." He sighed. "Except my darling Libby-kuchen."

Libby forced a laugh. It was a toss-up whether the pet name or the puppy-dog eyes that accompanied it were more disturbing. "Seriously, though. Why do you have a room full of women's clothes?"

"My mother's boudoir," he explained, with unmistakable pride. "She has quite an eye for fashion. This way we can match. Like a real couple."

"Because I'll be dressed like your mom?" Libby looked to Jean for support, but her best friend was laser-focused on the rack of gumdrop-colored outfits.

"It's about taste," Mr. L explained. "Being on the same level."

Jean pulled out a pale aqua shift with embroidered silver curlicues around the collar and sheer sleeves that puffed at the shoulder before fastening at the wrist with fabric-covered buttons. It looked like it should be worn with matching eye shadow and a 1960s bouffant.

"Oh hell yes." She waved Libby closer so she could jab the hanger under her chin. "Now we're talking. The piece of resistance."

The dress was beautiful, although clearly made for someone half Libby's height. She could probably squeeze into it, thanks to a boxy cut and her lack of curves, but she was going to be showing a lot more leg than Mr. L's mom. Not to mention the part where she'd have to worry about sweating on fabric that practically screamed, *Dry-clean only.*

"The shoes won't fit," Libby said, grasping at excuses. The tiny slippers with sparkly embellishments looked like a size-six, tops. This Cinderella needed an eleven. On a good day.

"I'll wear the shoes," Jean announced, like she was taking one for the team. "You can rock the earth goddess look. That's more your jam anyway, *Lillibet.*"

Right. Because Lillibet probably got weekly pedicures. No cracked heels for her.

"You're sure your mom won't mind?" Libby asked Mr. L. She was hoping to get through this experience without causing too much collateral damage.

"She is in Vienna for the summer, so it will be our little secret." He held up both hands, showing his crossed fingers. "I am happy to do a favor for a *friend.*"

Libby slid Jean a look that said, *Did you hear that? The weird emphasis on* friend? *Like we're spies and "friend" is the secret password?*

Jean was too busy pawing through the closet to notice. She snagged another hanger, this one holding a pale rose caftan that would probably hit Libby just below the knees. "We should try a few of these on." She gave Mr. L her best run-along-now smile.

After turning the lock, Jean blew out a long breath. "At least now we won't have to pretend your *old* Old Navy aesthetic is an environmental statement." She waved a hand at Libby's droopy sweatshirt and stained cutoffs, as if Libby's lack of fashion sense were the major stumbling block to selling their story.

"Why not? Lillibet is on the record about her opposition to fast fashion."

"Yeah, but this retro-Eurotrash art cinema vibe is way more believable than Lillibet going thrifting." Jean rubbed a sherbet-orange sleeve between the pads of her fingers. "Kind of amazing how all the loose threads are getting tied up. Bada bing, bada boom."

"Like a noose." Though a straitjacket might be more appropriate, since they had clearly both lost their minds.

"I thought you were excited to meet your mountain man."

"While pretending to be a real housewife of Honolulu? He's going to think I'm the worst."

"You don't know that."

"I'm faking being a fake, Jean."

"So it cancels out! Like a negative plus a negative."

"Is even more of a negative."

"Whatever. It's not my fault math makes no sense." Jean draped the caftan over the back of the lounge chair. "You need food."

"I think my problems go beyond low blood sugar."

"Stop by the kitchen and ask Keoki for a sandwich, then we'll talk." She was using the soothing tone that meant she was "managing" Libby, the way you'd placate a small child.

"I'm capable of making my own sandwich."

"Not like Keoki. And when someone has a talent, you should *honor the gift*." She poked Libby in the shoulder for emphasis.

"I hate it when you talk Lillibet to me."

"Doesn't mean I'm wrong. Eat something, then go get some freaking shells."

"Why do you need shells?"

"Because we have a bunch of crap to decorate."

"But I can't do the artsy part."

"Duh. I'll handle it, but I'm going to be too busy with the Me Tree to go beachcombing." Jean glanced at her phone. "We have three hours. Plenty of time for you to cool your jets and then come back here and get gussied up."

"Why didn't we invent someone who dresses like a cave troll and forgets to wash her hair?" Libby shoved her messy bun back to the middle of her head. "That's relatable."

"Nobody wants relatable. They're looking for the fantasy, so they can pretend they have a snowball's chance in hell of living that life, once they win the lottery and magically turn beautiful from all the great sex they're having with their perfect lover while someone else washes their dishes."

"That's the most depressing inspirational speech I've ever heard."

"You're welcome." Jean tipped her head at the door. "Now go, so we can get this show on the road."

"Yes, mistress." Hunching her shoulders, Libby gave the full Igor shuffle-drag as she lurched off in search of her last supper.

Chapter 6

The town car slowed before turning off onto a narrow lane studded with warning signs. PRIVATE PROPERTY. KEEP OUT. NO PUBLIC ACCESS. YOU ARE TOO POOR TO LIVE HERE. The kind of person who created a holiday devoted to herself obviously wasn't going to share a strip of asphalt with commoners.

They stopped in front of a tall metal fence. Hildy bounced in place as their driver entered the code she'd given him and the gate swung open.

It looked like a museum of architectural styles, the choose-your-own-mansion approach to designing a neighborhood: modern glass box, faux-Mediterranean, a Victorian cottage on steroids. A sandy path threaded the gap between two houses, offering a glimpse of blue. Jefferson rolled down his window. He wanted to follow that trail to the end.

Hildy leaned forward to address their driver. "Can you stop for a second, please?" When he obliged, she turned to face Jefferson. "I think it's best if Lillibet's first impression of me is as a strong, independent businesswoman. Someone she wants to partner with for the next phase of her career. You know what I'm saying?"

For once, he did. "Why don't I get out and stretch my legs, let the two of you get acquainted?"

"Great idea."

He grabbed his camera bag with one hand, reaching for the door with the other. "I hope she's everything you want her to be."

Hildy nodded. As the driver pulled away, she stuck her head out the window. "Don't get eaten by sharks. I still need you."

He saluted, watching until the car pulled into the driveway of a pistachio-colored house with a tile roof. Most of the structure was obscured by foliage, a climbing hedge that had been clipped into a wall of deep green leaves and woody vines. It wasn't quite tall enough to conceal the size of the building, the wraparound veranda, or the general opulence of the place—all of which were exactly what he'd expect of someone as blatantly entitled as Lillibet.

That was for Hildy to discover in her own time. Shaking his head, Jefferson started down the path.

The transition from pavement to sand was gradual. First there was a gritty shiftiness on top of the sidewalk, then a few patchy clumps of grass, and finally softness, underfoot and all around. Jefferson stood still, letting the breeze wash over his skin, like maybe he'd felt it wrong the first time.

His brain struggled to make sense of a wind that didn't bite or burn, that smelled like flowers instead of cold rocks and frozen water. *Relax,* said the air and the sunlight and the murmuring waves. It was like sinking into a warm bath on dry land.

Jefferson wasn't sure he trusted all this lulling. The perfection struck him as suspicious, or at least unreal. He hadn't even taken his camera out of the bag. There was nothing to photograph that wouldn't seem clichéd, like a thousand mass-produced post-cards already tacked up behind refrigerator magnets.

Except the woman sitting in the sand with her back to him, long tawny hair pulled to one side to expose the curving line of neck and shoulder.

The sun was in front of her, edging her silhouette in a buttery glow. It wasn't quite the golden hour, but the light was gentle— like everything else—and even without clicking the shutter he knew in his bones this was an image he would remember. Jefferson told himself it was mostly aesthetic, the way his eye traced the guitar-like curve of shoulder and hip. He was in the habit of cataloging compositional details, even when they weren't this visually pleasing.

She half turned as he approached, and he saw that her hand was buried in an open cellophane package. Her cheeks bulged as if he'd caught her mid-chew.

"Hey, uh, hi," she choked, wiping her fingers on her bare thigh.

He wouldn't have let himself take a second look at her legs if she hadn't used them as a napkin. They were very long, it turned out, and bronzed. He suspected she would be tall, if she weren't sitting with her toes buried in the sand.

"Would you like some?"

It took him a second to realize she was talking about the bag of food. "What is it?"

"Shrimp crackers."

He frowned at the surf. "A little insensitive."

Her smile revealed slightly crooked incisors that told him she'd never had braces. The warmth of her skin tone and streaky highlights in her hair spoke of a life spent in the sun. She had unexpectedly dark brown eyes and a small bump in the bridge of her nose. Her lips were pink and maybe a little chapped, though that could have been the residue of the crackers. It was an interesting face, as opposed to a perfectly symmetrical one. He wanted to keep looking at her. But that would have been weird, so he took in the view instead.

This strip of beach felt almost like a secluded cove, thanks to the rocks that stretched out into the water on one side and the heavy vegetation on the other. Up close the ocean appeared more blue-gray than turquoise, churned up into whitecapped peaks as it raced toward shore.

"Do you want to sit?" She patted the sand beside her.

The invitation took him by surprise, but not in a bad way. Until she started to get up.

"I assume you're here for the sunset, not Portrait of Scruffy Girl Stress-Eating." Her chin lifted to indicate his camera bag. "I'll get out of your shot."

He waved at her to stay. "I wanted to see the ocean."

"Oh good. Because you're like two hours early for sunset. And on the wrong side of the island. It's still pretty but, you know. Rises in the east, sets in the west."

"The mites crawl up, the tights fall down."

She blinked at him.

"That's how I remember stalagmites versus stalactites. In caves."

"Ah." It sounded like she wanted to laugh. "I take it you're not from around here."

"Is it that obvious?"

Her nod was solemn. "You're wearing a lei. Which could mean luau, except the outfit is all wrong."

"No aloha shirt?" Hildy had tried to coerce him into wearing one, but he'd held firm that pink was not his color, even if you called it salmon.

"I was thinking more of the shoes." She pointed at his feet. "And socks."

Now that she'd mentioned them, he was acutely aware of how sweaty and confined his feet felt.

"You should take them off," she said, as if reading his mind.

Jefferson didn't know whether it said more about her voice (low and a little throaty) or his life (short on excitement, at least until recently) that this was the most titillating suggestion he'd heard in months.

"Not to boss you around," she added. "It's just the sand gets in them, and you can't wear slippers with socks."

"Because of fashion?"

"And the toe divider." She held up a battered red sandal.

"Ah. We call them flip-flops. Or thongs." Unless that word had been given over entirely to stringy underwear? He was not going to ask.

"Take a load off," she said, when he continued to stand stiffly on the sand.

"You don't mind?"

"Pretty sure this beach is big enough for the two of us. I don't really believe in private beaches anyway. How do you own the ocean? These exact grains of sand? Good luck with that."

He smiled as he settled beside her, not so close that she'd feel like she had to talk to him, but not so far that it would shut the door on further conversation. Also this way he could strip off his socks at a safe distance.

When neither of them spoke, other sounds filled the air. The whoosh of the surf tugged at Jefferson's pulse, slowing his breathing to match the rhythmic rise and fall. He watched the fizzing wake mark the limit of each wave's reach, rushing across the sand before being sucked back to sea. The beach was striped in rippled bands, from dry to damp to drenched. The high-water line seemed clearly defined, until a random wave skidded right past it, forcing him to lift his feet to keep them from getting wet.

"Aw, go on. You can't come all this way and not at least dip your toes in." Standing, she brushed sand off the back of her shorts as she moved toward the water, beckoning Jefferson to follow.

Maybe there was something to this act-like-a-different-person-on-vacation idea. Could Jefferson become the kind of guy who frolicked through the surf in slow motion with a beautiful stranger? He rolled up the bottoms of his jeans, ready to find out.

"You live someplace cold?" she guessed, and he could tell she'd been checking out his legs. Or at least his spring-in-Wyoming tan.

"Very."

"I've never seen snow. In real life. I've only been to the mainland once, and we got off the plane and went straight to Disney. My mom decided my childhood wouldn't be complete without Space Mountain. 'What are credit cards for, sweetie?' " She relayed the last part in a breezy falsetto. Then her brain seemed to catch up with her words and she frowned at the sand, clearly embarrassed. Jefferson couldn't tell her not to worry—that he liked her honesty—so he pretended not to notice.

"It's a little like this," he said, as his feet shifted in the sand, slipping backward with each step. "Snow. Except it doesn't hold you up. Unless you're on skis. And it's a lot colder. Obviously." Was he babbling? It was possible he'd spent too much time around Hildy.

"Speaking of cold, are you ready?"

He watched the foaming edge of the water surge toward them and then away again, hissing as it disappeared. It was at least seventy-five degrees and sunny, high summer conditions where he was from. "I think I can handle it."

"Okay. On three." Her eyes locked on his as she counted down, one finger at a time.

Jefferson was so busy watching her face he was a beat behind when she darted forward, splashing in up to her shins. It took another second for his brain to process the sensation of a thousand ice knives stabbing his lower legs. Gasping, he hobbled back onto dry sand, bending down to make sure his feet were still attached.

"People swim in that?"

"You get used to it. It's better to go for it. Little-by-little will kill you."

He frowned at the waves cresting farther offshore. "What happens when you run into one of those?"

"Either you catch a ride or dive under and let it wash over you."

"I'm game if you are." Vacation Jefferson was off his rocker. He wasn't mentally or physically prepared for an ice bath in churning seas, and definitely didn't have the right gear. But apparently his inner twelve-year-old would do anything to impress a girl. Or at least this one.

Her laughter was a shot of adrenaline to his heart. "Wait, are you serious? In your jeans?"

He wasn't sure whether she was worried he was about to strip, or that he might drown in waterlogged denim. "I hadn't thought that far," he admitted. "But I'm not wearing—" Jefferson broke off, trying to think of a way to reassure her without being crude.

"Underwear?" she whispered, like maybe he'd forgotten the word.

"No. Or yes, I am wearing underwear. But they're . . . decent. Uh, modest." Now it sounded like he was part of a religious sect. The only phrase that came to mind was nut sack. *Thank you, Hildy.* Apparently she had also packed him a bathing suit in case his taste was "stuck in the eighties," as she put it. "Full coverage."

"No Speedo? Bummer." Her smile faded when her gaze snagged on his watch.

"I'll leave it with my bag." He started to unbuckle the strap.

She touched his wrist. "Wait." His entire body stilled at the skin-to-skin contact. "What time is it?"

"Four twenty-seven."

"Damn." She blew out a breath. "Jean's going to kill me."

Jefferson waited for her to elaborate, hoping the next words out of her mouth would be *that's my boss* or *pit bull* or even *parole officer,* anything but the other half of a couple.

"I should probably go," she mumbled.

"Okay." He tried to summon what Hildy called his *resting dead face.*

"Here." Reaching into her pocket, she pulled out a shell, rubbing it on the front of her shorts before handing it to him. "Let's make a wish first."

"You're not going to steal my voice, are you?"

"Was that . . . a *Little Mermaid* reference?"

"I have nieces."

She bit her lip to hide a grin. "Okay, Ariel. Make your wish, then kiss the shell and throw it as far as you can out to sea."

He watched the wind play in her hair. "Are you doing one, too?"

"You know what, why not?" There was a defiant edge to her voice as she pulled out another shell, this one spotted brown on the pale pink underside. He wondered if her pockets were always full of perfect seashells or if she'd collected them today, before his arrival. If she often wandered this beach—and whether she'd mind company.

"That's probably where my mom got it. From a cartoon. I can't believe I never made that connection. Though a lot of hers were more like curses." Her eyes crinkled at his look of surprise. "Nothing too dark. Sometimes she'd drag me down to the beach so she could pour out a little white zinfandel and symbolically purge her troubles. *Damn you, Bobby. I hope your stupid golf shirts shrink in the dryer.* That kind of thing." She paused, as if replaying her last words, before grimacing. "Oversharing, party of one."

Jefferson cocked his arm and threw the shell as far as it would go. They watched it plop beneath the surface, breaking the tension.

"What'd you wish for?" she asked.

He pretended to zip his lips.

"Come on, it's not like blowing out candles on a cake." Her face fell. "Crap. Crap, crap, crap."

"What?"

"I was supposed to help with dessert, too." She winced like she'd stepped on something sharp. "We're hosting a dinner tonight. Very important guests." Turning, she hurled her shell into the breaking surf, lips moving in a silent plea to whatever higher power was in charge of seashell wishes.

"It will be fine." Who wouldn't want to have dinner with a beautiful woman who shared her crackers with random passersby before luring them into the sea?

"I'll probably be too nervous to eat. But thanks." She looked up long enough to flash him a smile. "Um. I better go." He watched her fidget, shifting her weight back and forth. "Nice to meet you," she said in a rush, already turning away.

"I was thinking about checking out the sunrise tomorrow," he said, before she could get too far. "I hear it's nice on this side of the island."

At the sound of his voice, she had stopped moving. Now she glanced back. "I'm not a morning person. You'd have to drag me out of bed."

Jefferson cleared his throat, which had gone dry. It was too easy to imagine her sleepy-eyed and warm-skinned with her hair spread out across a pillow, like his subconscious was whispering, *You wish.*

And maybe her thoughts were traveling along similar lines, because she seemed to be having trouble meeting his eyes. "I mean I sleep late." She put a hand to her flushed cheek. "Okay-bye," she blurted, breaking into a run.

He realized he was smiling. The sticky haze of travel had washed away as if he'd plunged headfirst into the Pacific after all. Jefferson wasn't superstitious by nature, but he had a feeling his wish would come true.

And when they did meet again, he'd be sure to ask her name.

Chapter 7

"It's fine," Libby said to the empty path. The plane wasn't due to land until five thirty, and there was bound to be a wait for luggage—maybe one of their bags would be lost!—and then they'd have to drive around the island, which would take forever with rush-hour traffic.

There was plenty of time, in other words. She hadn't flaked out and fucked up because of a guy. Suck it, genetics. They could still pull off a fancy welcome dinner, Lillibet-style.

The first thing to do was change her clothes. Libby couldn't meet a potential future employer while wearing her period shorts (pre-stained and therefore worry-free) and a tatty sweatshirt the color of split-pea soup. If she'd known there were going to be attractive men wandering the beach, she would have dressed up. Not that he'd seemed to mind her old clothes or unbrushed hair or lack of makeup . . . or anything about her, really.

Libby shook herself. Head in the game. She sniffed her armpit, frowning as she revised her to-do list. World's quickest shower first, then clean clothes. Or, no, check with Keoki to see if he still needed help in the kitchen. On the off chance they managed to keep the charade going until dinner.

"It will be fine," Libby repeated, lowering her voice like the man on the beach. He'd sounded so certain, not bullshitting or blowing her off, but calm and unshakable, looking at her with those pale eyes. Maybe he was right. All they had to do was survive the next few days. Either she'd get a job offer at the end or not, and somehow life would go on. There would be walks on the beach and people to meet . . .

Oh no. Did that sound like a Lillibet-ism? What if it was like an infection, spreading through her soft tissues? Soon she'd be a walking grid of inspirational quotes and general pretentiousness.

"No, you won't, because it will be *fine.*" It sounded grimmer this time. Deep breath. "What's the worst that could—*ahhhh*!" Libby's strangled scream died out when she realized the figure leaping out from behind the naupaka bush was Jean.

"There you are! Come on."

"What are you doing?" Libby protested as Jean dragged her onto the grass. "We can't cut through these people's yard."

"They don't have an alarm. The mynas kept setting it off."

She shuddered to think why Jean knew so much about neighborhood security. "Listen, sorry I stayed at the beach so long," she said as they detoured around a massive outdoor kitchen. "I forgot my phone and . . . lost track of time." The rest of the story could wait until Jean wasn't vibrating with agitation. "It's going to be fine," she added, attempting to slow her friend's headlong rush.

"Ha!" Jean tightened her hold on Libby's arm, picking up the pace.

"Why are we running?"

They'd reached the back of Mr. L's property, distinguished by the in-ground pool and spa designed to resemble a natural lagoon, complete with waterfall and rocky outcroppings. Jean hauled Libby all the way to the outdoor shower hidden among the trees before whirling to face her.

"Because they're *he-ere*!" she announced in a singsong falsetto. "I have no idea why I said that like a creepy little girl in a horror movie, but you get the point."

"I do?"

Flinging open the slatted wooden door, Jean shoved Libby into the shower. "Clean up. I put a dress in there."

In a haze, Libby stripped off her clothes, then pulled the cord disguised as a vine, turning her face up to meet the splash of sun-warmed water. It was supposed to feel like standing in a gentle rain, Mr. L had explained, though the relaxation factor was diminished by Jean opening the door after five seconds to throw a towel at her.

"They can't be here," Libby said as she wiped her face.

Her best friend held out a sleeveless lavender shift. "You're going to have to fast-forward past the denial stage. They took an earlier flight, because *someone* likes to be spontaneous."

"Oh yeah, like taking that trip to the mountains—"

"Not her. *You*. 'Some days I flow where the wind blows me, drifting on the breeze like a dandelion seed.' "

"You try coming up with eight thousand ways to caption pictures of flowers."

"Speaking of which." Jean plucked a hibiscus bloom and stuck it in Libby's hair. "Did you get the shells?"

"I—did. Yes. Three really pretty ones. Because you said group-ings of three are better. But then I lost two." Lost, threw into the ocean because of a hot guy; it was a fine line. "Sorry! Can we get by without them?"

"I told them you were out foraging. To create tonight's cen-terpiece."

As opposed to last night's centerpiece, because what kind of plebe used the same table decorations twice?

"I'm sure we can find something. Here." Bending, Libby scooped a handful of crushed shells from the ornamental border lining the path. They looked more like broken teeth than some-thing that had washed up on a beach. "How about this?"

Jean stared at the crunchy bits of white. "You know what? YOLO. Maybe tomorrow we can use gravel. Or dirt clods. Because she's so earthy." She nudged Libby in the direction of the house.

"Anything else I should know?"

"I'm your housekeeper. My life imploded but you gave me a second chance, because you're all about women helping women."

"Imploded how?"

"I didn't go into details."

Libby nodded, relieved. They had enough lies to juggle with-out one of Jean's embellishing sprees.

"Sort of hinted it involved prison." Jean waved at her shoulder, as if the delicate constellation of plumeria and ravens she'd designed could pass for jailhouse ink.

"Oh boy."

"Also I'm Irish," Jean mumbled, like she didn't really want Libby to hear.

"You're kidding."

"It slipped out. I was trying to get in character."

"Lillibet has an Irish ex-con housekeeper." Was it too soon to give up? "In for a penny, in for a pound, I guess."

"Or a wee tuppence, as me mam used to say." Jean sent her a hopeful look.

Libby shook her head. They'd have to pray their guests didn't know any real Irish people. Or watch a lot of PBS.

"The good news is that Keoki is mixing up a batch of his li hing mui margaritas."

"Is the plan to get them drunk or are we numbing the pain?"

"Yes," Jean replied.

"It's *you*," the young woman in the purple maxidress said on an awestruck exhale. In person, she looked about seventeen, with flawless skin that seemed to barely contain her buzzing energy. She moved toward Libby as if in a trance, arms extended.

Was Lillibet a hugger? Libby had no idea. To be on the safe side, she opted for a ladylike hand squeeze, and a lean that stopped just shy of air kisses.

"In the flesh," she replied. Wherever possible, Libby hoped to stick with lies of omission rather than straight-up untruths.

"You're literally glowing. Wow."

If she were being herself right now, Libby would have admitted that her alleged radiance was the result of Jean flicking shower water in her face while ordering her to "snap out of it." Instead, she offered a faint smile that hopefully read as quietly confident, like a full-of-it Mona Lisa.

Glowing was the last thing she felt she was doing, especially compared to the vibrant youthfulness of their guest, with her bright eyes and abundant curls. Libby might not be that much older in years, but she was hunched like a crone under the weight of deception. And not only on the inside. A series of pokes between the shoulder blades, courtesy of Jean, let her know she was slouching.

"I can't wait to see JJ's face. That'll teach him to question me. Or you!" Hildy grinned at Libby as if the two of them were in on a joke.

"I've always preferred *quests* to questions." *And if I had a blunt instrument, I'd bludgeon myself with it.*

"Speakin' o' which," Jean cut in, "her young fella's gone walkabout, so he has."

"That's nice," Libby replied on autopilot, mainly concerned with filling the space where a reasonable person might begin to question Jean's Lucky-Charms-by-way-of-Outback-Steakhouse accent.

"He doesn't like to be cooped up. It's all about the great outdoors with Jefferson. Just a man and his camera. That's not bad, is it?" Hildy shook her head. "Look at me, talking business. Plenty of time for that, after we get to know each other better."

No, please, let's talk about work, Libby thought, as a knock sounded on the front door. She waited for someone to answer.

Oh right. This was supposed to be her house.

"I'll just get that," she said, angling her thumb at the door like a totally normal person who hadn't learned human behavior from sitcoms. Her footsteps were silent against the satin smoothness of the floor, drowned out by the pounding of Libby's heart. Because a terrible suspicion had taken root in her brain, throbbing like the beginning of a migraine.

Maybe she was wrong. Hundreds of tourists arrived every day, giant planes disgorging passengers from all over the world. What were the odds? She paused with her hand on the heavy iron knob, taking a deep breath before adjusting her expression to a serene smile.

He looked up at the sound of the door opening. A spark of recognition lit his eyes, a warm flare of pleased surprise that said, *It's you.* Like that was a good thing.

Libby had no idea what her face was doing, but her brain was stuck on a single thought: *I was right.* Iceman was hot—in a lean, serious, wolf-eyed way.

Then again, he was also the guy from the beach, which was

pretty strong evidence that Libby's intuition sucked. Because she could not possibly have been less Lillibet with him.

She drafted a silent letter of complaint to the universe: *When I said I wanted to meet someone like him, I didn't mean the exact same person!* Especially since he already had a charming, young, successful girlfriend.

"What do you say, JJ?" Hildy stuck an arm between them, wiggling her fingers. "Is she gorgeous or what?"

He looked startled, less by the question than by the presence of other humans. His gaze flicked to Hildy before sliding back to Libby. Did all his friends call him JJ, or was that a pet name, just between the two of them? Not that Libby was a friend, as evidenced by the fact that all traces of warmth had fled his expression. It seemed unlikely he was looking to expand his social circle with a thirsty phony who accidentally hit on people who were happily coupled up.

"I don't just mean superficially," Hildy continued. "Your inner beauty shines through. Lillibet, it is my very great pleasure to present the one and only Jefferson Jones. Winter warrior, savior in the storm, my personal guardian angel, et cetera."

"Hildy." His voice was a grumble of warning. Libby tried not to feel it in her bones, but it was a losing battle. He didn't have a drawl, exactly, but the low-and-slow thing was undeniably sexy.

"Fine." Hildy rolled her eyes. "JJ, this"—she twirled her hand like the ringmaster at a circus—"is Lillibet. Who by the way is *exactly* how I pictured her."

Libby waited for him to say something like, *Did you also picture her snarfing an entire bag of shrimp crackers while wearing shorts that should have been thrown away ten years ago?* But he only held out his hand, like a civilized adult. The palm-to-palm contact should not have seemed too intimate for a public setting, and yet the slot machine of Libby's nervous system was flashing lights and making dinging sounds so loud she worried everyone could tell she was losing it. Sensory overload.

"Pleased to meet you," she mumbled.

"Likewise."

"He thinks you're great," Hildy translated. "We both do."

"Oh, well. You, too." *Both of you.* Libby kept that part to herself, but her face flushed anyway.

"Is it time to do the centerpiece?" Hildy asked, glancing at the dimly lit dining room behind them. "I was hoping we could watch. If that's okay?"

"Certain and sure," said Jean, rolling each *r* like a bowling ball. She made a flicking motion at Libby. If that was supposed to be a hint, it flew right over her head. And it wasn't like "Lillibet" could ask someone else for pointers. Aesthetics were her bread and butter.

Libby walked to the approximate middle of the table, which appeared to have been carved from the trunk of a massive tree. The surface was lacquered to a glossy shine, but the edges dipped and flared like a coastline, still rough with bark in spots. A river of translucent blue glass ran from end to end.

One by one, Libby unfolded her fingers to reveal the damp fistful of crushed shells. Some of them were probably embedded in her skin. How hard could it be? She'd watched Jean make art out of scraps plenty of times. After quickly discarding the idea of scattering them like glitter, she dumped the whole thing at once.

"Minimalist," Hildy said, staring at the grayish white mound.

"Mmm." Libby debated sticking her finger into the center of the pile to make a hole. Like what, a salty donut? "It's an iterative process."

"She'll be pickin' up bits o' this and o' that," Jean chimed in. "Like a birdie buildin' its nest."

Hildy turned wide brown eyes on Libby, clearly expecting more.

"Because a lot of people only choose the perfect shells." As opposed to the ones that had been ground up for landscaping. "But someone has to love the broken pieces." She ventured a glance at her audience to see how this was going over. Hildy gave a solemn nod.

"I like to think these shells have been through things," Libby continued, confidence growing. "There's a story there."

"If only the poor wee bairns could talk," Jean said on a sigh.

Libby ignored Jefferson's raised eyebrows. *Off limits,* she reminded her brain. *No staring allowed.* It made a desperate grinding sound in response, like the fan in her ailing laptop.

"Live. Laugh. Love," Jean went on, when no one responded. "That's what I reckon they'd tell us."

"And find beauty in the unexpected." Hildy's eager expression clued Libby in that this was another of Lillibet's greatest hits.

"Right." She forced a smile, making a mental note to slap herself later.

"Is the no-ring thing a choice, or did you take it off to go gathering?" Hildy nodded at Libby's left hand.

"Um." They'd talked about this, agreeing that no wedding band was better than any fake they could afford, but the ready-made excuse flew straight out of Libby's brain.

A sharp poke in the kidney returned her to the present. " 'Tis about hands, tisn't it?" Jean prompted. "Touching hands. Reaching out. Touching this and that."

Thank you, Neil Diamond.

"Yes! I don't like anything to block that connection. Between me and the earth. Or the sea. Sand. Grass. Flowers." Libby looked for something to demonstrate her point, but it was tricky indoors. In a moment of desperation, she stuck her hands in her hair. It probably looked like she had a splitting headache.

"Likes touchin' herself, too," Jean said.

The silence felt like an empty swimming pool Libby was about to topple into. Somebody needed to say something. Like maybe the hostess of this *Titanic* of an evening.

"Cocktails will be ready in a jiffy." And won't that be peachy keen? At some point during her programming, Lillibet must have been fitted with the 1950s housewife chip.

The door to the kitchen swung open. Keoki emerged carrying a tray laden with drinks. Libby sent up a silent, *Hallelujah*.

"Who's this?" Hildy asked, looking him up and down. "The mysterious Mr. L?"

Keoki froze, shooting Libby a panicked look. He didn't share Jean's terrifying flair for improv, largely because it was hard for him to be anyone but himself. That was reason number one they'd never considered having him play Libby's husband, even before Mr. L leaped at the chance to fulfill his thespian dream. The second was the borderline-incest squick factor.

"Ha! Not at all. This is my . . . old friend," Libby stammered, at the same time Jean said, "Cousin."

They glared at each other.

"A cousin-friend," Jean amended. "Doon ya ken." She plucked a glass from the tray, draining it in one go. It looked like an excellent idea to Libby, who was headed in that direction when Jefferson's voice brought her to an abrupt halt.

"Is your husband joining us?"

She smoothed damp palms over her hips. Talk about a loaded question. Had anyone else picked up on the subtext of, *The one you failed to mention when you were making eyes at me on the beach*?

"Uh, yes. He'll be here soon." It sounded like a death sentence.

Keoki approached with a glass, having already handed one to Hildy. Jean grabbed it before Libby had a chance.

"Beg pardon," Jean rasped after sucking down half of Libby's drink. "I've always had a terrible thirst. Curse of me ancestors. The demon liquor in our blood!"

Libby made a throat-slitting gesture but was forced to play it off as fixing her hair when she realized Jefferson was watching.

"Aye," Jean continued, like a car sliding off the road. "Both of me grannies drank like there was nae tomorrah. I was named for them, you know."

"Oh?" Hildy said politely. "I didn't catch your first name, Mrs. O'Malley-Gilligan."

"Jean. Er, Jean-Colleen, that is."

Keoki pried the glass out of her hand. "Save some for the fishes."

"Shall we have our drinks on the lanai?" Libby said brightly. It seemed like something a hostess would propose, especially if her jailbird housekeeper with the dodgy accent was too busy getting loaded to do her pretend job.

A clap of thunder sounded, rumbles fading slowly into silence.

"Or not," Libby muttered.

Jefferson's amused glance lighted on the tray full of empty glasses, Hildy having dispatched her own in record time.

"I'll make another batch," Keoki said. "And I'll bring out something to snack on, so you can pace yourselves." He narrowed his eyes at Jean. "But not shrimp crackers, because *someone* ate them all." The disapproving stare swung to Libby.

She tried not to look at Jefferson, but the temptation was too strong. He turned away before she could guess whether he was going to spill her secret.

"Ooh, one of your legendary pupu platters?" Hildy directed the question at Libby, who watched Keoki open his mouth to answer before remembering.

It turned out there was a world of difference between talking up Keoki's recipes online, for an invisible audience, and taking credit for them in real life. How was she any better than the chef at Chez Jacques, who slapped his name on Keoki's best dishes? That was another reason her oldest friend needed his own place—to finally get the recognition he deserved. And put a roof over his family's head.

I owe you a month of karaoke, she promised him with her eyes. *All the diva hits your heart desires. I'll even do Celine.*

Being a better friend than she deserved, Keoki sighed. "Lillibet wanted to keep it light tonight."

"A liquid diet," Jean suggested. "Like them newfangled smoothies and suchlike."

"No, we're having seared furikake ahi and marinated ogo. Real food." Shaking his head, Keoki headed for the kitchen.

Hildy leaned closer, face lit with anticipation. "So. Tell me everything."

"About what?" Libby started to tuck her hair behind her ear, then worried it was one of those gestures that said, *I'm totally hiding something right now.*

"What we're drinking. Is it one of your signature aperitifs, or a special Me-mas concoction?"

"Ah." That was an easy one. "It's a margarita."

Hildy pursed her lips. "There was something different about it. Didn't you think?" she asked Jefferson.

"I wouldn't know."

Jean leaned against him, batting her lashes. "Sorry about that, laddie. You wouldn't begrudge a lady her tipple."

"Li hing mui," Libby snapped, dragging her friend off him. "That's what you're tasting."

"What's that?" Hildy pulled out her phone, like she was going to take notes.

"Um." Libby didn't think *salty dried plum powder* was going to land the right way. "The secret ingredient in my Me-mas margaritas."

"Mysterious! Provocative! I love it. And the red is so bold. We should have gotten a picture. Next time." Hildy nodded at Jefferson, like he was keeping a master list of photo ops.

"Is that the royal we?" he asked.

"Yes. Princess Hildy commands it."

It was impressive how she managed to laugh it off while still making it clear she expected her orders to be obeyed. Of the two of them, Libby suspected Hildy had a lot more to teach people about personal fabulousness.

"Ahem."

Speaking of fabulous, their host was standing at the top of the stairs. He'd traded his suit for a blue version with a faint sheen. His ascot and pocket square were a pop of brilliant teal. Peacock colors.

That was fine. It was all fine. She reminded herself to breathe. "Here he is."

"Who?" Jefferson seemed genuinely puzzled.

"Her man," Jean replied, when Libby found herself unable to say the word husband.

Mr. L continued his slow descent, pausing from time to time to pose as though traversing a red carpet. "My friends," he said, stopping a few steps from the bottom, where he was almost as tall as the other adults in the room. "Welcome to my home."

Jean coughed.

"Where I live with my beautiful Lillibet," Mr. L added. "Who is my wife. And so it is also *our* house. You might say."

The wink wasn't even the worst of it. But at least he looked happy, like someone had complimented his faucet. *Good for you, Rudy.* One of them should enjoy this train wreck.

The only person having more fun was Hildy, who was drinking in every detail of Lillibet's invented life, her mouth puckering in a soft O. Though that might have been the lingering tartness of the li hing mui. Jefferson's face remained unreadable, but Libby felt the weight of his attention even when she resisted the urge to look in that direction. He probably thought she was a gold digger, shacking up with an oddball older man to fund her ridiculous lifestyle. Could this night get any more awesome?

"So this is what you've been hiding." Hildy lowered her voice to a confidential murmur.

"What?" Libby hoped she didn't sound as guilty as she felt.

"There's your life and then there's your '*Life*.'" Hildy underscored the last word with finger quotes. "You have to keep some things private."

"Aye," Jean concurred. "A woman has many hidden chambers. Attics and basements. Proper full of secrets, they are."

Outside, the wind picked up, rain lashing the windows. No wonder Jean thought they'd been transported into a Gothic novel.

"I hope the goats are okay," Hildy said as a flash of lightning illuminated the storm-tossed yard.

Mr. L clapped his hands. "Is that what we're having for dinner? I love a good goat curry."

Everyone stared at him with varying degrees of horror. Jean was the first to recover.

"They're at the groomer." Realizing she'd dropped the accent, she added a hurried, "doon ya fash, lassie."

That's Scottish, Libby mouthed. Though what she really meant was, *Please stop*. And also, *No more Outlander for you*.

"I'm excited to see your Me Tree." The artificial brightness of Hildy's tone said Subject Change. Thank goodness one of them had social skills. "JJ and I have been dying to know which theme you settled on."

Me, too, Libby almost said out loud. The only thing Jean had let slip was that it was going to "rock your world." Which could mean a lot of different things, Jean being Jean. At the very least, it had to be less pathetic than the shell heap on the dining room table.

"And what presents you got yourself," Hildy added.

"We'll have to wait a few days." *Or at least until we find something to wrap.* "I can't open my Me-mas gifts before—" Libby's throat closed, refusing to say the word twice in the same sentence.

"Me-mas?" Jefferson supplied.

"We so appreciate you inviting us into your home," Hildy cut in, linking her arm through Jefferson's. "It's an honor to witness the very first Me-mas. History in the making!"

"Right." Libby dragged her gaze from the trusting way Hildy was clinging to Jefferson. "The, um, Me Tree is in here."

She set off confidently in what she thought was the right direction, only to be hit with a wave of doubt in front of the pocket doors. *Was* this the living room?

The doors slid apart with the whispering glide of expensive engineering. Libby peeked inside.

So many books. Shelf upon shelf of them. Floor-to-ceiling, in fact.

"I thought you might like to see the library first," she chirped, like it was a special treat. "And now we can—continue our journey together. To the living room. Because it's not the length of the journey that matters as much as the spirit of . . . discovery."

Jean flashed her a covert thumbs-up.

Hurrying to the other end of the corridor, Libby flung open a nearly identical set of doors with a game-show worthy, "Tada!"

Her fist clenched in victory at the sight of the "tree" in the corner, and not only because it meant she had the right room. Jean had strung together driftwood branches of varying lengths, backed with brown butcher paper, the straight edges suggesting a frame. The whole thing was suspended from the ceiling by metal rods and cables, the industrial elements contrasting against the weather-bleached wood strewn with bits of coral and fresh flowers.

Despite the pressure-packed situation, Libby took a moment

to appreciate her friend's artistry. Jean's found-object kinetic sculpture phase had been one of Libby's favorites, even though she'd developed a permanent forehead bruise trying to walk through their apartment.

This might work after all. The flush of hope brought prickles of sweat to Libby's hairline.

"As you can see," she said, crossing to the sliding glass doors to let a little fresh air into the room, "the Me Tree is a focal point for the meditative aspect of Me-mas. A place to sit and contemplate your place in the universe."

Libby sucked in a lungful of rain-scented evening before turning back to her guests. She expected Hildy at least to appear interested, but no one was paying the slightest attention to her rambling. Their startled expressions were trained on the Me Tree, which had spun in the breeze. The side facing Libby was the same rustic evocation of a trunk and branches she'd seen before. Apparently there was something surprising on the back, judging by the reaction it was getting.

What did you do? She tried to catch Jean's eye, without success. Swallowing a spike of dread, Libby walked slowly to that end of the room to see what they were seeing.

It was a naked woman. Or, to be more precise, a gigantic painting of an undressed lady—with Libby's face.

The larger-than-life figure wasn't totally nude, if you wanted to get technical about it. Long hair snaked down to cover her pubes and she was feeling herself up with one hand. That left her other pale round tit hanging out like a fried egg.

It was a good enough copy of that famous painting of the blonde standing on a giant shell that you recognized the reference, but Jean had given her version a hot-pink-and-pistachio palette, like you were seeing it through a druggy haze.

It was outrageous. Unbelievable. And also a really cool piece of art, if you could get past the shock value. In other words, totally

Jean. Libby could feel the unholy glee emanating from her best friend.

"Oh my goddess," Hildy breathed. "That is amazing. It's like the Birth of Me-mas. Is it a self-portrait?"

"No!" It came out a little too emphatic. "It was a commission," Libby improvised.

"It's striking." Hildy cocked her head to one side, considering the epic nude. "As if you're saying, *Here I am, au naturel, with nothing to hide.* A glycolic peel for the soul." Libby nodded as if that made perfect sense. "Was it a local artist?"

"Yes." Libby didn't look at Jean. "Who unfortunately died shortly after painting it."

Hildy made a noise of sympathy. "Were they in poor health?"

"It was murder." *Some might call it justifiable homicide.* Everyone stared at Libby, waiting for the gory details, until Keoki rounded the corner.

"My eyes," he groaned, nearly dropping the tray he was carrying. He stopped in the doorway, as if he couldn't bear to get any closer.

"Not to be tasteless, but that makes your portrait even more valuable." Taking the tray from Keoki's unresisting hands, Hildy set it on the marble-topped coffee table and started pouring drinks. "Which obviously you would never sell, but still."

"Aye, she's a keeper, all right," Jean chortled into the glass she'd grabbed before anyone else was served.

"I've seen the original," Mr. L informed the room.

Not me, Libby wanted to scream.

"The Botticelli is in the Uffizi Gallery," he went on. "In Italy. It was almost as lovely as my liebling. Wonderful fountains." He made a spurting gesture with both hands that felt slightly lewd.

"That's . . . sweet," Hildy said uncertainly.

He edged closer to Libby, arm outstretched as if to wrap it

around her waist, before pulling back with a shudder. "I keep seeing my mother in that dress."

Hildy looked from Libby to her supposed spouse. "How Freudian of you."

"Thank you." Snapping his heels together, Mr. L bowed.

As Libby reached for a drink, a feeling akin to resignation settled over her. So this was how their cursed experiment was going to end. Definitely more of a whimper than a bang. Maybe some high-pitched keening.

"Cheers," she said to no one in particular, throat burning as she swallowed. "I hope you like your drinks strong."

"Like you like your men?" Hildy teased, with a significant glance at Keoki.

He and Libby exchanged matching ew-yuck frowns. The insinuation was so far off base, it hadn't even factored into the long list of "things that will give away the game."

It wasn't like Libby could quickly explain how she and Keoki ran wild together as kids because her mom was never around and his grandmother had practically raised her. Or tell Hildy that once you've helped someone wash his sheets to keep his older brothers from finding out he wet the bed, you might as well be related by blood. Not to mention the pending arrival of Keoki Jr. None of that belonged to Lillibet.

"Keoki is very talented," she said instead.

"Oh, I bet he is." Hildy's tone was twice as suggestive as a brow wiggle.

"He's going to open his own restaurant." Which was way more impressive than anything Lillibet had pretended to do.

"With my help." Mr. L patted his lapel, indicating either his wallet or his heart.

"So you're a patroness of the arts." Hildy was still focused on Libby. "Generous with your assets."

Generous was not the first word that came to mind when people described Libby's assets. There was a reason Keoki's older brothers had called her Tiny Lychees, and it wasn't because she could put away so many of the spiny little fruits. Though that was also true.

"I need to get into that," Hildy said. "The arts. I worry the symphony is too obvious. So then I was like, maybe theater could be my thing?"

"Oh, aye begonia. 'Tis your lucky night. Luck o' the Oirish!" Jean's arm twitched in a salute. Sticky red liquid splashed from her glass onto the floor. Mr. L hissed like a cat.

"I've got it," Libby said before his head could spin around. She knelt in front of Jean, grabbing a napkin from the tray to wipe up the spill.

Hildy set down her glass. "This is so educational."

As a PSA about drinking too many margaritas, or the importance of hiring a dialect coach? Libby kept those thoughts hidden behind what she hoped was a smile of polite interest. As opposed to the look of a woman on the verge of losing it.

"Sometimes it's easier to take care of business yourself." Hildy gestured at Libby, who was trying to rise from the floor without flashing anyone. "Other times you delegate. Preferably to someone who looks like the Rock, only soft."

"Dad bod," Keoki said with unmistakable pride, jiggling his belly like Santa. Libby half expected him to bust out the ultrasound pictures to prove it, but he was too busy patting his topknot. "And I have hair."

"Excellent hair," Hildy agreed, fluffing her own curls. "Although I'm kind of off men lately. Besides JJ, of course."

Who wouldn't swear off other guys after finding someone like him? Libby guzzled more of her drink.

"Good on ya," Jean slurred, tapping the side of her nose.

"Menfolk canna be trusted, with their lying eyes and wee wandering willies."

"I think somebody could use a sandwich," Keoki said, reaching for Jean's arm.

"I've heard a sandwich can fix anything." Libby gave Jean a syrupy smile, wondering how she liked being on the receiving end of patronizing sandwich discourse. Keoki raised his eyebrows (unlike the Rock, he couldn't do one at a time), reminding her that Lillibet was too evolved to be passive-aggressive. "Did you know I grind my own millet?"

Hildy looked delighted by this non sequitur, but before she could ask for details, Mr. L cleared his throat. "Has anyone used the bathroom?" It sounded like he was about to accuse one of them of leaving a floater.

"My—he designed all the plumbing himself," Libby explained, gesturing at her faux-husband.

He preened. "Let me know if you experience any problems. Not that you will."

"The pipes, the pipes they're callin'," Jean warbled. "No doubt everything's flowin' like a river for these spry young things. Unlike me poor old uncle Malachi. Speakin' o' dribs and drabs, can I get a refill?" She rattled the ice in her glass.

Hildy had gone back to studying Lillibet's Me Tree centerfold. "So do you decorate a Me Tree?"

Sure, Libby thought. *It's like Pin the Tail on the Donkey, only with nipple tassels.*

"Aye," Jean said. "She'll be needin' the finishin' touch."

"A beret?" Mr. L guessed.

"Nay. Though she can wear it on her head if she likes. Sure, an' our Lillibet can reach that high, bein' the tall drink o' water that she be."

Libby was always aware of her height, but the combination of too-short dress and everyone staring made her feel particularly giraffe-like, as if her knees were growing knobbier by the second. Since she wasn't really twelve feet tall, she set down her drink and headed for the ladder propped against the wall. Jean must have left it there after setting up her special surprise.

When Mr. L showed no inclination to move, Jefferson walked slowly across the room to join her. The set of his mouth was grim, like she was a hitchhiker he'd picked up despite the high probability she'd turn out to be an ax murderer. "Let me help you."

She was too tongue-tied to argue. Now that they were sort of alone, as they'd been on the beach, Libby was painfully aware of the undercurrents filling the room like one of those crisscrossing laser security systems in an action movie. In silence, they lifted the ladder, positioning it next to 2D Naked Libby.

"It's just there," Jean called out to Jefferson, pointing at a box on one of the end tables. "Be a love and fetch it for her."

If the accent was the main problem with Jean pretending to be a domestic, a close second was her habit of ordering people around while she lounged and guzzled cocktails.

Jefferson started to reach into the box. "Are you sure?"

Libby's first guess was *severed head,* followed closely by t*he shriveled remains of my personal dignity.*

He held up the desiccated corpse of a fish that would have been hideous even in life. It looked like a cursed experiment in papier-mâché, round-bodied, with nasty needle teeth and beady eyes.

Even Hildy was temporarily at a loss for words. "Is it— symbolic?"

This was clearly directed at Libby, or rather Lillibet, which meant Hildy expected more than, *Hell, no! It's a joke.*

"Toxic waste." The words seemed to come from nowhere, boxing Libby into a corner. How was Lillibet supposed to bring that back around to Me-mas? "Sort of like with the food chain." She looked at the fish for inspiration. "And mutations. Because I'm using the occasion to . . . shine a light on environmental issues."

"It's just an ugly fish—" Keoki began, but Jean cut him off.

"Change! Always nipping at our heels." She made a biting motion with her hand. "Our Lillibet loves all the little beasties of the sea."

"Deep thoughts," Libby said, hoping that would put an end to the conversation. "Brought to you by Jose Cuervo," she added under her breath as she stepped onto the ladder.

It wasn't until she paused to hold her hand out to Jefferson that she realized the mask had slipped. He'd heard her make a highly un-Lillibet remark. Libby wasn't sure how she knew, since he didn't so much as twitch a brow, but the zing of awareness when their eyes met was undeniable.

Great. More fuel for the fire. Or maybe *pyre* was more accurate, since she was kindling her own funeral, one lie at a time. He'd probably added "basic bitch" to her cv. Right under "exhibitionist."

He turned the fish so she could take it without touching the spiky fins, then braced the ladder as Libby climbed another rung. She was so acutely conscious of his presence, her legs trembled.

"Careful," he said, and she tried not to jump at the phantom sensation of his breath caressing the back of her knees.

"Eyes over here." Mr. L snapped a hand in Libby's direction, and she felt the ladder vibrate as Jefferson stiffened. When she glanced down to make sure everything was okay, he was staring determinedly in the other direction.

Oh right. Because otherwise he could see up her dress. Libby wasn't used to taking the geometry of miniskirts into account.

Her clothing was not Mr. L's issue, however. He gestured at the hideous fish, sketching a sightline from its protruding eyeballs to his own face to make sure the angle was just so. She might need to pull him aside later to explain that as her "husband," he should pretend to care if a ruggedly attractive man had his face up his wife's dress. *Think of me like your favorite showerhead.*

Libby was close enough to read the suppressed amusement on Jefferson's face as he studied the fish, which had come to rest in her portrait's hair like a demented fascinator. She wondered what he thought of the rest of it, assuming he'd looked. *That's not really me,* she wanted to say. *I have a lot more moles.*

"Guess that's his good side," Jefferson's voice rumbled, for her ears alone.

Something about the moment cut through all the pretense, transporting them back in time. He was talking to Libby, the girl on the beach, like he knew she was still in there. Without meaning to, she leaned toward him. Jefferson must have thought she was losing her balance, because his hand cupped the back of her calf for an instant before jerking away like he'd touched something hot.

"Okay?" he asked.

She nodded, telling herself to climb down before she did something stupid. Stupid*er*. "Vertigo."

"Maybe you shouldn't be on a ladder?" He side-eyed her supposed husband. To be fair, even if they were actually married, it wouldn't make sense to put someone that vertically challenged on climbing detail.

"Hold on to your knickers," Jean called out, hiccupping as the lights switched off, plunging the room into darkness. There was a rustling sound, and then a click. Electricity hummed as a network of tiny bulbs flared to life behind Libby's portrait. One of them had been positioned directly behind the exposed nipple.

Libby felt for the next rung down with her toes, ready to put some distance between herself and this glow-in-the-dark peep show. She assumed Jefferson would move away as soon as she started to descend, but his hands stayed braced on either side of her body until it was almost as if those strong, warm arms were cradling Libby.

She knew she needed to move, but maybe she could get away with a few more seconds. He was close enough that she felt the cotton of his shirt brush her bare shoulders when he exhaled. Libby really needed a hug, even if it was an accidental one. Not a sexy hug necessarily, but that was a nice bonus.

The overhead lights flickered on. Libby froze in place for a tortured instant before hopping to the side and then back, like a solo line dancer.

"I think we should have a toast." Hildy raised her glass, and Libby braced for the kind of scorched-earth speeches she occasionally witnessed as a cater waiter. Like the anniversary party at which a wife had thanked her husband of forty years for "honoring at least one of his wedding vows."

Maybe Hildy was about to let it rip with something like, *To my shameless hussy of a hostess, who clearly doesn't want a job with my company, since she can't stop throwing herself at my boyfriend!*

"To new friends and new beginnings," Hildy said with a cheerfulness that gave no indication she'd noticed Libby fawning over Jefferson.

Jean leaned forward to clink glasses with their guest. "Hear, hear. And to the old ones. May the road rise up to meet them, so's they ne'er forget where they're meant to be a-going. Especially them what has a great deal on the line. Ahem."

Okay. Hint taken. Time to get back on the Lillibet train. Libby looked around blankly, trying to remember where she'd left her glass.

Silently, Jefferson held it out to her. *He* hadn't lost track of her drink. Or failed to notice she was empty-handed. If he was this nice to a vapid, philandering disaster, Libby could hardly imagine how well he must treat Hildy. Young, rich, and oh-so-lucky Hildy.

"Thanks," she said quietly, before tossing back half of her margarita. Without thinking, Libby licked some of the tangy red salt from the rim. *Oops.* That wasn't a very Lillibet thing to do. She rubbed her lips together, hoping no one had noticed.

Jefferson was staring at her mouth. Even though she knew he probably thought she had the manners of a preschooler, the cold drink turned to hot coals inside her.

"So what time is sunrise?"

Libby jumped at the sound of Hildy's voice.

"We're all doing yoga together, right?" the younger woman continued. "On the beach?"

The power of speech deserted Libby. All she could think of was blabbing to Jefferson that she wasn't a morning person.

"Ach, no," Jean said, shooting Libby a get-it-together glare. "She'll not be a-stretching and a-panting like a doggie."

It was Hildy's turn to frown at Libby. "But I thought you said the countdown to Me-mas would start at dawn? With the union of body, breath, and spirit?"

Libby swallowed. "I did. Say that." *Because I am completely full of shit.* "The truth is—"

"She's gone and hurt herself, hasn't she?" Jean supplied when Libby faltered.

"Yes! I . . . must have strained something. Doing my other yoga moves."

"Hamstring?" Keoki guessed, apparently forgetting they were making the whole thing up.

Libby thought of Jefferson watching her run across the beach. "No, it's not that."

"She sprained her bloomin' arse," Jean announced. Like that would smooth over the awkwardness.

"Yes," Libby forced herself to say. "I did. Strain a butt muscle."

Keoki sucked in a breath. "Glute injuries are tough."

"You should take a soak in the hot tub. With your friends!" Mr. L clasped his hands, delighted by his own suggestion. "I designed the jets to provide powerful deep muscle palpitation. Like making schnitzel." He demonstrated the pounding motion.

"Sweet Jaysus," Jean muttered, holding out her glass.

"Anyone else?" Keoki asked, clearly hoping to keep her from drinking it all.

"Why not?" said Hildy. "Since we're sleeping in."

Keoki filled her glass before giving the dregs to Jean.

Libby looked around the room. There were so many different agendas at play, and that was only counting the ones she knew about. Meanwhile, their cover story had sprouted more weird growths than an aging potato. It would take a spreadsheet to track the added flimflam, and this was only the first night.

Her attention strayed to Jefferson. Again. He shouldn't be her main concern right now, and yet her thoughts kept tugging in his direction, relentless as the tide. Would he still tell her everything was going to be fine now that he knew who she was?

Or *thought* he knew.

Probably not. Because Lillibet would never let on that she was worried. That would require her to admit she didn't have everything perfectly under control.

"Could I grab a quick shower before dinner?" Jefferson asked.

"You smell fine," Hildy assured him.

Libby caught herself nodding and tried to pass it off as a cough, like she hadn't noticed any intimate details about him. Not the way he smelled or his calf muscles or the color of his eyes or his body heat. Nope. Not her.

"My feet are sandy." He didn't look at Libby. "If that's okay? I don't want to mess up your plans."

Ha! Too late for that. Before Libby could think of a less damning response, Mr. L leaped into the breach.

"A shower is never 'okay,' " he sniffed. "Not in this house."

"Because our showers are so very exceptional," Libby said into the confused silence.

Her pretend-husband nodded. "Indoor, outdoor, steam, monsoon, thermostatic—"

"I can show you," she cut in, hoping to spare them the full catalog.

"Are you sure that's wise, now, lassie? What with the servin' o' dinner to supervise and all?"

If only I had—I don't know—a housekeeper *to help with things like that,* Libby glared back at Jean.

"Go ahead." Hildy picked up the bowl of mixed arare crackers, tossing one into her mouth. "Maybe JJ can try one of your scented oils?"

Was the condensation on the windows from the rain, or had Libby fogged the glass by imagining her hands gliding across Jefferson's chest?

"Hurry back." Jean tapped the corner of her eye, their signal for, *I'm watching you.*

"Time is honey, as I like to say. Sticky and everlasting." While everyone grappled with that stunningly opaque Lillibet-ism, Libby tried to slow her galloping pulse. It wasn't only the prospect of alone time with Jefferson making her heart race. Or the showering, though that was certainly front and center in her consciousness. Full frontal, you might say.

Escaping this room would be like stepping offstage, away from the harsh glare of the spotlight—some of which was emanating from an artistic rendering of her left breast.

She turned to Jefferson, swallowing to keep her voice from coming out too husky. "Follow me."

Chapter 8

"You have a beautiful home," Jefferson observed as he followed his hostess up the stairs.

It seemed like the right thing to say, even if the word felt wrong. A home suggested something scaled for humans. This was more of an estate. And it might not even be their main residence. He vaguely recalled Hildy referring to this as a beach house, which implied the existence of other homes.

"It's what's on the inside that counts," Lillibet replied, after a pause so long he wondered if she'd heard him. There was a microscopic flinch before she added a smile.

"You're not what I was expecting." He meant it as a compliment, but the glance she gave him over her shoulder was wary.

"No?"

He couldn't think of a socially acceptable way to explain that Hildy had made Lillibet sound like a spoiled nightmare, as opposed to the warm and appealing human in front of him. With the long limbs and softly swaying hips.

"Why do you do it?" he asked instead.

She stumbled over the top step, righting herself as she turned to face him. "I'm sorry?"

"Putting your life online." He gestured at the foyer below them. "It's not for money. And if you don't mind my saying so, you don't seem like an attention-seeker." She'd spent half the night trying to fade into the woodwork. Apart from the giant nude portrait. Possibly she hadn't anticipated company when that particular piece of art was commissioned.

"I like writing." She half whispered it, like she was trusting him with a secret, waiting for his nod before she went on. "Stories about people. And their lives." Her mouth opened and then closed again, accompanied by the rapid blinking of a person who has remembered something important. "By which I mean *lifestyles*. The art of, you know, finding beauty in the everyday. Because that's a way to help people . . . help themselves." She slid him a sidelong glance, as if to check whether he was swallowing what she was dishing out.

"I see," he said, pretending not to notice that the benevolent part of that little speech had the distinct air of a postscript. Not that he was in any position to criticize. Jefferson had done plenty of work-for-hire in the early days of his career. He wouldn't have wanted someone to judge him for taking glamour shots of show dogs to pay the bills.

They continued down the hallway in silence, passing several doors before she stopped in front of the second-to-last on the left. "We gave you and Hildy adjoining bedrooms. For comfort."

"Ah." Their alleged coupledom had completely fled his mind. She opened the door and waved at him to go in.

His backpack looked as shabby and out-of-place as a dust bunny in the immaculate vastness. Everything was wood and white and pale gray, from the raised four-poster bed with its gauzy hangings to the tall shutters closing off what he guessed must be a balcony. The overall effect could have been antiseptic, but it tilted slightly over the line into soothingly organic.

Or so he imagined Hildy would say.

Lillibet cleared her throat.

"It's very nice," he said. "Thank you."

"I was going to tell you the bathroom is there." She indicated the door with her thumb. "For your feet."

They both looked down at his shoes. It was true that he had sand between his toes, but he'd mostly been looking for a moment alone, or at least away from the atmosphere in the living room. Being on his own with Lillibet was a different kind of tension, one that made him feel more alive—unlike the slow suffocation of the scene downstairs.

"Okay," he said. "I can take it from here." As if his ability to bathe himself had been in doubt. Or she'd offered to stay and help. He started to toe off his shoes, then worried that seemed rude. Luckily Lillibet had already turned away, so she didn't notice him standing there with one bare foot and one shoe, his socks still balled up in his pockets.

"This is a new prototype," she explained, as he kicked aside his other shoe and followed her into the bathroom. The shower was rimless, with what looked like river rock lining the floor. She was frowning at the far wall, on which there did not appear to be anything resembling a knob. "It has a lot of settings." She poked at the tile. "Very cutting-edge."

"Is it motion-activated?" he asked, dodging the arm Lillibet was waving over her head.

"Um." She gave up on the arm movements and started pressing different spots on the floor with her toes. "Sometimes."

That probably meant the technology was glitchy, but she didn't want to insult her husband's work. Jefferson bent to study the other wall, looking for some type of control.

"It's because this is a guest room," she said, an explanation and an apology rolled into one. "That's why I never come in here."

"That's okay. I like a challenge." Crawling around a deluxe yet water-free shower with a virtual stranger wasn't even the weirdest thing that had happened to him this week.

"I can do this." Her eyes were closed, the words spoken under her breath. "I need to *relax*—"

They both jumped at the sudden *plink* of harp music playing from invisible speakers. The overhead lights dimmed, taking on a soft lavender glow.

She beamed at him. "Something happened!"

He nodded, not wanting to spoil her moment of triumph by pointing out that they still hadn't unlocked any of the more traditional shower functions.

"Now all we need is water." As she spoke, the harp sounds were replaced by the echoing call of whale song, interspersed with the rush of waves. The light changed to a pulsing blue, as if they were lying on the bottom of the ocean.

It might have been Jefferson's imagination, but he thought he caught a whiff of salt in the air. The only thing that would have made the ambience more aquatic was some form of liquid. "You're getting warmer."

She flinched as the whale sounds gave way to shrieking monkeys and the low hum of insects. Clouds of steam puffed out on all sides, scented with tropical flowers.

"I'm almost damp," she said, cupping a hand to catch some of the condensation. "I mean, from the mist."

Of course that was what she meant. He stared at the moisture caught in the hollow of her throat. Sweat or condensation from the shower? The only way to tell would be to taste it.

Whoa, there. He had no intention of going from cheated-on to cheater. Time to dial it back.

"Might be easier to stand outside in the rain." *Especially if it's cold.* He was only half joking, a distinction lost on the shower, which released a slow trickle of droplets from overhead.

"You did it!" She clapped her hands together, delight fading as the water cut off. "Do you think it's because we have our clothes on?" She tugged at the waist of her dress as if debating whether to take it off.

He swallowed. "What?"

"Maybe it senses that we're not naked. Like a safety mechanism, so it doesn't start spraying people when they come in here to clean—or whatever."

Part of Jefferson wanted to wait and let her propose the obvious solution, but his better nature forced him to speak up. "I think it's voice commands. Sound in general."

"Oh." She bit her lip. "That makes more sense. So it was the—" she clapped three times, and water shot out from several directions at once. They dodged the jets until the spray shut off.

"It's like trying to wash your hands in a public restroom."

"Makes it tricky to scrub."

"What is the sound of one hand clapping?" Lillibet mimed washing her armpit with one hand while slapping her thigh with the other. "There's probably a rhythm to it."

"Or else it's a two-person job." It was an innocent remark; there was nothing sexy about having a designated clapper, even if you were naked at the time. But the shower had other ideas. Apparently "two-person" was the cue for a sultry saxophone solo and potent aroma of rose petals. Jefferson tried very hard not to imagine Lillibet and her husband frolicking under the hot-pink heat lamps.

"Normal!" Lillibet tipped her head back to address the ceiling. "Regular. Basic. Humdrum. Calgon, take me away!" She shook her head. "How is it that none of those work? I just want a simple shower."

They waited for something to happen. It occurred to Jefferson that this was the opposite of Lillibet's usual approach, which relied on complicating everything. Or, at least, that was true of her online persona. The Lillibet wiping scented mist of her forehead with the heel of her hand while grunting in frustration didn't seem to be a fan of fussiness.

"Niagara," Jefferson yelled.

"What are you doing?"

"Just curious." He thought for a minute. "Irrigation?"

"Super-soaker," she called out, shoulders sagging when nothing happened. "I should go get Mr.—my husband." Her smile was rueful. "I didn't think it would be this *hard*."

Water sprayed them with ballistic force. It was like a scene from a war movie, and they were the doomed platoon caught in heavy enemy crossfire. Jefferson expected the music to change to whistling grenades and rat-a-tat machine guns, but what he could hear over Lillibet's stream of profanity sounded more like chanting. Operating on pure instinct, he reached for her, spinning around so that her back was against the wall and his body arched over hers, blocking most of the spray.

It was the closest they'd ever been to each other, and even the assault on his kidneys wasn't enough to distract Jefferson from the way her eyes—and lips—lined up with his. They fit together like dovetail joints in a wooden drawer. She was breathing hard, her rib cage pressing against his chest with every inhale. Jefferson could feel how easily the moment could turn into something more.

When the water cut off, it took a few seconds for his brain to process the clapping sound. It was not applause. A pointed *ahem* followed.

"I don't advise starting with level three," Lillibet's husband scolded, as Jefferson peeled himself away from her. They stepped out of the shower, meek as children busted with their hands in the cookie jar.

"It was an accident," she said, speaking over Jefferson's simultaneous confession:

"My fault."

"Sophisticated systems like this one require a delicate touch. Observe." With the grace of a dancer, Mr. L raised his hands to shoulder-height, slapping his palms as he said, "Gentle." A soft patter of droplets fell. He shot them a did-you-see-that? glance before saying, "Medium."

The steady spray was almost like a regular shower.

"Why didn't I think of that?" Lillibet muttered.

"Because you weren't ordering a steak?" Jefferson replied, for her ears only.

"Once you're ready for a more aggressive shower experience," Mr. L continued, as if they were in the middle of a symposium, "you can intensify the force."

Jefferson nodded. No need to repeat that experience. Or at least not the water-blaster part.

"We have also many other options. A shower for every mood. Bellagio." Geysers spurted in a dancing rhythm until Mr. L clapped them to silence. "Winter's journey." The temperature plummeted, accompanied by a hissing that sounded like freezing rain. "Night swimming." Total darkness, apart from a single floodlight that was probably supposed to be the moon. "Morning dew." The lights rose in washes of yellow and coral, while invisible birds chirped.

"He's what you might call . . . a visionary," Lillibet said, after a pause that suggested she was searching for an adequate word.

The door to the adjoining room flew open. "I knew it!" Hildy glared at them, hands on hips. "You're all up here having fun without me."

Mr. L cut short his demonstration with an authoritative double-clap. Likely for the best, considering he'd just announced something called the wheel of fire.

Hildy's sharp gaze traveled from Jefferson and Lillibet (still dripping) to the dapper figure of their host. "I didn't realize this was a group outing."

Beside him, Lillibet stiffened.

"We were experiencing technical difficulties," Jefferson explained.

"Hmm." Hildy stalked closer. "I hear they make a pill for that." She glanced at the shower. "That is a serious shower. You could scrub down a whole rugby team in there."

"I would be delighted to share with you some of the features, but for now I must speak to my *liebchen*," the shower guru said. "Privately."

With a quick smile of apology, Lillibet followed her husband out of the room.

As soon as the hall door closed, Hildy pounced. "Well, well, well. Jefferson Jones, ladies' man. Didn't know you had it in you."

"I have no idea what you're talking about."

"Nice try, Casanova. Sell stupid somewhere else. What were you and my Lillibet up to that got you all wet and bothered? Go on." She clapped her hands at him. "Spill."

From the shower, there was a gurgling rush of liquid, as if it were being poured from a massive pitcher.

Hildy scowled at him. "What the hell is going on in there?"

"That's the question of the hour."

One of them, anyway.

Chapter 9

> **lovelillibet** How do you keep things fresh in a long-term relationship? Mr. L and I have a grab bag of tricks, from travel to role-play. The real secret? Stop making assumptions. Instead of crushing your partner under the weight of expectation, allow them the freedom to surprise you. Spontaneity is a great way to manifest more fully in the moment.
>
> Love, Lillibet
>
> Image: A page torn from a calendar, folded into a paper airplane.
>
> #freeyourself #beherenow #thepresentisapresent

This is it, thought Libby, as Mr. L led her down the hall. *The big reveal.* Whatever ulterior motive he'd been hiding was about to be unveiled.

Instead of mentally preparing herself for this critical development, her thoughts veered back to Jefferson pressing her against the shower wall, sacrificing himself to protect her. Did he have bruises? Would she get to see them?

Focus.

She should be worrying about Hildy. Thank goodness her future boss hadn't walked in on them a few minutes sooner, while Jefferson was so close Libby could have drowned in his eyes. They were almost the color of a swimming pool, aqua shading into green— She pinched the skin between her thumb and index finger.

That was a thought for later, when Libby was alone. Assuming she survived what Mr. L had in store for her. After experiencing that shower, she was rethinking her first impression of their host. Maybe he was more of a mad genius than a single-minded corporate bigwig.

Hopefully not the kind with a freezer full of corpses.

They turned a corner and continued to the end of the hall before Mr. L opened another door, gesturing for Libby to precede him.

"My office. One of them," he corrected himself, laughing as he indicated the seating area opposite the desk. "Please."

The decorating theme seemed to be Antique Navigation. There were globes and brass instruments she assumed related to sailing (in days of yore), and sprawling maps with fancy calligraphy mounted on the wall. They looked authentically old but could have been reproductions. Or a record of his global plumbing empire.

Mr. L watched Libby approach a leather armchair. Her supposedly sprained hindquarters were inches from the seat when he threw up his hands like a traffic cop. "Stop!"

She froze, bent in half. It brought her almost to his eye level.

"You're dripping," he chided, pointing at her dress.

Oh, that. "Sorry. I—can go change?" In fact, that sounded like a brilliant idea. Straightening, she took a sideways step toward the door.

"No need. I have a prototype of the Sirocco Flow right here." He opened one of the cabinets lining the wall behind his desk, pulling out a sleek rod with a rounded end.

"You make blow dryers?"

The answer was apparently yes, as he proceeded to blast Libby from hem to collar, finishing with a few touch-ups to her hair and face.

"The travel-size is small enough to fit in a pocket," he announced, switching it off. "I call it my magic wand."

Libby sent up a silent prayer of thanks that Jean wasn't there to hear that part.

"Please, sit." Mr. L gestured at the chair behind Libby as if the ambush drying had never happened. He waited until she was perched on the edge of the butter-soft armchair before settling onto the matching love seat. "This is pleasant. Just the two of us."

After a brief delay, during which she could almost hear him think, *A smile would be a nice touch,* he smiled at her.

Libby felt her mouth jerk in response, like they were androids teaching each other to mimic human expressions.

"We should get to know each other better, don't you think? Naturally, I've heard a great deal about you from our mutual friend Keoki. I refer of course to your troubled early years. No father, distracted mother, economic insecurity, lackluster academic performance." His hand flapped a careless *et cetera.* Like it was the same old story, not worth going into the details.

Technically she *had* a father. Libby hadn't spontaneously generated herself. He just wasn't around. The rest was true, in a brutally factual way. Although Libby didn't think of herself as a charity case, the way he seemed to. She'd never considered herself poor until college, because everyone she knew lived the same way she and Keoki did.

"Is it any wonder you've had so few opportunities to better yourself, with such inauspicious beginnings?" Apparently it was not a rhetorical question, because he looked expectantly at Libby until she responded.

"I don't know. I'm not a sociologist."

"Certainly not!" He laughed as if she'd made a joke. "You need a college degree for that."

Libby was still reeling from the casual insult when he leaned forward, uncorking a carafe of what appeared to be water and filling one of the empty glasses beside it. "Drink this."

"I'm fine," she said, despite being parched from the drying incident. Even poor girls with no education had street smarts.

"Straight to business. I like that." He took a sip of water, set down the glass, then leaned back, carefully smoothing his trousers before crossing his legs at the knee. It was like watching an uptight person act out the clue "relaxed" in a game of charades. The effect was further undercut by the intensity of his gaze as he asked, "Do you enjoy helping people?"

Warning, said Libby's brain. *Potential trap ahead.* "I—guess?"

"Hmm." His mouth curved downward. "I believe in helping yourself. It builds character. However, there are exceptions to every rule."

She gave a cautious nod, more to the latter part of the statement than the pull-yourself-up-by-the-bootstraps bit. Classic rich-man thinking.

"I'm prepared to help you." He smiled at his own generosity.

"You already are," Libby reminded him. "Helping us, I mean. A lot. The house, the clothes, the cover story." She could have gone on, but Mr. L beat her to it.

"Don't forget the car."

"Right." He'd been significantly more chill handing over the keys to a shiny black SUV than he was about people touching his faucets.

"But now I'm talking about a far more *significant* commitment."

"Like for Keoki's restaurant?"

"This would be a venture of a *personal* nature."

"I'm not sure I follow." Translation: *I'm not sure I want to follow.*

"Imagine what you could do with, say, twenty thousand dollars?"

Shit. It is the kidney. Libby kicked herself for not googling the risks of being a living organ donor.

"College tuition," he continued, oblivious to her growing panic, "rent, dental insurance. A fresh start."

Libby lowered the hand she'd unconsciously raised to hide her less-than-perfect teeth. "You want to give me money?"

He nodded eagerly, pleased with her quickness on the uptake.

"Why?" Somehow she doubted he was running a secret scholarship fund for underachieving twentysomethings.

"In exchange for one small favor." The pinching motion that accompanied these words did nothing to dispel Libby's fears.

"Which is what, exactly?"

He held up his left hand, fingers waggling as if they were in a martial arts movie and he'd paused for some mid-fight taunting. Libby doubted Mr. L was saying, *Come at me, bro.* She shook her head, giving up.

"Marrying me." He whipped out a silk hankie, offering it to Libby for her inevitable tears of joy.

Chapter 10

The discovery that their shower had a summer storm setting (complete with rumbling thunder) could only distract Hildy for so long.

"So they're swingers? I had my suspicions."

"What?"

"The Lillibets. Pretty sure that relationship is all the way open." She waved at the door through which their hostess and her husband had disappeared. "Hence the alleged *chef*. Probably the so-called housekeeper, too." Hildy settled onto the edge of the vanity, tapping her lip as she thought out loud. "Gives new meaning to the term live-in help, if you feel me."

Jefferson had to admit that the woman who'd been introduced to them as Lillibet's housekeeper didn't seem particularly concerned with anything that fell under the "keeping house" umbrella.

"She's always been cagey about her husband," Hildy said, as though piecing together clues. "Like he's semi-part of her brand but she's really a solo act. I always wonder in cases like that if it's about respecting the other person's privacy or a sign of cracks in the foundation. Don't you?"

"Can't say that I do." The lack of agreement didn't slow Hildy down.

"Although it's not as bad as the ones who are all, *I love my husband sooooo much, he's so sweet and handsome and perfect, here we are on date night,* and it's like, mmmkay, you're definitely having an affair. Total overcompensation." She pretended to turn a dial. "Set the timer for the divorce announcement."

"You think those two are splitting up?" He could have kicked himself for asking, even before Hildy snorted in triumph.

"I knew it. You think she's pretty."

"Not what I said."

"Listen, I ship it," she continued as if he hadn't spoken, picking up a decorative soap and sniffing it. "You're both kind of light-haired and lanky, but not *too* similar-looking, to the point where it's creepy. You ever see one of those couples that one hundred percent look like siblings?" She gave a theatrical shudder.

"Hildy."

"I know." She held up a hand. "You're on the rebound, a vacation romance is super-fun even when you're not stuck in the Sahara of dry spells—which we both know you are—and she's empirically smokin.'"

"That's not what I was going to say."

"Whatever they called it in your day. Foxy. Babelicious. I don't know."

"*Married.* I was trying to remind you that Lillibet is married."

"Ish." Hildy seesawed her hand. "But it doesn't really matter, does it?"

"No," he agreed.

"Because of our thing." She grimaced in apology. "Sorry to cockblock you, buddy. I didn't realize you'd want to get hot in the tropics."

He shook his head, recognizing the futility of arguing.

"I need you to stay in my corner a little bit longer. Let our love story play out in the press. It's not really lying," she added, noticing his frown. "They started it. All we're doing is letting them run with it."

Jefferson wasn't so sure. Ignoring a bunch of online chatter wasn't the same as pretending in front of real people, one of whom was turning out to be a lot less artificial than he'd been led to expect. "How much longer is this going to go on?"

"Our showmance, you mean?" It was a game with Hildy to try to get him to use the word. So far, he was winning. "It's hard to give an exact time frame. When the moment's right, we'll know. *I'll* know," she amended, after a quick glance at him. "But you'll be the first person to find out after that. Well, among the first."

If the media thing didn't pan out, she had a bright future in politics.

"Think of it like surfing," she suggested.

He waited for her to recall the landlocked nature of his home state.

Hildy sighed. "I'll dumb it down for you. Right now we're standing on a massive pile of potential energy. Before this wave crests, I need to get myself on a solid footing so I can ride it all the way to shore." Her hand sketched a smooth glide through the air. "If that means letting the sharks get a little nibble, so be it."

"I was with you until the sharks."

"The hype machine. Faceless masses of media consumers. Gossip rags. Take your pick." She shrugged before hopping off the vanity. "We have to feed the beast. Let them believe the fairy tale."

"Including Lillibet?"

"At least until I know she's not going to sell me down the river to boost her own stats. Once she's on Team Hildy, it'll be a different story. If I work fast, maybe you can still get some. It'll be like we both sealed the deal." She squeezed his forearm. "I know it's a lot to ask, and I wouldn't put this on you if it wasn't really, really important. This week is the key to my *entire future.*"

Jefferson suspected there was more than a little exaggeration happening, but he didn't want to offend Hildy by pointing out that she was young, and this one week wasn't likely to change the direction of her life. Still, he felt compelled to urge a little caution.

"Probably best not to get your hopes up too high."

"I know you think I'm being dramatic. Which, it wouldn't take much by your standards, but that's beside the point. I have plans within plans. And if I pull this off, I'll be in a position to give your career a major boost, too. *When* I pull this off." Her eyes closed like she was giving herself a mental pep talk. "With a little assist from my uber-competent wingman."

The flattery was almost worse than the bribery. "I said I'd help, Hildy. It doesn't have to be tit for tat."

"I know, JJ. We're strictly platonic." She laughed at her own joke before turning serious again. "I'm just saying I appreciate your sacrifice, and I fully intend to make it up to you. Maybe you can meet a nice ranch girl when you go home. Sow your wild oats or whatever they say in your world. Ride that bronco."

"Yes. All our personal ads have a rodeo theme."

"You should tell Lillibet about your chaps."

"I don't—"

"Shhh. Don't spoil the fantasy. Anyway, Methuselah, it's called playing the long game."

"Which game are we talking about?" He hoped it didn't involve leather pants.

"You, me, Lillibet, new jobs. Friends helping friends. Put this on your dream board. Time passes." She made a whooshing sound effect. "The two of you work for me. You're my favorite older people couple friends, like a reverse protégé relationship. If I get a flat tire, you'd come fix it. And bring Lillibet, and then we'd all go out for tapas."

"I'll teach you how to change a tire." It was upsetting that she didn't already know. That was a basic life skill, important to her safety—Jefferson tabled that topic for a later discussion. At least she was handy with bear spray. "I doubt you have much call for wildlife photographers in Chicago."

"Our headquarters may be in Chicago, but Johnson Media is an international enterprise. I'd find something for you to do." She pointed a finger in the air as inspiration struck. "You and Lillibet could be a team! You take the pictures, she writes the words. Plus all that other stuff you want to do with her, off the clock."

He ignored the cheesy wink, refusing to let his mind go there. "I'm a grown man, Hildegarde. I can find my own work. And I don't chase married women."

Yawning, she headed toward her room, patting him on the cheek in passing. "Being a lone wolf may be fun for now, but eventually you're going to want someone beside you, scarfing down raw antelope in your little dirt den. Think about that."

Hildy paused in the doorway. "And for future reference, the wet shirt thing is probably not your best play. Ryan Gosling set that bar pretty high. What women really want is someone who will sensually shampoo their hair." She made scrunching motions next to her head before tossing him a towel.

Chapter 11

lovelillibet Do you ever think about how something as simple as a bubble can have so many different meanings? In a glass of champagne, it's effervescence and joy. If we're talking about the blue bubble of a Portuguese man o' war drifting on the surface of the ocean, it's time to swim the other way unless you want to get stung. That's why when some people refer to me as a content creator, I tell them I'm a context creator. Because no woman is an island.

Love, Lillibet

Image: A tiny blue-tinged man o' war with trailing tentacles draped across the sand, waiting for an unwary beach walker.

#watchyourstep #tinybubbles #contextisqueen #veuveclicquot

I'll take insulting marriage proposals for a thousand, Libby thought. *Or no, twenty thousand.*

"You want to pay me to . . . ?"

"Marry me," he filled in the blank.

Because that made everything crystal clear. "Meaning what, exactly?"

It looked like he was going to repeat himself a third time, in case Libby really was that slow, until his eyes widened in understanding.

"Not sexual congress." His expression was mildly repulsed, as if Libby were the one who'd propositioned him. "I'm married to my work. We make each other very happy."

He smiled at Libby with a smugness she struggled to interpret. Did he want her to congratulate him or stew in the knowledge that she could never compare to his faucet empire?

"Also I need a green card."

Ha! Guess your weird shower can't help you with that. Libby gave herself a mental shake. She was not in competition with bathroom fixtures. At least now she knew why he'd agreed to play along. Except for one thing.

"Why me?" As opposed to any of the less pathetic candidates he might have chosen. Someone who'd made it through college without running out of money, for example.

"I am a man who recognizes an opportunity. A gap in the market, let us say. A space for growth." He cupped his palm, holding it out to Libby. Was she the blank space in this equation? "When you bring together timing, inspiration, and potential, innovation happens."

"I don't really understand corporate jargon." As opposed to personal wellness BS.

"You are available and—with a few cosmetic refinements— will look the part. Blond is a desirable color."

It was also available from a box in every drugstore. Which didn't stop people from making snap judgments based on Libby's appearance. That had been part of Jean's argument for starting *Love, Lillibet*: thumbing their noses at everyone who looked at Libby and saw long blondish hair and a tan and assumed she was Beach Barbie.

"I considered the other one. It's true she is neater in her proportions, but also"—his nose wrinkled as he searched for the right adjective—"*unpredictable.* You know the Irish." He mimed raising a bottle to his lips. "So you see, you are perfect for my purposes. No family, low social standing, physically attractive. The total package."

It was eerily reminiscent of a serial killer's checklist.

"Perhaps I will be inspired to name a fixture in your honor." He looked her over like a fish at the market. "French gold, I think. Brushed finish or brilliant? What do you say?"

"Um, both sound nice?" She assumed he wasn't talking about real gold. A tooth was one thing, but a showerhead? That was some Marie Antoinette business.

"You misunderstand me. I don't require anyone's opinion about my creations."

"Oh." Libby stopped herself on the verge of apologizing. What else could he have been asking? *Ohhh.* "You were talking about . . . the other thing."

"Our marriage," he confirmed, as if she'd correctly solved a basic math equation. *One plus one equals green card.*

"That's, you know, a big decision."

"How so?" The faintest hint of testiness had crept into his voice. "The advantage is almost entirely on your side."

"I don't know if I'd go that far." When Mr. L looked ready to argue with this mumbled protest, Libby hurried on. "I'm not saying I would say no . . . necessarily." She drew out the sentence, stalling for time.

Mr. L leaned forward.

"At least, not at this exact moment." Certainly not without talking to her friends, in case they had some idea how to get her out of this with minimal blowback.

"I think we are back to yes, no?" He made a circling motion with his finger.

"No! No yes!" Libby didn't totally blame him for losing track, considering the number of negations she'd thrown out while also trying really hard *not* to sound like she was shutting him down. How was she still this bad at spewing nonsense after all those months as Lillibet?

She opened her mouth to try again, but at that very moment Jean burst into the room. "There you are!"

Libby leaped to her feet. "Coming!"

"But—" Mr. L began.

"Hold that thought. We'll circle back to this soon." Libby flashed what she hoped was an ingratiating smile before racing out of the room so fast there was probably a trail of cartoon smoke behind her feet.

Jean was half a step behind, her instinctive sense of drama (and when to flee the scene) kicking in without prompting. They hurried past the bedroom from which Hildy's laughter floated, light and delicate as a flute solo. Libby tried not to be bitter. It wasn't Hildy's fault she had a boyfriend who liked her for herself, as opposed to her citizenship and general lack of resources, especially of the educational and orthodontic variety.

When they were safely inside Mr. L's mother's dressing room, which Jean had claimed as her command center, Libby pulled away.

"Why are we skedaddling?" Jean asked. "Did you plant a bomb in there?"

"He wants me to marry him."

Jean's bark of amusement died out when she saw Libby's expression. "You're serious?"

"Yes."

"I guess he hasn't dealt with morning Libby. Did you remind him you can't cook?"

"Nice."

"Sorry. It's an unexpected twist."

Libby dropped onto the chaise longue. "Exactly what we need right now."

"So he is into you? Because he barely looked at the Me-mas centerfold."

"Hard to believe, considering my nips were flashing like a fricking lighthouse."

"Exactly my point," Jean said, ignoring the sarcasm. "He would have been more titillated if I'd done a portrait of one of his faucets."

"It's not me personally. He needs a warm body, and apparently blond hair is a bonus."

"Ah." Jean knew how Libby felt about being valued for her appearance—and only that. "Remember when your mom was like, 'You know she won't always look that way.' I still don't know if the message was, *Don't feel bad, mousy one,* or *Don't get attached to having a cute friend, her days are numbered.* Like, are you her mom or her wicked stepmother?"

Looks had always been a big deal to Libby's mother, to the point that their relationship could be divided into phases based on how she felt about Libby's appearance at a given time. Stage one: Libby is a cute-enough kid to make a flattering accessory. Stage two: Libby is all awkward angles and acne, a warped mirror for her attractive mother. Stage three: Libby finally grows into her height, only now she looks like a younger model of her mom, with longer legs. And the last thing Rachel Lane wanted was a living reminder of her age.

"She's a mystery," Libby said, with a lightness she didn't feel.

"I think the word you're looking for is monster." That was one of the unsung roles of a best friend: giving voice to the things you couldn't let yourself think, much less say.

"Maybe we should introduce her to Mr. L. She'd set him straight." Though it didn't sound like their hypothetical arrangement would outlast the oft-mentioned day when Libby's metabolism crapped out.

"Hold on, there, blondie. Let's think this through." Jean paced back and forth in front of the dresser. It was a new habit; there wasn't enough floor space at their apartment to get a decent circuit going. "How can we make this work to our advantage?"

"Besides the twenty large he offered to pay me?"

Jean stopped mid-stride, slowly lowering her foot to the floor.

"That's a lot of frozen dinners. If he came in at twenty, we can definitely negotiate up."

"What?"

"If he really wants you to be his trophy wife, let's make him pay." Jean raised both hands in the universal sign for, *Just listen before you freak out.* "Take the money and fake it for a few months. You need a job, and it's a hell of a lot easier than temping. At least nobody will monitor your bathroom breaks."

"Um." Libby let the skeptical arch of her brows do the rest of the work.

"Okay, bad example. You'll get more than fifteen minutes for lunch. In fact, it could go on for hours. With multiple cocktails, *and* dessert. You won't get to eat most of it, but still. It'll be there. Not to mention the access."

"To what, his tennis club? You know how I feel about racket sports."

"I'm talking about real access. It'll be like you're a Trojan horse, taking them down from the inside."

"Number one, he wants a green card. That's it. And number two, this is not your eat-the-rich moment."

Jean sank onto the lounge chair beside her. "You turned him down?"

"I'm not sure."

"Did you black out?"

"I got nervous and started rambling."

"Yikes." Jean winced. "You didn't totally shut the door, though, right?"

"I don't think so. I kind of got the feeling that no matter what I said he was going to hear 'yes,' because I'm so pathetic and he was doing me this huge favor."

"Romantic."

"Every girl's dream."

Jean rubbed her face with both hands. "Okay, let's regroup. The good news is, we're still in with a chance."

"You sound surprised."

"Honestly? I figured we'd be out on our asses by now."

Libby stared at her.

"You needed encouragement, so that's what I gave you. And it worked. Hashtag winning."

More like hashtag we're-all-gonna-die, from where Libby was sitting. And the night wasn't technically over. "What about dinner?"

"They're pretty wiped from traveling. I suggested they eat in their rooms. Rest up for tomorrow."

That was both a good idea and surprisingly housekeeper-like. Maybe they were growing into their roles. "Are you bringing up a tray?"

"Hell, no." Jean looked disgusted by the mere suggestion. "What am I, their servant? Are their arms painted on?"

Or not. "Maybe we should go listen outside their door?"

Jean made a *tsk*ing sound. "All these years, and I had no idea you were such a perv."

"To hear what they're *saying*. If they suspect anything."

"We should have bugged their room." Jean clenched her fist in frustration. "I can't believe I didn't think of— What?"

"What, what?"

"Guilty face." Jean demonstrated, looking down and to the left. Libby was pretty sure her roommate was exaggerating the lip nibble. And the hunched shoulders. She definitely hadn't wiped her sweaty palms on her thighs.

"I think I might have messed up."

"I thought you said you were ambiguously vague? We need to stay on your pretend-husband's good side. Don't forget about K's restaurant."

"I know! But I wasn't talking about Mr. L. It's Jefferson."

Jean looked confused. "Who cares about him?"

Libby pressed her lips together, hoping her strangled *mmmm* didn't sound too much like *me*.

"Did he bust you?"

She shook her head.

"Then why are we talking about him?" Jean moved to the closet, clearly more interested in Lillibet's wardrobe options for tomorrow than talking about Jefferson.

"There was sort of an incident, I guess you could call it. In the shower. Between the two of us."

"Did it involve you getting up close and personal with his package? A little FedX-rated role play? Special delivery in his pants?"

Leave it to Jean to make it sound like he'd lost control of his bowels. "He was being a gentleman. Protecting me."

"From what?"

Libby hesitated, aware it wouldn't sound right. "The water."

"Was anyone naked?"

She shook her head, hoping the silent *unfortunately* didn't show on her face.

"Okay, then. No big deal. Moving on."

"You're not mad?"

"I'm mostly disappointed."

"Sorry."

"That you have no criminal instincts," Jean clarified. "How many years have we known each other? My skills should have rubbed off on you by now. But no, there you are, confessing like a punk."

"Excuse me for being honest." Intermittently honest, anyway. Libby still hadn't mentioned the meeting on the beach. Or how hard she was finding it to think about anything else.

"Listen, we both know you broke your brain watching that

video a truly unhealthy number of times, but you need to let go of that fantasy man. He doesn't exist."

"He's right down the hall." Libby neglected to add that she could still feel the very real impression of his body against hers. That was not her imagination talking.

"And he's an ordinary guy. Not whatever Thor-meets-Mr.-Darcy you cooked up in your head."

What if he's better? That was a dangerous thought, so she shoved it aside. "It's a lot harder to fake it to someone's face." Especially if what you really wanted was to make that person like you—the *real* you.

"It helps to think of yourself like one of those Russian dolls. You unscrew it and there's another one inside. They're all part of you, but not the only version, because people have layers. Show one to the world and keep the others hidden until you need them."

That wasn't terrifying at all.

"Anyway, I'm not worried about your little water aerobics with Mr. Fro Yo. He already has a girlfriend, and I'm not gonna lie, she's pretty rad."

"I like her, too." Beyond the possibility of a job, Hildy seemed like someone Libby would want to hang out with. If only it didn't require her to make asinine comments about personal enlightenment the whole time.

"As far as he's concerned, you're also taken," Jean reminded her. Crossing to the dresser, she helped herself to a squirt of hand lotion, rubbing it in as she considered Libby. "Maybe you should make it official. With Mr. L."

"Seriously?"

"It would be like tying a string around your finger. *Note to self, don't cross any lines with that one dude because I'm hella married.* On top of which, you pocket the cash. Sounds like a sweet deal to me."

"He did offer to name a towel rack after me. Or was it a bath mat?"

Jean was silent for a moment. "I was going to say, *He's full of surprises,* but it's actually the opposite, isn't it?"

Libby nodded glumly.

"I know how much you want this, Libs. And I'm not going to let you blow it. We'll figure it out. All the its."

Jean *had* put a lot of effort into this ridiculous scheme. More than Libby had ever seen her devote to, say, a legit job. Libby might not be blessed with a college degree or perfect teeth, but she had loyal friends.

"I did have one idea." Libby watched her roommate kneel on the floor and reach for something under the sofa. It turned out to be a bottle of wine, no doubt smuggled from downstairs.

"Hit me." Jean sliced through the foil with the tip of her keychain corkscrew.

"Put off giving him a final answer as long as possible and then pretend I died?"

Jean paused with the cork halfway out of the bottle. "That's a little extreme."

"How is it any more out there than the rest of this?" Libby could have made a list, with her giant nudie portrait near the top. "You're the one who used to talk about faking our deaths to get our student loans canceled."

"That was different. Lillibet can't disappear. It defeats the whole purpose."

"We could say I had amnesia? Like when I resurface a few months from now."

"I have a better idea. Let's drink this wine, go to bed, and start fresh in the morning." The cork emerged with a *pop.* Jean set it aside, holding the bottle out to Libby. "We made it through the day. Here's to us!"

Libby took a long drink. "Whoever we are."

Chapter 12

Jefferson had never tasted papaya. The teardrop shape and mottled green-and-yellow skin suggested something in the squash family, until he watched Keoki's knife slice one in half without visible effort. After scooping out the fat black seeds, Lillibet's chef placed an entire half on a white plate, squeezed a wedge of lime over the exposed orange flesh, and pinched a purple-and-white blossom from the floral arrangement on the counter, placing it next to the papaya.

"Don't eat the flower," he said, handing Jefferson the plate and a spoon.

They were the only ones in the kitchen. Jefferson had already walked down to the beach, hoping to see the sunrise—and anyone else who might be there to greet the day. He'd struck out on both counts. Lingering cloud cover muted the colors on display, and he'd been alone at the water's edge.

"There's a table in back," Keoki told him, nodding at the kitchen door. "I'll bring out coffee when it's ready."

"You don't have to wait on me."

"Might as well enjoy the quiet."

Jefferson heard the unspoken *while it lasts.*

The chair was still damp with dew, but the temperature of the air was pleasant enough that it didn't matter. Jefferson sat with his back to the pool masquerading as a lagoon, preferring the view of swaying palms above the deep green hedge.

He took a deep breath, letting the feeling of the place settle over him. Sunshine, salt-tinged breeze, the distant murmur of the ocean: If this were a real vacation, it was the moment he'd know he had arrived at his destination, with nothing but relaxation ahead. But if he'd learned anything last night, it was that he couldn't afford to let his guard down—least of all around Lillibet.

Jefferson could mostly forgive himself for the beach, when he hadn't known better than to be dazzled. Some of the blame for yesterday evening could be laid at the feet of jet lag and tequila fumes. Today he needed to keep his head on straight. Fade into the background and pay a lot less attention to their hostess.

The spoon dipped into the soft flesh of the papaya as if he were scooping ice cream. Jefferson's experience of tropical fruit was mostly of the canned variety, so the flavor ambushed him, impossibly mild and sweet, with a hint of tang from the citrus. It was rich but also delicate, almost perfumed. A perfect summer peach dripping with juice came close, but the difference between this papaya and the grocery store fruit Jefferson typically brought home—the mealy apples and bland bananas—was like comparing homemade pie to a goop-filled lump from a vending machine.

"Are you in love?" Hildy asked, pulling out the chair next to his.

Jefferson swallowed before he choked.

"With the papaya." She slapped him on the back, sounding even more pleased with herself than usual. "Because your face got kind of dreamy, by Jefferson Jones standards. Like you were thinking about having an emotion."

"I was enjoying a quiet breakfast."

"Poor baby. Hermit time is over." She had her own plate, with several other types of fruit, including a tiny banana, next to her papaya half. He watched her take the first bite.

"That is so freaking good. Did you try the mango?" Hildy transferred a slice to his plate. "No offense to everyone I've ever dated, but it's better than sex."

"I'll have to tell my grandmother," Keoki said, setting a carafe and two mugs on the table. "Not the sex part." He pulled a sugar shaker from the pocket of his apron, placing it next to the mugs, before reaching back in for spoons. "It's from her tree. I'll be right back with coconut yogurt."

After he disappeared into the kitchen, the sliding glass doors to the living room opened. Jefferson made a conscious effort to slow his spiking pulse before looking up.

It wasn't Lillibet.

Her housekeeper slouched onto the lawn, one hand to her temple. What he could see of her face around the dark glasses was pale.

"Ouch," Hildy murmured, watching her cross the grass to join them. "Looks like somebody has a te*quil*-er headache. That's one thing spring break in Cabo will teach you. Check yourself before you get wrecked."

Mrs.—the last name escaped Jefferson; McGillicuddy, maybe?—collapsed into a chair, sliding down until her head came to rest against the back of the seat.

"Coffee," she rasped. Jefferson hadn't touched his, so he slid the mug over. "Do you have any pain pills?"

Hildy rummaged in her bag, pulling out a travel-size metal

container of Advil. "Would you like some fruit?" she asked the new arrival, watching her wash two tablets down with coffee.

"Ugh, no." The hungover housekeeper gulped more coffee. "Where's Keoki? We need a bell."

Jefferson held up the carafe, refilling her mug when she set it down.

"That's better," she said halfway through the second cup. "A wee bit better."

Her accent wasn't quite as strong this morning. Jefferson had once worked with a Hungarian photographer who reacted to alcohol the same way, his otherwise precise English twisting into borderline incomprehensibility after he'd had a few.

"Will Lillibet be joining us?" Hildy asked. "I know she likes to meditate first, to start the energy flowing from the inside. And she prefers not to rely on artificial stimulants." She sighed at the mug cradled in her hands. "I tried switching to juice, but it's not the same. I need coffee to wake up enough to make the juice."

"Sure, an' he'll make it fer ya." The housekeeper nodded at Keoki, who had emerged from the kitchen with a tray bearing yogurt and bowls.

"Make what?" he asked. "French toast? Omelet? Soufflé?"

"Juice us up some o' that kale and ginger. Like Lillibet likes."

He scowled as if she'd asked him to flambé roadkill. "I only cook real food. She needs eggs and Portuguese sausage. Safer for everyone," he muttered, heading back to the house with his empty tray.

"I'll have some as well," the housekeeper called after him. "He dotes on her," she confided to Hildy and Jefferson.

"I can tell." Hildy shot Jefferson a knowing look.

"Aloha and guten morgen." Their host, dressed in another suit, waved from the steps leading down from the porch, as if to make sure everyone watched his approach. He stopped behind an empty chair, scanning the table several times before settling his attention on the housekeeper.

"Where is my charming *wife* this morning?" He seemed to take pleasure in saying the word, though the extra emphasis wasn't enough to get the housekeeper's attention. She stared into her cup, ignoring his existence.

"My wife *Lillibet*," he added, clearing his throat. "I've been looking for her."

"She'll be about her business, won't she?" the housekeeper said. "Hither and yon."

It looked as though he wanted to press the point, until another glance around the table reminded him they had company.

"Please tell my wife, Lillibet, that the lawyer will be here to speak with us this afternoon."

The housekeeper lifted her cup in an ironic salute. "No rest for the wicked," she sighed when his back was turned, before heaving herself out of the chair.

"You see what I'm talking about?" Hildy said when the two of them were alone with the housekeeper's dirty dishes. "There's something going on here. Besides the staff phoning it in."

"Maybe it's her day off." That was at least as likely as Hildy's swinging sexcapades theory. "What do you think he meant, about the lawyer?"

"Eh." Hildy scraped the skin of the papaya with the edge of her spoon. "Lawyers are always sniffing around this kind of house-hold. Taxes, estate planning, money laundering, who knows? Mo' money, mo' paperwork."

A flutter of fabric caught his eye. Lillibet peeked around the corner of the house, looking both ways before tiptoeing barefoot onto the grass. There was a sneaky quality to her movements that—combined with their host's earlier interrogation—made Jefferson wonder if she was avoiding her husband.

As she crossed the lawn, her black-and-white dress floated in the breeze, exposing flashes of tanned calf.

"I can't wait until I'm old enough to rock a caftan," Hildy informed him. "That's definitely vintage, by the way, which is so cool. Sustainable *and* chic. Mind you, Lillibet could wear anything and make it look good. Did you see her portrait this morning?"

Jefferson shook his head, unsure what the subject of clothing had to do with that picture.

"She's wearing the cutest little shorts. You know those ones with the suspenders, like they wear in Switzerland? The OG hot pants. You should check it out. Even though we both know you prefer the real thing. Lillibet, that is. Not short shorts." She snapped her fingers. "Lederhosen. That's the name."

They watched her approach, long hair shining with the rich gold of old brass where it caught the sun.

"Did a slow song start playing in your head?" Hildy whispered. "I listen to a lot of oldies, so I know things from your generation. Is it that 'you look wonderful tonight' one?"

There were no flies on Hildy. He'd give her that much, even if she apparently thought he was a Boomer.

"More of an instrumental track? Harp? Pan flute? Saxophone solo?"

"Cowbell. That's how we roll in Wyoming."

That made her laugh, which gave Jefferson an excuse to grin, as he'd wanted to since Lillibet stepped into view.

Hildy hopped out of her chair and threw her arms around Lillibet before springing back with a chagrined expression. "Sorry. That's not appropriate for a professional relationship. Not that I'm trying to wheel and deal before you've even had breakfast. Although I am really excited to open that dialogue. Most likely in your office—unless you want to be somewhere more organic? To unharness our energies?"

"Breathe," Jefferson murmured.

"Right." Hildy gave an exaggerated inhale, and Lillibet took advantage of the brief pause to claim a chair. "Oh, did your husband find you?"

Their hostess shot to her feet as if she'd landed on something sharp. "It's about curtains. For the shower. That's why he's looking for me."

"So, shower curtains," Hildy translated.

Lillibet pointed at her. "Exactly. I'll text him." She patted her pocket but didn't take out her phone. "Um. We should go out," she said, glancing at the house. "Exploring. I'd love to show you some of the island."

"Yes!" Hildy pressed her palms together in prayer pose. "That would be *amazing*. JJ can take pictures while the two of us talk shop." She looked down at her flowy pants. "Should I change? Are we thinking beach or brunch?"

Lillibet's head jerked at the sound of the kitchen door opening. Her face relaxed as the housekeeper rejoined them, a piece of toast in one hand.

"I was telling them about our plans," Lillibet said.

The housekeeper scowled. "Were you, now?"

"You know. A little sightseeing. Away from the house." A silent message seemed to pass between them—something they didn't want to share with guests. Maybe one of the showers had gone rogue and they needed to clear the premises before it killed again.

"Reckon it'd be a bonny day fer snerklin. Down Tartle Carve way. Sure as me name is . . ."

"Jean-Colleen," Lillibet filled in when the other woman trailed off. Though that was by far the least mysterious part of her statement.

"Aye." It sounded a little Popeye, squint and all. "Shake the lead out, mates. We leave in five."

❀ ❀ ❀

It turned out they were going snorkeling, at a place called Turtle Cove. When Jefferson admitted he didn't travel with flippers or a mask, the housekeeper assured him he could rent whatever he needed. The second Hildy slid into the backseat beside him, Lillibet threw her husband's luxury SUV into reverse.

"Sorry," Hildy said, apologizing for the two extra minutes it had taken her to put on a bathing suit and pack her beach bag. "I couldn't find my invisibility hat. So we don't get papped," she explained, when Lillibet sent her a wide-eyed look in the rearview mirror. Hildy held up a blue baseball cap with a faded smiley face logo. "Even if we weren't keeping this story on lock for our properties, I don't do unstaged candids."

"Perish the thought," Jefferson said under his breath.

Hildy whacked him with the hat. "I brought something for you, too. Even though you don't need a disguise because no one's going to recognize you unless you put on a snowsuit and carry me across the sand."

"No," he said, preemptively.

" 'Meme, Myself, and I—That Time I Accidentally Went Viral.' The Jefferson Jones story." Hildy held up a finger to signal a new idea incoming. " 'A Hero Comes Along.' Too on-the-nose? I'll have to make sure there isn't a porno with that title. And Mariah Carey is a little out there for you emotionally, JJ. In the sense that she expresses them. I'll save that one for me."

Jefferson waited to see if the merry-go-round was going to pick up speed, but with a self-conscious glance at Lillibet, Hildy broke off, running her hand up and down the strap of her seat belt. "Enough of that. It's hard to shut off the packaging part of my brain. It's so ingrained. Which is why I'm going to be a boss bitch editor. But we are not talking about that right now, because we are in the moment. Let's go see some fishies!"

❀ ❀ ❀

Jefferson had never considered underwater photography, there not being much call for it in the mountains. A different quiet held sway when your face was submerged, both like and unlike being alone in the woods. A slow current instead of wind, the undulating of marine plants, fish flashing past in bursts of brilliant color that put the earthy camouflage of four-legged creatures to shame.

If he thought of himself as an observer, hovering over the aquatic metropolis, Jefferson could forget what he was wearing. Hildy had waited until they were at the beach to hand him the rash guard. At that point there was no going back; they'd spent half an hour driving a handful of miles on the two-lane road, because even the rich had to contend with the traffic of too many people trying to enjoy the same small patch of impossibly beautiful island.

It hadn't always been this crowded, Lillibet explained from the driver's seat, while her housekeeper napped against the passenger window. At least not when she was a kid, out here away from the tourist hot spots of Waikiki. Jefferson added that piece of information to the rough mental sketch he'd been drawing of her background, while she went on to explain how locals were caught between needing the influx of cash from all those visitors and wondering at what point they would hit critical mass.

"Only room for so many on this floating door," the housekeeper, whom Hildy had taken to calling Mrs. OMG, said through a yawn. "Someone's got to be thrown into the deeps or we're all goin' down."

Jefferson had been here less than a day and could already see why so many people were desperate to visit—and, having come once, would dream of returning. That was one thing you could say for his part of the world: It didn't appeal to everyone. Especially in winter, which could mean anytime from October to June. If you wanted bare skin, warm breezes, and outdoor swimming, it was easy to resist the siren call of Wyoming.

Nor did you need special beachwear to live there, which was how he'd wound up at the mercy of Hildy's twisted sense of men's fashion.

"Fit check," she'd announced, circling a finger to get him to turn around after he squeezed himself into the long-sleeved shirt. "Oh. Oh my." She pressed a hand to her mouth, as if overcome with some strong emotion. (Jefferson suspected it was joy.) "It's even better than I thought it would be."

He looked down at the patterned faux-gold, giving way at the elbows to swirling turquoise . . . gloves? "What the hell am I wearing, Hildegarde?"

"You're Aquaman." She poked him in the belly, where a series of shadowy curves suggested an overdeveloped chest. "SPF50 *and* I gave you a six-pack, Grandpa. You're welcome."

Hildy had tried to convince him to put on the matching leggings, but he was wise to her game and used sunscreen everywhere his swim trunks didn't cover. The fish didn't care that he was dressed like an overgrown child on Halloween, but Jefferson wasted no time peeling off the superhero swim shirt as soon as they were on dry land.

"You better lube yourself up if you're going to run around topless." Hildy pulled a tube of sunscreen from her bag and tossed it at him. "I'd help, but my hands are sandy, so I might take off all your chest hair. Your first foray into manscaping should probably be in a more hygienic setting."

"I'll manage."

"What about your back?" She turned to Lillibet. "Would you mind? I don't want him to fry. You can teach him your special technique. The Wagyu massage. The relaxation helps with absorption," Hildy explained for Jefferson's benefit. *Enjoy,* she mouthed.

Lillibet hesitated before holding out her hand. Jefferson passed her the sunscreen with equal reluctance. Mostly reluctance.

She started at the top of his spine, stroking up the nape of his neck before letting her fingers trail down over his shoulder blades. What began as a light touch grew firmer as she rubbed the sunscreen into his skin, working it over his deltoids and then lower, her fingers slipping between his arm and his side to make sure everything was covered. Jefferson's body desperately wanted to lean into her touch, so he tensed his muscles to keep from giving in. Hopefully she didn't think he was flexing to impress her.

"How is it?" Hildy asked. "Soothing?"

What was a word that meant the opposite of that? His brain was too scrambled to play thesaurus. Jefferson had one clear thought, and it wasn't something he could say out loud. *I wish I had more skin so she would never stop touching me.*

"Bloody hell," growled the housekeeper, standing up from her towel. "Give me that."

"I'm almost finished," Lillibet said, holding the sunscreen out of reach.

"It's me job," the housekeeper argued.

"Sunscreening people?"

"Helping you. Afore you can help yourself, missy." This time Mrs. OMG succeeded in yanking the tube away. After squirting sunscreen onto her palm, she slapped it onto his back with both hands, wasting no time on gentleness.

"There," she announced, capping the sunscreen and handing it to Jefferson. "Yer on yer own for them wee hairy man nipples."

Hildy choked on her can of Passion Orange juice. "Waxing is quick and easy, JJ. Well, it's quick."

"Thanks for the tip."

"Don't mention it."

"Might as well get one o' them spray tans while you're at it." The housekeeper thumped him in the gut.

He was beginning to understand why Keoki had opted to stay home.

"Who needs a snack?" Lillibet asked, sparing him further commentary on his personal grooming. Maybe she thought he was beyond hope. That would explain why she seemed to be having a hard time looking in his direction. "We should get shave ice!"

"Aye," the housekeeper agreed. "Reckon *someone* needs a cool down."

Chapter 13

lovelillibet What are the simple pleasures that take you back to childhood? For me, it's the delicate richness of lobster bisque, which we had for dinner on Saturday nights. Nothing makes me feel young again like dipping a sterling soup spoon into a vintage porcelain dish of creamy seafood goodness.

Love, Lillibet

Image: Hundreds of tiny crabs crawl across a sandy beach.

#homesweethome #islandlife #comfortfood #foreveryoung

"I couldn't let you come all this way and not sample the most famous local delicacy," Libby said when they joined the line outside the shave ice parlor Island nICE, as if bringing them here had been a selfless act of hostessing duty.

It was a relief to talk about something she understood, instead of faking her way through another lifestyle humblebrag. When it came to shave ice, Libby's opinions were firm and backed by years of experience. Her guiding principle could be summed up as "yes." Ice cream, azuki beans, sweetened condensed milk, mochi: yeses across the board. Jean tried to argue with her about flavor combinations but was hampered by an inability to pronounce most of them with her accent. Guava became guab-er and lilikoi picked up three or four new syllables before she managed to spit it out.

"Is this the place Obama likes?" Hildy asked, as they neared the register.

"The line's even longer at that one," Libby said as they shuffled forward a step. "We don't go near it this time of year."

"A charry leem man, he is," Jean chimed in. There was a pause as they all worked out that she was saying *cherry lime* before she turned to Jefferson. "You strike me as more vanilla."

"Not today. JJ needs to get something exotic, because I'm going with the house special. Always start with a baseline menu item. I learned that from one of our food critics. It's like putting a racehorse through its paces. At an Italian restaurant, you order the lasagna first, to check how they handle the classics, and so on. Hence why I'll get the tropical trio." Hildy linked her arm through Jefferson's. "And you can choose something different. As long as it's awesome. Like melon. And lychee. Or pickled mango. With some of that li hing mui."

"Anything else?"

"Just some extra mochi."

"I live to serve," he said dryly.

"Another reason we're so perfect together." She gazed up at him from under the brim of her hat, which was working overtime to hide her distinctive curls.

"Because you live to give orders?"

"Bingo, babe."

Libby pretended to study a rack of postcards, sparing herself more of their cute coupleness. When Hildy insisted on paying for everyone, calling it a business expense, Libby didn't argue, because (a) she was afraid her card would be declined, and (b) when she reached into her bag for her wallet, the first thing she found was a brochure for Invisalign. Mr. L must be trying to sweeten the pot. She shoved the glossy bribe to the bottom of her purse before summoning a (crooked) smile of thanks.

They found a bench outside, ignoring the sticky patches left by previous customers.

"Is this giving you flashbacks?" Hildy asked Jefferson, helping herself to some of his sunset-colored shave ice.

"To my Snoopy snow cone machine?"

"Our *blizzard*, Iceman. The deadliest meet cute." She frowned. "Still workshopping that one. But you know what I mean. Mounds of snow everywhere. The helicopters circling."

"Shork wortch," Jean attempted to say.

"Shark watch," Libby translated. "That's what the helicopter is doing."

Hildy shivered. "That's one thing we didn't have to worry about on the mountain. You know what was weird? There we were, surrounded by snow and ice, which is basically water, and yet I got so thirsty." She clutched Jefferson's arm. "Remember when you melted snow in your little collapsible cup? Get you a man who can light a fire in the middle of an ice storm, ladies. You would not believe the things he had in those pockets."

"We'll not be needin' to see any o' that." Jean narrowed her eyes at Jefferson as if he might be on the verge of whipping out his equipment.

"So you spent the night outside." Libby nodded at Hildy to continue.

"In our little snow fort, yeah. Which has honestly cured me of any desire to ever go to one of those ice hotels. And then the helicopter found us in the morning, as soon as the wind died down. Thanks to my little signal."

"Flare gun?" Libby guessed.

"That would have been badass." She pretended to cock a bazooka. "But no. This was inspired by one of my sorority sisters who got married on the beach last summer. The photographer did these aerial shots where they spelled out 'Mrs. and Mrs.' with driftwood and then they took pictures with a drone. Black-and-white, so tasteful. Although some people"—she cut her eyes at Jefferson—"are too old school for drones."

"They're a nuisance," Jefferson countered. "It has nothing to do with my advanced age."

"How old are you?" Libby tried for casual, but judging by Jean's glare, she'd missed the mark.

"Askin' as a journalist, she is. Likes to have all the facts. 'Tisn't that she's personally interested, mind you."

"He's thirtysomething," Hildy said, as if the exact number didn't matter once you got up that high. "Anyway, there we were in the middle of this vast expanse of white. Absolutely no way they were going to be able to spot our snow cave from above. I could tell JJ was worried, but he didn't want to say anything because he's so protective."

Libby found herself nodding and hurriedly assumed a neutral expression. "And then?"

"I suggested we drag some branches over to make an arrow, pointing at the cave. And it worked." She gave a modest shrug.

"It was a good idea," Jefferson said.

"All's well that ends well, am I right? Look at us now." Hildy plucked a piece of mochi from his dish, popping it in her mouth. "Alive and thriving."

It was hard not to be charmed by Hildy, even when she was causing Libby acute stress, with a side of envy. "I'm glad you're here."

Hildy gave an eager nod. "It's like coming full circle. The whole reason I was out there is because of you."

The shave ice reconstituted inside Libby's stomach, a lump of frozen dread. "What do you mean?"

"Remember that post about how getting lost can be the quickest way to find yourself? You were describing that silent retreat you went on."

" 'I speak to myself with the voice of the trees,' " Jean quoted, puffing out her cheeks to make whistling-wind sound effects.

"It—can be, uh, good. Spending time on your own. Alone." Libby was clinging to a buoy of make-believe in a sea of guilt. There were a lot of things you could say about Lillibet, but she'd never guessed "accidental murderer" would be among them.

"Right? And like you said, surprising things can happen when you open up to inspiration. Like, I thought it was going to be a weekend of mountain air, digital detox, and thinking deep thoughts in my yurt. The perfect conditions to put together a killer business proposal. Which is a whole other topic." She made a swiping motion with one hand, physically shoving it to one side. "Back to our adventure. All my plans went out the window when I met JJ."

"And almost died," he reminded her.

"Because an experience like that makes you realize there's no time to waste. You have to pay attention to the signs telling you, *This is your moment. Grab it while it's hot.*" She looked to Libby for affirmation.

"Yes," Libby said slowly. "Although, there are signs, and then . . . there are signs."

Jean gave her a look that said, *Are you stupid or just an idiot?*

"Do you believe in coincidence?" Hildy asked.

"That depends." Libby would have left it at that, but Hildy was hanging on every word. "On your definition of coincidence."

"Like take me and JJ. He wouldn't have been out in the woods that day if his girlfriend hadn't dumped him. Personally, I think it's good riddance, because she sounds like a nightmare. Have you ever met someone who adopts a new personality based on who they're sleeping with, like why figure out your own mess when you can date your way to an identity?"

That one hit a little close to home. Rather than saying, *Yes, and she was my mother,* Libby pretended to take the high road. "You met her?"

"No, but she has a big digital footprint. Unlike JJ. So right

there you have a mismatch. My read is that this Genevieve"—
Hildy made air quotes around the name as if it were just as likely
to be an alias—"is an emotional vampire. She's looking for someone to be obsessed with her and tell her how beautiful she is
twenty-four seven."

"Is she?" Libby couldn't stop herself from asking. "Very beautiful?"

"Eh." Hildy tipped the paper bowl to her mouth, swallowing
the last of the melted ice and sugary syrup before setting it on the
bench beside her. "Under the makeup and filters, who knows? But
she must think this new guy is going to give her more status, or
stroke her ego, even though he seems pretty into himself. Look
at me, I'm a butcher who does interpretive dance. Pretentious,
much? Guess what he calls his business."

Libby glanced at Jefferson, whose stony expression made it
clear there would be no hints from that quarter.

"Bite Me?" Jean guessed. "Stuff My Sausage? Porky LaBeef?"

Libby frowned, silently encouraging her to stop there.

"Deep Cut." Hildy paused to let that knowledge settle in. "I
left him a one-star review on Yelp for having terrible taste in
women. No offense, JJ." She leaned her head against his shoulder
for half a second before sitting up again. "If anyone understands
the pain of giving your trust to a two-faced user, it's me."

Libby pretended there was something in her eye, rubbing it
with her finger to hide the twitching of her lid. *Two-faced? How
terrible!*

"Just the one face on our gal." Jean smacked Libby's cheek like
she was waking her from a faint. "But it's a good 'un."

"With a skin care routine like hers? Of course it is!" Hildy
stroked her own firm young neck. "And speaking of what goes
around comes around, it's lucky for me this guy was such a tragic
loner, or he wouldn't have been out in the woods that day. And
then I wouldn't be here, alive *and* on the brink of realizing my

professional goals." She shifted on the bench, taking one of Libby's hands in both of hers. "Which is where *you* come in."

"Ye hear that? Listen up," Jean hissed.

"I am listening." Libby squeezed the words out of the side of her mouth, maintaining eye contact with Hildy. "We're both listening. Very, very quietly."

Hildy let the silence build as she stared into Libby's eyes. "Are you for real?"

It was hard to say whether Libby's strangled laugh sounded more like a rusty screen door or a Muppet facing a firing squad. "What?"

"You strike me as very self-aware. A savvy businesswoman who knows her audience and creates the content they want."

For an endless, excruciating moment, Libby was sure her secret was out.

"Your feed is highly curated," Hildy prompted, before Libby could blubber a confession and beg for mercy.

"Yes, well. Aesthetics are—so important. I've always felt." Libby's nose was probably growing by the second.

"Proper actualized, she is," Jean chimed in. "More herself than most anyone else."

Hildy waited to see if Lillibet had anything to add to this ringing endorsement before continuing. "And what do you envision, moving forward? Because I sense the hunger. To put yourself out there. To express yourself. To be known."

It was so stirring the way she described it, one fist clenched, that Libby was halfway convinced. Had they forged a magical mind meld across an ocean of flimflam . . . and also a real ocean?

"Do you want to stay the course, grow *Love, Lillibet* into a global brand? Because I can help with that."

Womp womp. "I'm not necessarily locked into a specific paradigm." Or, you know, saying things that made sense.

To Libby's infinite relief, Hildy looked pleased. "Then you're open to other possibilities."

"Yes." So open. The Grand Canyon of openness. How to put it in Lillibet terms? "I truly believe that I am ready to . . . manifest my freedom. Of self-expression. In a fluid and evolving way."

"Like one o' them lamps," Jean suggested. "With the swirling blobs."

Libby paused. "A lava lamp. Indeed. But less, you know, lampy. Lamps can be beautiful and, ah, light-giving, but they're also so *contained*. If you see what I mean."

"Yes! We have to break the glass! Ceilings, walls, all of it." Hildy bounced with excitement. "That is exactly my struggle." She took a deep breath. "Okay, I think the time has come. Can I be completely honest with you?"

Please don't. That was Libby's first, conscience-stricken thought, since there was no chance she could return the favor. But she nodded anyway, and not only because Jean was glaring at her. If this had anything to do with the reason Hildy had flown here to meet Lillibet, then Libby was all ears.

"I'm still working on the pitch, but it's like you said. Practice is progress." Hildy leaned back and then forward again, rolling her shoulders. "Okay. I'm going to dive in. What if there was a magazine that was like the big sister you never had? A place to turn for advice, inspiration, a sense of community, or when you just want to hang. It would be warm yet light, deep but also a distraction when you need one. Impeccably designed but with enough meat to sink your teeth into, only not to the point where you feel like a bad person if you don't read every single word and then you wind up with a stack of shame on your living room floor. Cough *New Yorker* cough."

"Sounds bloody fantastic," Jean said.

"What do you think, Lillibet?" Hildy's expression was so vulnerable, Libby would have said anything to reassure her. Only this time there was no need to pretend.

"I love it."

"Yeah?" Hildy flashed a dimple. "Is that an environment—and a way of approaching the world—you might want to be part of?"

"It sounds like my dream job," Libby said truthfully.

"Maybe even the Me-mas of careers?" Hildy asked, face shining with hope.

Libby hoped her faint smile would read as agreement. She tucked a flyaway piece of hair behind her ear, trying to quiet the uproar in her mind. Was it time to tell Hildy something real? It felt like trying to step off a moving treadmill. Her gaze flicked nervously from Hildy to Jean before landing on Jefferson.

He looked back at her with an air of calm that settled something inside Libby. It was like pulling on a sweatshirt when the temperature is just cool enough to make you shiver, and feeling your tensed muscles relax. She'd already shared this sliver of truth with Jefferson, and he hadn't laughed.

"I've always wanted to write human interest features. In-depth profiles of people." *Who are not me.* "There's one I've been working on, about Keoki's grandmother . . ." Libby trailed off at Hildy's frown. "Does that not fit with your vision?"

For once, Hildy seemed to be at a loss for words. "I guess I was thinking we would do something more you-focused," she said at last. "Advice and stories from your life. Meet Lillibet, our in-house adulting consultant, here to share a woman's wisdom—that kind of thing. Expanding on what you've already created, only on a much bigger scale." Her laugh was closer to a sigh, heavy with self-deprecation. "I had this picture in my head that you would be the beating heart of *Life-comma-Styled.* Which is the name of my magazine. Although the comma is silent. Obviously."

"That's—wow." Libby had never imagined feeling simultaneously flattered and horrified. Jean was shooting her murderous looks, silently urging Libby to promise the moon and worry about the details later.

"No pressure. Just because I've been building the entire concept around you doesn't mean you have any obligation to take the job. And by 'you' I really mean 'us,' " Hildy clarified. "I'll be a presence behind the scenes. Unless you're a person who checks the masthead, in which case my name will be right there." Her shoulders sagged. "I came on too strong, didn't I? I've been told I can be a lot."

"You're the exact right amount." Libby had spoken without thinking, wanting only to wipe that doubtful look off Hildy's face, and the result was a strange hybrid of her real self and something Lillibet might say. Probably another sign of the end times, but at least Hildy perked up.

"I think this is one of those release-and-reflect moments," she said with renewed confidence, patting Libby's thigh. "We both need to *ask the mirror* and then reconvene to share our insights. Am I right?"

Jefferson's brows lowered in confusion. "You have a magic mirror?"

"It's a form of soul-searching," Hildy corrected. "Lillibet can explain it better."

Libby turned her gaze to the sky, as if hunting for the perfect words. That were not a stream of profanity. "Well, it's a lot like it sounds. You stare into a mirror and wait. To see what bubbles up."

"Like that *Candyman* movie?"

"No, JJ." Hildy swatted his arm. "It's about self-reflection. I look myself in the eye and sink deeply into my own consciousness, swimming through the layers of resistance until I make contact with my core feelings. What did you call it again?"

"Mirror diving." Which was almost as bad as Me-mas. One of

Libby's main takeaways from the last twenty-four hours was that Lillibet's thoughts were even more vomit-inducing when you had to say them out loud.

Mercifully, Hildy's phone dinged. She checked the screen, huffing with impatience. "I better take this. My uncle's been calling all day. Like it would kill him to send a text."

She stood and walked a few paces before accepting the call. "Hi, Uncle Richard," Hildy cooed, using the singsong cadence of a preschool teacher. "You know your camera is on, right? Because I'm getting a really intense close-up of the inside of your ear. Seriously, what happened to that trimmer I got you for Christmas?"

She moved out of earshot before they could hear more, leaving behind a thicker-than-usual silence.

"Anyone see the game?" Libby prayed there had been a game. Any game.

Jean's only response was a what-is-wrong-with-you? scowl, but Jefferson shook his head.

"Keoki used to play," Libby rambled on.

"That so?" he asked, with what was clearly more politeness than interest.

"Yes. He did. Football." Too bad it wasn't track and field, so he could run up and javelin Libby right now.

"But he's reinvented himself." Jefferson didn't phrase it as a question. Did he know something? Or suspect?

Libby gave a nervous laugh. "I wouldn't say *that*, exactly. I mean, it's not like he *invented* anything. Per se."

"Being a chef," Jefferson clarified. "It's a departure from football."

"Ah. Yes. That much is true." She couldn't seem to stop nodding. "Oh, look! Here comes Hildy." Libby pointed like a sailor spotting dry land. Then she got a better look at the younger woman's face. "Is everything okay?"

"In a word, no."

"What is it?" Jefferson asked, and in spite of the dread pinching her stomach, Libby paused to appreciate his gruff concern. It sounded like he was ready to do battle with whatever Hildy was facing. Blizzards, bears, poor cell reception—you name it, he was the man for the job.

Hildy blew out a frustrated breath. "We're hosed. Well, mostly me. But also the rest of you." She scrunched her loose curls into a bun, holding it with one hand. "It's my uncle."

"Aye," Jean agreed. "We got that much."

"He's squelching my independence. Again. How far do I have to go to get some breathing room?"

It was impossible for Libby to tell whether this was a legitimate complaint or more along the lines of, *He canceled one of my seventeen credit cards!*

"So annoying," Hildy muttered, letting her hair fly free. "I suppose we better go back. Before he gets into trouble."

"You're leaving?" Libby and Jean asked, almost in unison.

"I'm not leaving." Hildy clutched her heart. "*I* was here first. If anyone should leave, it's Uncle Richard."

"Here as in *here*?" Libby checked the shave ice line, not spotting anyone who looked like the head of a media dynasty. Surely there would be suspenders.

"He's at your house." All the bubbliness had fled Hildy's voice. "That's where he was calling from."

"My house? Here? On this island?" As opposed to her many other homes.

Hildy grimaced an apology. "Surprise."

Chapter 14

---

lovelillibet Do you ever think about how our bodies are like the husk of a coconut or the ti leaves surrounding the succulent center of a laulau? When I make my deconstructed laulaus, I try to use unexpected fillings like caramelized pork belly and sweet potato. It reminds me of the fun of meeting new people, peeling back their layers to find the truly tender bits within. But to do that, we have to be willing to serve our own hearts on a platter.

Love, Lillibet

Image: A green banana leaf with charred edges unfolds to reveal succulent bits of pink pork and orange sweet potato, next to a perfect mound of rice.

#parfaitfordays #wecontainmultitudes #flavoryourjourney #seasoning soflife

---

"Hey," Hildy said, as they pulled into the driveway, next to an unfamiliar car Jefferson presumed was her uncle's rental. "What about the goats?"

Lillibet's shoulders hitched upward. "Ginger and Poki?"

"Aye," the housekeeper said, with a grimness that made Jefferson wonder if she had something against them. "Those be their names."

"Does the groomer do boarding, too?" Hildy had unfastened her seat belt but made no move to exit the car.

" 'Tis true." Mrs. OMG nodded vigorously. "They keep them

longer for the extra treatments. They'll be puttin' bonny ribbons on their wee horns and painting their sweet baby devil hooves."

"She's kidding," Lillibet said. "The real reason is that . . . our goats have social anxiety. Sometimes meeting new people can give them—a rash."

"Oh." Hildy sighed. "Too bad. I could use some emotional support right now."

Lillibet twisted in her seat to offer a smile of reassurance. "Your uncle probably wants to make sure you're okay."

Hildy's bottom lip jutted. "I'd be more okay if he trusted me to be a responsible adult. Not that I'm not. Everything I said about working for us was totally legit."

"I feckin' hope so," the housekeeper muttered. Lillibet opened her mouth to reply, but the muffled sound of voices drew everyone's attention to the front porch. Mr. L was shaking hands with another man in a suit, the latter holding a briefcase.

"That's not my uncle." Hildy sounded relieved, but Lillibet didn't move from her crouched position, body angled sideways to hide behind the dash.

"Why don't you go ahead?" she said. "Find your uncle. Talk it out. We'll give you some space. Take the whole house, and I'll . . . make myself scarce." Reaching behind her, she opened the door and slid onto the driveway, all without lifting her head. Jefferson watched her sneak around the back of the vehicle, still bent double.

"Um," Hildy said.

"That'll be one of their games," the housekeeper assured them. "Proper kinky little fellow, our Mr. L."

Hildy made a noise of agreement. "I got that from the shower."

Jefferson watched Lillibet dash across the grass, yank on the door of an older-model truck, and throw herself into the backseat. After the man with the briefcase backed carefully out of the driveway, Mr. L surveyed the front garden through narrowed eyes before heading inside.

"Get on with you, then." The housekeeper made a shooing motion.

Hildy sent Jefferson a we'll-be-talking-about-this-later look before climbing out of the car.

"In my opinion, the bidet is the most misunderstood of bathroom fixtures . . ." Mr. L was saying when Jefferson walked into the living room behind Hildy. It sounded like they'd arrived in the nick of time.

"There you are!" A middle-aged man with a thick head of salt-and-pepper hair rose from the couch, holding his arms out.

Apart from the bow tie, Uncle Richard did not resemble the picture Hildy had painted. Jefferson was expecting pinstripes and baldness, with the pasty complexion of someone who spent most of his time indoors. The actual man was tall and round-bellied, with wide blue eyes blinking behind round tortoiseshell frames. He'd taken off his jacket and rolled up the sleeves of his white button-down, either as a concession to the heat or because this was his off-duty mode.

"Here I am," Hildy agreed, not quite stomping across the room to hug him.

Maybe she had a point about her uncle's undermining. His arrival seemed to have de-aged her straight to adolescence.

"And this must be the Iceman."

Jefferson expected the bone-crushing handshake of a man who believed testosterone could be measured by grip strength, but at the last minute Hildy's uncle pulled him into an embrace.

"Thank you," he said hoarsely, slapping Jefferson on the back, "for saving my baby."

Jefferson inclined his head as he pulled away, hoping they could leave it at that.

"How did you even find me?" Hildy demanded. "I know for a fact I turned off location sharing."

Her uncle wagged a finger. "Not with Thelma."

"Thelma would never sell me down the river."

"No, but she has been known to leave her phone unattended. Everyone needs the bathroom eventually."

"Hear, hear," said Lillibet's husband. "The cornerstone of my business philosophy."

"Thelma is my uncle's executive assistant," Hildy explained for Jefferson's benefit. "The power behind the throne."

Uncle Richard looked like he was about to argue the point before visibly gathering himself. "The important thing is that you're safe and sound."

"Um, yeah. You saw the press conference."

Jefferson made a mental note to tell Hildy later that her bid for independence would be more effective without the eye-rolling.

"I'm talking about you running off like this. 'I've found a mentor who can help me realize my full potential.' All that about 'going into seclusion' and the need to do a 'spiritual detox' while you 're-orient your priorities.' It sounded like you were joining a cult! You know they prey on college girls. For what I'm paying, you'd think that school would keep closer tabs on you."

"And there it is," Hildy muttered. "Always comes back to the money." She flounced to the nearest armchair, looking up at her uncle with a mulish expression. "Number one, I'm a competent adult, not a chump. And two, Lillibet isn't a cult leader. She's a hugely positive influencer."

"Yes, I've seen her picture." Uncle Richard waved a dismissive hand at the portrait of Lillibet, which had acquired a toga-like drapery of what appeared to be bedsheets. "Where is the legendary Lillibet?"

"I would also like to know," Mr. L chimed in. "What happened to my spouse? *Lillibet*," he tacked on, in case there was any doubt who he was talking about.

"*She* understands that I need room to operate," Hildy told her uncle. "It's so refreshing to deal with someone who respects my autonomy."

"Had I known the Iceman was with you—"

"It's Jefferson." His correction was drowned out by Hildy's snort.

"Right, because a Y chromosome makes everything so much better."

"I'm merely saying that it's nice to see a steadying presence in my niece's life."

"In the sense that he kept me from falling off a mountain to an icy death? And getting eaten by bears? While vultures plucked out my frozen eyeballs?" She paused to let this image (however unlikely) sink in. "Or do you have another reason for being glad I didn't bite it?"

"I'm sure I don't know what you mean." Her uncle's fiddling with his glasses suggested otherwise.

"Why did you really crash my vacation? Be honest. It's about the story, isn't it? You haven't seen engagement like this since we broke the news about the astronaut love triangle. Or the orphaned hippo bonding with the three-legged dog."

"Hildy, you're my niece."

"That didn't stop you from going full Missing White Girl." She held up a hand to silence his protest. "I would have done the same. A good leader maximizes every opportunity. Hence why I've been providing Johnson Media with a steady stream of A-plus-plus content."

"Which has tapered off dramatically since your disappearance. The more recent one," he clarified.

"And I bet you think we should keep cranking it out, without any strategy or sense of pace, until everyone gets bored and moves on? Or, worse, there's a backlash and we burn through all our viral capital in a matter of hours?"

"What you have to understand, Hildy, is that these things have a built-in expiration date. It's the nature of the beast." It was the indulgent tone of a grown-up explaining basic facts to a child. Not an approach Jefferson would have recommended, but Uncle Richard hadn't asked for his advice.

"Yeah, because you follow the same tired playbook every time. Have you ever heard a pop song that's nothing but chorus for three minutes? No! And you know why not? Because it would be annoying. That's why there are lulls. A quiet moment to catch your breath. Which you would know if you weren't stuck in the stone age of hype."

Uncle Richard puffed out his chest. There was only so much criticism a man like him could take, in Jefferson's experience. It reminded him of the photo safaris he'd helped run when he first moved to Jackson, for corporate types who wanted to spend a weekend stalking wildlife with their fancy cameras. They were all jovial male-bonding in their immaculate Patagonia gear until someone served the wrong mineral water at lunch, or there weren't enough paleo options at breakfast. That was when the real my-way-or-the-highway personality peeked through.

"The public has a vested interest in your story," Uncle Richard said, stiff with dignity.

"Do you honestly think I wasn't going to leak a beach shot tomorrow?" Hildy fired back. "The perfect scenic thirst trap?"

Jefferson thought, unhappily, of his Aquaman rash guard before remembering that he would almost certainly be the one taking the picture. Still, the whole discussion left him with the clammy feeling of squeezing into a damp bathing suit. It was such a clinical way to approach a relationship: as a product to be manufactured and sold. He thought of Lillibet confessing—as if it were an embarrassing secret—that she wanted to write "stories about people." *That* he could understand. Then again, Jefferson's job could be summed up as "taking pictures of animals," so maybe he was too simpleminded to appreciate the business decisions that happened this far up the chain.

Hildy kicked her legs up, heels thudding against the floor. "I'm busting my butt to play this situation like a maestro *and* save you from your own terrible instincts, and where's the respect? The acknowledgment?"

"There's no need to get emotional. I know you're a hard worker." Uncle Richard smiled like he was thinking about patting her on the head, a misread so extreme Jefferson was beginning to understand why the other man's marriages were short-lived. "You're probably still recovering from your ordeal. Why don't you come home and have a nice rest? We can redecorate your bedroom!"

Hildy dramatically widened her eyes. "Really? With a canopy bed? Can I have some glitter stickers, too?"

"I don't see why not," Uncle Richard began.

"Are you kidding me right now?" Hildy yelled, jumping to her feet. "I don't believe this."

She ran out of the room, leaving behind a silence punctuated by the pounding of her feet on the stairs.

"Maybe you should talk to her," Uncle Richard suggested, looking hopefully at Jefferson.

Mr. L nodded. "You could suggest a bubble bath. My new glass soaking tub is like a trifle dish for humans. Minus the pedestal, for reasons of structural integrity."

Privately, Jefferson thought they were both nuts. Hildy obviously needed time alone, and who wanted to roll around in a giant serving dish? But he was glad of the excuse to leave the room, so he kept those thoughts to himself.

"I'll check on her," he promised, without specifying when.

Chapter 15

It was amazing how much a mountain of sticky rice and shrimp drowning in garlicky butter could improve your mood. Libby licked the back of her hand, catching a trickle of sauce before it slid past her wrist. Delicious, even with the base note of skin.

Running away from Mr. L had been a spur-of-the-moment decision, but in hindsight it felt like one of the few good choices she'd made lately, and not only because of the carbs. Escaping the Lillibet charade let her breathe freely for the first time all day. It reminded Libby of the time she and Jean had signed on to advertise a new burger joint, not realizing the job consisted of standing on a street corner in full-body foam costumes: a smiling milkshake for Libby, and an evil-looking sleeve of fries for Jean. Stripping off that sweaty food suit at the end of a shift had felt a lot like this—a weight off her back and the thrilling taste of freedom. Who knew wearing your own face could be such a rush?

It didn't hurt that this was a regular hangout spot in their real lives, a roadside collection of food trucks where you could get a killer meal for cheap. There were plenty of shrimp shacks along the North Shore, and Keoki knew (or was related to) most of the people running them, but the one at the old sugar mill in Kahuku was their favorite. Sitting at a picnic table in the open-air pavilion while string lights swayed in the breeze was the essence of relaxation. No more worrying about your posture or saying the wrong thing to the rich, powerful strangers you were trying to bamboozle.

"So she sort of offered you a job but not exactly the one you wanted." Keoki set down the tail of his last shrimp, wiping his mouth with a recycled paper napkin. "Did I miss anything else?"

"I mentioned the story I'm writing about Tutu."

"Good one." He had absolute faith in the quality of Libby's work, even though he hadn't been allowed to read it. "Did you give it to her?"

Libby shook her head. "It's not done."

"All that running around like the Hamburglar is distracting you," Jean said, slamming down her can of coconut stout. "Why don't you tell Mr. L okay, but you want a long engagement? And maybe a small cash advance?"

"Did he say anything about kids?" Keoki asked, frowning at Libby's stomach.

"No, no, no, and no. A world of no." Libby cupped a protective hand over her food baby—the only kind she was planning to have anytime soon. "But I did find an application in my room for nontraditional degree seekers at Kapi'olani."

"Community college?" Jean frowned. "Make him shell out for UH."

"Did you forget the part where I don't want to be his mail-order bride?"

Jean sighed. "If this is about your future boss's boyfriend, it's not going to happen."

"I know." Was it necessary to rub Libby's face in it? "You heard what Hildy said. They can't stand two-faced people. It's a matter of time before all this blows up in my face."

"Good thing you have a spare." Jean elbowed Keoki, who shook his head.

"Not funny," Libby told her roommate. "It's going to get ugly."

"Ah, go on." Jean burped into her fist. "Things are looking surprisingly good. Not for your doomed romance, but it's not like that's a big loss."

Keoki frowned. "I like Jefferson. He's solid."

"You like everyone," Jean reminded him. "It's disturbing. You're going to have to bring your children to me so I can help them wise up before they get taken in by the first scam artist who tries to steal their lunch money."

"I'm going to pack their lunches."

"Really not the point." Jean reached across him to grab his water. "You can find guys like Jefferson anywhere. If slightly generic dudes do it for you."

"Jefferson isn't generic," Libby said.

"Name one interesting thing about him."

What *wasn't* interesting about Jefferson? Libby found it hard not to hyper-focus on his physical presence: his voice, the planes of his face, the line of his shoulders, that slight frown tipping into quiet amusement. Libby was torn between relief that Jean didn't feel the same pull and wanting to yell in her face, *WHAT IS WRONG WITH YOU?*

"Um, he hangs out with wolves and mountain lions? He saved someone's life? He has wilderness survival skills?"

"So he's a Boy Scout. That's like the white bread of men." Jean turned to Keoki before he could interrupt. "I know, you like white bread, too."

Keoki shook his head. "Not just white. All kinds of bread. The essence of bread is goodness."

"But you have to admit some are better than others," Jean persisted. "They have more flavor. Texture. A nice firm crust."

"For the record," Libby cut in, raising a hand, "I don't want to date anyone with a crust."

"You know what I mean." Jean groaned, like Libby was the difficult one. "Sharpness. Grooves and ridges. *Edge*."

"So I should be looking for someone from a biker gang?"

"They could be crusty," Keoki said.

Jean tossed a blob of rice at him. "I'm just saying, what if there's no there there? He's a blank slate. Reasonably handsome, has all his teeth, probably pays his taxes on time. You can project whatever fantasy you want onto him. I think you need someone a lot less normal, Libs."

"Because I'm such a weirdo?"

"Totally." The reply came without an instant's hesitation.

"Uh, thanks?"

"You're welcome." It probably was a compliment, in Jean's mind. Her filing system for people relied less on good vs. bad than the bizarre-to-snoozeville spectrum. "That's why we're soul sisters. The wilding is just buried a little deeper in your case. Like an ingrown hair."

"Aw, geez." Keoki shoved his tray away. "I asked you not to talk about hairs when I'm eating."

"You're totally done." Jean gestured at his empty plate.

"I might have dessert."

Libby perked up, leaning sideways to see if the smoothie truck was still open.

"No time," Jean informed them, checking her phone. "You need to give me a ride to Dolphin Bay. I'm covering the overnight shift."

"When are you getting another car?" Keoki asked.

"When our ship comes in." Jean tipped her head at Libby, like she was a walking lottery ticket.

"Mopeds are cheap," he grumbled.

"Sorry." Libby didn't even have enough cash to offer him gas money.

"It's okay. I need to get home for Cici's foot rub."

"Wait, neither of you are coming back to the house?" Libby swallowed a bubble of panic. Was she really equipped to run this shell game on her own?

"Don't worry, Mr. L will be crashed. He asked me to make the mushroom soup for dinner."

Libby nodded. That stuff was at least half brandy—to the point you had to be careful around open flames.

"That doesn't mean you can run wild, missy." Jean kicked Libby under the table. "Solo showers only."

"Haha," Libby said as they stood and threaded their way through the grid of picnic tables. "Actually, I've been thinking."

"Don't hurt yourself," Jean fired back.

Libby ignored her. "Our lives aren't *that* bad. When you look at the big picture. We have all this." It would have been more convincing if she hadn't waited until they were standing in front of the industrial-sized garbage cans to make her expansive arm-flinging gesture.

"You feeling okay there, Mary Sunshine?" Jean tried to put her shrimpy garlic hand on Libby's forehead.

"What if we didn't go back?" Libby stepped out of range. "We could cut our losses and disappear right now."

"Except my restaurant," Keoki reminded her.

"And we'll be living under a bridge by next week." Jean rubbed her fingers together. "Since we have no cash monies."

These were valid points. Not to mention the part about never seeing Jefferson again. "You're right."

"Of course we are. No walking away from your dream job," Jean said.

Keoki slung an arm around Libby's shoulders, squeezing her to his side. "That's kind of exciting, Libs! Right?"

She shrugged. It was certainly one possible outcome.

"You know what else?" Jean said with sudden gravity, grabbing Libby's hand.

Libby leaned closer, eager for words of comfort. Normally Jean expressed affection through sarcasm, interspersed with threats of violence against anyone who did Libby wrong, making these occasional glimpses of sentiment that much more precious.

Rising onto her tiptoes, Jean whispered, "I call shotgun." And then she was off, laughing as she sprinted toward the truck.

"It's okay, Libs. It'll be your turn one of these days," Keoki said.

But when? And for what?

Chapter 16

The stairs creaked, alerting Jefferson that someone else was awake. He knew it wasn't Hildy, because she was on or off like a toddler, going full speed until she hit the wall and crashed—as she'd done around eight, worn out from her earlier spat. The footsteps were too light to be her uncle and too slow for Lillibet's husband, who tended to scamper.

Which left the lady of the house.

Jefferson pushed back his chair. He didn't want Lillibet to find him sitting in her dark kitchen, staring at the shadow play of branches in the moonlight. Although she might understand his need for quiet, having made the choice not to come home until the rest of them had gone up to their rooms.

The sounds of descent stopped. After a beat of silence, he heard another footfall, fainter this time. The movements were almost furtive, which didn't make sense for someone walking through their own house, even in the dark. Jefferson looked for something heavy, settling on a shallow wooden dish. Slowly, he eased himself upright and around the table, sticking close to the wall.

Soft steps moved closer. A circle of light crept across the floor, coming to a stop a few feet from his hiding place. As he listened, a door slid open, followed by the crinkle of plastic.

Huh.

Sure enough, there was a tearing sound, then a dry rustle. Jefferson stepped into the open, not surprised to see Lillibet with her arm buried in a bag of snack food.

She jumped into the air, throwing the bag at his face with a strangled, "Hiyah!"

He tried to catch it, instead managing to eject half the contents on its way to the floor.

Libby clutched her chest. "You scared the crap out of me."

"Sorry." He set down the wooden platter, belatedly disarming himself.

"No, I'm sorry." She stepped toward him, plucking a cracker from the inside of his collar. "I shouldn't have attacked you."

"I'll probably survive."

Lillibet shook her head as she brushed salty powder off the front of his shirt. "Did they get in your clothes?" Her hands froze at a telltale crunch. "Oops." She poked him, confirming the cracker's location. "That's not in your pocket."

"No," he agreed, feeling the crumbs work their way into his chest hair.

"I guess it's better than getting rice crackers in your pants." She bit her lip as her gaze traveled past his belt buckle. "At least you know how to work the shower now."

Speaking of showers, the atmosphere in the kitchen seemed to be getting steamier by the second.

"Pretty sure the floor got the worst of it," Jefferson said, seizing on a safer topic.

She crunched over to the wall and turned on the overhead light. Together they surveyed the mess. Crackers were scattered like confetti.

"I get snacky when I'm writing." It sounded like an apology. "I didn't think anyone else would be awake, or I wouldn't have come down like this."

She crossed her arms over the front of her thin T-shirt. The neckline was stretched out enough that a bra strap would have been visible if she'd been wearing one. Jefferson made an executive decision to concentrate on her face.

A trio of freckles marked the delicate skin under her right eye. Knowing that tiny detail felt almost as intimate as seeing her in pajamas.

"I have shorts on." Lillibet hiked up her shirt, offering a glimpse of plaid flannel to reassure him she wasn't running around in her underwear.

He nodded, acknowledging this important distinction. Even though the shorts were the size of a handkerchief. And she'd inadvertently flashed a few inches of tanned stomach. Jefferson dragged his thoughts in a less dangerous direction. "Where do you keep the dustpan?"

"Um. It's—around here somewhere." She opened one cabinet after another, frowning at the contents.

"You don't always live here?" he guessed.

"No." She half laughed at that. "I mean, I'd love to. I wasn't trying to be like, *What, this shack?* But no."

Her tone was hard to place. Wistful? Amused, but not really? Maybe she didn't get a vote on which of their many residences they called home.

"And you have a housekeeper."

"Right. Hard to know what to do with all that help—aha!"

She raised the dustpan in victory before kneeling in the sea of snack food.

"I can do it."

"It's my mess." There was a crunch as her shin made contact with a cracker.

"I think you could claim self-defense," he said, joining her on the floor. For every cracker he picked up, another was pulverized into dust. "Might be more of a vacuum job."

"I don't want to wake anyone up."

He nodded, less out of consideration for the other people in the house than from a selfish desire to be alone with Lillibet, even if they weren't doing anything more exciting than cleaning the kitchen. When they finished, he stood first, reaching down to offer Lillibet a hand. She hesitated before letting him pull her to her feet.

"I lav you?" he asked when they were facing each other.

She jerked her hand away, as if she hadn't realized she was still holding on. "What?"

"Your shirt." He dipped his chin to indicate the peeling red letters.

"I *Lava* You. It was a barbecue place. They went out of business," she added, in case he'd been about to propose a middle-of-the-night excursion. Her fingers twisted the fabric, pulling it taut across her chest.

Jefferson developed a sudden interest in the lines of grout at his feet. "So, Lillibet. What were you writing?"

"Libby."

He risked a glance at her face.

"That's what I usually go by, with my friends. Lillibet is for . . . the public-facing stuff."

"Libby," he repeated. It suited her—like that soft-looking shirt. And the blink-and-you'd-miss-them shorts.

"I was trying to finish the story about Keoki's grandmother."

Jefferson understood the part she didn't say out loud: *So I can give it to Hildy.* "How's it going?"

Lillibet—*Libby*—shrugged. "Can't tell anymore. Hence the snacks." She tugged on the end of her braid, brushing it against her palm. "Is that why you were down here? I think there's more papaya in the fridge. Since I noticed you were holding the fruit bowl."

"I thought you were an intruder."

"Oh! Ha. No. I'm definitely supposed to be here." She rubbed the sole of her foot against the opposite leg, no doubt brushing off crumbs. Jefferson wasn't sure why she seemed to be trying to convince herself.

"I came downstairs to call my sister," he said. "Meant to do it earlier, but it was hard to find a quiet time."

"Do you talk every day?"

He shook his head. "It's my birthday."

"What?" Her eyes were enormous. "It's been your birthday this whole day? You should have said something."

"It's no big deal. Susan wanted to make sure she got a chance to wish me a happy birthday. And she was up late, so we're good."

"The two of you must be really close."

"Pretty much."

"And you get along really well?"

"Most of the time."

"Is that where you would be tonight if you weren't here? Your sister's house?"

"Probably. She and the girls like to do it up. Streamers. Trick candles."

She absorbed this in silence, like she was interviewing a head of state. "Is it just the three of them? No dad in the picture?"

"He took off when the youngest was a baby. That's why I moved back to Wyoming."

"To be there for your sister?" Libby blinked rapidly, like her eyes were welling.

"I'm sure Susan could have handled it, but I wanted to be close. Get to see the girls grow up a little." Jefferson wasn't sure what had loosened his tongue, but now that he'd started, he couldn't seem to stop. Maybe he liked that she was interested in his life.

"What does she do? Your sister."

"She's a vet. Has her own practice now. That's why she was still up. There was an emergency call. The dog's going to be fine," he added, at Libby's worried intake of breath.

"So you're both animal people? I mean, people who like animals. Not like—werewolves."

He smiled at the distinction. "We used to watch all the nature shows. Hour after hour of *Animal Planet*. Kind of an obsession. It got to be a competition to see which one of us could absorb more facts about capybaras or blue whales."

"You would have killed at trivia night."

"As long as the questions were about vertebrates." He stopped himself there, worried he'd been talking too much. "Is this going in your next story?"

"Sorry. Am I being nosy? I just think it's so cool that you knew what you wanted to do when you were a kid and then actually followed through. I wish I'd been that focused."

"Probably fewer kids' shows about journalists."

"That's true. I didn't really think about reporting as a job until college, and then . . . other things happened." More tugging at her shirt. Jefferson wanted to ask, but could tell she didn't want to go there.

"Looks like it's coming together for you now," he said instead. She shrugged, and he got the impression she didn't enjoy being the topic of conversation. Odd, for someone who had dedicated a holiday to herself. "Speaking of which, did Hildy find you?"

"Why? Did something happen? Is she upset?"

It surprised him that a person as positivity oriented as Lillibet would leap to catastrophe first. "She's fine. It's about tomorrow. She was hoping you could take us someplace where her uncle won't follow."

"Oh! I know the perfect spot. You'll love it." Her eyes lit. "We could have a do-over birthday celebration. I'll ask Keoki to bake something."

"I'd just as soon not make a big deal out of it. Hildy already thinks I have one foot in the grave."

Her mouth worked like she wanted to ask why his alleged girlfriend didn't know his birth date. To his relief, she didn't push it. "We should do something right now, before it's over. Your birthday, I mean. Not your life." Libby hurried to the pantry, not giving him a chance to argue.

"The crackers are toast, so that's a no-go." She pulled out a lower shelf, sighing in disappointment. "Why so healthy? There should at least be some coconut balls in here." Closing the pantry door, she crossed to the refrigerator. "Birthday salad would be a crime against humanity. Aha!" She rummaged through the bottom of the produce drawer. "Jackpot. I found the secret stash. He probably thought I'd never look behind the lettuce."

She sounded so pleased with herself Jefferson couldn't help smiling. It was the pure triumph of a child winning a board game, nothing like the notice-me superiority he'd expected of Lillibet.

"What is it?"

"It's a surprise. Go sit over there." She waved at the table. "It needs to warm up a little. You want to know something terrible?"

"Yes."

"Sometimes I put them in my pockets. If they've been in the fridge a long time."

"When you have pockets." Maybe he should have made it less

obvious how much he'd noticed about her nightwear. To his relief, Lillibet only nodded.

"But you know what would work? A candle!" She pulled open a series of drawers before holding up a slender taper. "Perfect."

Jefferson watched her grab a plate from an upper cabinet and place something on it, stabbing it a few times with the pointy end of a paring knife before inserting the candle. A wand-style lighter flicked to life in her right hand, and the wick caught right away.

"You're good at that," he observed.

"Restaurant work. We light a lot of candles. I mean, lighted. Lit. I used to light candles when I waitressed. A long time ago." She cleared her throat. "Anyway. Are you ready?"

"I think so." Or, if not ready, at least willing.

She turned off the overhead light. "Your present is that I'm not going to sing."

The candle flickered as she approached, casting a soft glow on her face. "I'll say it instead. Happy birthday to you. Happy birthday to you. Happy birthday, dear Jefferson." Her voice faltered, their eyes meeting in the dark. It should have felt more casual to hear her recite it like a poem instead of serenading him, but between the dark kitchen, the candlelight, and her half whisper, the moment shifted into something intoxicatingly intimate. And that was before she called him her dear.

"Happy birthday to you," she finished in a rush, setting the plate in front of him. "And many more."

"Should I make a wish, or do I need a shell for that?"

"It's your birthday. Get crazy." She pulled out the chair next to his, tucking herself in beside him.

His other wish had already come true, although it wasn't exactly how he'd imagined meeting her again. Jefferson kept this one simple. *More time.* Then he blew out the candle.

"Are you going to eat it?" She nudged the plate a little closer.

"What is it?"

"A Maui Caramac. Macadamia nuts and caramel and choco-late. They're really good. Even if it looks like a little brown lump."

A brown lump on a plain white plate with a mismatched can-dle: the presentation didn't scream "lifestyle guru," but Jefferson preferred Libby's late-night ease to Lillibet's in-your-face extrav-agance.

"I can share," he said, more out of politeness than from any expectation that she'd take him up on the offer.

"You don't mind?" She was already breaking it in half. "Here. Have the big piece."

"Thanks."

She watched him take a bite. "It's good, right? I could eat a whole box of these."

"It's perfect." A birthday he'd never forget.

Chapter 17

The sun was peeking over the horizon as they pulled into the parking lot, dipping the world in pale lemony light. Operation Evade Hildy's Uncle (and coincidentally also Libby's would-be husband) was a go.

Libby led the procession through the trees, followed by Hildy, then Jefferson, and finally Jean. She'd debated whether to wake her best friend after her late shift at the resort, but Keoki was registering for baby gifts with Cici, and Libby worried that without either of them around she would shrink into the awkward and tongue-tied version of herself.

To her relief, Jean had bolted upright as soon as Libby crept into her room with a jumbo travel mug of coffee.

"Today's the day," she croaked, rubbing her eyes. "Mark my

words, something big is going to happen. She's going to offer you the job."

"She probably hasn't even read the story yet. It's been like four hours."

"Don't argue with my intuition. I feel it in my bones."

"You know you're not actually an old Irish wise woman?"

"I could be. In another life." Jean grabbed the coffee and took a swig, wincing at the burn.

"Are you sure you're up for this? You barely slept."

"You know me. I love the nightlife."

"You've got to boogie," Libby finished. This was one of Keoki's greatest hits, though not everyone appreciated the novelty of a disco standard performed as a ukulele dirge.

Fully caffeinated, they escorted their guests along the familiar trail to the beach, donning their reef shoes and checking that everything was safely loaded into the wet bags before starting across to Mo'o Island. It was not a casual stroll. The surface of the water looked like mercury where it was deep enough, but enough of the reef was exposed that you could see the uneven surface. There was barely room to place a foot between the knife-edged ridges and sudden dips. If you didn't want to slice open your leg or step on something poisonous, you had to move with caution.

Between the hush of early morning and the concentration required to stay upright, they made most of the trip in silence—until they were halfway across, and Hildy burst out laughing.

"You okay?" Jefferson asked.

"I was imagining my uncle doing this. In his loafers. With the little tassels." The giggles trailed off as she found another foothold. "Although golf shoes might not be a bad idea."

Jefferson was still standing with his legs braced, staring at the reef below.

"You want your camera?" Libby asked, coming up beside him with the larger of the two waterproof backpacks.

"Not sure my balance is that good."

"It'll be easier on the island. There are tide pools." Did this place fit the bill of "inaccessible to Hildy's uncle"? Absolutely. But Libby had mostly been thinking of Jefferson. This was his kind of setting, beautiful but rough, with the otherworldly quiet she sensed from his pictures.

There was no one on the island when they arrived. It was just far enough offshore to make people think twice before swimming over, which was for the best. Between the rocks and the riptide, it was a trip better taken at the right time of day, preferably with someone who knew the area. An influx of tourists would also be a concern for the shearwater nesting grounds at the center of the island.

One of the gray-and-white seabirds circled overhead as they trekked along the narrow path. Libby unzipped the wet bag, handing Jefferson his camera. His eyes met hers in a silent *thank you* that made her blush.

After he snapped a few pictures, they continued around the protected habitat, traversing the uneven terrain at the far end of the tiny island. The rocks ended in a sheer cliff battered by waves. Droplets sprayed over them, leaving puddles where the ground dipped. Hildy peered over the rim.

"That's a legit death trap. Rule number one. Nobody goes over. I'm not sure even JJ could save you from that. Hashtag common sense social media." Popping her hip, she twisted to the side, pivoting to face the opposite direction when the wind blew her hair in her face. "How's the light, JJ?"

"It'll do."

Libby watched in fascination as Hildy cycled through poses: looking down, looking up, hand in the hair, hand at her neck, sad smile, poker face, touching her lip. It was a master class in knowing your angles.

"I want this to say, *I've lived, I've loved, I've learned. I'm a wiser woman today than I was yesterday. It's better to have loved and lost than never loved at all."*

Jefferson lowered the camera. "That's a tall order, Hildegarde."

"A thousand words. That's what a picture's supposed to be worth. I'm barely over twenty. Anyway, this is just describing the mood. We'll get Lillibet to help with the caption." She smiled winningly at Libby.

Libby tried to look like she had some idea what was going on, but it was a losing battle. "What is this for, exactly?"

Hildy held up a finger. "Before we get to that, I need to apologize. I haven't been completely honest with you, Lillibet."

One of Libby's feet slipped on a slick patch of rock and Jefferson reached out to steady her. He was wearing the rashie inside out to hide the Aquaman muscles, but she could feel the strength in his grip. She wasn't sure it would be enough to hold her up if Hildy was about to take back the job she'd never officially offered.

"What's all this, now?" Jean demanded, tugging Libby away from Jefferson. Libby was grateful to her friend for asking, since she couldn't get the words past the tightness in her throat.

"Let me finish the preamble." Hildy hopped down from the boulder she'd been using for her impromptu photo shoot. "I'm sorry I lied to you. That's a shitty thing to do to someone you want to build a relationship with, professional or otherwise."

Libby could only nod numbly.

"However," Hildy continued, "in my defense, it was more of a misdirect than straight-up falsification and I have trust issues due to previous experiences with personal betrayal. It's hard to know if someone is being nice to me for me or because of my family name."

"I'm sure you had a valid reason for—embroidering the facts. Life is complicated. We've all made certain choices that in retrospect could have been . . . better." Libby would have gone on if Jean's warning glare hadn't stopped her cold.

"Thank you for understanding," Hildy said. "I was afraid you'd be mad. But I should have known you'd get it, being such an empathetic person. In fact—cue the dramatic pause—that's why I loved your story so much. About Tutu Lua."

"You read it?" Libby flinched as Jean punched her in the arm.

"No, she's a frickin' psychic. Let the poor wee lassie talk."

Hildy put a hand to her heart. "I feel like I know her. Tutu. This is *exactly* the vibe I'm going for with the magazine. Gentle lessons in living an authentic life, with a delicious aesthetic. I want to go to her house and hear her stories. Maybe meet some of the big hunky grandsons."

"I didn't say *that*," Libby began, stealing a glance at Jefferson.

"I can read between the lines. It's okay," she assured a frowning Libby. "Wilderness Daddy doesn't mind. You know *Speed*, right?"

It was Jean's turn to scowl. "The drug?"

"The movie. Sandra Bullock and Keanu Reeves. Where she tells him relationships that start under intense circumstances never last. And then some other stuff about the bus blowing up. But the main thing is the love story. You know what I mean?"

"Not—exactly," Libby admitted. She'd seen it, of course. Keoki made them watch every Keanu movie, except the one where the dog gets hurt.

"I'm thinking that's how we frame it. We flew too close to the sun, it was fun while it lasted, et cetera. Keep it archetypal. Easy to understand. Never underestimate the stupidity of the public."

Libby was feeling pretty stupid herself at the moment. Like she'd been hit in the head.

"I know." Hildy raised both hands in a be-patient gesture. "It needs your magic touch. And professional photography. I'm staring out to sea. Sun sparkles, maybe a rainbow. Or one of those birds swooping in! Lonely but beautiful and proud. What do you think, JJ?"

He shook his head. "I'm not an animal trainer."

"We'll hang around, see what happens. And then Lillibet will help me craft a poignant message about people who touch our lives for a season and then fade away, like autumn leaves or—something less trite. Every ending is a new beginning, lightly hinting that I might be available soon, after an appropriate period of mourning." Hildy beamed at Libby. "I trust you."

"You do?" Realizing she'd sounded a little too incredulous, Libby tried again. "Trust is—a river that flows in both directions."

"Strange kind of river," Jefferson murmured.

None of it fazed Hildy.

"You are the perfect person to bring our story to life. Like you did with Tutu. Two hot, young—or young*ish*—people from different worlds meet on the side of a mountain, finding life and quote-unquote love, until it slips away." She bent to scoop up a handful of sand, letting it trickle through her fingers.

"You're dying?" Jean sounded more outraged than concerned.

"No. My health is immaculate, thanks to JJ. We're *breaking up*." Hildy let that settle for a few seconds. "Well, fake-breaking-up. In the sense that we were never together. Maybe we should sit down?" she suggested. Probably because Libby looked like she was about to pass out.

They walked onto a sandy strip on the sheltered side of the island that faced the shore. Someone had arranged a half circle of driftwood logs around the ashy remains of a fire. Hildy settled herself on a weathered trunk, threading her fingers together and resting them on her knee like it was a boardroom table.

"Where were we?" she asked.

"You didn't find love in the snow cave?" Not the most intelligent way Libby could have phrased the question, but her brain was too scrambled for logic. What next, they'd tell her the footage of Jefferson carrying Hildy through the snow was a deepfake?

"No. But we did discover a healthy platonic bond based on mutual respect and teamwork, so yay us." Hildy patted herself on the back. "The real treasure was the friends we made along the way, and so on."

"I—did not see that coming." Either the sun had climbed high enough to warm the space between Libby's shoulder blades, or Jefferson was watching her.

"Really?" Hildy looked delighted. "See, JJ? I told you we could do it. He was worried."

"I don't like lying," Jefferson corrected.

"I approached him at a weak moment. Under the influence." Hildy spoke with a hand shading her mouth, like the last bit was a secret.

"IV fluids," he rumbled. "It wasn't a morphine drip."

"I'm talking about the euphoria of not dying. That's a powerful high, especially when you factor in the rescuer/rescuee bond. He was *so* relieved I was alive and well."

Jefferson shot her a wry look. "Sometimes I still am."

"Thanks to your heartfelt paternal affection for me," Hildy teased. Not about the affection; she seemed pretty confident on that front. Libby suspected the game was to crack Jefferson's stoic façade, though in this case Hildy had to settle for a shake of the head.

"I wanted to get a read on your character before we brought you into the circle of truth." She smiled at Libby, as if that were no longer a concern. "You're a lot like me. Ambitious but also loyal and discreet. That's how I know I can trust you."

"Oh," Libby choked. "That's really nice of you to say—"

Jean threw a twig at her. "Learn to take a compliment, Miss Lillibet. She's ever so modest," she added to Hildy, who accepted this with a brisk nod.

"The way I see it, you're a storyteller, and I'm a story *seller*. It's a language I grew up speaking. When everyone jumped on the May-December romance angle, I immediately saw the potential."

"For fame?" Jean asked.

"For *power*. I control the story because I am the story. Well, technically we." She circled a finger between herself and Jefferson. "But mostly me."

"What's in it for him?" Jean asked. "Is he on the payroll?"

"A little offended you think I'd have to bribe someone to fake-date me, but we'll let that slide." Hildy fluffed her windblown curls. "Besides doing me a solid, JJ is here to show his ex he's not sitting at home crying while she plays stuff-the-sausage with Prince Caspian."

"Crispin," Libby murmured.

"Ahem." Jean sent her a look that said, *Try to be less obsessed, loser.*

Libby gave herself the mental equivalent of a double slap. "Your uncle doesn't know?"

"Nobody does except me and JJ. And now you two."

"He'd be mad?" Libby guessed. "Is that why you're not telling him?"

Hildy gazed at the brightening sky. "He'd respect the hustle. But I'm not going to give away my leverage before I have an iron-clad commitment. Johnson Media is making bank off us. It's not just the news coverage. TV movie rights, a novelization, there's at least one memoir in it . . . if I can bring this all the way home, *and* claim the credit, I'll be able to write my own ticket. No more, 'Wait your turn, Hildy. You have to pay your dues.' Like Uncle Richard isn't the ultimate nepo baby."

"And that's when she gets the job?" Jean asked, cutting through the Johnson family drama like so much plastic packaging.

"Yes! It finally came together in my head—thanks to you." Hildy directed that part to Libby. "I've been stressing over how to play the ending, because I think we all know it's tricky to make the leap from tabloid darling to respected public figure. What am I going to do, go on *Dancing with the Stars*? No. I have a better way to stage my metamorphosis from *being* the story to *producing* content." She paused as if one of them might want to venture a guess. "A classy, thoughtful, yet still highly entertaining profile of *moi*. Including strategically placed references to my exciting new magazine venture. Which my uncle will have no choice but to bankroll if he doesn't want to look like an out-of-touch buffoon with money problems. And then *you* can be my star columnist, anchoring every issue with a deep-dive human-interest feature." Hildy winked at Libby. "You talked me into it. No offense to what you've been doing, but this new direction feels fresh and forward-thinking. From self-care to caring about other people. It's a radical approach."

"Devious. Risky. Unnecessarily complicated," Jean mused. "I love this plan."

She was already taking it in stride, unlike Libby. In all their plotting and scrambling, Libby had never really believed the Lillibet experiment would work. It was more comfortable to keep her expectations low and imagine disasters, instead of letting herself dream that Hildy would offer her a golden ticket.

"Are you okay, Libby?" Jefferson spoke as if the two of them were alone on the island, earning a sharp look from Jean.

"That's Lillibet to you, laddie."

"It's a lot to take in," Libby said.

"Speaking of the job, she is," Jean explained. "Proper gob-smacked."

"I am. It sounds incredible." Better than she deserved. That much at least Libby could say with complete honesty. A surge of hope sent her heart flying skyward. It was everything Hildy was offering but also the knowledge that Jefferson wasn't in love with someone else. And maybe Libby hadn't imagined the heat in his eyes last night, or the way he said her name—her real name—like it was something of value.

"Let's not be a-countin' our chickens afore they hatch," Jean cautioned. "What's our play?"

"We need the keys to the kingdom," Hildy said, getting down to business. "Aka a fully autonomous executive-level editorial position for yours truly. So let's dot every *i* and cross every *t* and serve this to my uncle in a package he won't be able to resist. By which I mean a PowerPoint presentation. He has a troubling weakness for those."

"All we have to do is—a slideshow?" Libby was sure there must be a catch.

"And keep my uncle happy and distracted. We're selling him the narrative—I found love, sadly it didn't last, but it's okay because Lillibet helped me discover my true purpose, which is to be the next Anna Wintour. Only happy and not just about the clothes. Feed the illusion, so he doesn't get suspicious and make me leave empty-handed." Hildy paused to give Jefferson an encouraging nose-wrinkle. "Don't worry, JJ. All you have to do is stand around looking stern. My uncle is always more comfortable with male energy in the mix. He'll probably cry when we break up. But what was I going to do, live on a ranch?"

"Still not a cowboy, Hildy."

"Your jeans beg to differ."

Jean snickered.

"It's today, tomorrow, and then Me-mas. Which will obviously have its own magic." Hildy spoke as if they were home free. "And who better to curate a perfect vacation experience than Lillibet? Flex those hostess muscles before you transition to your ace reporter phase. Not that you won't be able to maintain your lifestyle," she added, like Libby might bail if she had to give up her sunrise yoga. "I'm totally down with you working remotely. I wouldn't want Mr. L to think I'm stealing you away."

"That—won't be an issue."

Jean elbowed Libby. "Sounds simple enough, eh? While we're out here clearing the air, there's something else you should know."

Was she—she wouldn't, would she? Libby was surprised by the force of her silent *no.* Of course she wanted Jefferson to know she wasn't married, but that would require unmasking herself as a pathological liar.

"Turns out I'm not Irish," Jean announced. "And I've never been in the slammer."

"This is my shocked face." Hildy pointed at her deeply unsurprised expression. "And the housekeeper thing?"

"Nah. I'm her roomie."

"From college," Libby jumped in. "Back in the day. You know what they say. Once a roommate, always a roommate."

Jean nodded as if this were in her top three catchphrases. "I wanted to be here for moral support. Since this opportunity means *so much* to Lillibet. But like in the background, so she can do her thing. And who's more invisible than a housekeeper?"

That really depended on the housekeeper, Libby thought.

"I figured the accent would set the mood," Jean continued, forcing Libby to nod like that made perfect sense. Nothing like the world's worst brogue to create an ambience!

"Aww, that's sweet. Like me and JJ," Hildy said. "Only without the accent, because I didn't think of it. But he's still my big manly binky. Not in a dirty way."

"Good." Libby hadn't meant to say that out loud. "Um, Jean—who is just Jean, by the way, not Jean-Colleen . . . or whatever—is an artist. She did the big painting. In the living room." In case they thought Lillibet had filled the whole house with naked pictures of herself.

"Your Me Tree?" Hildy gasped. "I love your style. I'm giving serious thought to commissioning illustrated covers for my magazine. I don't suppose you'd be interested?"

"Reckon I jest might—I mean, yeah. Totally." Jean corrected her accent midsentence, sending Libby a look that said, *Did you hear that? Ka-ching.*

They spent another half hour on the island, Jean and Hildy chatting strategy while Jefferson took pictures and Libby kept an eye on the tide—and tried to look like she wasn't coming apart at the seams. As soon as they got back, she'd text Keoki to see if they could do dinner at Tutu's house tonight. Tomorrow she would . . . think about later.

One step at a time, Libby reminded herself as they picked their way back to shore. The water rose higher by the minute, swirling over their feet and sucking at their ankles. It was a precarious position: wobbling along spiny ridges of rock, halfway to dry land, but Libby was only part there, her mind spinning off in a dozen directions.

What was she really moving toward right now, beyond the safety of the beach: A job? A better life? The truth?

All Libby knew for certain was that turning back was no longer an option. She had to keep inching forward, hoping the next step wouldn't send her plunging onto the unforgiving reef.

Chapter 18

Jefferson leaned back in his folding chair at the edge of the lawn, sipping an excellent local porter. The air had stayed balmy as dusk eased into darkness, the first stars winking overhead. There were torches staked into the grass, their flames shifting in the light breeze. He couldn't remember the last time he'd felt this peaceful.

He was no stranger to beautiful places, the kind that drew tourists by the busload. What was different here was that the best parts weren't hidden away in a tower or a penthouse or behind a fence, where only the rich and connected could gain access. The fruit, the weather, the flowers, the beach: it was part of normal life. He doubted anyone at the resort down the road was enjoying a better meal or more appealing company than what was on tap here. Keoki's grandmother had welcomed them into her home with a warmth that put everyone at ease, insisting they call her Tutu. Uncle Richard was immediately smitten, gluing himself to Tutu's side. Even Hildy had mellowed out, dropping her energy level from an eleven to a six.

Everything felt easier now that they'd come clean to Libby about their non-relationship. A weight Jefferson hadn't realized he was carrying was gone, leaving his entire body lighter—until he filled that space with kalua pork and greens, slow-roasted in a pit behind Tutu's garage. Now he was well-fed, under the open sky, with a beer in his hand, enjoying the soft layers of laughter floating from the picnic table where Tutu and Cici were being waited on like queens.

It was traditional for the men to handle the cooking, he'd been told, and not only because Keoki's slight Japanese girlfriend had what looked like a rubber ball under her shirt. Jefferson had helped unbury the meat from its nest of ash and banana leaves, which was the most they would allow a guest to do.

The screen door swung open. Libby stepped outside, wiping her hands on her hips. She'd been carrying dishes in and out of the kitchen as if she lived there, more comfortable at this modest one-story than her own home. It wasn't only the teasing of Keoki's brothers, who communicated mostly via headlocks and noogies, or Tutu treating her like a granddaughter. Her movements were looser, her face more relaxed. The fancy dresses with their stiff fabrics and fussy embroidery had been replaced by a faded cotton skirt and one of those shirts that tied around the neck, baring her shoulders. She looked younger and softer, more Libby than Lillibet.

Jefferson wondered how much her husband's absence was contributing to her mood. He hadn't missed the undercurrent of relief when she announced Mr. L would not be joining them.

The artist/ex-roommate/not-Irish non-housekeeper was also otherwise engaged, news that seemed to disappoint several of Keoki's brothers.

Hildy caught his eye, blowing a kiss that Jefferson grudgingly pretended to catch in one hand, tucking it into his pocket. Since her uncle's attention was split between Tutu and his plate, this performance was almost certainly for Hildy's personal amusement. Jefferson had drawn the line at letting himself be reeled in by her invisible fishing pole.

The whole thing was ridiculous, and yet he was right there in the thick of it, unwilling to let this interlude end—even if it meant playing ventriloquist's dummy. Allegedly, Uncle Richard suffered from a condition Hildy had diagnosed as "estrogen deafness," so if there was something she particularly wanted him to hear, she fed the line to Jefferson first.

"Everyone has flaws, JJ," she'd patiently explained. "My uncle isn't going to suddenly shed his chauvinist tendencies at his advanced age, so we have to work around his limitations."

Things he had been instructed to pass along so far this evening:

Tutu Lua has led a fascinating life.

It would make a great story.

You'd need the right person to tell it.

I bet Lillibet could do it.

Jefferson made a mental note that the next time Hildy proposed a plan, he should assume the wheels were already in motion.

"Is this a luau?" Hildy's uncle asked in a booming voice. "Is that what makes a luau a luau? Eating squid luau?"

Tutu slid the bowl of creamy spinach and squid closer to his plate. "Less talk, more eating."

Uncle Richard laughed, like all he'd ever wanted in life was to be bossed around by Keoki's grandmother. "You're a very vivacious woman. And such magnificent hair. Have I mentioned that?"

"It's okay. You can say it again," she replied graciously. "You got a helicopter at home?

"No, but I do own an impressive collection of model planes."

"Huh." That was the extent of Tutu's commentary on a grown man playing with toys. "How about my story? You going to put it in your newspaper or what?"

He held his phone up to his mouth. "Set a reminder to remind Thelma to remind me to look into a story about Tutu."

Hildy grabbed the phone out of his hand. "Cancel reminder," she huffed. "Don't poach my exclusive." She circled a finger at Jefferson.

"The story has already been assigned," he translated.

"To Lillibet," Hildy added.

Uncle Richard frowned. "I thought her area was more place mats and things."

"One, they're called tablescapes." To Jefferson's relief, Hildy didn't ask him to repeat that part. "And two," she continued, "you can care about aesthetics and still be a skilled professional. It's called multitasking."

"Yes, but her poor husband," Uncle Richard pointed out. "Where does he fall on the list of tasks? The demands of running a business empire are too heavy to shoulder alone."

"He's at a builders' association meeting." Hildy's tone suggested this was on par with cleaning the bottom of a birdcage. "I'm pretty sure Mr. L can sell his own faucets."

"You'll understand when you settle down and start a family of your own." Uncle Richard reached across the table to pat Hildy's hand. Luckily for him, they were using plastic silverware, or he might have pulled back a bleeding stump.

"It's never enough. We make everything beautiful and stroke your egos and bear your children and then you try and nickel-

and-dime us when it comes to pursuing our own ambitions." Hildy shook her head. "Where's the justice? Is it any wonder we need a Me-mas?"

"You need a what?" It sounded like Uncle Richard was ready to pull out his credit card.

"Are you seriously telling me you don't know about Me-mas?" Hildy huffed. "That is so culturally insensitive."

Uncle Richard caught Jefferson's eye, raising his brows in a clear bid for man-to-man sympathy. "She's always been dramatic. I hope you don't mind her little outbursts. I'm used to it, of course. Like water off a duck."

Keep telling yourself that, Jefferson thought. Hildy's uncle might be in charge on paper, but there was no question who was driving the emotional bus.

"I can't believe you would show up here without at least taking the time to educate yourself about something so important to me." Hildy added a hitch in her voice that made Jefferson wonder if acting classes had been part of her business school curriculum.

"But Hildy! Sweetheart. That's why I'm here. Flying all this way to check on you should count for *something*. I'm a very busy man."

"Uh-huh. All that golf isn't going to play itself."

Libby, who had walked outside in time to hear Hildy's muttered retort, froze. Her gaze found Jefferson's, and he suspected they were wondering the same thing: *Is this what she meant by keeping her uncle happy?* Then again, their argument had the familiar rhythm of an established routine. Maybe this was the Johnson family's love language.

"How about some music?" Keoki held up a ukulele. It looked like a child's toy in his hands.

"Wonderful," said Uncle Richard, already applauding. Either he really loved live music, or he was grateful for the interruption.

As Keoki's smooth baritone served up a medley of pop hits from the 1980s, Hildy left her place at the table to join Jefferson.

"They're playing your song," she said, plopping down beside him with a plate balanced on one hand.

"Yes. Phil Collins was huge in my day. Pretty sure I danced to this at prom."

"No way! You went to prom?" She laughed at her deliberate misunderstanding of his joke, forking up another mouthful of pie. "I don't know what this haupia stuff is, but I could eat a truckload."

"Coconut pudding," one of Keoki's hulking brothers said in passing. He tried to ruffle Hildy's hair, but she ducked out of the way.

"Respect the curls."

He pretended to be scared, backing away with his hands raised defensively as Keoki launched into a melancholy version of "Private Eyes."

"What did you think?" Hildy asked Jefferson.

"It was very good." He was running with the assumption that they were no longer talking about the music. "The pork was extremely tender."

"Not about the food, JJ. Respectfully, you're probably the least gourmet person here. Although you're right about the pork." Hildy nodded at Lillibet, who was laughing with another of Keoki's brothers. There seemed to be an infinite supply of them.

"She's in her element." If the full belly, dark beer, and gentle breeze were lulling him to sleep, awareness of Libby kept him on the alert. The chance of catching her eye, or a fleeting smile, was a constant hum at the back of his mind. She was part of the slip-through-your-defenses magic of this place, as pleasing to his senses as the rest of the scene.

Hildy's gaze sharpened. "I was talking about how I handled my uncle. Got him on the defensive. That's how I soften him up so he's in a more receptive frame of mind. To give me what I want," she added when Jefferson looked at her blankly. "But I guess you were too busy thinking about someone else to notice my sick moves."

"Hildy."

"*Jefferson.*" She mimicked his long-suffering tone. "I know you're super-sad and lonely right now, but life is long, Emo Oldster. For some of us more than others, but still. You never know what the future holds."

This time he knew exactly what she meant, even without the head tip in Lillibet's direction. Or the wink.

"I know what it doesn't hold."

She scraped up more of the coconut filling. "What?"

"Breaking up a marriage."

"Hmm."

Jefferson sighed. "Yes, Hildy?"

"At any point today I could have said, *Hey, Lillibet, where's Jefferson?* and she would have been able to answer without even thinking about it. Same goes for you."

"That's beside the point."

"Then I guess you have no interest in coming to work for me and seeing if your paths cross again one day. Like if someone were to put you and Lillibet on the same assignment. In a remote location. With lots of alone time."

"We barely know each other," he said, sidestepping the question.

"When you know, you know. That's the kind of guy you are."

"You barely know me, either," Jefferson reminded her.

"Are you really going to sit there and nitpick my brilliant insight into your life? This is quality life coaching."

"Should I write you a check?"

"How modern of you, JJ. Will you send it to me via the United States Postal Service? With a stamp and everything?"

A flash of blue caught his attention, his brain instantly cataloging the shade of almost-lavender as Libby's skirt.

"You obviously like her," Hildy said, watching him watch Libby disappear into the house with a serving bowl in each hand.

It wasn't technically a question, so he kept his mouth shut.

"That's the essential fact, right?" She grabbed his beer and took a sip. "I see you as a person who doesn't overcomplicate things. You call 'em like you see 'em."

He reclaimed his beer before she could finish it. "Maybe I don't make things complicated enough."

"Said absolutely no one ever. Why would you want to do that?"

"To learn from my mistakes."

Hildy sighed. "Is this about your ex? Better question, is Lillibet anything like her?"

"Not so I can tell." He frowned. "But I didn't know Genevieve was like Genevieve until it was too late."

"Okay, I need there to be like ninety percent less Genevieve in this conversation. That's the first thing. And secondly, no one's asking you to marry Lillibet. Because that would be bigamy. Maybe it's a fling, driven by pure physical attraction. Think about that for a second." She waggled her brows.

Jefferson didn't feel the need to share that the most casual hookup of his life had lasted three months, until her research grant on the western glacier stonefly ended and she went back to her teaching job in Florida. The real issue was that it didn't feel right to think of Libby like that—as an itch he could scratch and be done with.

"Was it like this when you met she who must not be named?" Hildy prodded, twisting sideways in her chair.

He thought back to his first meeting with Gen, at a gallery downtown. In hindsight, he guessed she'd liked the fact that he was one of the photographers whose work was on display, putting him over the very, very low bar for local celebrity. All he'd seen at the time was a lively, attractive woman who made a joke about the cheap wine they served at these things. Or maybe it hadn't been a joke, any more than Genevieve was genuinely interested in his work. She wanted to be part of a couple that fit a certain image—and had mistaken him for the type of person who spent his Friday nights making the rounds of the "right" parties and restaurants. They all felt wrong to Jefferson, the uncomfortable clothes and awkward conversations in crowded rooms, whereas Gen thrived on dressing up and being seen.

"The thing with Gen just kind of happened." A not very inspiring summary of that year of his life, but true enough.

"Totally different scenario this time," Hildy said.

"There's no scenario."

"Not if you don't lower the drawbridge at your Fortress of Solitude. I don't mean that in a sexual sense, by the way. I know men of your generation are scared of talking about their feelings."

"It comes up at all my AARP meetings."

"Good. Then you're not as rusty as I thought." She raised an arm over her head, waving it like a checkered flag. "Hey, Lillibet? Can I talk to you for a second?"

"Whatever you're thinking of doing, don't," Jefferson warned.

"I'm not going to do anything. This is all on you."

They watched Libby approach, feet bare and skirt swaying in the breeze. Her smile was uncertain, possibly because Keoki was singing the saddest version of "Rhythm Is Gonna Get You" ever performed.

"What's up?" she asked.

"It's been such a great night, hasn't it, JJ?"

"Yes."

Hildy shook her head when he left it at that. "We wanted to thank you. For *everything*."

"It's not me." Libby contemplated the grass at her feet. Jefferson wasn't sure whether the praise or the subtext made her more uncomfortable. "All the credit goes to Keoki and Tutu. They have the magic touch. If you overlook their taste in music."

"You grew up around here?" Jefferson heard himself ask, ignoring Hildy's smug look.

"Right here, most of the time. At Tutu's house. Sometimes for days on end. My mom was big on needing a break, because of how hard it is to be a single mother. Which I'm sure is true, but maybe don't mention it in front of your kid all the time." Her eyes squeezed shut. "Sorry, party foul. Didn't mean to kill the mood. Can I get either of you something to drink?"

"I'm fine," Hildy assured her. "Jefferson's sharing with me."

Sighing, he handed over the bottle.

"Okay, everybody, bring it in. Time to talk story." Keoki's brother Michael bellowed the announcement, while Jimmy pounded the bottom of a Tupperware bowl like a drum.

"Here we go." Hildy rubbed her hands together in anticipation. "I cannot wait. You're going to sit with us, right?" She pointed Libby toward the empty seat next to Jefferson.

"Um, okay." Libby sat, her arm brushing his before they both rearranged themselves, hands on laps.

Good to know a half second of forearm contact could give him a coronary. He seriously needed to get a grip. As soon as that half of his body stopped tingling.

"You were out at the island today?" Tutu asked.

Hildy nodded with the eagerness of a star student. "Yes, Tutu."

"Powerful place. Especially for women."

"I felt that," Hildy agreed. "The energy."

"Want to hear the story of how it got its name?"

"Yes," Hildy said, only a beat ahead of her uncle's, "Hear, hear!"

Tutu inclined her head, like a queen acknowledging her subjects.

"There was once a great king." She let her gaze stray to Uncle

Richard, who bounced with excitement. "Strong, with plenty of taro to feed his many wives."

Hildy choked a little. Her uncle remained rapt.

"But this king was getting older. He asked his queen, 'Who will rule my kingdom after I am gone? I need a son.' "

"I have two," Uncle Richard whispered, holding up two fingers. "Sons."

"The king was very lucky. The next full moon, his wife gave birth to a fat, healthy baby."

Keoki rubbed Cici's stomach.

"The baby"—Tutu paused dramatically—"was not a son."

"Shark baby?" one of Keoki's brothers asked.

Tutu frowned at him. "The baby was a girl. A beautiful daughter. Any man would be proud—except that stubborn king. He only wanted a son. So the queen hid her daughter away in a cave, and told the king the baby was stolen by menehune."

"Uh, Grandma?" Keoki sounded nervous. "That's a little dark." He tipped his head at Cici.

"*Pshht.*" Tutu flicked her hand at him. "She's a lot tougher than you." Cici patted his shoulder.

"This princess grew up wise and strong," Tutu continued. "Skilled at hunting and fishing, weaving lauhala, tending her garden. They called her Malaekahana, and word of her bravery spread to the old king. 'If only I had a son like Malaekahana,' he said to his queen, for there had been no more children. 'Then I would know my kingdom will live on, even after I am gone.' "

"The queen said, 'Why not make Malaekahana your heir? Everyone loves her. And she has great hair.' But the king said, 'Bah. A woman cannot rule. It has to be a son.' And so that stubborn king never saw what was right in front of him. On the day he died, with no daughter to comfort him, or keep his kingdom strong, he could barely whisper, 'Bring me Malaekahana.' But it was too late!" Tutu raised her index finger. "By then, Malaeka-hana had her own kingdom. After the king passed, she took his land, too, and that's why her name is spoken to this day—but the king is a nameless ghost."

"So sad," Hildy said after the applause died down. "It was right there in front of him the whole time. A worthy successor. If only he hadn't been blinded by his outdated patriarchal assumptions. He must have so many regrets." She side-eyed Uncle Richard.

"Is that a real story?" Jefferson pitched his voice low so only Libby could hear.

"Tutu made a few modifications. Too on-the-nose?"

"I think the intended audience liked it."

They watched Hildy throw herself at Tutu in an exuberant hug, while Uncle Richard told anyone who would listen that he'd always considered himself a feminist.

Keoki picked up his ukulele and started strumming. He didn't sing the lyrics, so it took Jefferson a few measures to recognize the tune as "I'm Every Woman."

"Do you think it'll make her happy?" Libby asked quietly. "If she gets her way about the job—whatever it costs. Will it be worth it in the end?"

Jefferson tapped the neck of his beer bottle as he considered his response. He was close enough to sense the tension in Libby's body, even without touching her. There was a question behind the question, and he couldn't deny the spark of curiosity it lit within him. Was this about working with Hildy, or something more personal?

Maybe it was all his imagination—with a little help from Hildy's insinuations—and Libby was perfectly happy in her marriage. He forced himself to take the high road, playing it cool and neutral.

"I don't suppose there's any way to know before it happens."

She opened her mouth to say something else, but before she could speak, Keoki called down the table.

"Li'l Bit. You need to get back to the house."

"So soon?" Uncle Richard pouted.

Keoki nodded. "It's Goat Time."

"Did he say Go Time?" Hildy's uncle asked, looking from face to face to see if anyone else knew what was going on.

"Goat," Keoki corrected. "*Baaaaaa.*"

"That's a sheep, bruh." His brothers started making noises of their own, a chorus of bleating and shrieks rising in volume and pitch.

Hildy clapped her hands in delight. "Goats!"

Beside him, Libby rubbed her temples. When she realized Jefferson was looking, she pasted on a smile.

"Let's go meet the goats. I mean, you'll be meeting them. Obviously, I already know them. Since I bottle-fed them from infancy. After they were tragically orphaned. As you may know."

Jefferson nodded slowly. "I do now."

Chapter 19

"I don't know what I'm more excited about, their little bouncy hops or the sweet noises they make. They're just so *cuddly*." Hildy had spent most of the car ride hyping herself up to meet the goats, steadily raising Libby's blood pressure. There was no way her pretend pets could live up to this level of anticipation.

"There's this one YouTuber I follow who taught her goats to dance," Hildy said from the backseat. "I wish I could have goats. And chickens. Maybe an alpaca. But I was never allowed to have pets." She didn't have to look at her uncle; they all knew who she was targeting with that tragic disclosure.

"It's very hard to travel with pets," Uncle Richard said. "We all make sacrifices."

"That's funny. I distinctly remember Albie having an aquarium."

"Doesn't ring a bell," her uncle replied unconvincingly, as Libby pulled into the driveway of Mr. L's house.

She bent to pick up her purse, buying herself another moment to gather her courage. Something hit the front of the car with a loud thump. In the passenger seat, Uncle Richard screamed.

Libby jerked upright, convinced she'd rear-ended someone even though they were parked. The headlights illuminated the terrifying face of an animal, front hooves propped on the hood of the car. It stared at them with one demented eye before tipping its head back and shrieking again.

Good to know the scream hadn't come from Hildy's uncle.

"You were saying?" Jefferson remarked from the backseat, earning a shove from Hildy.

A sharp tap on her window made Libby jump. She expected to see hot goat breath fogging the glass, for some reason imagining the furry beast circling the car like a killer whale in search of a weak point.

The reality was worse. Mr. L stood inches from her door, tapping the watch on his raised left wrist. Out of sight, the goat screeched again.

You and me both, Libby thought, reluctantly exiting the vehicle.

"Do you see this?" he sputtered, waving at the grass. "They relieve themselves everywhere!"

Libby stopped herself from suggesting he design a goat-friendly outdoor commode. This was more of a diaper situation, judging by the trail of pellets littering the path.

"I need to speak with you," Mr. L continued, ignoring the curious looks from their guests. Well, Hildy seemed interested. Jefferson's face was harder to read.

"How was your meeting?" Libby asked, belatedly realizing it would be the wifely thing to say.

The tense line of his mouth relaxed into a curve of satisfaction. "I was able to preview the Scylla and Charybdis. The prototype of my personal drying station," he explained as Uncle Richard joined them. "But that's not what I wanted to speak to you about."

"Ah." Libby scanned the yard, in case there was an escape hatch hidden under the bushes.

"How's your back?" Hildy asked suddenly, clutching her uncle's arm. "It must be acting up. From the trip and all."

"Not really. I had a private cabin on the plane—"

"You don't have to be brave in front of me, Uncle Richard." She looked up at him through trembling lashes. "I know that old fencing injury is a torment."

"I don't like to complain," he started to say, yelping as the goat tried to ram him in the thigh. Jefferson grabbed the trailing rope, pulling it away from Hildy's uncle.

"I know." Hildy patted Uncle Richard's sleeve before turning to Mr. L. "I don't suppose you have anything that might help with a stiff lower back?"

Libby's pretend-husband puffed up so fast, she was surprised he didn't float off the ground. "The Kitzlochlamm." The consonants were so guttural Libby was afraid she'd have to Heimlich him. "Named for the mystical ravine with crystalline geysers hidden behind ancient rock."

"That sounds intriguing." Uncle Richard put a hand to his back. "Perhaps a soak wouldn't go amiss."

"This is the pinnacle of home spa technology," Mr. L promised, leading him away. "I fear it will make your own plumbing appear inadequate."

"I hope your uncle knows he means literal plumbing," Libby said as the door closed behind them. "He wasn't trying to emasculate him."

"Eh. His ego can survive a few dings." Hildy bent to address the goat. "And now we can have fun with these precious babies. This must be Ginger?"

The brown goat twisted out of reach before doubling back to lunge for a mouthful of Hildy's skirt.

Libby *hmmed* in agreement. It sounded as likely as anything else. "I'll take—it from here," she told Jefferson, covering her stumble by confidently holding out a hand for the rope. Was "Ginger" a boy or a girl? She couldn't think of a way to discreetly check without getting kicked in the face.

Behind the house, the other goat was still tied to the patio furniture, next to an overturned chair.

Hildy frowned. "I thought Poki was white."

Everyone turned to look at the black-and-white-spotted animal dragging the table across the flagstones.

"It was a privacy issue," Libby explained.

"For the goats?" Jefferson asked, in the tone of someone pretty sure he'd misunderstood.

"I felt it was important to maintain healthy boundaries. In terms of social media. We don't like to expose them to the public too much. Technically they're still minors."

Hildy nodded. "Goat years must be like dog years."

"You could say that. They're definitely in their teenage phase right now." Libby raised her voice to make herself heard over the bleating. "Acting out. Typical adolescent behavior."

The goat seemed to take offense at this description, forcing Libby to dodge a flying hoof.

Hildy squinted at the goat's hindquarters. "I could have sworn Poki was the boy."

Libby started to nod, before noticing the dangling udders.

"Did they give you the wrong ones?" Hildy asked. "That happened to my step-aunt, with her Pomeranian. It was a lot harder to tell with all the fur."

"Animals are funny that way." Libby tried to casually pet the black-and-white one, but it nipped at her hand. "I'm sorry. I shouldn't have said that. They're very sensitive."

"Have you tried antidepressants?"

Jefferson frowned at Hildy. "For the goats?"

"They had to do that for Mitzi. The Pomeranian. Her therapist recommended it, to help with the separation anxiety."

"Your aunt's therapist?" Jefferson asked.

"Mitzi's. My aunt has a different one."

"They do prefer peace and quiet," Libby said, as the brown goat rammed the leg of the table, shrieking in outrage when it didn't budge. "Why don't you two go inside and get some sleep? I'll get them settled for the night. I'm sure they'll be calmer in the morning." She crossed her fingers behind her back.

Hildy looked from Libby to Jefferson. "You stay, JJ. Maybe you can get some action . . . shots. If you remember how to use your *zoom lens*?"

"Good night, Hildegarde," he said through a sigh.

The swish of the door closing was the last sound for several long, sticky moments—if you ignored the bleating. At least the presence of barnyard animals kept the scene from feeling too romantic, despite the moonlight and softly waving palms, with the gentle lullaby of the surf in the distance.

Libby's brain provided a helpful series of what-ifs. What if she and Jefferson were alone out here because they'd met under normal circumstances, and gotten to know each other, and started dating, and she'd brought him to Tutu's house as her boyfriend, and now they were going for an evening stroll? Preferably holding hands. Or maybe his arm around her shoulders? Definitely no goats.

Except her real self would never have met Jefferson, so in a twisted sense she owed "Lillibet" for bringing him here, even though pretending to be someone else was the thing keeping them apart. If that qualified as irony, Libby decided she wasn't a fan.

"Where do they sleep?" Jefferson started to untangle the black-and-white goat from the outdoor table. His mind was clearly on practical matters, not torturing himself with romantic hypotheticals.

"Don't worry about it." She turned in a circle to keep from getting tangled in the other lead. "You're a guest."

"Seems like you could use the extra pair of hands." He came to stand beside her, pivoting when the goats started to crisscross. "These two hooligans look like trouble."

"I don't know what's gotten into them." Libby cringed at the sound coming out of her mouth. She should have rehearsed her fake laugh. "We can tie them up over here."

"They spend the night in the open?" Jefferson asked, following her across the lawn.

"Yes. We—let them be free-range." At least until Keoki got back and told her otherwise. "So they don't get claustrophobic." A terrible thought struck her. "Do you—know much about goats? From your work?"

It was Jefferson's turn to look uncomfortable. "Mountain goats are an invasive species in the Tetons. People, uh, hunt them."

"Oh. The poor things." Libby hopped sideways to avoid a head butt to her calf. "I mean, balance is obviously important. Ecologically. And internally."

Jefferson paused in case she wanted to throw in a few more inanities about her digestive tract. "Your goats are lucky."

"We try not to stifle their individuality."

"They seem very un-stifled." He dodged a pair of dancing hooves while tying his goat to the trunk of a palm tree, then held out his hand for Libby's rope. "What else?"

"Hmmm?"

"Is there a nighttime routine?"

"Oh. *That*. Usually I start with their affirmations. *You're so pretty, you have the softest fur*, et cetera. And then a bedtime story—nothing too scary—and finally a song."

He blinked at her. Libby tried very hard to hold on to her poker face.

"But that's only if they've been good. There'll be none of that tonight," she told the goats with mock-sternness. Libby looked back at Jefferson with a smile that turned into a startled *oof* when one of the goats rammed her in the thigh.

The sneak attack sent her toppling into Jefferson. He caught her by the arms, steadying her before she could take them both down. She was pretty sure he could feel her heart thundering, especially since her chest was pressed against him. If this were a middle school dance, they'd be declaring their coupledom for all the world to see.

"Bad goat." He spoke over Libby's shoulder, still holding on. The brown one made a noise that almost sounded apologetic.

"I think they like your voice." Libby touched her fingertips to her breastbone, knuckles grazing his shirt. "You feel it right there. The rumbliness."

Jefferson's throat moved as he swallowed. Libby's gaze traveled upward from his throat, past the strong jaw, lingering on his mouth.

"Libby!" screeched a voice that was neither low nor soothing.

The goats bleated in alarm, and Libby used their distress as an excuse to lurch away from Jefferson, turning to check on her alleged pets before acknowledging her roommate.

Jean stood at the back door, annoyance radiating from her narrowed eyes to her tapping foot.

"I better see what she needs," Libby mumbled, hurrying toward the house.

She was ninety-eight percent certain Jefferson was watching

her walk away. The heat of his gaze was almost enough to offset the chill in her best friend's eyes.

Inside the kitchen, Libby offered a tentative smile. "The goats are here."

"It looks like they machine-gunned the front yard with poop. Did you try to milk them or something?"

"Uh, no. I wasn't going to walk up and start squeezing their— *teats*." Libby half mumbled the word, less out of modesty than being iffy on the pronunciation. "Also I thought one of them was a boy."

Jean grabbed a bottle of water from the refrigerator.

"I put a plate in there for you," Libby told her.

Her roommate's nod was perfunctory. "I'll take it with me."

"Upstairs?"

"I have to go back to the resort."

"What? Why?"

"A shift came open, so I grabbed it. I'll get time-and-a-half. And until you have a job with an actual salary, somebody needs to step up and pay the rent. I don't want to be homeless because you suddenly went boy-crazy."

"That's not fair."

"No, what's not fair is that this situation affects all three of us, but you act like it's just you. What you want. Your dysfunctional hormones."

"You think I don't care about Keoki's restaurant? Why else would I be running around pretending I'm going to illegally marry a strange man who thinks my teeth are weird?"

Jean shushed her with a finger to her lips, frowning at the ceiling. After a few beats of silence, she turned back to Libby. "And me?"

"What do you mean?" Libby sensed a trap.

"Think about the doors this would open for my career. Johnson Media must have a crap-ton of artists on their payroll. I could do graphic design, illustration—for serious money."

"You want a steady job?"

"Not necessarily. But I wouldn't mind making bank for some freelance work, so I have more time to spend on my own stuff. You heard what Hildy said. A *magazine cover*. Can you imagine?"

"That would be incredible. And of course I want to help."

"Great. You can start by not screwing this up." Jean stalked out of the kitchen.

"What did you mean about the dysfunctional thing?" Libby asked, half a step behind.

Her roommate sighed. "This is not the time."

Libby accepted the subject change because she wasn't in a place to push her luck (and didn't really *want* to know). As they passed the living room, she glanced through the open doors, eyes landing on the giant nude. "Should we change her clothes?"

Jean had taken to dressing up the Lillibet portrait in different outfits, mostly (Libby assumed) for her own twisted amusement, though Hildy also found the ritual delightful, like a supersized paper doll.

Tonight, however, painted Lillibet was still wearing the seaweed bandolier and panties she'd had on that morning. With a huff of impatience, Jean retraced her steps to the kitchen, returning with a frilly white apron wadded up in one hand. Dragging the ladder into place, Jean climbed high enough to reach the sandy bikini, stripping it off and dropping it to the floor. With the same care she would have used to throw a pair of dirty socks in the hamper, Jean tossed the apron at the portrait.

"There," she said, jumping down the last few rungs.

"Have you gotten any sleep in the last twenty-four hours?" Libby asked, struck by the lack of manic energy.

"I'm fine." Jean was already on the move. Libby followed her up the stairs, feeling like the big dopey sidekick who didn't get it.

"Tutu told the story about Malaekahana tonight," she said to Jean's back. When in doubt, pretend everything's normal.

"Where the dude tries to murder his kids?"

"She made it an allegory about women in the workplace. So Hildy could get in a little dig at her uncle about taking over the family business." Libby waited for Jean to give her a gold star for promoting their cause, but all she got was a grunt as Jean stepped into her temporary bedroom.

"That's good, right?" Libby pressed, shutting the door behind her. "And I think everyone had fun—"

"Especially you and Ranger Dick?" Jean interrupted. "Did you show him a good time?"

"Jean, nothing happened." Nothing explicit, anyway. You couldn't put someone on trial for heated looks. "I was really good."

"As in, you spent the whole evening with Hildy, hashing out the details of your new job?"

"It was a party! Not a business meeting." An unpleasant memory surfaced. "Speaking of paperwork, Mr. L's lawyer apparently left some documents he wants me to go over." As a person more familiar with waiting tables than signing contracts, Libby's first thought had been that her pretend husband was signaling for the check, until the true meaning of his urgent hallway pantomime landed.

Jean rifled through her gym bag, sniffing a bra before dropping it on the floor. "Well? What do they say?"

"I don't know."

"Because you were too busy playing Dirty Heidi in the backyard with Vanilla Ice?"

There was too much to unpack in that Mad Libs of a sentence, so Libby avoided the whole thing. "We could look at it now?"

"I have to go to work, Libby."

"Right. I know. I just feel more confident when you're here."

Jean's cheeks puffed as she exhaled. "Listen."

Uh-oh.

"I can't always be there to hold your hand. At some point you're going to have to deal with things on your own."

Libby blinked against the sting in her eyes. "Oh. I'm sorry."

"It's not—" Jean broke off, pressing her lips together. "I'm trying to be an adult. I have to put on my own oxygen mask first. Especially if this plane is going down."

"Is that what you think is happening?"

Jean shrugged. "Hopefully not. But it wouldn't be the first time you've crapped out before the finish line."

"Me?" Libby was aware that she hadn't exactly girl-bossed her way through life, but since when was that her fault?

"One day you're going to have to ask yourself, *What do I, Libby Lane, really want? More than anything else.*" Jean underlined the last part with a swipe of the hand. "And then go for it. All the way. Let the chips fall where they may."

In typical Jean fashion, she didn't wait for a comeback. Libby caught up with her halfway to the stairs.

"I am doing that," she started to say, only to fall silent at the sound of a door opening at the end of the hall. Libby cringed at the scuffing footsteps, even before Mr. L's voice hailed her.

"Libblibet," he said, holding up a file folder.

"Lillibet," she corrected under her breath.

"I have the papers for you to sign."

Jean had moved closer, trying to peek at the densely printed page in his hand. "What is it?"

"Our prenuptial agreement. Very straightforward."

Not the word Libby would have chosen, but she kept the snort inside. Her eyes met her best friend's. Libby could tell Jean expected her to beg off.

"Is there a problem?" Mr. L asked. "I am merely protecting my business interests."

"No," Libby said, so firmly he flinched. "I promise not to come for your faucets. Do you have a pen?"

From the pocket of his suit jacket, he produced an ornate silver writing implement that probably cost as much as he was paying Libby to marry him.

Not that a prenup was the same as saying, *I do*.

She opened the folder, fumbling with the cap until she realized it screwed off. It wasn't easy to write without a desk, especially with what turned out to be a fountain pen. The gesture lost some of the intended drama when Libby had to go over the first letter of her name four times. Still, she got it done, sending Jean a defiant look as she scratched the final *e* on the last page of a contract she hadn't read.

How was that for follow-through?

Chapter 20

You look tired. That was one of the things Jefferson's sister had taught him never to say to a woman. Right up there with, *When is the baby due?* and *You should smile more.* According to Susan, all of that was code for, *Your appearance is my business, because I am a pig.*

So instead of asking Libby if she'd had a bad night when she came into the kitchen looking pale and puffy-eyed, he poured her a cup of coffee.

"Thanks."

He held on to the mug a little too long, caught by her smile.

"I am so sorry," Hildy said, skidding into the room with her curls bouncing around her head like a personal typhoon.

Jefferson took a step back.

"What is it?" Libby asked.

"My freaking uncle. Trying to quote-unquote strengthen our bond by taking an interest in my 'hobbies.' He actually said that. What does he think I'm doing here, making friendship bracelets?" Hildy squeezed her eyes shut, rubbing the center of her forehead with two fingers. "Also, we were in the same family therapy sessions. Don't try to pass off a basic exercise from the Showing You Care worksheet as your brilliant insight you came up with by yourself."

Libby took a long sip of coffee before setting down her cup. Placing both hands on Hildy's shoulders, she stared into her eyes. "You lost me."

"*Love, Lillibet.* He looked it up last night. Allegedly he read a bunch of posts himself, which probably means he asked Thelma to summarize it for him. What do you think his main takeaway was?"

Jefferson caught the slight flinch before Libby smoothed her expression. "I can hardly begin to guess."

"He wants Crepes Lillibet for breakfast." Hildy threw up her hands. "Can you believe it? An ocean of profound spiritual insights, and that's what he gets out of it. *Me hungry. Woman make pancake.*"

The door to the patio opened to admit Keoki, whistling as he stepped into the kitchen with a handful of fresh herbs. "Who wants a frittata?" His cheerful expression dimmed as he got a whiff of the tension in the air. "No eggs?"

"Could we maybe do Crepes Lillibet instead?" Libby asked.

Keoki frowned. "I thought that was for tomorrow."

"Slight change of plans."

"Um. Actually." Hildy wrinkled her nose in apology. "He wants to watch Lillibet make them. I told him you weren't our bitch, and he said, 'I thought you wanted her to be our bitch,' and then I said, 'You can't say bitch, Uncle Richard,' and then he wanted to know why I could say it if he couldn't—it was a whole thing. Long story short, it would be great if you could dazzle him with your crepe-making skills."

"Sacrebleu," Keoki said under his breath.

Hildy glanced from him to Libby with a stricken expression. "I hope this doesn't ruin Me-mas. We can save the Me-mosas for tomorrow, at least."

Libby's friend, the un-housekeeper, sailed into the kitchen in time to overhear. "What's going to ruin Me-mas?" Her eyes went to Jefferson, as if he were the most likely culprit.

"Nothing." Libby stood a little straighter, lifting her chin. "We'll just have to make it work."

"Crepes," Keoki filled in, tipping his head at Libby. "He wants to watch *her* make them."

"Crap," Jean whispered.

"Am I too early?" Uncle Richard asked, pausing to sniff the air.

"Go sit down and drink your coffee," Hildy told him, flicking her fingers in the direction of the breakfast bar.

"I had a wonderful night's rest," her uncle informed the room at large as he settled himself at the counter. "It must have been that exceptional bathtub. Hildy, are we doing enough plumbing coverage?"

"Yes," she said, with the finality of a slamming door.

Libby and Keoki were huddled near the refrigerator, conferring in hushed voices, while the housekeeper looked on, offering the occasional nod.

"What are we discussing?" Libby's husband asked, wandering in with a leather-bound notebook.

"We're having crepes for breakfast," Uncle Richard informed him, patting the stool at his side.

"Really? How wonderful." He did not sound like a man who regularly enjoyed that particular menu item.

"You should watch and learn, Hildy." Uncle Richard gestured to the stove, where Libby was adjusting the heat beneath a flat-bottomed pan. "So you can make crepes for your own family one day."

"Because that's going to happen," his niece replied through gritted teeth.

"What's that, dear?" Uncle Richard cupped a hand to his ear.

"I said, this is the kind of work I do in the kitchen." Hildy snapped her fingers twice. "JJ, I need you to take some pictures of Lillibet while she works. We can use them to promo the story."

"Which story would that be?" her uncle asked, with the trep-idatious air of someone who knows he's supposed to know the answer.

"The one about me. And JJ. We'll do a whole behind-the-scenes bit about our tropical vacation and meeting Lillibet. The story itself will be part of the story."

"And that young man's charming grandmother?" Uncle Richard nodded at Keoki.

"A totally separate story." There was a strongly implied *duh* at the end of that sentence. "Trust me, it's handled. This is what it looks like when someone is a tastemaker *and* a rainmaker."

"That was one of my first showerheads," Mr. L said with a dreamy smile. "The Rainmaker 3000. Obviously I've come a long way since then."

That was Jefferson's cue to pick up his camera and move away from the plumbing talk. On the other side of the kitchen, Libby had lined up a pitcher of batter, a mason jar with a handwritten label ("lilikoi-guava puree") and a plastic tub with a sticky note that read "yuzu-infused crème fraîche."

"She likes to prep everything in advance," Keoki explained, as Jefferson snapped a close-up of the ingredients on the sunlit counter. "All she has to do now is warm up the caramelized mango." He spoke with the slowed-down, slightly-too-loud cadence you might use with someone who wasn't fluent in a language.

"I just take the pictures," Jefferson said, assuming he was the one being talked down to.

"Is she flipping them yet?" Uncle Richard called.

"No," Keoki said, before Libby could answer. "She always makes sure the pan is nice and hot first. Which she can tell because she flicks some water droplets on it first and hears the sizzle."

Keoki stepped aside to let Jefferson get a better angle on Libby. She shifted uneasily, turning the handle of the pan toward the back of the stove before twitching it back to its starting position.

"Does the camera make you nervous?" Jefferson asked, lowering it.

"It's not that so much as having an audience. Watching me." She bit her lip. "Which is what an audience does. Redundant, party of two."

"Because she likes to wait and show the finished product," her ex-roommate volunteered. "When it's been attractively plated. With an eye to composition and color. Not blobbed together like a melting sundae." She cleared her throat, as if she suspected Jefferson of being the glop-and-run type.

He moved to Libby's other side, trying not to crowd her. He was better at this with animals. Hard to imagine what kind of camouflage he'd wear to blend in with this kitchen, unless Carhartt introduced a stainless-steel-and-marble print.

"Not your usual assignment," Libby said, reading his mind.

"Not exactly." Sunlight hit the back of her head, and Jefferson took a picture of her long ponytail. It was a useless shot for any purpose other than recording the exact shade of her hair. "Like a mountain lion."

She glanced over her shoulder at him, and Jefferson realized he'd said the last part out loud. Too used to working in solitude, apparently.

"What is?" Libby asked.

"Your hair."

Jean clucked her tongue. "Are you calling her mangy?"

"Do I really?" Libby touched the side of her head. "Have mountain lion hair?"

"Gag me," her friend muttered.

"I thought you had wolf eyes," Libby told Jefferson. "The first time I met you."

He was instantly transported back to that day on the beach. Maybe they'd both felt it—the sense that something out of the ordinary was happening.

"Sizzle," Keoki whispered.

Libby put a hand to her red cheek.

"The pan." Keoki pointed at the stove. "It's ready." He demonstrated by flicking more droplets at the surface, which immediately evaporated with a hiss of steam.

She picked up the pitcher.

"Remember what you always say. The secret is in the wrist." Keoki mimed tipping the pan from side to side. "No hesitation."

"I certainly am full of helpful advice," Libby said tightly.

The batter hit the pan with unexpected force, splashing droplets onto the surface of the stove. Libby grabbed the handle and made a slightly more violent version of Keoki's gesture. She frowned at the resulting shape—more octopus than circle—before placing the pan back on the burner.

"Now is it time to flip it?" Uncle Richard asked.

Keoki shook his head. "First one's always a dud."

"Certainly true of marriage," Uncle Richard quipped, chortling at his own joke.

"Very funny," Mr. L agreed.

Jefferson looked at Libby to see if she was offended, but she was focused on the crepe, like she could make it cook faster by staring.

"Do you do weddings?" her husband asked.

It took Jefferson a second to realize the question was directed at him. "Not as a general rule, no."

"Too bad." The other man sighed. "I'm in the market for one."

"A wedding photographer?" Hildy asked, giving voice to Jefferson's confusion.

"It never hurts to plan ahead," the other man said with a wink.

Hildy raised her eyebrows at Jefferson, confirming he wasn't losing his mind. Libby's husband had just openly discussed his next marriage—in front of his current wife.

"Too bad you won't be able to take the pictures at your own wedding." Uncle Richard beamed at Jefferson, who shot an immediate don't-even-think-about-it look at Hildy.

"A wedding would be a ratings bonanza," Hildy agreed. "Especially a beach ceremony."

Jefferson was seventy-five percent sure she was teasing.

"You can't get married here, Hildy. Your aunt would murder me in my sleep. You know she's been dreaming of planning your wedding for years."

"Um, yeah, not to mention the part where I'm twenty-one."

"And still in school," her uncle added.

"For now," Hildy said, too low for him to hear.

Libby, who had heard, turned to face her. "You might regret it later. Not finishing college. People look at you differently."

"That's a good point," Hildy admitted.

"Why is she allowed to say that and I'm not?" Uncle Richard protested. "Is it one of those words I don't have permission to use?"

"Yes," Hildy said. "Don't say college. It shows your privilege."

"It's never too late to improve your circumstances." Mr. L smiled at Libby's back, like she was Exhibit A.

"My circumstances are magnificent, thank you very much." Hildy fluffed her curls for emphasis.

There was a commotion at the trash can, and they all turned to see Lillibet peeling the blotchy remains of the first crepe off the pan.

"She'll flip the next one," Uncle Richard announced, with the prophetic confidence of a man used to getting his way.

"Whatever she does, she'll do it with intention." Hildy smiled at Lillibet, who was pouring more batter into the pan.

"And a two-handed grip," her uncle continued his sportscaster-style narration. "Like Albie's backhand. For the added power."

"You *would* think it's about power," Hildy scoffed. "Finesse is what matters."

While they continued to mix tennis metaphors, Jefferson saw Libby wince in pain before sticking a finger in her mouth. He was moving before he realized he'd made the decision.

"Let me see," he said, low enough that no one else noticed.

Reluctantly, she showed him the pink pad of her finger. It didn't look like it was going to blister, but he held her hand under the tap for a minute just in case, cupping her wrist in his hand.

"I think you'll be okay," he told her.

"You're not going to amputate?"

Jefferson shook his head. He wouldn't have minded holding on to her a little longer, but he was already playing with fire. Not that her husband was paying any attention.

"Here's a perfect example." Hildy pointed at Jefferson, though the speech was clearly for her uncle's benefit. "You jump straight to our wedding, which is totally OTT."

Uncle Richard looked at her blankly.

"Over the top," she translated. "Why not throw in, 'Our Secret Baby Joy,' with a full nursery photo spread while you're at it?"

"Not before the wedding, Hildy. Our midwestern readership skews conservative. You know that."

"What I know is that it's a waste of resources to put on an actual wedding when all we really need is to get the rumor mill going with a lightly staged shot of JJ shopping for a ring. Isn't that right, JJ?"

He was still trying to untangle the layers of presumption in that statement when Keoki spoke up.

"You like black pearls?" he asked Hildy.

"Yes, please," she purred. "Do you know a place?"

"And do they also sell ukuleles?" Uncle Richard interrupted.

Hildy spun her stool to stare at him. "How much apology jewelry have you bought over the years? In all that time, have you *ever* seen a combination jeweler and music store?"

Jean raised her hand. "Pawnshops."

"There! You see, Hildy?" her uncle crowed, though Jefferson would eat the spiky part of a pineapple if the CEO of Johnson Media had ever set foot in one himself.

"That caramel smells really, really perfect," Keoki said with an urgency that drew everyone's attention back to the stove. Libby yanked the saucepan off the heat.

"About my uke," Uncle Richard began, breaking off when Hildy made a throat-slitting gesture.

"Add that to the you-don't-say list," Hildy interrupted. "Ukulele or nothing for you, and personally I vote nothing."

"It's not for me. I thought Albie would like one. He was always very musical."

Hildy eyed him skeptically. "You mean before his voice changed?"

"You could go to PCC," Keoki said, cementing Jefferson's impression of him as the peacemaker of the group. "They have everything. Jewelry, ukuleles, Dole whip—"

"Yes!" Libby burst out.

For a beat, it seemed like she was really excited about Dole whip, whatever that was. Then they noticed the perfectly browned crepe resting (mostly) in the pan. If Jefferson hadn't been holding his camera, he would have clapped.

"Darn," Uncle Richard said. "I missed it. I'll catch the next one."

"Easy come, easy go." Hildy's voice turned syrupy. "Why don't you eat the first one, Uncle Richard? I know your blood sugar gets low in the morning."

There was something to be said for the Good Niece/Bad Niece routine, because her uncle brightened at this scrap of encouragement.

"Thank you, Hildy. Don't mind if I do."

The erstwhile housekeeper handed him a plate. It was the most domestic gesture Jefferson had seen from her yet.

"I'll make a few calls, and then we can get our shopping on." Hildy glanced at their hostess. "Is that okay with you, Lillibet?"

Libby wiped her forehead with the inside of her elbow, smearing batter all the way to her hairline before offering a weary thumbs-up.

"She'll need to freshen up first," Jean said, throwing her a dish towel.

Chapter 21

It was late afternoon by the time Libby herded the entire crew down the highway to Laie. Their destination, Hukilau Marketplace, was a collection of shops, restaurants, and souvenir stands that filled the entrance plaza at the Polynesian Cultural Center. It was absolutely geared toward tourists, but with offerings that attracted the occasional local, too—more for the food than for the aloha shirts and ukuleles.

"This is exciting," Hildy's uncle said, rubbing his hands together. "It's been ages since I personally supervised a photo op."

"Technically this is my operation, but okay." Hildy handed him a sun hat. "I'm glad you could join us. There's no substitute for getting out in the field. Is everyone clear on the drill?"

Jefferson shrugged, visibly uncomfortable, but Mr. L piggy-backed on Uncle Richard's nod with a crisp salute.

"Good." Hildy checked the time on her phone. "Let's project ourselves into the present, collecting each moment like a pearl to be strung on the necklace of our lives." She glanced at Libby, inviting her to add her two cents. Or, in this case, nonsense.

"It's about gathering treasure," Libby improvised. "From the—deepest part of our inner core."

"The appendix?" Uncle Richard guessed, pressing a hand to his lower back.

"Those are the kidneys," Jean informed him.

"I had mine removed," Mr. L confided.

Hildy's uncle blinked at him. "Your kidneys?"

"Appendix. But I still have my gallbladder."

"We all have empty spaces," Libby said, before anyone else could join the roll call of missing organs. "And yet we find a way to be whole."

"Some holes are easier to fill than others," Jean quipped, helpful as always.

"Amen, sister." Hildy stationed herself at Jean's side. "Speaking of treasure, you're coming shopping with me, right?"

Libby watched the two of them link arms, trying not to feel like the odd woman out.

"We'll leave Lillibet in charge here," Hildy said, offering Libby a trusting smile that somehow doubled as marching orders.

"I'm perfectly capable of overseeing matters," Uncle Richard said.

"I'm talking about the jewelry," his niece informed him. "Lillibet's sense of style is on a different plane from yours. No offense. Besides," she added, cutting off Uncle Richard's sputtered protest, "you're too recognizable. Whereas Lillibet can still go incognito—for now."

That perked him right up. "We should have disguises."

No sooner had Uncle Richard spoken than Mr. L trotted off, returning with free maps of the park from a nearby kiosk. He and Hildy's uncle immediately unfolded theirs, holding them in front of their faces.

"Surprise me," Hildy told Jefferson in parting. "But let Lillibet choose, because I don't want to look like a rodeo princess."

"So no horseshoes?"

Libby caught the trailing end of his almost-smile. His eyes looked even brighter now, set off by the tan he'd picked up since arriving on the island. How was it possible she'd only known him for a handful of days? It was as if every minute they'd spent together weighed ten times as much as an ordinary one. Maybe that was a side effect of living a double life—especially when part of it felt so real.

If she hadn't been halfway to infatuated already, his gentleness when she burned her finger would have tipped her over the edge. Being taken care of was Libby's emotional Achilles' heel. She had formed attachments to drugstore employees who helped her choose the right shade of lipstick, never mind emergency first aid.

"Um, the jewelry place is over here." Libby rotated her arm like she was backstroking on dry land, almost taking out Mr. L. He frowned, possibly reevaluating his choice of fake wife.

"The photographer is in place," Uncle Richard reported as they wove through the crowds.

Despite having most of a journalism degree, Libby had been unaware until today how many of the paparazzi shots on the pages of celebrity magazines were prearranged by a publicist. Hildy and her uncle had placed a few calls to ensure that someone with a camera would be on hand to "surprise" Jefferson while he "shopped" for rings. Nice to know she wasn't the only one on the fringes of the media ecosystem with a dubious relationship to truth.

At the Pearl Diver booth, they left Jefferson staring down at a display case while Libby and her businessman buddies hovered awkwardly out of the frame. She almost looked like one of them, thanks to the powder-pink suit Jean had strong-armed her into wearing. The sleeves barely reached her elbows and there was a brightly patterned scarf around her waist, concealing the fact that the skirt was too small to fasten, but it was still twenty times snazzier than anything in Libby's closet.

Think of it like Spanx, Jean suggested when Libby complained about the itchy fabric and tight fit. *It's a reminder to keep sucking it in.*

At least she'd gotten to wear her own clothes at Tutu's last night, since Mr. L wasn't there to notice. Plus Keoki's brothers would have teased Libby mercilessly if she'd shown up dressed like an uppity Realtor.

"On your six," Uncle Richard murmured. "Our shutterbug has arrived."

If it hadn't been for the glint of sunlight reflecting off the camera lens, Libby wouldn't have spotted the photographer. Blending into the background must be part of the job. Sort of like Jefferson's work, only more predatory.

"He's not smiling," Mr. L observed, peering around the edge of his map at Jefferson.

Uncle Richard gave a thoughtful nod. "It is a weighty decision. I don't like the pressure myself, which is why I generally leave such things to Thelma."

Libby stopped herself from pointing out that he wasn't really going to propose to Hildy. The less talk about fake engagements the better, especially in present company.

Uncle Richard's phone buzzed. "Yahtzee," he said, checking the notification. "He got the shot. We're in business."

They rejoined Jefferson, who was still scowling at the glass display case as if it contained rotting meat.

"See anything you like?" Mr. L asked Libby.

Uncle Richard pointed down at a massive black pearl flanked by diamonds. "That one's nice."

She almost choked when she saw the price.

"I won't count it against your . . . allowance," Mr. L assured her. "Think of it as a *bonus*."

Jefferson frowned at him.

"A bonus *gift*," her would-be husband corrected himself, smiling at his own cleverness. "To commemorate our pre-anniversary."

"I'm good," Libby said.

"What about a seahorse?" Uncle Richard was still studying the jewelry. "Hildy loves horses. She'll talk your head off about them."

Somehow Libby doubted that Hildy was still in her horse girl phase.

"Does she know the Lipizzaner stallions of Vienna?" Mr. L made a series of prancing hops, arms held in front of him like a second set of legs as he turned a slow circle around them.

The woman staffing the cash register flashed them a bright customer-service grin. "Are we shopping for a special occasion?" Her blue uniform shirt had a hibiscus print, and she was wearing a silk lei that partially obscured her name badge. Something ending in *-cia*.

"Wait, don't tell me," Felicia or Patricia said, after surveying the group with a practiced eye. "I hear wedding bells. You two must be her proud dads." She smiled at Uncle Richard and Mr. L. "We do monogrammed cuff links, FYI."

"I do love a cuff link," Uncle Richard said, clearly pleased she'd recognized that about him.

"He's not my father," Libby told Maybe Morticia. "Neither of them are. And they're not a couple."

"Though I would be honored." Mr. L bowed to Hildy's uncle as if they were about to waltz.

"Likewise, I'm sure," Uncle Richard replied.

"Okay." The saleswoman nodded her understanding. "I get it. You have a complicated family."

"I feel I've learned something from each of my marriages," Hildy's uncle mused. "Like water under a bridge. Turning the wheel that makes grist for the mill."

"Did you know they have a waterfall here?" Mr. L asked.

"I did not." Uncle Richard sounded intrigued.

Libby's pretend husband extended an arm. "Shall we?"

"After you," Uncle Richard said.

The saleswoman sighed as the two titans of industry walked off. "They're sweet."

"I've always thought so," Jefferson deadpanned.

"Now, what about you two lovebirds?" Possibly Alicia asked.

"He needs a gift." Libby fully intended to explain that it wasn't for her, but the woman behind the counter didn't give her a chance.

"And you're here to make sure he doesn't cheap out. Say no more. Wish I'd done that with my last boyfriend. He gave me lingerie for Valentine's Day. *No tags,* I thought to myself. *He must be pretty confident he got the right size.* But was that why the tags were off?"

"No?" Libby guessed.

"No," the other woman confirmed. "It was because he borrowed the whole set from his other girlfriend. Who had already worn it, by the way. What kind of person does that?"

This time Jefferson filled in the blank. "Your ex?"

"The tightwad! A nightie, maybe, but a G-string? No, thank you." She stared into space, lost in memories.

"Sounds like you're better off without him?" Libby ventured, when an uncomfortable amount of time had passed.

"Dropped him like he was hot. Which he wasn't. A tiger in the sheets, though. Short guys." The other woman tapped her temple. "They have more to prove, if you get what I'm saying."

"I—think so," Libby said.

"File that away for later. In case you don't always have this tall drink of water to quench your thirst." She eyed Jefferson appreciatively.

"It's not like that." Libby was pretty sure her cheeks were hotter than the crepe pan she'd burned herself on this morning.

"Can't get enough, huh? I thought I was picking up those crazy-in-love vibes. You're going to want something to help you remember this feeling later, when you start to get on each other's nerves. A tasteful pendant, perhaps?"

The speed of the pivot left Libby dizzy. "He's not here for me. I'm helping him choose—for someone else."

"My sister," Jefferson said.

"Susan, you mean? Or do you have another one?" Was it pathetic how excited Libby was to show off her insider knowledge of his life? A little. Was that going to stop her? Nope.

"She's the only one. What about you?"

"No siblings. It was just me and my mom." When her mom was around. "She used to bring me here. To try her luck." Libby nodded at the shallow tank of pick-a-pearl oysters, fifteen dollars a pop. "Never stopped believing she was going to find a huge one, worth way more than she paid."

Jefferson considered this for a moment. "Gambler or romantic?"

"Yes." Also easily distracted by a bit of sparkle. Ready to buy into a good story, even if she'd made it up herself. Always chasing something new instead of being satisfied with what she had. Once, Libby had opened a tin on her mother's dresser, expecting breath mints, and found a dozen mismatched pearls, dusty and forgotten. It was the getting that mattered to her mom, not the keeping.

And yet she constantly complained about how hard it was to find lasting love, never considering that maybe she only *thought* she wanted to settle down. Her mother's choices—still serial dating, after all these years—told a different story. The last time they talked, her mom was in Vegas with someone new. Libby hadn't bothered committing the guy's name to memory. As a kid, she'd made the mistake of believing one or two of her mom's boyfriends were stepdad material, in it for the long haul, but it always turned out that *she* was more attached to them than her mother had ever been.

Was that what she was doing with Jefferson? Deluding herself into a broken heart?

"Should we give it a try?" he asked.

It was an effort to wrestle her thoughts back to the present. "An oyster?"

He nodded.

"Okay." She would do it for Susan, whom she would probably never meet. "What are your nieces' names?" Libby asked suddenly, wanting to collect another piece of Jefferson.

"Abby and Louise."

"Pretty."

"I'll tell them you said so."

The thought of Jefferson mentioning her to his nieces lodged in Libby's chest like a warm little ember of hope.

The saleswoman put down the mirror she'd been pretending to polish. "What are we thinking, secret lovers?"

"We'd like to pick a pearl," Jefferson informed her.

Even though Libby knew the reason he hadn't corrected the "lovers" part was that this lady lived in her own reality, she couldn't help reading into it a tiny bit. Watching Jefferson distracted her from the familiar ritual of choosing the perfect oyster, then counting down until it was pried open, at which point another salesperson rang the bell mounted on the side of the booth to alert passersby that someone had been lucky enough to discover a pearl. (Even though it said right there on the sign: GUARANTEED AUTHENTIC PEARL IN EVERY OYSTER!)

"What a beauty! See that hint of pink?" Felicia, whose name had been revealed when she bent to measure the pearl's diameter, continued to praise its exceptional specialness, as if it were somehow set apart from the hundreds of others she saw in a week.

"Here you go, sir." She deposited the pearl in Jefferson's palm. "Why don't you hold it up to her skin? Are you more of a white or yellow-gold person, ma'am? Or platinum?"

"Um." Libby was tempted to say, *Whatever's cheapest,* because the real answer was that most of her necklaces were on wire or string. The fancy pendants, from Jean's glassblowing phase, got a leather cord.

"Yellow," Felicia decided, handing Jefferson a gold chain.

It seemed easier to play along instead of arguing. That was definitely why Libby unfastened the top button of her borrowed jacket, and he brought his hand up to rest ever so lightly against her throat, holding the pearl and the strand of yellow-gold in place. There was no doubt in Libby's mind that he could feel the throb of her pulse, so close to where his fingertips brushed her skin.

"Try a little lower," Felicia suggested. "Down in the valley, as they say."

Libby blushed as she undid the next button, and not only because she didn't have a valley so much as a pair of speed bumps. Jefferson let the chain slide lower. It felt cool and smooth, though it was only a matter of time before her internal combustion heated the metal until it burned them both.

"I can show you a few of our settings." Felicia slid an album with laminated pictures of necklaces and rings across the counter. "We have options at every price point."

Libby was grateful to have a place to point her face. Jefferson joined her in studying the catalog, both of them as serious as if they were shopping for a house instead of a souvenir trinket.

"Which would you choose?" Jefferson asked.

"I like simple."

"Me, too."

"My favorite is the whale tail," Felicia volunteered. In case they were wondering. "Though we are running a special promotion on rings. Twenty percent off if you buy one of our premier settings with the matching band. Free engraving." She glanced at both Libby and Jefferson, like they were all in on a secret.

It was a bold sales pitch: *Maybe you should get married while rings are on sale?* Libby should have been used to playing along by now, but this was a step too far. She hit the wall, unable to stand there another minute and pretend it meant nothing, that she didn't wish they were a real couple with a future that might or might not involve semiprecious jewelry.

Lie about her name? No problem. Fake being a self-obsessed housewife? Sure! Act like she didn't want to melt every time Jefferson looked at her? Forget it.

"I'll let you finish up," she mumbled, already walking away.

Chapter 22

> **lovelillibet** Few things compare to the dynamism of open flames. My candle game is strong, but I aspire to level up one day. Wouldn't it be atmospheric to live in olden times, with a flickering torch on the wall? Or one of those darling oil lamps? We all need more warmth in our lives, so why not start with fire?
>
> Love, Lillibet
>
> Image: The red-and-white lighthouse at Makapu'u Point with the Pacific Ocean in the background.
>
> #eternalflame #homefires #hotornot #oldschool

Jefferson found Libby on a bench in the shade, out of the flow of tourists moving between the park and the shops. He thought the heat might have gotten to her, but the slumped shoulders and hanging head suggested the problem was on the inside.

He watched her as he approached. She hadn't spotted him yet, so her expression was unguarded. If he had to put a name to it, Jefferson would have said she looked a little sad. It reminded him of his sister Susan in the last year of her marriage, always tensed for the next argument. Libby's husband sure seemed to keep her on a tight leash. Financially, anyway; he didn't appear too worried about her physical whereabouts. Or how she was feeling.

Susan had once accused Jefferson of suffering from a mild case of white knight syndrome. Her point had been driven home with a solid punch, shortly after picking him up from the hospital where he and Hildy had been kept overnight for observation.

Don't you dare pull another stunt like that. And you better not fall for another wounded bird, she'd warned, before he could explain that he wasn't really dating the "Snowbound SoCal Socialite."

As it turned out, the "wounded bird" comment had been in reference to Genevieve, who—once he thought about it—had been known to showily fall apart when she wanted something. That left it to Jefferson to step in and save the day. He was honest enough to admit liking his role in their dynamic: the one who kept calm and solved problems. Compared to Gen's revolving array of crises, his issues were easy to ignore.

In the months since their breakup, Jefferson worried he'd worn a groove in his brain, programming himself to respond to drama. Was that why he'd been immediately drawn to Lillibet? Was she a closet disaster?

She looked up then, as if she'd heard him thinking about her, and Jefferson watched her face light up as their eyes met. He knew he wasn't imagining their connection, and he was willing to bet she was equally aware of it. Hard to say if that made the situation better or worse.

He sat down beside her, leaving a respectful distance between them. "Everything okay?"

"It turns out I'm a tiny bit weird about people buying things. There's a little voice in the back of my head that's always whining, *Are you sure that's a good idea?* So, yeah. That's what it was. Money stuff."

That tracked with what he'd gathered about her early life. It also sounded like a partial truth, but he wasn't going to push for more. She'd talk when she was ready. Or not at all, considering he probably wasn't her top choice of confidant.

"It's a ti plant."

It took Jefferson a few seconds to catch up. He'd been letting his eyes wander while he thought about Libby, but it must have looked like he was captivated by the pointy fuchsia leaves.

"The gardens here are beautiful. I bet you'd love to take pictures, if we had more time."

He nodded, though he wasn't thinking about plants. "Are you going to say something wise about sand and hourglasses?"

"No." She spoke without looking at him. "But I do wish I'd met you under different circumstances."

Jefferson knew what she meant, though he wasn't ready to trade the memory of that day on the beach. He felt like a teenager, sitting in the dark next to a girl he liked, both pretending to watch the movie while totally focused on each other. *If I put my arm here, will she move away? Was that an accidental foot touch or something more?*

Only he and Libby were both grown-ups, so the question of whether she was putting out feelers or throwing up a wall carried much higher stakes.

"Are you talking about your husband?"

"Hmmm?" She seemed genuinely puzzled. "Oh, him? No." Libby started to shake her head, before rapidly correcting course. "I mean, of course that's part of it. In a way." She gripped the back of her neck with both hands, squeezing as she tipped her head back. "You must think I'm a monster."

"No." There was an understatement for the record books.

"You know that saying, 'You've made your bed, now you have to lie in it'?"

Jefferson nodded. That was a pedestrian one, by Lillibet standards.

"It's like that. Except I didn't make the bed, or wash the sheets, and the mattress sucks, and somebody stole my pillow. I'm lying in a big mess, basically. It might as well be an old lumpy futon on the floor. With fleas. And what if this is the only bed I ever get?"

Even before he heard the hitch in her voice, Jefferson recognized the signs of a doom spiral. Next the mattress would be on fire, surrounded by quicksand and piranhas.

"Hey." He put a hand on her shoulder, forcing himself not to dwell on the shape of it, or the warmth of her skin. "Do you need ice cream?"

Libby sniffled. "Yes," she said in a small voice. "How did you know?"

"I've seen the symptoms before."

"Your nieces?" she guessed.

"Sometimes."

She smiled at him through damp lashes, and Jefferson had a vision of a cartoon tombstone with his name on it. *Wounded bird,* said the voice of reason. *Wedding vows.* But it was like telling someone to pack an umbrella when they were already soaked. A waste of breath.

"There you are!" Hildy cut through a sunburned family whose coloring screamed *Upper Midwest,* raising both arms to keep her shopping bags from whacking the occupants of the double stroller. "I know you're supposed to choose your own Me-mas gifts, but I couldn't resist. Also I feel like we've reached a place where we really *get* each other, so it's not like I'm going to love something you'd hate, or vice versa."

"You shouldn't have." It wasn't a knee-jerk response; Libby sounded genuinely distressed.

Hildy wedged herself onto the bench between them, depositing her loot on the ground. "This is cozy. Just the three of us."

"Where's Jean?" Libby asked, scanning the passing traffic.

"I was supposed to tell you. She had to go. Said not to expect her for dinner. Oh, and we ran into Keoki as he was leaving, and his cousin got us VIP seats for the show tonight. Hot shirtless men and open flames! My uncle is going to love it."

"Is that so?" Jefferson was curious to hear Hildy's rationale.

"Are you kidding me? Percussion, burning stuff, and audience participation are like his three favorite things. You should see him at Cirque du Soleil." Hildy leaned in to Libby. "I also took the liberty of buying tickets to the dinner buffet. So you don't have to worry about cooking."

"I guess it makes sense, if we're staying for the show."

"Plus I picked up on it not really being your thing. The actual making of food."

"Oh?" Libby said faintly.

"No shade," Hildy assured her. "This is social media we're talking about, not testifying in front of a grand jury. Everybody gives themselves a glow-up. You're still you, underneath the filter."

Libby's smile was strained. "That's one way of putting it." She hesitated. "It seemed like something people would expect. From Lillibet."

"Branding. Sure." Hildy checked her phone. "Breaking news. Uncle Richard is drinking out of a coconut. Dreams do come true."

"I need some men," the emcee intoned, his mouth an inch from the mic. "Big guys, little guys, or in between. Doesn't matter as long as you're brave enough to come up here." He angled a hand above his eyes as he peered at the packed tables.

At Hildy's look of challenge, Uncle Richard stood, dropping his napkin next to his empty plate before marching toward the dance floor. Libby's husband sprang out of his chair to jog after him, a terrier shadowing a Great Dane. They were joined by a dozen or so hapless husbands and young kids.

"What about you, JJ?" Hildy asked as the performers tied grass skirts around the waists of their volunteers.

"I don't want to show anyone up," he replied, as the group on the dance floor began swiveling their hips in time with the instructions from the stage.

"Whatever you say, Shakira."

They both looked up at the sound of Libby's laughter. She was shaking with it, that first choking burst giving way to silent spasms. Jefferson suspected it had something to do with seeing her husband and Uncle Richard do pelvic thrusts.

A pair of young, shirtless dancers flanked Hildy. Earlier in the evening, she'd watched with vocal appreciation as they scaled palm trees in nothing but a loincloth. It appeared they'd both oiled their muscular chests since then, smooth pectorals glistening under the lights.

"Fine. You talked me into it," she said as they led her away. "Let's show the old folks how it's done."

Every day with Hildy was an education.

"Jefferson."

How many times had Libby said his name? Not enough for the effect to wear off.

"Can I ask you something?" Her warm brown eyes were fixed on his face.

He nodded, embarrassingly eager to be of service—even if it was just passing the salt.

"Do you think we could pretend, for tonight, that we're not ourselves?"

Jefferson's confusion must have shown on his face.

"Forget everything you know about me." She leaned toward him. "No past, no complications. I'm just a girl you met on the beach."

"Libby—"

"I'm not really married."

She might as well have dumped the pitcher of ice water over his head. "You mean you want me to pretend you're not married?"

"I mean I'm really not. He only asked me because he needed a green card. It's a temporary arrangement. There was never any kind of . . . personal relationship."

That explained a lot. And yet, however easy it was to accept that Mr. L was only her husband on paper, Jefferson was struggling to grasp what it meant for *him*.

"It's a secret," she said into the silence. "I'm not supposed to tell anyone." Libby frowned at the spoon she was flipping over and back again. "I guess that's what secret means."

"And you're telling me because?" Jefferson wanted to be sure he understood. And if part of him hoped she would say, *Because I trust you and want you to know me*, he was also braced for disappointment. The answer could just as easily be, *You're leaving town in two days, and we'll never see each other again.*

Libby set down the silverware to clasp her hands on her lap. He could almost feel her gathering her courage.

"I was thinking we could leave," she said, with only the slightest tremble in her voice. "Right now. You and me."

Jefferson was already on the edge of his seat, but those words pulled the chair right out from under him.

Chapter 23

He could always say no. Part of Libby even wanted him to be the responsible one. *No, I won't follow you off this ledge.* He was probably trying to think of a nice way to turn her down. She decided to offer him an out.

"Unless you'd rather not?"

He looked at Hildy's uncle, wreathed in leis and shaking his moneymaker for all it was worth. "The show goes on for a while?"

"Hours."

Jefferson turned that quiet, knowing gaze on her. "Let's go, girl from the beach."

Her heart tried to launch itself into orbit. "Libby is fine."

"Then I'll be Jefferson."

"Great." It was all she wanted. A few stolen hours to be themselves, nothing fake getting in the way.

Except the part where she was pretending to pretend to be her real self, instead of admitting the truth. That was suboptimal. If Libby wasn't careful, she'd tie herself in so many knots, it would be impossible to untangle. But in the meantime, she'd have this one evening with Jefferson.

For a moment she'd wavered, torn between saying nothing and spilling the whole thing. This was the middle road. Not totally brave, but not completely dishonest, either. If Jean complained, Libby would point out that it was partially her fault, for telling her to get real.

What do I really want? This.

They slipped out a side door and down the path to the parking lot. It wasn't until they reached the car that Libby realized the flaw in her plan. This was why she never took bold spontaneous action. What was the point of going for broke if you sucked at logistics?

"Problem?" Jefferson asked.

"I don't have the keys."

He nodded.

"It would be a jerk move to strand them here anyway."

"Too far to walk," he agreed.

She opened her mouth to suggest the bus, before realizing that would be the least Lillibet thing she'd said yet.

Jefferson pulled out his phone, tapping the screen with one finger. "Six minutes." He looked up at her. "Until our ride gets here."

"You called us a car?" It felt almost as heroic as carrying her through a blizzard.

"I have a few apps. Don't tell Hildy."

The sound of drumming drifted down the hill. Libby's heart

kept time with the pounding beat. What if someone came look-ing? She knew herself well enough to imagine her response. *Why are we out here in the dark? Because I . . . lost a contact. Jefferson was helping me.* And then she'd squint up one eye to sell it, and Jefferson would think she was a freak.

It was easier to worry about that kind of what-if than ask her-self what she was doing. Having a light bulb moment was one thing; following through was a lot scarier. Before Libby could convince herself to retreat—back to the people and music and bottling up her embarrassingly huge crush on Jefferson—the car arrived.

He opened the door for her, a questioning look on his face.

Which would she regret more: Going for it or playing it safe? If she only had this one chance, a single evening to be alone with Jefferson, the choice was clear.

Let the chips fall where they may.

The house was locked. Rather than explaining why she didn't have access to the place where she supposedly lived, Libby led Jefferson through the side yard as if that had been her destina-tion all along.

"Hot tub?" she asked, hoping it sounded more confident than she felt.

Their bathing suits were hanging from a drying line behind the shower. Without waiting for an answer, Libby grabbed hers and stepped into the cabana to change. She kept on the lei they'd given her at the luau, because it was pretty and smelled good and she needed the ego boost. When she came out in her bikini, Jefferson was holding his swim trunks.

"I'll meet you over there." She nodded in the direction of the man-made lagoon, one end of which curved into a roughly cir-cular whirlpool.

The faux-lava-rock surround felt like actual pumice, smooth without being slippery. She picked her way across and then lowered herself into the bubbling water. Okay, that felt amazing. Maybe the hot tub was a stroke of genius. Libby willed her muscles to relax. She could do this. Act like a normal, functional adult.

And then Jefferson walked up, and she stared as if she'd never seen a man's chest before. She remembered that first day on the beach, when seeing him with his jeans rolled up made her all wobbly inside. It was strange how the same thing—an ankle, the shape of a calf muscle—could mean something completely different, depending on the person. Libby was pretty sure she'd never looked at another guy's leg hair and thought, *Hot damn, that's sexy.*

"How's the water?"

"Hot." She sounded weirdly emphatic, like it might be burning off her top layer of skin, but she wasn't really thinking about the temperature.

"No torpedoes?" Jefferson dipped a foot in, feeling for the ledge with his toes.

"What?" She was a little distracted by the flexing of his arm muscles as he slowly submerged himself to the shoulders.

"Special features. Robot sharks. Geysers. Like the shower," he added, when she continued to look at him blankly.

"Just me." *Devouring you with my eyes.* Libby had moved to the other side to give him room, so they were sitting opposite each other, the twelve and six on a clock face. She stretched a leg out, wondering if he was close enough to touch.

He jumped when her foot made contact with his shin.

"Sorry," Libby said, more out of reflex than because she meant it. Seduction game: on point. She should have practiced on a doll first.

Jefferson shifted a few inches to the side. Maybe he thought he'd be safe there, although this being a round hot tub, he was closer than before. He frowned at the rippling surface of the water. "So it's not a real marriage."

It wasn't quite a question, but she could tell he needed to hear her say it, one more time.

"Really, really not real. Purely practical. He wanted a green card for business reasons, and I—" *You what, Libby?* She thought furiously. *Were willing to whore yourself out for a fancy house?* "Have U.S. citizenship. But I promise, I am deeply single, in all the ways that matter. Single like . . . a bicycle with one wheel."

Now his mouth relaxed. "You're single like a unicycle?"

"Yes. And it doesn't get much more single than that. In the area of wheeled transportation."

"Is that right?" He reached for her as he spoke, hand sliding down the wet skin of her arm until it closed lightly around her wrist, squeezing once before continuing on to trace the contours of her palm.

The sensation was just shy of ticklish. Libby's fingers clamped onto Jefferson's like a Venus fly trap, a half involuntary movement. They stayed with their arms stretched between them, like he knew she needed a minute to adjust to the sensation of holding his hand for the first time. Or maybe it felt momentous to him too.

"Hi." She raised and lowered her arm like they were shaking hands. "I'm Libby."

"Jefferson." He didn't let go. "Have I seen you somewhere before?"

"We ran into each other on the beach. It's definitely not because a giant nude portrait of me exists."

"And I have never been in the tabloids." He shifted closer. "You're the girl with the crackers."

She nodded, taking another step toward him. "You're the guy with the camera."

"That's me. Can I kiss you?"

"Yes, please."

Libby tried to do a sexy saunter, but it was more of a determined wade until her foot slipped. Jefferson caught her by the waist before she went under. She grabbed his shoulders as he pulled her onto his lap. His hands slid below the surface, guiding her legs around his hips.

If she'd thought touching Jefferson's hand was a lot, straddling him was a different order of intensity. It took several breaths to process the closeness. Like finding out she'd won a million dollars and trying to compute the magnitude. How many twenties was that? Because right now, she and Jefferson were lined up thigh-to-thigh. Libby had the irrational thought that their legs were hugging.

Her eyes drifted shut as his head dipped, lips pressing against the hollow of her throat. When she opened them again, he was watching her. She leaned forward until her mouth touched his.

Finally. Her lips parted on a sigh, breathing him in. A slow, soft kiss turned into something hotter. Jefferson's tongue met hers, the grip of his hands turning urgent. She slid forward on his lap, wanting to get closer.

Some endless but also much-too-short span of time later, he pulled back. "Nice to meet you. What did you say your name was?"

"Libby." No trace of Lillibet tonight.

He cupped her cheek with one hand. "I'm not seeing anyone, Libby. In case you were wondering."

"I'm not married." It felt like diving off the cliff at Waimea Bay, almost totally telling him the truth.

"Glad to hear it."

"I've also never gotten into a complicated situation I later regretted." If it was time for wishful thinking, Libby might as well go all the way.

He traced the curve of her bottom lip with his thumb. "I can honestly say I don't regret anything right now."

That was enough of a green light for her. Permission to live in the moment. It was like going from a dark room into the midday sun. *We do this now.* Touching was on the table. Staring, too. After days of trying to keep her distance—at least physically—the sheer sense of possibility short-circuited Libby's brain. She smoothed her hands over his shoulders, molding the muscle with her palms the way she'd seen Keoki do with a ball of dough.

His hands were doing their own wandering. A light, caressing pressure settled first on her legs, fingertips skimming slowly up the outside of her thighs. When he reached her waist, he tested the sloping curve above her hips, the merest hint of a squeeze as he tried different placements, looking for the best grip. He wasn't racing to get to the obvious destinations, pumping her ass like a stress ball. Some guys treated a woman's body like a ticking bomb, scrambling to cut the right wire before the countdown clock hit zero. Jefferson operated like he had all the time in the world and was going to take it.

She held her breath as his fingertips trailed across the softness of her stomach until his thumb was pressed against her belly button. Libby got the sense he was making a tactile record, charting the space her body occupied, in case he needed to find her in the dark. *This is Libby,* he would say. *I recognize this inch of skin at the bottom of her rib cage.*

He was so focused on her, with his eyes and his hands. Libby relaxed into his touch, half hypnotized despite the hummingbird beat of her heart as his other hand traveled over her lower back, continuing his slow survey. Had anyone ever paid this much attention to her before? In the past, she'd felt like physical parts first and a person second. This was the opposite of that. She knew Jefferson wasn't comparing her to an airbrushed image.

The look in his eyes said he wanted to touch *her* because she was Libby, and he wanted to know everything about her.

"I can't believe you're real." His voice was even gruffer than usual, scraping Libby's nerve endings.

"Same. About you, I mean." But it was also true that Libby had never felt more anchored in her body, fully inhabiting every inch of her skin. That had to be what mattered, more than the fine print about her life.

Their eyes met as his hand slipped lower, cupping her hip. He shifted sideways, adjusting her position on his lap. His thumb traced the elastic of her bikini. She was sure he could hear the catch in her breath.

Are we going to have sex? Right now? In this hot tub? The wondering was a cricket chirp, barely audible over the typhoon of lust. Jefferson's fingers tangled in the ties of her bikini top. The knuckles of his other hand dragged along the underside of her jaw, then across her collarbone, before sliding between her breasts. He paused there, one finger skimming the string linking the thin triangles of her top before sliding beneath the fabric. The pleasure hit her bloodstream like a shot of tequila, making her dizzy.

"I like you," she blurted, managing to be a huge dork and totally inadequate at the same time.

Jefferson's eyes lit as if she'd written him a love song. "I like you, too."

She kissed his smiling mouth, wrapping herself around him to keep from floating away from sheer happiness. It was a perfect moment. Libby had never felt anything close to this—

Her sudden hiss of pain startled them both.

"Sorry," he said at once, pulling back.

"No, it's okay. Just a pinch. Your hand . . ."

He lifted the fingers resting at the top of her thigh. Libby shook her head. "The other one. On my neck. I think some of my hair got caught in the straps."

As she followed the direction of Jefferson's gaze to where his right hand cupped her breast, his thumb applying the exact right amount of pressure, Libby realized something didn't add up. Specifically, the number of Jefferson's hands.

"What the heck?" she said at the same time he reached behind her.

"Bad goat," he scolded, trying to pry the lei out of Poki's mouth. The goat pulled harder, not caring if Libby got clotheslined in the process.

"I think we might have to sacrifice the flowers," Jefferson said, holding the lei away from her throat. She lowered her head so he could lift it up and over, tossing it onto the rocks. The goat bleated its thanks. Or possibly it was saying, *Sucks to suck, losers.*

"You okay?" Jefferson asked.

"Yeah. Kind of a mood killer." Sinking down until her chin touched the surface, Libby swished back and forth, pulling the rubber band off her messy bun.

"I wouldn't say that," he murmured, watching her hair swirl around her.

Maybe their evening wasn't ruined. He didn't have to know she was rinsing off goat slobber.

Smooth and sultry, Libby coached herself as she started to stand. Like a Bond girl rising from the surf. The air felt cool on her shoulders as she thrust them back. She reached behind her, ready to untie her bathing suit and toss it aside. *Feast your eyes on this!*

There was a plop, like seaweed sticking to her skin. Libby looked down, where she was surprised to see her breasts on display, even though she had yet to untie her bikini. She felt under her hair. No straps.

Which she probably should have guessed, considering the dripping thing that had slapped her stomach was the remains of her bathing suit.

"That is not how I imagined that going." Libby crossed her arms over her chest. It wasn't the toplessness that embarrassed her. That had been the plan all along, minus the epic failure of her first ever attempt at a strip tease. "I can't believe a goat ate my bikini."

It was from the clearance rack at Target, but still.

"Hold on." Jefferson reached into the waistband of his shorts. Libby's first thought was that he was going to take off his bathing suit to make her feel better, but the trunks stayed on as he pulled the drawstring free. "Turn around."

She did as he asked, wondering if he was about to reveal a secret fondness for bondage. That would be an unexpected twist, though no more out of left field than bringing barnyard animals into the mix.

"I should be able to rig a strap out of this," he explained, putting an abrupt end to the spicier scenarios Libby was imagining.

She tugged the clammy bikini top into place, holding it as she passed the longer strap over her shoulder. Jefferson carefully brushed her hair to one side before tying his drawstring to the intact portion of Libby's halter. The other side was trickier.

"It's just a stub," she warned as he reached over her shoulder.

"It's not the size that matters." His breath skimmed the back of her ear.

"Are you doing a fancy knot?" she asked, to distract herself from the fact that her boob was jiggling like a pocket full of change.

"Yep. They call this one the Mulligan."

"Really?"

"No." Jefferson rubbed his cheek against hers, since all two of his hands were occupied. "This is my first bikini repair. I'm improvising."

"It wasn't part of your wilderness rescue training?"

"We focus more on cutting people out of their clothes."

That really shouldn't sound as hot as it did. Maybe there was something wrong with her, beyond the wardrobe malfunction.

He gave the string a final tug. "How's that?"

She wiggled her shoulders up and down. "Seems secure." One of her breasts was hoisted significantly higher than the other, but they'd never been perfectly symmetrical anyway. As she turned to face him, Libby felt strangely shy. "Thanks."

"What is it?" he asked, studying her face.

She hesitated. Frank conversations were not Libby's strong suit. In a weird way, knowing how many things she couldn't talk about made it easier to be brave about this one awkward subject. Or maybe it was her bedrock sense that it was safe to be vulnerable with Jefferson that gave her the courage to say, "Did you not want to see my boobs?"

He rubbed his mouth, stifling a laugh. "I promise that's not the issue. You looked upset, so I wanted to help."

"I was trying to be sexy," Libby admitted. "Not *whoopsie!*"

"Trust me, you don't have to worry about that." The heat of his gaze burned through any possibility of doubt. "I wanted to be sure it was your choice."

"As opposed to the goat's." She took a step closer. "You were saving me from being chewed into a corner. Non-consensual gnawing."

Jefferson reached for her, wrapping an arm around her lower back. "For the record, I have no objection to you taking off your clothes."

"That's too bad," she said, before kissing him again.

"Why?"

"You have me tied up pretty tight." She curled a finger around the part of the strap that wasn't a thick white drawstring, lifting it away from her body.

His eyes tracked the up-and-down slide of her hand. "Good thing I always carry a utility knife."

In those shorts? Libby thought not. She'd spent enough time on his lap to know better.

He turned her so they were back-to-front, one arm anchoring her to him while the other brushed her hair aside to expose the nape of her neck. "I like a challenge."

If she had a cosmic remote, Libby would have hit pause right there, with Jefferson surrounding her, solid and warm, his lips against her shoulder.

"Cold?" he asked when she shivered.

She shook her head. "You?"

"Nope." He splayed his hand over her stomach, the heat of his hand melting her from the inside. "Where were we?"

A goat answered before Libby could, bleating something that sounded like, *I finished the flowers, dickwads. What's for dessert?*

"Go away," Libby grumbled, though it was hard to feel too much annoyance when she was slathered over Jefferson like the filling on an open-faced sandwich.

"I assume you're not talking to me," he said, lightly biting the lobe of her ear.

"No." *Please never leave.* Libby buried that thought deep before it could cut her.

In the distance, the goats made more noise. *Remember us? We're still here!* It was like having an annoying chaperone. At least they weren't right up in their business. In fact—

Libby abruptly pulled herself out of Jefferson's arms. "Did that goat sound really far away to you?"

He frowned. "Now that you mention it, yes."

She waded to the edge of the hot tub, standing on the bench for a better view. The brown goat was quietly nibbling grass. Beyond that, Libby spied the chewed-off end of a rope.

It was the number one thing Keoki had warned her about. *Those goats are escape artists. We have to make sure they don't run away because they're hella expensive. The cheese sells for forty dollars an ounce.*

This was standard goat behavior, not a karmic slap on the wrist. And yet Libby couldn't shake the feeling she was being punished. Maybe it was a law of the universe: tell too many lies, and you were doomed to get cockblocked by your fake pets.

"I have to find her," she told Jefferson. "Before something happens."

The way her luck was running, the goat was probably dancing in the middle of the highway by now.

Chapter 24

> **lovelillibet** When people say the age of adventure is over, it tells me they've forgotten how to take risks. You can turn your whole existence on its head anytime. For example, the other day I traded my swishy layers for curtain bangs and now it feels like I'm vacationing in my own life.
>
> Love, Lillibet
>
> Image: Gauzy white drapes swirl behind a wrought-iron railing.
>
> #renewyou #hairtodaygonetomorrow #chargeintochange

Jefferson was right behind her, ready to go on goat patrol. Except then Libby climbed out of the hot tub, all endless glistening legs and a scrap of barely-there fabric inches from his face, and his brain went offline, frozen on that accidental close-up. He considered bashing his head on the fake rock border to restart his executive functioning.

This situation was rapidly slipping out of his control, and it had nothing to do with runaway goats.

What am I doing? On this island, with this woman, in this hot tub?

A better question was why he hadn't stopped to ask himself any of those things until now.

The answer seemed to be that cool, calm, and collected Jefferson had left the building. New Jefferson was in charge, and this version of him was driven by wants instead of plans. Leaving the luau, putting his hands all over her, thinking about doing more . . . that was base instinct behind the wheel. In his normal life, Jefferson would have seen the obstacles ahead and pumped the brakes.

They lived thousands of miles apart. She was about to start a new job that could send her life in a completely different direction. He barely knew her.

And Libby had a husband. Even if she hadn't married for love. Was there such a thing as being a little bit married? Jefferson would have called it a load of malarkey if he wasn't so desperate to believe she was free.

None of that slowed him down. A switch had been flipped, and suddenly Jefferson was a heat-seeking missile. She offered, and he leaped at the chance, following Libby like she had him on a leash. It had never been like this before, an all-consuming wave of feeling sweeping doubt and hesitation out of its path.

He needed to talk to her, even though there was no guarantee she was on the same page. What did she want? What was she willing to risk? If there was any chance of this becoming something real, he wasn't willing to leave it to guesswork. Cards on the table—but not until they found the damn goats.

"At least you can see which way they went." Libby nodded at a bare patch in the otherwise lush hedge, right at goat height. She tossed Jefferson a towel, hanging the one she'd used on a hook outside the shower. They shrugged on their clothes, yanking them into place over still-damp skin, and set off in pursuit.

"Are there any predators we should be worried about?" he asked, as they followed the trail of missing leaves and broken twigs.

"Some of the neighbors might come after them if they mess up their landscaping."

"What if they try to swim for freedom?"

She paused to look back at him. "You think they might drown?"

"I know goats are strong swimmers. I was thinking sharks."

Her face fell.

"I'm sure they're too smart for that," Jefferson assured her.

"They ate one of the cushions on the patio furniture," she reminded him.

Among other things. Jefferson's fingers twitched at the memory of touching the skin underneath the strap of her bikini. "It's not like you hear about a lot of goats getting eaten by sharks. As part of the food chain."

A security light flashed on ahead. "I'm going to go out on a limb and guess they went that way," Jefferson said.

"In your expert opinion. As a wildlife tracker."

"If I'm reading the signs right. Are you friendly with your neighbors?" he asked as they moved toward the puddle of light.

"Why?" The question seemed to make her nervous. Maybe there'd been a spat about parking, or someone's obnoxious wind chimes.

"If they recognize you, they won't think we're trying to break in."

"They're probably asleep." She moved farther into the shadows.

"Eureka," Jefferson said a few steps later, pointing at the grass.

Libby squinted at the pile of pellets. "It's like bread crumbs. Only poop."

They followed the trail of droppings and gnawed-off branches to a narrow path through the brush, the whoosh of the surf increasing in volume with every step. Jefferson stopped to inhale, tasting salt. The ocean was vast and dark apart from a wedge of reflected moonlight. The entire scene felt impossible: impossibly beautiful, impossible that he was here, with Libby. He had the urge to reach over and take her hand, fast-forwarding to a time when that was part of their relationship.

When they had a relationship, period.

As if he'd willed it, Jefferson felt the brush of her fingers, wrapping around his.

Look, she mouthed, when she had his attention. The goat was asleep on the sand, head bent back to use its body as a pillow.

"She looks so peaceful," Libby whispered.

"A jailbreak takes it out of you."

"Seems like a shame to disturb her."

Given the choice of going back to Libby's house or lingering on the beach, Jefferson knew which he preferred. He considered the trailing end of rope. "Want to see if we can tie her to that tree?"

When Libby nodded, he took it as evidence of a question asked and answered: *Want to stay here with me a little longer?*

Yes.

"I'll text Hildy. Tell her I went to bed early."

"And I have a headache," Libby suggested, "which is why you were nice enough to take me home."

Jefferson had a vision of taking her back to his place, where he could be even nicer. Preferably for more than one night. But even if she were willing to leave with him, she couldn't, could she? A pretend marriage was still a commitment.

Text sent, he silenced his phone before tiptoeing toward the goat.

"Does bending make you quieter?" Libby imitated his half crouch.

He put a finger to his lips as she crab-walked to his side. Jefferson fished the rope out of the sand with exaggerated care, like it was a high-stakes game of pick-up sticks, and passed it to Libby.

When she had a solid grip, he started feeding out rope, edging toward the nearest palm tree. There was plenty of slack, since the goat had been dragging as much yardage as the average rock climber. He hitched the rope to the trunk, tight enough to hold while still allowing access to the leafy green plants beyond the sand.

At Jefferson's thumbs-up, Libby let go of the rope and backed away. He joined her at a safe distance, where they could keep an eye on the goat without waking her.

"You probably earned a new badge tonight. Level-Two Knot Master." She fiddled with the strap of her bathing suit.

"Too tight?"

"I might just— Give me a sec." Turning her back on him, she reached under her sundress. After some shimmying and squirming, she stuck her hand down the front and pulled out the bikini top, yanking it over her head before facing him with a look that said, *Tada!*

"That's better," she sighed.

"Quite a trick."

"I know. And I didn't even need a knife." She blew on her fingernails. "Just call me Houdini."

He would have been happy to keep standing there grinning at her, but it was time to do the hard thing. "Listen, Houdini."

Libby tensed, like a rabbit poised for flight. So much for easing into a difficult conversation.

"That wasn't a move, by the way. Taking off my top. I could do much better than that. Not that I would, if you're not into it. Since it seems like the mood might have changed." She took a careful step back, giving him space he didn't want.

"It's not that." He gripped the back of his neck. "I wanted to talk to you. Seems like I might have jumped the gun. Before."

"And now you regret it ever happened, because you realize you made a terrible mistake, and you'd rather forget the whole thing?" Her tone was friendly and understanding. *No hard feelings.* But she wouldn't meet his eyes.

"Libby." Jefferson waited for her to look up. "I don't regret anything." He kept his eyes on her face, letting her see that he meant every word. "I won't forget anything about tonight. Or these last few days."

She swayed toward him. "Really?"

He grasped her by the shoulders, quickly realizing physical contact wasn't a good idea. Opening his hands, he pulled away before he could slide them down her arms and onto her hips.

"I don't think we should take it any further." It killed him to see her face fall, so he added a hurried, "Not yet, anyway."

"Oh." She rocked back on her heels, worrying her bottom lip. "Why?"

Because I'm an idiot. But not enough of one to dump the whole thing on her before he'd thought it through himself. *Now that we've kissed, how would you like to turn your life upside to be with me, somewhere, somehow?*

"Sorry," she said, when he didn't answer right away. "I shouldn't have asked. You don't owe me an explanation."

He took hold of her hand. "I don't want to do this the wrong way. While you're married to someone else."

"But—"

"I know it's not a real relationship, but I don't want to pretend with you, and it feels like there's something in the way. A barrier. Maybe I'm imagining it?" He looked at her hopefully, waiting for a denial.

She kept her head down, making a noise that sounded like *mmmm-hmmmnnn.* That seemed to be her full statement on the subject.

"It hasn't worked out too well for me in the past, letting the physical relationship come first. You end up sweeping stuff under the rug. And the thing of it is . . ." Jefferson hesitated, gripping the edge of the cliff with his toes. "It feels like this could be a good thing. And I don't want to screw up something important."

He waited for her to offer a response, preferably along the lines of, *It's not just you, I feel it, too.* "Does that make any sense at all?" Jefferson asked, when he couldn't take it any longer.

"I can't believe you just . . . said all that. Out loud. With words."

"Too much?"

"Oh no. Keep it coming."

Some of the tightness constricting his lungs eased. "I want to know you, Libby. And I want you to know me. Before we cross that line—"

"In the sand."

"Or wherever. Maybe I am an old man at heart. This is probably not the sexiest conversation you've ever had."

"No, I'm pretty sure it is, actually." She broke off, laughing under her breath. "You talked to me about your feelings. Voluntarily. You *thought* about emotional stuff. Like an adult. You thought about *me*. I'm basically a puddle right now. You could scoop me out of the sand. Like . . . a giant litter box." Her eyes squeezed shut. "Speaking of sexy."

He wanted to kiss her again. Not because she'd compared herself to cat pee, though that was part of it. The odd mixed in with the funny and vulnerable.

"This is where we met," he said, glancing at the silver-crested waves.

She nodded.

"But we're not in the same place."

"No."

"I don't mean geographically." Jefferson was miles ahead of where he'd been that day, although part of him had already been falling for her—a gradual lean that picked up speed the closer he got.

Her grin was a lasso around his heart. "I figured. And also it's night." She pushed her hair back from her face, like she wasn't sure what to do with her hands. "Do you want to stay and see the sunrise?"

"Yes." He knelt to smooth the sand before spreading out the towel he still carried. "Come here."

She settled herself beside him, hip to hip, her head resting on his shoulder.

If he had a seashell, he'd make another wish: *Let this be the first of many sunrises we watch together.*

Chapter 25

---

lovelillibet Don't let dark thoughts scare you away from trying something new. So many people told me that baking a soufflé was hard, and I made the mistake of letting their negativity take up space in my head. Well, guess what? My first try came out perfectly. Light as a cloud, with a heart of molten perfection.

The only thing I regret is letting doubters hold me back.

Love, Lillibet

Image: A wire basket of eggs, the shells ranging in shade from pale brown to celadon.

#breakyourshell #digforgold #selftrust #reachforthesky

At some point Libby must have drifted off. As much as she wanted to stay awake, savoring every second of this time together, the last few days had taken a toll.

But she'd learned things last night, coloring in whole new sections of her picture of Jefferson. Giving her most of the towel while he stretched out on his side at the very edge. The soft kiss he'd pressed against her forehead as she was falling asleep. Pulling her closer when she shivered, his arm draped over her like a blanket.

And that moment when she'd opened her eyes and found

him looking back at her, their faces inches apart. They were near enough to count each other's eyelashes. Everything faded away except Jefferson, as if they were drifting in the silence of deep space.

Libby didn't usually go in for goopy sayings about eyes being a window into the soul (that was more Lillibet's speed), but she found herself hoping it was true, because that would mean he could see right down into the depths of her real self, without the need for any of the words she was too afraid to speak.

"Just in time," he said, brushing her hair away from her face.

Belatedly she realized the sky must be lightening if she could see him this well. Glancing away from his face, she clocked the first hints of morning overhead, a gradual undarkening that presaged the big display of color and light.

Libby sat up, a little stiff but not caring in the slightest. She leaned against Jefferson, and he put his arm around her shoulders. Together they soaked it in. And while Libby knew she was happy, she also felt like crying. Just a little—from the beauty, and the improbability of finding someone like Jefferson, and needing to release a backlog of emotional pressure.

She had a good fifteen minutes of peace and tranquility before the first lash of panic.

"She's fine," Jefferson assured Libby, when she looked around for the goat. "Having a morning snack."

Libby's stomach rumbled. The crayon-box sunrise was starting to disappear. Soon it would give way to the blue of a regular summer day, with all its practical concerns. She stood and stretched, shaking out the towel while Jefferson untied the rope. Get the goat home, clean herself up, and—no. Coffee, then shower. God, donuts would be so good right now. Could she borrow a car to drive to Ted's?

As they made their way back to the house, Libby let herself imagine an alternate reality where Jefferson was her steady, committed boyfriend (because what other kind of boyfriend would he be?) and the two of them were about to cruise to the bakery together. A lazy morning, with nothing on the agenda but hanging out.

"Libby!" Keoki's voice snapped her out of the daydream. His eyes landed on the goat Jefferson was leading along the path. "Where were you?"

"On the beach." It was true-ish, if you collapsed the timeline. "We—took him for a walk. I mean her. The goat."

Keoki crossed his arms. "Did she eat anything weird?"

"Define weird." She thought of her bathing suit. Had it really eaten the strap or just given it a good nibble?

"I'll take her from here," he told Jefferson, who handed him the rope. "Rush order for chèvre." Which hopefully wouldn't taste like Spandex.

Jefferson nodded as if that made perfect sense. *Chev-ruh* must be showing up on charcuterie boards in the wilds of Wyoming. "See you back at the house," he said to Libby.

She watched him walk away. It was stupid to feel sad, like the sand was running out of the hourglass. Libby scratched her scalp. Speaking of sand.

"This is a really important supplier." Keoki kept his voice low in case Jefferson was still in hearing range. "I can't mess up my relationship with them. Reputation is everything in this business."

"Sorry."

He shrugged off her apology with the usual Keoki no-big-thing attitude, but she could tell it was an effort. This was a much bigger mistake than Libby accidentally eating an important ingredient he'd foolishly left at their place.

"How was the appointment?" she asked, as Keoki tugged the goat into motion. Libby felt another lash of guilt at how close she'd come to forgetting his big day. In a normal week, Cici's twenty-week ultrasound would have been the number one topic of conversation.

"She's a girl." He beamed at Libby over his shoulder. "Big kicker. I'm thinking soccer."

The goat stopped to nibble on a patch of grass. Three seconds later, she was pulling on her lead, bleating something that sounded like, *I'm finished with my snack, asswipes. Get a move on.*

"I gotta go, Libs. You can do this. Believe in yourself, okay?"

"Are you quoting *Love, Lillibet*?"

"It's a mug Cici has. With the Loch Ness monster." He patted her on the shoulder. "Good luck."

Keoki veered toward the front of the house, where Libby could just make out the diesel rumble of the truck waiting to take the goats back to the farm. Her feet carried her slowly toward the backyard. Jefferson was waiting on the terrace.

"You okay?" he asked.

"Yeah." Libby managed a smile, drawing on the part of her that was purely happy to see him, despite everything. "It feels like we're coming back down to earth. From, you know."

"Planet Last Night," Jefferson filled in. He was looking at her like he wanted to smile, or even laugh.

"Bedhead?" Libby patted her hair. "Or should I say beach-head?"

He ran a finger along her hairline, drawing it across her temple and then behind her ear. Even after he stopped, the trail of warmth continued, all the way down to her toes.

"Did you fix it?" she asked when she found her voice.

"I just wanted to touch you." His knuckles brushed the side of her neck. "Before we go inside, there's something you should know."

"Your name isn't really Jefferson?"

He paused like she'd strung up a trip wire. "Uh, no. That is my name."

"Of course," she said quickly, before he could question why

the first place her mind went was *false identity.* "Go ahead. I shouldn't have interrupted you."

"That's okay." He swallowed. "I like you. A lot. And I'd like to keep seeing you, when all this is over. I don't know how or where, but if there's a way, I'm willing to try. If that's something you want."

"I do want," Libby said, before her conscience could scream, *I'm not worthy.* "All of it. With you."

He was so honest and brave. Jefferson deserved someone who didn't suck. *I'm going to confess everything,* she decided. *Today.* And then come clean to Hildy, bringing the Lillibet hoax to a merciful close. Like an exorcism.

She slid an arm around the back of his neck, drawing herself against him. Libby didn't usually throw herself at people. Too many of the guys she'd known were wishy-washy, one foot out the door. Lean on someone like that, and you'd both eat dirt. With Jefferson, she trusted him to be there, solid and real, meeting her halfway. Not just because he was an upstanding person, but because he wanted her there, in his arms, as much as she wanted to be wrapped around him.

I like you, too, she told him with her lips. *A scary lot.*

His hands traveled down her sides, squeezing the curve of her waist before sliding back over her shoulders to pull her closer. Every time she kissed Jefferson was like discovering a new flavor. *Oh, I like this one, too.* One quick kiss was building into something more when he pulled away, resting his forehead against hers.

"Next time we spend the night together, let's go someplace less sandy."

It was a rain check that felt like a promise: *This will happen.* All Libby had to do was eliminate the obstacles standing between them. Which happened to be slightly different than the ones Jefferson knew about, but that was all part of the process.

She breathed deeply, letting the cool morning air fill her

lungs. There was something hopeful about this time of day, like you were literally seeing the world through rose-colored glasses. Maybe that was Libby's problem: she'd always slept through the optimistic hours. Right now, with Jefferson at her side, it was just barely possible to believe it would all work out.

"I guess we shouldn't go in together." Libby didn't have Jean's gift for strategy, but instinct told her she wouldn't be able to act normal around Jefferson so soon after having his tongue in her mouth.

"We could say we were doing yoga."

"What about my butt?"

"Seems perfect to me." He pulled her against him, hands cupping her cheeks (the lower ones). "On closer inspection."

"You know, I didn't actually have a sprained ass." Because that was definitely the right place to start her confession. Really ripping off the bandage.

Jefferson nodded, unsurprised. "I figured it was the morning thing. Wanting to sleep in. Especially on Me-mas."

She hoped the *oh shit* didn't show on her face. Mother freaking Me-mas. "Right. That's today. I was supposed to start the day me-ditating. Next to the Me Tree. Aka Big Naked Me." She bit her lip.

"I prefer you in 3D."

"Even though you can't use my nipple as a night-light?"

"Not high on the list of qualities I look for in a woman."

"Imagine in the wilderness, though. If you're camping. It could be handy."

"Libby," he said with mock-sternness. "Are you stalling?"

"Puh. Me? No. I can't wait to get in there. Get this party started." It would have been more convincing had her voice not dwindled to a sigh by the end.

"Why don't you tell them you want to spend the day in bed?" Color flooded his face. "Reading, I mean. Or sleeping. Alone. I thought the whole idea of Me-mas was getting to do whatever you want."

"I feel like I owe Hildy a Me-mas to remember."

"That's nice of you." His thumb brushed her cheekbone, lightly touching her bottom lip before he lowered his arm. For someone so reserved with his facial expressions, Jefferson was surprisingly free with physical affection. He kissed the spot he'd marked with his thumb before taking a step back. "I'll go in through the kitchen. See you on the other side."

Libby watched him lope across the grass. One way or another, the moment of truth had arrived.

The mirrored finish on the doors reflected the deepening blue of a clear, sunny day. Libby decided to take it as a positive omen. Carefully sliding open the massive wall of glass, she stepped inside, pausing to let her eyes adjust to the dimness.

"Oh." The occupants of the not-empty-after-all living room stared back at her, champagne flutes in hand. "Me-mosa time already?" Libby tried to sound cheerful, but it was hard to hear herself over the roaring chorus of *nononononononononono* in her brain.

Hildy. Her uncle. Mr. L. And Jean, shaking her head in a silent, *I wouldn't bother.*

"What was the meaning of *that*?" Uncle Richard demanded, pointing at the glass.

Libby glanced behind her, confirming that, yes, from inside, the terrace might as well have been a stage, brightly lit and visible to all. Maybe they hadn't been sitting here long. If they arrived after the butt grab, Libby might be able to salvage the situation.

"We were . . . doing yoga?" She glanced at her audience to see how that had gone over.

"That didn't look like any yoga I've ever seen," Uncle Richard huffed. "And I've seen plenty in my day!"

"It's probably a Me-mas thing." Hildy sounded only slightly less desperate than Libby. "She gets a freebie."

If anything, her uncle's outrage grew. "With your fiancé?"

"Hello? We're not really engaged." Hildy snapped her fingers at Uncle Richard as if that would jog his memory.

He waved this off, champagne sloshing dangerously in his glass. "A technicality. It doesn't excuse this disgraceful behavior."

Hildy took a swig of champagne. It looked like she was fortifying herself for what came next. "Jefferson isn't my boyfriend."

"He broke up with you?" Uncle Richard set down his glass so hard Libby was surprised the stem didn't snap. "My poor Hildy! You must be devastated. Not even speaking of how upset our advertisers will be. This is quite a blow—for everyone."

"I'm sure we'll cry ourselves to sleep," Hildy muttered. "News flash! This is all—well, mostly—part of my plan. Besides, not everyone in this family is into weirdly huge age gaps. Ahem."

"My marriage is not on trial," her uncle sniffed. "Furthermore, there is no such thing as a 'freebie.' In my experience, they're terribly expensive."

Jefferson entered the room, taking stock of the situation in a rapid-fire slideshow: Libby still standing by the door, tense and unhappy; the transparent-from-inside glass; the worst possible audience gathered to watch.

Uncle Richard gestured angrily at him. "What do you have to say for yourself, young man?"

"We ran into each other on the beach," he said, after a blink of hesitation. "Watching the sunrise."

"It's okay, Jefferson." Libby didn't want him to lie for her, on top of everything that had already gone wrong. There was a glug and a splash from Jean's direction as she refilled her glass. "It's true that I was kissing Jefferson. As you all apparently saw. And the reason is that . . . I like him."

There was an extended silence, like they were waiting for Libby to go on. But that was really it. The headline and the story. One bullet point.

"That's rather brazen, in front of your husband!" With a look of sympathy, Uncle Richard turned to Mr. L, who plucked at the cuffs of his dress shirt, basking in the attention.

"I'm not actually married," Libby told Hildy's uncle.

"Yet!" Mr. L sprang into action as if he'd been awaiting his cue. Hurrying across the room he knelt in front of Libby. From his pocket, he produced a small velvet box.

Surely not, Libby thought, heart sinking past her ankles. Even Mr. L had to realize this was not the moment.

"Rock me like a hurricane," Hildy gasped, when he cracked open the lid.

"Blimey," Jean chimed in, forgetting she was no longer Irish.

Libby had never seen a diamond that size in real life. You could gouge someone's eye out in hand-to-hand combat. Which was a totally normal thing to think when a person was about to propose.

"My darling Lillibet, will you do me the honor of accepting my hand in marriage?" Mr. L raised the back of his hand, wrist bent.

Does he want me to kiss it? Is the ring for him? Libby was lost, thoughts iced over by the most intense secondhand embarrassment she'd ever experienced.

"Aren't they already married?" Uncle Richard stage-whispered.

Libby shook her head. "No." On all counts.

"You're not?" At the note of confusion in Jefferson's voice, she forced herself to look at him.

"He wanted to marry me for a green card—like I said." Sort of. "But I wasn't going to actually do it."

"I beg your pardon?" Mr. L stood up. "Then why did you sign this?" He pulled the prenup from an inside pocket, brandishing it like a smoking gun.

"I wanted a little more time." A taste of what might have been, even though Libby knew it wouldn't last. They probably thought she was talking about money, and all the luxe lifestyle trappings it could buy, but what Libby really envied was the sense of possibility. *That* was what she'd tried (pathetically, naively, catastrophically) to borrow from Lillibet: the illusion of being a person who could have it all—a great job and a greater guy. It was like blowing your tiny reserves of cash on a night out instead of saving for the future. When you were never going to get everything you wanted, might as well grab what you could before it disappeared.

"For what?" Uncle Richard demanded. "Is this one of those bling rings?"

Hildy threw her head back. "How many times do I have to tell you the whole world is not conspiring to steal your stuff?"

"We—I didn't want to ruin everything," Libby said, hating how weak she sounded.

"When did you sign that?" Jefferson asked.

"A day or two ago," Libby replied, unsure why that detail mattered.

"After I got here?"

She nodded, and saw the flash of hurt in his eyes before he looked away.

"I still don't understand who was fooling who," Hildy's uncle muttered, clearly fed up with all of them.

"Maybe we should talk about this over breakfast?" Libby suggested. "And more champagne." Gallons of it.

"Why, so you can poison us?" Uncle Richard scoffed, before turning to his niece. "I don't trust this person you've taken up with, Hildy. She's married, she's not married, she's getting married, she isn't—the story keeps changing. It shows a lack of commitment."

"You're one to talk," his niece retorted, not quite under her breath.

"He's right." Libby felt like she'd been playing an endless game of hide-and-seek, the kind where you get so tired of waiting for the ax to fall, you stand up and give yourself away. *Here I am. You can tag me now.*

"I have been lying. About some things. A lot of things," Libby amended. "This is not my house, for example. Since that is not my husband."

Mr. L struck a pose, hand under his chin.

"Wait, hold up." Hildy made a stop sign with her palm. "The house part," she clarified, when Mr. L started to interject. "Not him."

"It was part of the act. Pretending to be Lillibet."

"Oh my god." Hildy's hand flew to her mouth. "Is she dead?"

"What?" Libby glanced at Jean, who shrugged.

"Did you kill her and steal her identity?" Hildy pressed.

"Nooooo." Libby drew out the word, hoping Jean would jump in with a preposterous explanation that would still be more plausible than the truth. Barring that, she'd settle for a sinkhole opening under the house.

No such luck.

"That would be hard to do," Libby said quietly. "Considering she doesn't exist." Jefferson looked at her sharply. "I'm just Libby. That's all I ever was. There's no such person as Lillibet."

"She's talking about curation," Hildy said with a confidence Libby didn't deserve. "Standard operating procedure for social media. We all craft our online persona."

"Yeah." Libby scratched her head, watching a few grains of sand sift onto the floor. "It was a little more than that."

"We invented her," Jean snapped. "Lillibet. She's like the tooth fairy, but more, you know." She stuck a finger down her throat, gagging theatrically.

"You were right about the cooking," Libby told Hildy. "That's all Keoki. I suck in the kitchen. And I don't arrange stuff prettily—Jean's the artistic one—or take care of my skin or have a perfect life."

It should have been a relief to confess, but the truth was not setting Libby free. She felt humiliated and pathetic and had a powerful urge to disappear, but she forced herself to stay and watch her audience's shock and confusion tip into horror.

"You really don't live that life?" Hildy gestured at the palatial living room.

Libby shook her head. "I wait tables for a living."

"So no tinctures? Or body oils? Restorative exfoliation? Do you even do yoga?"

"I'm afraid not."

"Charlatans. They're everywhere," Uncle Richard huffed. "People in our position are always targets. They tell you what you want to hear. *I love baseball! This corned beef is delicious! What a full head of hair you have!* And then you find out it was all a game. They were playing you from the beginning."

"Black widows," Mr. L said.

"Nobody's getting murdered," Libby protested, but no one paid any attention.

"Why didn't you tell me?" Jefferson asked. "Last night."

"I just wanted a chance to be with you. One night together."

"Is that all it was to you? One night?"

"No!" Panicked, she scrambled for a way to make him understand. "I was . . . living my truth."

Everyone stared as if Libby had farted. It figured that the first time she tried to say something Lillibet-like and mean it, the words landed like a lead balloon.

"I mean, on the inside," she stammered. "Where the real me is. It's like those Russian dolls—"

Jefferson didn't storm out or slam the door. He walked quietly, shoulders hunched like he was shielding himself from the next blow.

A distant part of Libby's brain wasn't surprised that Jefferson was going off alone to lick his wounds, instead of throwing a tantrum, but she couldn't shake the feeling that once he was out of her sight, she'd never see him again. What was she going to say if she ran after him: *I'm a liar, please love me anyway*?

"I was always me to you." Libby mumbled the words at his departing back, but by then it was too late. Her timing was as bad as her moral compass.

"What about me?" Hildy's voice was plaintive, sounding even younger than she actually was. "Were you ever going to tell me?"

"Yes. I swear. I was waiting for the right moment."

Hildy shook her head, unconvinced. "You and JJ were my role models. I thought you were more mature than this!"

"I'm not that much older than you—"

"You're supposed to be an old soul," Hildy shouted, before drooping. "But I guess none of that was real."

"You see, Hildy? This is what I'm always telling you. Keeping a cool head is essential in business. It takes razor-sharp instincts to swim with the big dogs." Uncle Richard made a slicing motion with his soft white hand. "This is why you need to go back to school and live in a nice, safe, protected environment until you're ready to make your way in the world."

"Have you been on a college campus in the last three decades?" She clutched her head with both hands. "I can't believe this is happening. This is exactly what I was trying to avoid."

Just when Libby thought she couldn't feel any worse. "None of this is Hildy's fault. She's incredibly smart and motivated and full of ideas. Any company would be lucky to have her."

Uncle Richard lowered his glasses to give Libby a look of deep disdain. "You'll pardon me if I don't believe anything you have to say."

"Seriously—whatever your name is." Hildy didn't lift her head. "Don't do me any favors. The last thing I need is more help from *you*."

Keoki strolled into the room, his smile wilting. "Hey . . . everybody. I thought Me-mas was a happy day?"

"Me-mas is canceled," Hildy said. "Along with everything else." Jean offered her the champagne.

"I believe that is my property." Mr. L grabbed the bottle away from Jean, handing it to Hildy himself. "There's nothing here that belongs to you three. Except that." He pointed at the portrait, like they were doing a courtroom scene and Libby's nudie picture was on trial.

He might not be getting a green card out of the bargain, but at least they could give him this, Libby reflected. A moment to chew the scenery to his heart's content.

"I expect you to remove it from the premises, along with yourselves, in the next ten minutes." Mr. L paused to give them his most threatening look. Libby rated it about a four. "Otherwise, I will have to consider my legal options. I could sue for breach of contract."

Uncle Richard nodded his support. "A man is only as good as his lawyers."

"Good luck suing us for not doing something illegal." Jean sauntered to the ladder and started to climb. "And if you don't appreciate my art, you don't deserve it."

After unfastening the butterfly clips that held the painting in place, she carefully rolled it before descending. "Put that in your pipes and smoke it."

When Jean jerked her head at the door, Libby and Keoki fell in behind her. Neither of them could top that exit line.

Libby risked a final backward glance. She was clinging to the desperate hope that Jefferson might appear, but there was no sign of him.

The room, and the house, and her life, echoed with his absence.

Chapter 26

Keoki stared at the road in front of his truck. He was still dazed, which was probably a blessing. A shot of Novocain to the brain, before the real pain set in. "What happened back there?"

It wasn't quite an accusation, though there was an undercurrent of, *I was gone for an hour. How could you screw everything up that fast?*

"Libby Long Legs here decided to burn it all down." Jean pantomimed pulling the pin out of a grenade with her teeth and tossing it underhand, whistling as it descended to an invisible explosion. "It would have been impressive, if we weren't so totally hosed right now."

"Mr. L looked pissed." Keoki glanced to his right, like he was hoping they'd contradict him. When Libby shrugged to say, *Pretty much,* his brows drew together. "But he knew all about it. It's not like it was a surprise."

"Except she signed the prenup," Jean informed him. "That

might have gotten his hopes up." *And who could blame him?* She didn't say that part, but Libby heard it loud and clear.

"I didn't know, Libs." Keoki gripped her shoulder, shaking lightly. "I wasn't setting you up to marry the guy."

"I know."

"Were you really thinking about it?" Keoki's tone was harder to read. Disbelief, mostly; Libby didn't think *he* was disappointed in her. Or, at least, not for that.

"No." Was that completely true? "I don't know. I think I was trying to make Jean happy, and it got out of hand."

Her roommate snorted. "Right. I was definitely top of mind for you. Especially last night. And this morning." She leaned past Libby to address Keoki. "Mr. L will be fine. If anything, he'll come out ahead. Fancy new faucets in every Johnson Media property. That's how those people think. *I have money and you have money so together I bet we can make even more money. Wheee!*"

"Like their money had babies." No one could accuse Keoki of not having a one-track mind. He bent forward at the waist, like he had a stomach cramp. Or wanted to bang his head on the steering wheel. "What am I going to tell Cici?"

Keoki's restaurant. Another gallon of shame, in Libby's already overflowing cup. "You won't lose your job, will you? Jacques isn't going to fire you over this?"

"If he does, I'll tell everyone the secret ingredient in his *velouté de champignons sauvages* is Campbell's cream of mushroom." He winced. "I wouldn't really. That would be mean."

"We know, gentle giant." Jean punched him in the shoulder.

"Even though he's a pain in the booty."

"We know that, too," Libby said, more softly and without the violence.

"I thought this was my out. Me and Cici had a whole plan. She was going to run the front of house and Pohai would be a server. When she's not in school."

"Pohai?" Jean asked.

Keoki rubbed his belly. "The baby."

"So, like . . . in sixteen years she could wait tables?" Jean clarified.

"I might have had a second location by then. 'Just Desserts.' Because we would only serve desserts."

"That sounds nice." In a different world, Libby would have gone there every day. Most likely at closing time, to beg for scraps.

"It would have been. And I could have given Cici and P everything they want."

"I don't know that a waitressing job is every girl's dream," Jean pointed out. "A new phone, maybe. Or a car."

"I'd let her have one of those smashed-face cats," Keoki said, as if it were the ultimate concession. "And now what am I going to do?"

Not get a cat, Libby thought. Her brain was still fuzzy, though the numbness was wearing off fast.

"I feel you." Jean angled her body to make it clear she was only talking to Keoki. "You were ready to go big, take a leap, put it all on the line. And then somebody couldn't take the heat, so she decided to punt. As usual."

The problem with a best friend was that they knew all your fault lines—and how to slip under your guard and stab you right at your weakest point. It wasn't the first time Libby had considered the possibility she might be a fuckup by nature, too lazy or disorganized or just plain untalented to get ahead.

"I love how you're blaming this whole thing on me," Libby said, fear giving way to resentment.

"It was your gig, *Lillibet.*"

"Yeah, but it was your idea. I told you it was going to blow up in our faces, but noooo. We had to do it your way. All convoluted and borderline-criminal."

"At least I had an idea. An idea that was *working,* until you threw in the towel. And for what?"

Libby turned her face to the window so they wouldn't see her eyes well with tears. "Sorry I'm such a disaster you have to tell me how to live. What should I have done differently, Jean? Marry a random stranger so he could get a green card? Because lying has worked out so well for us, let's try defrauding the government!"

"I never said that."

"No, you told me to figure out what I really wanted. Which I did. And it turned out so well. Thank you for that helpful advice."

"I didn't think you'd choose the guy! That's like your whole deal. Not turning into your mom."

Keoki shot Libby a panicked glance. He knew her mother was a loaded subject, which was why they generally avoided it like a boarded-up factory filled with radioactive waste. "Hey." He reached across the seat to pat Libby's knee. "Let's not fight. At least we still have each other."

Jean snorted under her breath. "Lucky us."

"This is one of those times when I can't tell if you're messing with me," Keoki admitted.

"She's messing with you." By which Libby meant, *She's always messing with us.* It was easy to be Team Anarchy when you didn't care about the aftermath.

"That's not all. We also have—our health," he said, a little desperately.

Not even Keoki could find a silver lining. The air was still tight with tension. Libby felt it in her scalp, and her chest, and clenched fists. Her fight with Jean wasn't over. It was like a pimple you mess with, knowing you're only going to make it worse. Next time it would be a red, angry volcano.

The rest of the drive passed in silence. The three of them were right back where they'd started, with nothing to show for what they'd risked. Unless you counted a scraped and battered heart, a reputation for lying, and a truckload of regrets.

Chapter 27

If Libby had needed a reminder of how far she'd fallen, walking into their apartment would have done the trick. Spending a few days in the lap of luxury made their digs look even sadder, which was no small feat. The sagging secondhand couch, the cracked linoleum, the flickering fluorescent bar on the kitchen ceiling, the faint aroma of microwave ramen: It was a study in how not to flourish. Hashtag losing.

"Did this place get dirtier while we were gone?" Jean brushed off the counter before setting down her bag.

Libby recognized this as an invitation: *Let's talk about a thing we agree on—our shitty apartment—so we can be on the same team.* She could say something like, *I don't see how that's possible.* Then Jean would propose they treat themselves to a movie night and a pile of junk food to help forget their troubles. Tomorrow they'd wake up in their lumpy old beds, right back in their lumpy old lives, and everything would return to normal, as if they'd hallucinated the entire Lillibet experience.

But Libby didn't want to forget. And while Lillibet may have been a figment of their imaginations, the thought of letting the last few days fade into oblivion made her want to collapse on the stained carpet and howl. She was going to hold on, clutching the memory of everything she almost had like a ragged teddy bear.

Libby let the silence grow, watching Jean check the refrigerator and cupboards in case the grocery fairy had swung by during their absence.

"There's nothing." Libby let the heaviness of her tone convey the double meaning. No snacks, no job, no love. When that didn't get a response, she added a sigh.

"Just say it." Jean still had her back to Libby, peering into the empty cabinet as if she could see through to the other side. "Whatever you're stewing about, might as well get it off your chest so we can move on."

She sounded frustrated, like Libby was the immature one, pitching a fit for no reason.

"Is it really that hard to guess why I might be upset right now?"

Jean spun around, leaning against the counter with her arms crossed. "So we struck out. Shit happens. Don't do the crime if you can't do the time."

"That's it? I'm *crushed*, Jean."

"There are other jobs. We'll find a way."

Libby couldn't believe what she was hearing. "You think that's the only thing I care about?"

"It should be. It was a killer opportunity."

"Hey, thanks for the reminder! That's exactly what I need to hear right now. Like I could forget we're back to square zero." She threw herself onto the couch, covering her eyes with both hands. "Did you not even notice how much I liked him?"

"Uh, I'm pretty sure everybody noticed."

"What?"

"What do you want me to say, Libby? *Congrats on having the hots for someone*? Your timing could have been better."

"It was more than that."

"Oh come on. You knew him for, what, three days? Give me a break."

"What is with you right now? Did I ask for the tough-love special? Hey, bestie, think you could kick me while I'm down?"

Jean looked at the ceiling. "You're trying to make me the bad guy. I'm sick of it."

"So you brush it off like it has nothing to do with you. Must be nice."

"I didn't say that."

Libby gave her a skeptical look.

"Has it occurred to you that you wouldn't have met him if it wasn't for me? *I* made that happen." Jean thumped herself in the chest. "I'm the one who got the ball rolling and dragged you along, kicking and screaming. And do you know why? Because you were *never* going to do it yourself. So, yeah, you're welcome. Now do me a favor and take some responsibility for your own crap instead of trying to blame all your problems on me."

"What's that supposed to mean?" It was one of those questions you ask without wanting to know the answer.

Jean rubbed her forehead. "Do you really want to have this conversation right now?"

"It's not like my day could get much worse."

"Okay, well for one thing, you have major mommy issues."

"Uh, yeah." Libby was mildly relieved to be accused of something she'd admitted to herself ages ago. "I know it's not a great relationship."

"I'm talking about the damage it did to you." Jean twirled a finger next to her head. "Mentally."

Libby's heart pounded in her throat as she waited to hear how Jean was going to follow up that doozy.

"My theory is that's why you need someone like me around. You want to be the kid with a helicopter parent always telling her what to do, since you didn't get that when you were an actual child. I give you cover."

That was . . . a thought that had never crossed Libby's mind. "I assumed you were going to say I had abandonment issues."

"That, too. There's a whole array of things that pile up into a general tendency to choose the path of being chickenshit." She jabbed a hand at Libby. "You'd rather hide behind someone else than put yourself out there. If you never try, then nothing is your fault."

"Wow. That C in Intro to Psych is really paying off for you."

"And what did you get?"

"I got a B, thank you very much." B-minus, but whatever.

"Then maybe you should apply some of those skills to your life."

"Why bother? Sounds like you have me all figured out." Libby crossed her arms, staring at a sticky ring on the coffee table. "It's kind of amazing you've put up with me this long, since I'm such a wreck. Being the poster child for emotional maturity that you are, with your totally healthy family history. When's the last time you talked to your parents?"

"Now the claws come out," Jean muttered.

"I thought I was a chicken. Do chickens have claws?"

Jean checked her phone, a little too intently to be faking it as an excuse to look away. "I don't think we're going to get anywhere talking about this tonight."

"Why, are you afraid I'm going to scratch you with my scaly claw?" Libby pawed at the air with three fingers. "I thought you were all about facing up to reality instead of running away like a big baby."

"Maybe I have someplace more pleasant to be."

Libby huffed in disbelief. "Like where?"

"I don't know. Slaughterhouse? Paper mill? Women's prison?"

"Ha, ha." She watched Jean shoulder her bag before heading for her bedroom. "Where are you really going?" Libby called after her.

"To work. Because life goes on," Jean shouted back, before shutting her door.

She emerged from her room a few minutes later, detouring into the bathroom. Libby heard her rummage in the cabinets, then the sound of a zipper closing, before her roommate stepped into the living room.

"I can't believe you're leaving." *When my life is in the toilet and I need my best friend.* Libby didn't say that part out loud. She'd never had to tell Jean those things in the past. Jean's troubles were Libby's, and vice versa.

A tiny part of Libby had even hoped Jean would have an idea of how to fix this. Or, barring that, they could drown their sorrows together.

"I think we've said enough for today."

If you didn't know better, it might have sounded like a mature and reasonable response. But Libby was deeply familiar with her roommate's coping skills, and those words were not part of Jean's emotional vocabulary. The thought flashed through her mind that Jean was glad to be getting out of there. She might even have picked a fight so she'd have an excuse to bail.

"Must be nice," Libby said tightly. "To move on when you get bored. No skin in the game."

"Must be nice to fall apart and let someone else worry about the bills."

That got Libby right in the guilt gland. "I'll call around and see if we can pick up some shifts this weekend." Since there would be no fancy grown-up salary swooping in at the eleventh hour to save them.

"I'm booked. At the resort."

"Oh." It wasn't completely unprecedented; they didn't *always* work the same gigs. Only most of the time.

Jean fiddled with the strap of her bag. "Maybe we could use a little space. It might be good for both of us, to not be so tied at the hip."

It sounded like the worst idea in the world to Libby. Jean could pretend she was being practical, but it still felt like a punishment. *You messed up, now I'm leaving.* She must have known Libby would take it badly, because Jean kept her eyes on her phone.

"My ride's here," she announced, walking out before Libby could say another word.

Libby tried to smooth the crumpled page, but only succeeded in smearing peanut butter across the bottom half. Her aim had been better several glasses of vodka ago.

"I finally have time to try journaling. Check me out, looking on the bright side!" She tapped the pen against her lips. "Ow." That part wasn't going in the gratitude journal. Or whatever this was.

Thinking in full sentences was beyond her, so she switched to making a list. To get the juices flowing.

My best friend hates me.

Didn't get the job.

Said goodbye to best, hottest, most wonderful man—that didn't really capture the scale of her loss. She scribbled it out.

Blew chance at first real relationship and will never know love. And I don't even have a cat.

Okay, so it was more of a Bitch List. That felt on brand for her new life.

A roach stuck its head out from under the refrigerator. Libby couldn't muster the will to get up and crush it.

"Hey, little buddy. Don't worry, I'm not coming for you. Why shouldn't you live? You're probably happier than I am. Got a family, I bet. Dreams for the future. Hope. You could be a VIP in Roach Town. Part of a great love story. Rocheo and Juliet. Who am I to judge?" She pointed at the roach with the vodka bottle, before pouring herself more.

"I'm not Lillibet, that's for sure. Freaking Lillibet." Forgetting her glass, she took a swig straight from the bottle. "She has a lot to answer for. You know what I'm saying?"

The roach sat quietly on her kitchen floor, antennae twitching.

"You're a really good listener. Has anyone ever told you that?" She wiped her mouth on the neck of her T-shirt. "This is honestly more respect than I've gotten from some humans who were supposed to be on my side. And I probably murdered your entire family, so that's extra noble, you know? It shows real, um, generosity of spirit. And like moral fiber and stuff. Unlike yours truly."

Picking up her phone, she snapped a picture of her new friend. Possibly also her only friend. "I'm not going to lie, pal. I still find you intensely unpleasant to look at." Libby made a retching sound in the back of her throat. "I think it's the legs. But also the body, with the sections. And your face. But that's a me problem. I'm going to work on it. Not judging people by their appearance. Or insects. Live and let live. Laugh, live, love. I don't know what the roach version would be. Scurry, scatter, survive."

Libby poured herself more vodka to go with this deep thought. "Roaches probably don't put up with that kind of BS. *Say what you mean, Sally. Quit talking around the issue! Are we infesting this place or what?* That's why you're going to take over the world while humans stab each other in the back and then go *pffft.*" She blew a raspberry.

The roach was stoic. *Take all the time you need,* he seemed to be saying.

"Maybe words are the problem? We rely too much on all the blah blah blah when we could just rub our legs together." Libby tried to slide one calf over the other in the way she imagined roaches made tiny roach sounds, but only succeeded in losing her balance. Lying on her back with her legs splayed at an awkward angle, she grabbed her camera with an ironic squeal. "Selfie!"

The only thing missing was that yellow tape they used to outline corpses on TV.

"I know I've been talking your ear off—or your little antenna thingies—but if I could ask one favor. Please don't crawl on me." Pleading with him seemed easier than getting up. "You probably think I've hit rock bottom over here, but that would push me over the edge. A roach in my hair. Or up my nose. Anywhere above the shoulders. What is the opposite of self-care? I never really thought about it until now, but I think that would qualify."

When Libby glanced at the roach, she was surprised to see it halfway to the stove.

"You're leaving?" she asked, mildly insulted. Technically she'd asked for space, but in light of recent events it was hard not to feel like she was driving everyone away. "I'm boring you, aren't I? All this navel-gazing. Me, me, me! But nobody really tells the truth. We want people to see the going-out version, not what we look like at home in our ugly clothes with a shiny forehead and some kind of crust on our chin." She swiped at her face, hoping it was peanut butter rather than drool. Because that would be so much classier.

"Whatever. Filter this, mofos." She snapped another selfie, snorting at the result. "Can you imagine Lillibet posting something like this? *Here I am with my perfect life, rocking my perfect eye booger. Love, Lillibet.*"

But why shouldn't she post an unflattering picture? Lillibet had already been unmasked in front of the people who mattered. Might as well let all two of her followers in on the secret.

"You know what's not cowardly, Rocheo? Letting it all hang out. We are down here in the dirt, being our most authentic selves." She angled the phone to get a picture of her forehead with a roach in the background.

"Hey, fam, check out this gorgeous tablescape." Libby struggled to her knees, aiming the camera at the cluttered coffee table. "That wadded-up Kleenex is one hundred percent artisanal, bee-tee-dubs. I snotted on it myself. And did you know that potatoes, the main ingredient in potato chips, could also be used for vodka? That makes them a natural pairing for those late nights when you hate yourself enough to make bad choices!" She held her glass next to her face for another selfie. "Cheers!"

Libby swiped through her camera reel. "Guess this is where I live now. Might as well own it." She toggled to Instagram.

"New post? Don't mind if I do. Hashtag no more hiding."

lovelillibet To All the Bots I've "Loved" Before,

You know those Welcome, new followers, here are a few things to know about me posts? This is kind of like that, except without the new followers. And it's more of a de-introduction, which I guess is also known as a goodbye.

RIP, Lillibet. You total phony.

I don't mean that in the sense of, Oh, I'm just showing you the pretty parts, like standard social media fronting. "Lillibet" legit doesn't exist, and I'm your basic failing-at-life nobody.

Do you like my apartment? Me neither. But I guess it doesn't matter, since I'm probably going to have to move now that my roommate hates me and I can't afford my half of the rent. That's also why the top of my grid looks like a dystopian wasteland. I can't take pictures for shit, and my best friend isn't around to do it for me.

So, yeah, that's me. A lonely loser. I don't know if any real humans still follow this account, but just in case, I'm sorry if my pretend life made you feel bad. Trust me, no one could be more inferior to Lillibet than the real me, sitting here with blackheads and cellulite on a carpet that hasn't been cleaned since sometime in the last century. Try not to be jealous!

Something I realized recently is that I mostly care what a few very specific people think about me. Not an online me I perform for strangers, but the living, breathing, dry-shampoo-can't-save-you-now version.

I wish I'd been myself with them, while I still had the chance.

So screw it. No more lies.

Things are going to look a little different around here from now on.

Sincerely, Libby

Image: Woman with greasy hair talking to massive brown cockroach.

#partyofwon #mybestlie #getreal

Chapter 28

Do you ever look around your kitchen and think, Wait—am I supposed to clean that? The cabinet door, the wall, inside a drawer, a can opener, whatever. Like there's a whole list of basic things everyone knows except you, and you somehow missed the memo about brushing your teeth.

Yeah, me neither. Anyway, it's just going to get dirty again.

Sincerely, Libby

Image: The inside of a drawer lined with stained contact paper, peeling in patches, with particle board shavings and multicolored crumbs.

#hazmat #whendoesadultingstart #wegotthefunk

Jean didn't come home that night or the next, and she wasn't at either of the cater-waiter gigs Libby was lucky enough to pick up over the weekend, working through the pounding headache of her hangover and into a state of deeply dehydrated regret.

Libby checked her phone every time she had a break, but the only notifications were comments on her *Love, Lillibet* shit posts, which seemed to have struck a chord. Libby didn't remember ever getting this kind of response when they were faking content. She replied to a few, because she didn't have anyone else to talk to, and a couple of them were funny. One described her aesthetic as "half-empty vending machine in the darkest corner of a hospital basement," which struck Libby as exactly right. Some people understood her. Maybe there was something to be said for the kindness of Internet strangers.

On Sunday, Libby dragged herself up the stairs after an exhausting evening at a couple's baby shower. Being on her feet for hours in cheap shoes was hard, but the part that really sapped her will to live was watching the blissful lovebirds hold hands and smile at each other. It was a miracle she hadn't puked onto a tray of appetizers.

All she wanted was to scrub off the funk of feta cheese, overcooked puff pastry, and secondhand smugness, so of course that was when her roommate returned, locking the bathroom door behind her. Unless it was a burglar who'd realized there was nothing valuable in the apartment and decided to grab a quick shower before moving on to greener pastures.

Libby barely cared, unless whoever it was used all the hot water. It was enough to make you long for a house with twenty-seven bathrooms . . . and one very special shower.

She collapsed onto the couch in her sticky black pants. The fabric was shiny at the knees, worn to the brink of splitting even though she waited as long as possible between washes. Libby had been looking forward to throwing them away, but that wasn't an option now. Maybe her followers would know whether air freshener worked on clothing. Although she should probably take them off first.

After a few minutes, the bathroom door opened, releasing a cloud of steam. Jean walked into the living room wearing her bathrobe, a towel wrapped around her hair.

"You came back." Libby was going for nonchalant, like she'd barely noticed her absence, and if it *had* crossed her mind to wonder if Jean was ever coming home, it certainly wasn't because Libby minded one way or the other.

She rolled her eyes. "I'm not your mom, Libby." It sounded like a punch line, but neither of them laughed. Jean sat down on the edge of the coffee table, not quite in Libby's space but close enough to knee her in the shin.

"I'll always come back, you big loser. You're stuck with me. That's the deal. Even if I'm a dick sometimes."

"I wasn't sure," Libby admitted, knocking her legs against Jean's.

"That I'm a dick?"

"The other part."

"For an ace reporter, you can be a little slow on the uptake." Jean winced. "Too soon?"

"It's fine. I think we have some salt in the kitchen if you want to go ahead and pour that on the open wound."

"Just put it on my tab." Jean patted her leg. "Of dick things to say."

"Could you maybe stop saying dick, though?" Especially since Libby would be living in a dick-free universe for the foreseeable future.

Jean pretended to think it over. "Mmmm, probably not. I still have to apologize for being a dick about your boyfriend. Sometimes when I feel bad about something, I strike first, you know?"

"I think there's a psychological term for that."

"You'd know. Being the star psych student in the household."

"B-minus," Libby admitted. Once you started narcing on yourself, it was hard to stop.

"The point is, I get it. Love makes you crazy. Or lust. Whatever it is."

"You mean 'was,' " Libby corrected. "We're extremely past tense."

"Unless he sees your cry for help."

Libby got a vivid mental picture of a small airplane trailing a banner over his house in the mountains. *Jefferson, I'm sorry. Please come back. I'll learn to hike. Love, Libby.*

That probably wasn't what Jean had in mind. "What are you talking about?"

"This Watch Me Melt Down in Real Time bit you're doing." Jean pulled her phone out of the pocket of her robe, opening the *Love, Lillibet* profile. Which probably needed a new name, now that the posts were signed, "Sincerely, Libby."

The simple act of shedding the *L*-word—well, both of them, but especially *Love*—felt like a big step toward honesty. Libby's mother had been big on tossing a "Love you, kiddo," over her shoulder as she walked out the door, but she never looked back to see how Libby felt about being left behind or gave her daughter a chance to reply. Eventually Libby gave up—on the word as well as the feeling.

"I was afraid I was going to come home and see your little friend Jiminy in a top hat, doing tricks." Jean clicked on one of the shots of Libby's new acquaintance.

"I call him Rocheo."

"First of all," Jean said, passing the phone back to Libby, "no. And second, I'm pretty sure that was two different bugs. You had a ménage going."

That tracked. Maintaining stable relationships wasn't Libby's strong suit. Unlike showing her ass on the Internet. "I guess I kind of lost my filter."

"I like it." Jean shrugged. "Why let Lillibet go gently into the night when you can take the nuclear option?"

"You know what's weird?"

"Besides you making peace with the insect kingdom?"

"I think I might miss her," Libby confessed.

"Hildy?"

"No. Well, yes, but I was talking about Lillibet."

Jean gave a low whistle. "How the turn tables."

"I know. But there was something freeing about being her. The total confidence. She thinks it, she says it. Zero self-doubt."

"See? For an uppity hobag, she wasn't all bad. Nothing is ever completely black-and-white. Except old movies."

"I think maybe on some level I wish I was more like that. *Fearless*." Instead of timidly tiptoeing around the *idea* of being brave.

"Definitely not afraid to take up space." Jean shot Libby a significant look.

"Yeah." She was starting to realize that was part of putting yourself out there: Having the courage to want things and then reach for them, regardless of the consequences. For Libby, it had never been the "no" she dreaded so much as the possibility of pissing people off by asking in the first place. Which was not a super-healthy way to relate to other humans. "I'm not saying I'd ever go full Lillibet, but there might be times when a little of that energy could be useful."

Jean pointed at her. "Like Bruce Wayne and Batman. Your secret alter ego."

"Minus the crime-fighting and the rubber suit."

"And the butler." Jean sighed. "We could use one of those."

"I'm afraid we missed our chance."

"We're back to that one-bathroom life."

Libby's molars ached, possibly because of how tightly she was squeezing her jaw. "You don't mind? That I pulled the plug?"

In retrospect, those first anti-Lillibet posts might have been her way of lashing out, like she was kicking over the block tower they'd built together. But they'd morphed into something else. Self-examination. Apology. Emotional purge. Probably other stuff Libby wasn't even aware of yet.

"Art is ephemeral. We're always going to be growing and changing. Trying new things." Jean looked at her toes, which were painted her signature bloody red. "Closing the casket on the past."

"Um, ominous much?"

"Speaking of doom and gloom, I saw them."

"Who?"

"Hildy. And Mr. Freeze."

It was like that poem about fire and ice, only inside Libby's gut. "Where?"

"The resort."

Another stupid mistake: Assuming they'd gotten on the next plane home. Libby made a mental note to bang her head against the wall later. She had more pressing concerns now. "Did you talk to them?"

"I thought about it. But I was already hiding behind a planter, and it seemed weirder to jump out and be like, *Hey, remember me?*"

"Yeah. I can see how that would have been strange." Libby hesitated, not sure she wanted to know. "Are they still there?"

"They checked out this morning."

It was amazing how things could hurt all over again, even when you thought you'd felt the worst. "So, they're probably gone." For real this time. On a plane, off the island, across an ocean.

"Probably," Jean agreed. She slid Libby a sidelong glance. "Do you need a snack?"

"We don't have anything."

"Poor Rocheo."

"I know." Libby rubbed her chest like she had indigestion, but this was not a feeling Rolaids could cure.

"Do you want me to leave you alone?" Jean asked, in her trying-to-be-sensitive voice.

"Yeah, because I'm sure solitude is the perfect cure. What would help with this loneliness? Being more alone!"

"Hair of the dog," Jean said, plopping onto the couch beside her. "You're not alone, Libs."

"I know." She paused for effect. "I have Rocheo." A sharp elbow connected with her rib cage. "You were right about some of that stuff. Like how I'm scared of putting myself out there. I try so hard *not* to be something that I forget to be my own thing." And if Libby was serious about profiling other people, she needed to practice taking a hard look at herself.

"To be clear," Jean said, leaning her head against Libby's shoulder, "I'm also at least fifty percent full of shit."

"It's part of your charm."

"I like to think so."

"One thing you were wrong about." Libby glanced at the top of Jean's head, the smooth darkness of her hair divided by a razor-sharp part. "You are like my mom. Not my actual mom, but what I wanted her to be. Someone who wouldn't mind if her life was totally intertwined with mine, you know? Permanently connected, even if we hit a rough patch."

"We're like each other's moms." Jean hesitated. "Don't tell me if that's a messed-up psychological syndrome."

"We took the same class, Jean."

"I know, but I skipped a lot. Hence the lower grade. Though I basically had a C-plus."

Libby let that pass. "I don't think there's anything demented about accepting someone unconditionally. Flaws and all." She squeezed Jean's hand.

"Are you proposing?"

"You wish."

"Okay, but will you at least post something sappy about me? *And I owe it all to my best friend, who is also available for freelance art commissions.*"

"Maybe."

There was a knock at the front door. Libby's heart skipped a beat, pierced with the irrational hope that it was Jefferson, bending the rules of time and air travel to find her. She tried not to look disappointed when Keoki walked in, carrying bags of food.

"SOS," he said.

The fact that Keoki was delivering the message in person rather than by text sent a pulse of alarm up Libby's spine. Given how low her emotional reserves were running, she hoped this was one of his menu-related crises. *This garnish or that one? With the demi-glace or without?* Her stomach reminded her she hadn't eaten at work. Too busy during the event to take a break, and too blue to hang around afterward.

The smells coming from those bags were enticing enough to get Libby off the couch, at least long enough to grab plates and silverware from the kitchen. She returned to see Keoki unloading a six-pack of beer.

Jean pinched him, patient as always. "Are you going to tell us or what?"

"If it's about planning a baby shower, I have a whole list of what *not* to do," Libby assured him.

He cracked open a beer, taking a long swallow. "Didn't want to do that in front of Cici."

"Because she's pregnant?" Libby guessed.

Keoki shook his head. "She'd ask why I was upset. And then I'd have to tell her I quit my job."

"What the hell, K?" Jean shoved him with both hands, putting her full body weight behind it. Keoki didn't budge.

"Did something happen?" Libby asked.

"I think it's been building." He unpacked a family-size container of lo mein, peeling off the lid. "There I was, following Jacques' recipe for croquembouche, and I thought to myself, *You know what would take this to the next level? A lilikoi glaze.*"

"And that was the problem?" Jean prompted, when he lapsed into a reverie. "Jacky boy didn't like your special sauce?"

"I didn't even ask him about it." Keoki sighed. "I knew he would say no because he's not interested in trying new things. Especially if it's not his idea. And then I thought, *You know what was more fun than this?*"

"Dental surgery?" Jean guessed.

"Nah, having the freedom to create. Like when I got to invent all those recipes for Lillibet. That was cool. Really flexing my muscles. In a culinary way. That's what I want my daughter to see. Her dad stood for something. He went after his dreams. To make her proud."

Not it, Libby mouthed at her roommate, who was better at delivering harsh truths. Or in-your-face partial truths, depending on the situation. Jean patted Keoki's arm.

"That's beautiful, K. But she also needs diapers and shit."

He frowned at her. "You're the one who said we had to be bold."

"You guys seriously need to stop listening to me." Jean slid the container of noodles closer to her plate. "I try stuff on. Throw it out there and see what sticks."

"What are you going to do?" Libby cut in, hoping to distract Keoki from that terrifying window into their friend's mind. And maybe also pick up a plan she could loosely copy for her own life.

His shoulders sagged. "I don't know. That's why I came to you guys. You always have ideas."

Libby assumed he was talking about Jean, but he looked back and forth between the two of them, wide-eyed and trusting, like maybe Libby had something to contribute, too. Not as a wannabe influencer but as his friend.

"Okay." She set down her plate. "Let's figure this out."

Two hours later, Libby was folded up in a corner of the couch, a notebook balanced on her knees. Keoki reclined on the opposite end, feet propped on the table and his hands linked behind his head, while Jean was upside down in their only other chair, to increase the blood flow to her brain.

Righting herself with a groan, Jean checked her phone. "I think I've been awake for two days."

"Do you want me to leave?" Keoki asked.

"No." Libby glanced down at the list of search terms they'd already tried. Using Google as a Magic 8 Ball wasn't getting them anywhere except a state of depression, so it was time to switch tactics.

"What do you most want?" Libby asked Keoki, as if she were a therapist instead of his failing-at-life childhood friend.

"To be a good dad," he said at once.

"Right." Libby pretended to make a note. "I think we've established that."

"Gourmet baby food?" Jean suggested.

"I think I'd rather cook for people with teeth."

"See? That's good." Libby pointed the pen at him. "We're narrowing it down. What else?"

His cheeks puffed as he made popping sounds with his lips, like a fish on dry land. "Not having to do the same thing every day. Be able to go outside sometimes. Enough work for a small crew but not filling out paperwork for hours and hours. I want to be able to think about the food, you know? Seeing people's faces when they eat something amazing. Not stuck in an office. Or yelling at sous chefs."

"You never yell." It sounded like Jean was accusing him of something.

"Why start now?" he replied reasonably. "I want to be the person who says, *Hey, welcome. Let me feed you.* Like at Tutu's house. A place people come to relax. Sit awhile. No pressure."

Libby felt the first stirring of an idea, followed by a wash of doubt. Her faith in herself was at an all-time low.

"What?" Jean was watching her with narrowed eyes. "Do you have something to share with the class?"

"It's not that original."

"Libby, don't make me come over there."

"You would be a really scary teacher," Keoki told Jean.

"Excuse you, I'd be scary at a lot of things."

"I heard they're going to have a vacancy. At the food court in Kahuku." Libby waited for a reaction. So far her friends mostly looked confused. "The smoothie place is closing. They were talking about it at the party I worked on Saturday. Maybe that could be . . . something to consider?"

"A food truck." Keoki scratched the underside of his chin. "It's not exactly the same as a restaurant."

"No," Jean agreed, her voice slow and thoughtful. "But it might be easier to get up and running. Lower start-up costs."

"And we'd help," Libby volunteered. "I've got nothing but time." And sad feelings, but those were less helpful in launching a business.

"I'll do your logo and shit," Jean chimed in. "Menus, to-go boxes. We can paint the whole truck."

"Keoki's Kitchen could be right there next to the garlic shrimp and the mandu stand." Keoki squinted like he was looking at the picture through a haze.

"Good smells," Libby pointed out. "A lot of happy people."

"Okay." He stood and started gathering his dishes.

"That's it?" Libby set down her notebook. "You're going to do it? Just like that?" She might be on the risk-averse end of the spectrum, but surely this was too spontaneous. Even Jean looked taken aback.

"No. I'm going to go home and ask Cici what she thinks," Keoki replied. "She's way more practical than us."

Jean stacked her plate on top of his. "With all due respect to Cici, that's a pretty low bar."

Chapter 29

There were moments over the next weeks when Libby wanted to go back in time and slap her past self for suggesting Keoki open his own food truck. Not because the enterprise was cursed, unlike certain other recent schemes that sprang to mind. It was just a lot of sweaty, greasy, back-straining work.

Getting the lease was the easy part. All Keoki had to do was promise to be open for business by the end of the month. One of his cousins knew where he could find an old Airstream trailer, and he was able to source most of the cooking equipment secondhand. (There were perks to having worked in food service since your teens and being generally beloved.) They still had to rip out the interior of the trailer, retrofit it as a working kitchen, figure out the menu, clean up the lot, create a seating area, hang lights, paint signs, advertise, get permits, pass inspections, stock the pantry and refrigerator, and scrub an endless stack of pans.

That was Libby's main memory of those days, though she did a little of everything, including press releases. And then, because the clock was running down and Keoki didn't have time to train anyone else, she learned how to work the line, finishing dishes he'd prepped and doing the grunt work even she couldn't mess up.

"We're building your skills. First the crepes, now you can do a whole salad by yourself. That's a complete meal."

"I toss lettuce with a dressing you made. I'm not exactly Julia Child."

"But you're tall like Julia. Baby steps."

Toward what? Libby didn't ask. It was a relief not to think about her own life.

That didn't stop her from acknowledging the irony of her current situation. Libby was doing exactly what she'd been running from in the first place—food-related manual labor—and yet she was grateful for it. The sheer physical exhaustion, the rushing around, the endless to-do list, the tangible sense of accomplishment: it made her feel better, even when she smelled worse.

If Libby had ever managed to start a real gratitude journal, she would have written:

*I'm grateful for the chance to help Keoki, since I semi-ruined his life.** *

*Although Mr. L would have been a weird business partner.

I'm grateful I have someone to talk to who isn't a cockroach.

I'm grateful for the people who read Sincerely, Libby *because it tells me I'm not the only one flailing through life.*

I'm grateful I don't have time to worry about my personal problems.

That last one especially was a relief. It was like taking a vacation from herself, shutting down all the circuits that powered her worries about the future, and the past, anything beyond this moment. She was a rock deep underwater, sensing the movement of waves far above without feeling more than a surface vibration. The work was never-ending, but it was honest, and had a purpose beyond tricking people. Libby slept better at the end of a day of menial labor than "Lillibet" ever had while lounging in the luxury of her million-thread-count sheets.

It was a revelation she shared with the readers of the newly minted *Sincerely, Libby* account, among other guess-who-pulled-her-head-out-of-her-ass observations. Libby didn't pretend to have all the answers, any more than she fronted about her home life, but she did keep posting. *Behold my many and varied imperfections, all tied up with a hairnet and rubber gloves!*

Now that Jean was back, Libby even had artsy photos of her grungy state. A bandaged knuckle. Industrial-sized containers of cooking oil. Rorschach blots of teriyaki on a take-out napkin. A harrowing journey into the depths of their refrigerator, which was even more desolate now that they ate most of their meals at the food truck. But from cool angles that made it look almost intentional. The pictures were credited to Jean, with an additional disclaimer (*I DIDN'T TAKE THIS*), just as the pretty plates were clearly attributed to Keoki (*I DIDN'T MAKE THIS*). Which left Libby free to claim the words, even if the *I WROTE THIS* was only in her head.

And because the universe was contrary, or fond of ironic twists, or had a generally terrible sense of humor, plain old Libby was pulling more followers by the day. The numbers had easily tripled since her Lillibet days. That didn't make her an influencer in any sense of the word, but people were reading sentences that Libby wrote. And they were lines she actually meant this time.

No amount of sweat dripping into her eyes, parboiling her hands in hot soapy water, or making fun of herself online would have kept Libby from obsessing over Jefferson, if what she lacked in willpower hadn't been supplied by geography. It was as if he'd dropped off the face of the earth when he left the island. Libby couldn't find a crumb of new content online, and not for lack of trying. She kept waiting for the breakup story to appear, or a big glossy profile written by someone else. Apart from a single "Trouble in Paradise?" headline (reusing the photo of a frowning Jefferson from the jewelry booth, with the display of rings cropped out), there was nothing.

His photography website was as bare-bones as ever. Watching the famous video felt weird now that she knew the real him, like her tween self kissing a picture in a magazine instead of actual boys. Out of desperation, she even checked to see if he had a profile on any of the dating sites, though it was hard to think of something less Jefferson than advertising himself on the Internet. Plus, after narrowing her search to his part of the world, marketing algorithms decided she was a survivalist with significant quantities of facial hair and targeted her online ads accordingly. All that camo might come in handy if she decided to stalk him old-school, with binoculars. Maybe some face paint. A hat covered in moss.

But for that she'd have to fly to Wyoming. And to do *that* she needed money.

Libby's rational side tried to convince the rest of her to accept that she most likely would never see Jefferson again. Might as well go cold turkey and embrace her new life of useful drudgery.

But the part of her that believed in fairy tales secretly hoped that if and when their paths did cross, she would be worthy of him *because* of this time spent busting her ass.

Even though her heart felt more like a thick bruise than a functioning muscle, Libby was aware that her Sad and Lonely era could have been sadder and lonelier. She saw Keoki and Cici almost every day, and the food truck community was laid-back and welcoming. Her Internet friends provided commentary and occasional comic relief that helped her feel less invisible.

The person she saw least was Jean, despite sharing an apartment. Her roommate was still logging ridiculous hours at the resort. When Libby worried about her burning the candle at both ends, Jean swore she had it under control.

And she must have been getting some downtime during her shifts, because Jean often returned from the resort with new concept art for Keoki's Kitchen, gradually refining his logo (a cresting wave with an anthropomorphized pineapple holding a ukulele while riding a surfboard) and sketching out the mural for the street-facing side of the trailer.

Libby posted sneak peeks of Jean's drawings on her account, along with behind-the-scenes shots from the restaurant-in-progress. In the back of her mind, she was piecing together a longer story: "Local Boy Makes Good (Food)." A companion piece to the Tutu story, if that one ever saw the light of day. Because if you could make a restaurant out of spare parts and unexpected detours, maybe it was worth putting in that kind of work to build her career. Even if the steps weren't quite as straightforward as sanding picnic tables and scrubbing pots.

One night when she was alone again at the apartment, Libby started writing. It wasn't quite a food story, or a travel write-up, or a profile of Keoki, though it had elements of all three. The flavors of the North Shore, the locals who lived there, the tradition of hospitality. She was trying to capture a particular moment in a specific place. And hopefully attract as many customers as possible to Keoki's food truck.

When she finished, Libby sent it to Jean, who was yet again working the night shift.

Where are we sending it? Jean replied, ten minutes later. *Times? Tribune? New Yorker? Paris Review?*

Libby smiled at her phone, feeling a warmth that had nothing to do with the lack of air-conditioning. *Not sure yet. Probably someplace local.* She hesitated, afraid of sounding full of herself. *Or maybe an in-flight magazine?*

Dancing dots appeared and disappeared several times before Jean finally replied:

Hold that thought. I might have an in.

When Jean's key turned in the lock later that night, Libby forced herself not to run across the room and scream in her face, *Do you have anything to tell me about my story?*

"Hey," she said casually, peeling herself off the couch. "How was your— Is that a freaking hickey?"

"No." Jean raised a hand to her neck, covering the exact spot that had caught Libby's eye. "You don't want to hear my news?"

"Is it about your hickey?"

"No, it's about your story."

Trust Jean to play her trump card. Libby braced for disappointment. "Well?"

"I reached out to Hildy."

"What? Why?"

"Because she has sway and she likes your stuff," Jean said, as if it were that simple.

"Liked." Libby leaned hard on the final *d*. "I'm sure she hates me now."

"Time heals all wounds. I figured she was over it."

Libby doubted three and a half weeks was long enough to change anyone's mind. It certainly hadn't made a dent in her feelings about a certain reserved yet secretly tender and romantic photographer.

"And?" Libby forced herself to ask. Might as well take her medicine.

"Unknown. She hasn't gotten back to me. Which is weird, considering I told her you had a job offer from another magazine. I figured there was no way she'd back down from a challenge like that."

"Please tell me you're joking."

Jean dropped her bag on the floor. "Even if that would be a lie?"

"No more lying! I can't handle it. And besides, I want to get a job on my own merits. Not by tricking people."

"Hmmm." Her roommate moved into the kitchen, pulling a packet of ramen out of the cupboard. Libby watched her fill a mug with water and stick it in the microwave to heat.

"What?"

"Where are you applying for these hypothetical jobs?" Jean asked, smashing the packet of ramen with her fist.

"I don't know. I was thinking freelance to start. Build my portfolio."

"Why not someplace on the mainland? There are a billion times more opportunities there."

Libby would have been less taken aback if Jean had suggested job-hunting on the moon.

"Not that I'm trying to get rid of you," Jean said, as if she could hear the frantic whirring of Libby's thoughts. "I just want you to open your mind to the possibilities. In case you thought that was something you couldn't do. Because you could. Be the one to leave. If you wanted. You would be okay. *We* would be okay. And if it doesn't work out, at least you know you can make a mess and come out the other side in one piece. More or less."

There was so much packed into Jean's words. How well she knew Libby, and the exact shape of her fears. A silent acknowledgment of the fight neither of them had forgotten or wanted to repeat. The much-gentler-than-usual nudge: *Have you thought about this?*

And of course Jean was right. Even when Libby was angling for a job with Hildy, she'd never given serious consideration to moving far away. Deep down, Libby saw herself as a person who got left, not the one to venture out on her own.

Her mind was ever so slightly blown. Jean was often surprising, but never more than when she used her powers for good.

"She did like my story," Libby said, chewing her way through a new thought buffet.

Jean nodded, her expression saying, *And?*

"That means someone else might like it, too. It's not impossible." She glanced at Jean, collecting another nod of encouragement. "Because that really came from me. Not just my life but who I am." Some of the best parts of Libby, even—things she wasn't ashamed of. Her curiosity about human beings. The urge to understand how they live and why. Wanting to share those stories with other people.

She fixed Jean with a serious look. "We still can't lie." It was important to reinforce these messages as often as possible, in the hopes that someday they would stick. "I have to tell Hildy the truth."

"Fine." Her roommate shrugged as if this had been her goal all along. "You two can sort it out. I'll forward you the email."

To: hejohnson@students.cap.edu
From: lilane@gmail.com
Re: I'm sorry
Dear Hildy,

I am writing to respectfully request that you disregard the email from Jean. On the off chance you didn't delete it unread. To be clear, I do not have a job offer from anyone else.

I apologize for taking up more of your time. And everything else.

Best regards,

Libby Lane

Dear "Libby,"

Hello to you too.

I hadn't seen Jean's email but of course I went to look for it. If that was a clever ruse to get me intrigued, congratulations. It worked. So why don't you want me to see your pitch? Am I not big-time enough for you?

All best,

Hildy Johnson I

Dear Hildy,

I'm sorry if it sounded like I didn't want you to see my story about Keoki's food truck. I assumed you would rather be boiled in hot oil than ever hear from me again. Since I lied to you and messed up all your plans. Et cetera.

Pursuant to the above, I'm sure you won't want the story about Tutu either, so I am respectfully withdrawing it from submission at this time.

Best regards,

Libby

P.S. That is my real name.

Libby,

Stop apologizing and send me the freaking story about Keoki. As a friendly reminder, you gave me the piece about Tutu first.

If I decide not to run it, I will inform you in writing and provide the customary kill fee.

Please be advised that I have a legal team like you wouldn't believe.

I'll be in touch.

Hildy Johnson, Future Legend

Chapter 30

lovelillibet Do you ever have those days when it feels like you want to be alone because you're too grumpy for company but then you realize what you need is a friendly voice and maybe you shouldn't have gone dark and shut off your phone? It's like opposite day, with a side of self-sabotage.

Sincerely, Libby

Image: An overgrown trail with a rockslide blocking the way forward.

#snapoutofit #getoveryourself #pickupthephone

Hildy started the call by complaining about the fact that it *was* a call.

"This is so inefficient. You come from a dark time, JJ."

"You know how it is out here in the Wild West. It was this or a telegram. What can I do for you, Hildy?"

"I'd like to lodge a formal complaint. Where the hell have you been? I thought you might be ghosting me, but then I was like, *Be reasonable, Hildy. You're practically his best friend in the world right now.*"

There was a hopeful pause, which Jefferson filled with the expected noise of assent.

"So were you on a silent retreat? Sacked out on your couch eating ice cream straight from the container while binging K-dramas? Sitting in the dark crying?"

"Those are excellent guesses, but I was on assignment. As I told you I was going to be."

"Yeah, but I assumed you'd have your phone. What were you photographing, the eighteenth century?"

It could have been the past, given the near-total absence of civilization. "I was deep in the Alaskan wilderness. Not a lot of cell towers."

"You must have had satellite phones?"

"Yes, but people were using them to play Candy Crush."

"Haha."

Even if he'd wanted to call Hildy—or anyone else—it wouldn't have been an appropriate use of resources. And there wasn't a lot of privacy at camp. Certainly not enough for the kind of conversation he wanted to have.

Jefferson had wondered more than once if Libby would try to call while he was away. It seemed important that she be the one to contact him, so he'd know he meant more to her than a temporary distraction. The problem with this approach—well, one of them—was that she didn't have his number.

He probably should have asked Hildy for advice. It would almost have been worth the I-told-you-so's.

"What if it was an emergency and I needed to get ahold of you? Did you think about that?"

She was softening him up for something; he could tell that much over the phone.

"You're a resourceful person, Hildegarde. I'm sure you would have figured it out."

"Damn straight. Which brings us back to the reason I'm calling. Remember when you had to save me from my own poor choices, because of the blizzard and all?"

"It rings a bell."

"Well, now it's my turn. You're welcome."

He had a hunch she wasn't talking about surviving a night outdoors. "Could you be more specific?"

"I have your next job lined up."

"You're giving out assignments?" Jefferson tried to phrase it delicately. As far as he knew, Hildy was headed back to college in the fall, dreams of launching a magazine temporarily on hold.

"Work experience, babe. I set it up with my adviser. I'm finishing my last year off-campus so I can do what I want and still get enough credits to graduate. Technically I'm assisting the features editor at our Chicago paper, but that's a side hustle while I firm up the business proposal for my magazine. And then, look out world! It's Hildy time."

"Good for you. I'm impressed." Although it was a little deflating to learn that Hildy had fixed her life in a matter of weeks, while he was treading water, never getting closer to shore.

"Thanks, Reluctant Father Figure. That means a lot, coming from you. So, about this assignment?"

Despite his better judgment, Jefferson was curious. And his calendar wasn't exactly jam-packed. "What is it?"

"That's complicated."

He felt the first stirring of alarm. "Does it involve wildlife?"

"Not as such. Although, when you think about it, we're all part of the animal kingdom, aren't we?"

The sigh stayed on the inside. It was his own fault for getting his hopes up. "Then I don't see how I can help you."

"Come on, JJ," she whined. "Just say yes. Do this one little thing for me. I promise you won't regret it."

"So it's a favor for you." That made a lot more sense.

"Let's call it a mutually beneficial arrangement. What if I told you someone was trying to steal something precious from me? Would you or would you not rush to my aid?"

"Hildy. Surely you know the story about the girl who cried wolf?"

"I'm one hundred percent serious! I have turf to protect. Help me, Jefferson Jones. You're my only hope."

"I'll put some gas in the Millennium Falcon."

"I knew you'd come around. Okay, here's the deal. Are you ready?"

"Hard to say."

"Well, hold on to your pantaloons, because our girl Libby sent me a story."

Jefferson's throat went dry. A month of distance had done absolutely nothing if the thought of someone else getting an *email* from Libby kicked his pulse into the red zone.

"She did?" There. That sounded calm. If you overlooked the epic pause.

"More or less. We got there eventually. Technically our verbal agreement still applies, which obviously gives me first dibs."

"In your expert legal opinion as an employment attorney?"

"Sarcasm is not becoming in a person of your age, JJ. Now pay attention. She wrote something I want, and I need the visuals to go with. Which—if you're playing along at home—is where you come in. With your camera."

He paused to let the dust of that speech settle. "Is this another elaborate scheme?"

"What?" Hildy made a series of theatrical splutters and huffs. "You've gotten paranoid living out there in the woods alone. Why would you say that?"

"Because there are other photographers, and I'm guessing this alleged assignment is not in Wyoming. Am I getting warmer?"

"You would be. If you knew what was good for you."

Jefferson recognized that resistance was futile. Not that he'd been trying very hard to escape Hildy's machinations. "What's the story?"

"I take it you haven't been keeping up with her posts?"

"She's still doing that?" He wasn't sure why the thought bothered him; it was none of his business how Libby chose to represent herself online. Maybe he wanted to think her whole life had been turned upside down, the same as his, instead of going back to the status quo with barely a ripple.

"Just check it out, JJ. It's called *Sincerely, Libby* now. Unless you don't want the gig?"

"I want it." The words flew out before he had a chance to second-guess the decision.

"You mean you want *her*," Hildy translated. "I have to say, you might think it would get old, always being two steps ahead, but no. I'm still enjoying the ride. If you had a phone capable of FaceTiming, you'd be able to see me patting myself on the back right now."

"My loss." Though it would be nice to see her face. "You're not mad anymore?"

"I'm trying to mature into a more forgiving human being. Except with a very small subset of people who will be my sworn enemies until death, but there's only one person on that list so far. I'm willing to give Libby another chance, for your sake. And because the story is fantastic, which totally validates my initial instinct about her. Go, me."

"You're patting yourself on the back again, aren't you?"

"Hair toss, actually. Listen, between you and me, Lillibet was a teensy bit annoying. Trying to hit that love-to-hate, beautiful-monster niche is always a gamble, so this is a much safer bet, branding-wise. All the warmth, none of the smugness."

The Libby he knew *was* warm, with all the drowsy heat of a summer day, and just as golden. He'd doubted her at first, or at least his understanding of who she was, but it hadn't taken long for the fog to clear. Whatever story she'd been selling, the Libby he'd met that first day on the beach had stayed the same person all along.

"How soon can you fly out?" The clacking of a keyboard underscored her words. "I'll have my people make the arrangements."

"I'll buy my own ticket, Hildy." He wondered if she could hear the smile starting to break free. "But thanks."

Chapter 31

lovelillibet There's no way for any of us to know what we look like to other people. We might be out there stressing about our clothes or the weird thing our hair is doing and then someone passes us on the street and the only thing they notice is our earlobes.

I think the takeaway here is, why bother? You can't control it, so we might as well let it ride. Think of all the time I've saved over the course of my life by not brushing my hair.

Sincerely, Libby

Image: A person with long messy blonde hair covering their face.

#scruffyforlife #noskills #whodis

The rental car's navigation system directed Jefferson to a gravel lot off the highway. It was only a few miles from where they'd stayed before, but light-years removed in style. Everything about this place said, *Relax, feel the breeze, eat something good.* As opposed to, *Be careful with my museum-quality faucets.*

The sense of place was so strong it brought back all the feelings from the last time he'd experienced this honeyed light and the bracing tang of the ocean. It was like déjà vu, only instead of a prickle of awareness, he was swimming in regret and longing.

What if she didn't want to talk to him? He was the one who'd left without giving her a chance to explain.

Keoki's eyes widened when Jefferson approached the window of the food truck. He looked him over, lips pursed like he was considering whether to fry Jefferson whole or slice him into sashimi. When he saw the package of shrimp crackers sticking out of Jefferson's bag, Keoki gave a grudging nod.

"She's in back."

The "she" in question rounded the corner of the trailer before Jefferson could get there, pulling something off her head as she stepped into view. Her long hair tumbled free, glinting gold in the afternoon light.

For a heartbreaking second, Jefferson worried Keoki had tipped her off and she was running away. Then their eyes met, and the sun rose for the second time that day, filling him with the molten glow of morning.

"What are you doing here?" she whispered, still standing where she'd frozen at the sight of him.

"Hildy asked me to give you this." He handed her the marked-up pages that had been express-mailed to his apartment.

He watched the confusion give way to surprise. "My story?"

"She had some notes." Presented on actual paper in red ink, because Hildy figured that would appeal to a "more traditional audience," as she'd explained via Post-it. That was apparently a diplomatic way of saying "old."

"I—don't think I can think about that right now. I mean, thank you. But. Um. Words. What even are they?" Libby looked at the ground. "Is that why you came?"

"I'm your photographer." Hopefully in more ways than one.

"Oh." She scuffed the gravel with the toe of her sneaker. "Is that the only reason you're here?"

Jefferson shook his head, both as a negation and because he

couldn't believe how bad he was at this. "It seemed like a decent cover. In case you slammed the door in my face."

Libby made a show of examining the open space around them. "I guess I could clang the lid of the Dumpster."

"Do you want to?"

"Not really."

It was past time to stop talking around what was really going on. They'd had enough of not leveling with each other.

"I'm sorry," she said.

Her words overlapped with Jefferson's rushed, "I came back for you."

"You go first," she said.

"I was away."

"You were?" A hopeful note had entered her voice.

"Alaska."

"That's far."

"It felt that way." He took a few seconds to look at her, basking in the luxury of being this close. Even if he'd like to be closer. "I brought you something."

"From Alaska?" She sounded so excited, he kicked himself for not picking up a stuffed moose.

"Before that." He took a step in her direction. "I got you a Me-mas present."

"There's no such thing as Me-mas."

"Don't tell my nieces. They still believe."

Her gaze fell to his bag, expression softening when she spotted the crackers. "You brought me crackers?"

"Would you have preferred flowers?"

"No."

He smiled, in relief and fondness. "Good. These are your emotional support snacks." Jefferson handed them to her. "This is your real present." Reaching back into the bag, he pulled out a small satin pouch.

After a beat of hesitation, she took it from him, carefully un-snapping the closure to let the contents spill onto her palm. He'd wondered if she would recognize it; the immediate curving of her lips told him she did.

"For me?" She threaded the delicate gold chain through her fingers, letting the pearl they'd found together dangle beneath.

"It always was."

She blinked hard, brushing at the front of her apron. "I imag-ined this a little differently. Seeing you again. For some reason I thought I'd be in a ball gown."

"Why?"

"I'm not sure. I wasn't supposed to smell like fried food, either."

"Do you want me to come back later?"

She grabbed his forearm, holding him in place. A pulse of heat passed from her skin to his. "Don't leave."

He took a second to gather himself. "I missed you, Libby."

"You did?"

"Every day."

Hesitantly, she raised her eyes to his face. "I thought you were mad. About the lying."

"I freaked out a little." He was man enough to admit it. "I was afraid you were playing me. Or I read the signs all wrong. But then I realized that didn't feel right."

"And then what did you think?" She was a little breathless, like this was the most suspenseful story she'd ever heard.

"That I should have trusted my gut and stuck around long enough to hear what you had to say."

"It was kind of a tense moment."

"I still shouldn't have run out on you."

"You came back," she pointed out, like that evened the slate.

"I couldn't stay away."

Her eyes were huge, the afternoon sun turning them the color of a shady creek. "Yeah?"

"It felt like I left part of myself across an ocean." He touched the place on his chest that had ached for her.

"That sounds painful."

"It was. But now I can breathe again."

"Oh." It was a tiny puff of air, like that was all she could get out. And then she was crashing into him, arms twining around his neck. Jefferson staggered back a step, bumping into the side of the trailer.

When her tongue slid between his lips, it took him apart. He was distantly aware that they were making out in a parking lot. Losing control in public wasn't part of his plan for the day. Then again, he hadn't gotten much further in his plotting than finding her, and this was so much better than that.

She pulled away, studying his face. Jefferson had no doubt his pupils were blown out.

"You smell it, don't you?" She lowered her nose to her shoulder, sniffing. "Conch fritters?"

He put his face to her hair, breathing in. "I promise you I'm not thinking about fritters."

She sighed in his arms, like her main worry in life had been resolved. "I don't understand why you aren't running the other way. You haven't exactly seen me at my best. Or even as me, most of the time."

"You were always Libby to me. I don't think you ever tried to hide that." He stroked her back, fingers pressing along the sides of her spine. "I know where you come from. I know you take your coffee with cream, and you snack when you're nervous. I know you're kind to strangers and you like to make wishes. I know the difference between your real laugh and when you're pretending. I know what it feels like to wake up next to you." He raised his hand to cup her cheek. "That seems like a pretty good start."

Her eyes were wet when she tipped her face up for another kiss. "I know something," she whispered against his lips.

"What?"

"My roommate isn't home."

That was all Jefferson needed to hear. "My car's over there."

"It's kind of a pit," she warned him. "And I don't have a hot tub. Or a laser light show in the bathroom."

"That's a relief."

"Yeah," said Keoki's booming voice, as he stepped out the back door of the trailer. "It is a relief. You two are a health code violation waiting to happen." He turned his attention back to the phone propped between his cheek and shoulder. "They came up for air. Okay. Nice doing business with you. Mahalo. Here." He held the phone out to Libby. "She's going to run my story in her paper."

Libby was still frowning as she held the phone to her ear. "It's Hildy," she reported. "I'm supposed to put her on speaker."

It looked like she regretted the decision when the words, "I hope you have your clothes on, sex fiends," blared from the phone.

"We're in a parking lot," Jefferson told her.

"Like that would stop you. You're welcome, by the way."

"Thank you," Libby said, before adding a hesitant, "You're really going to run the story about Keoki?"

"Front of the Living section. Sunday edition. I'm saving Tutu for my magazine, so don't get any funny ideas. But I wasn't talking about that. You can thank me for playing matchmaker."

"I would have gotten here eventually." It was a mild protest; Jefferson liked to give credit where it was due.

"Like what, a message in a bottle? You're too old to play the waiting game, JJ. The modern world moves fast."

"Actually," Libby cut in, "about the magazine. I really want to start at the bottom and work my way up."

"That's between you and JJ. You're both consenting adults." Hildy cackled at her own joke. "Seriously, how bad do you miss me right now? Don't you wish we could all go get some shave ice and shoot the breeze?"

"It's not the top item on my agenda." Jefferson's eyes met Libby's.

"Okay, horndog. I get it. Don't worry, I'm sure we'll be in touch soon. I've got ideas for days. We'll figure out the job stuff later. Ciao, lovers." With a smacking *mwah,* she ended the call.

Libby blinked a few times before passing the phone back to Keoki, who exchanged it for a large paper sack.

"What's this?" she asked, looking at the sealed paperboard cartons stacked inside.

"Dinner." Keoki winked. "And breakfast."

Jefferson took hold of her free hand as they started toward his car. They kept stealing glances at each other, making sure this was really happening.

"One more thing," Libby said, when he let go to dig out his keys.

"What's that?"

"Shotgun." She pumped her fist, dancing a little in victory. "Frickin' finally."

He knew exactly how she felt.

Epilogue

lovelillibet I used to think that when I grew up, I'd automatically have fancy pajamas. Satiny, lacy things that actually match. I figured it would be like getting boobs, which never worked out for me either, to be honest. Unfortunately, it turns out you have to buy all that crap (pajamas, I mean, though you could buy boobs, too, if you had the money), and then take care of it, and I'm pretty sure most of that stuff is hand-wash.

Which is why I still sleep in T-shirts I've had since middle school. They're halfway to being vintage.

Sincerely, Libby

Image: A pile of ratty T-shirts strewn all over an unmade bed.

#whatisanegligee #silkcostshowmuch #handwashthis

"This bed is my new favorite place," Jefferson said the next morning. It was their private, clothing-optional island. If they had a source of fresh drinking water, he might never leave.

Libby fed him another bite of the reheated malasada from Keoki's care package. "Better than a sleeping bag in the woods?"

"Depends on the company." He stretched, careful not to dislodge Libby from where she'd perched beside him, one long leg draped across his hips like she was holding him in place. As if he had any desire to move. "You made it sound a lot worse. Your bed."

"I was in my exaggerating phase."

"And now?"

"Goldilocks era. Everything is exactly right." She bent to brush a sugary kiss across his lips.

"You even have art."

She leaned back, gazing at the ceiling above them. "I was hoping you wouldn't notice."

"Kind of hard to miss." Though in all honesty, it had taken him a while to register the giant painting suspended over the bed, given the more pressing distractions.

"I know. It's weird. Like I enjoy lying here staring at myself. Maybe I should put mirrors on the ceiling."

"I've heard worse ideas."

Libby fought back a grin. "I guess it wouldn't be me if there wasn't something bizarre." She settled a hand on his stomach. "You don't mind?"

It wasn't until she tipped her chin up at the familiar pink-and-green nudie painting that he was able to think beyond the movement of her fingers sliding up his chest. "I could get used to it."

Jefferson was talking about all of it. The two of them in a bedroom, however it was decorated. But Libby shook her head, a little sadly.

"You can't, actually. Jean moves it around. Once I opened the freezer and it was all rolled up so the head was staring back at me."

"Keeps you on your toes."

She made a hum of agreement. "Are you tired?"

"Sleep is overrated." He ran a hand up the curve of her calf. It wasn't jet lag making his heart race. Jefferson had never asked his body to contain this much happiness. He was a two-liter of carbonation and caffeine, all shaken up.

Being with her had always felt easy, since that first day on the beach. Now that all the walls of make-believe had been torn down, Jefferson could see the change in Libby. It was the same lightness he felt in himself. There was no more holding her breath, waiting for the crash. This Libby belly-laughed and fed him breakfast in bed and sprawled all over him like he was her personal body pillow.

And she told him stories. About silly things, like the time she and Jean spent the day at the airport holding up signs for fake passengers they were pretending to meet, just to see the double takes as people wondered if these two college kids were really picking up Bruce Springsteen or the second runner-up roller derby champions from Toledo, Ohio.

He couldn't remember the last time he'd talked to someone all night, peeling back layers until they were both half drunk with lack of sleep and the thrill of discovery. Lying together in the dark, she'd shared more about the work she wanted to do, connecting with people on a deeper level—instead of flitting from one person to the next, more interested in the surface than in what was underneath.

"I think we all want that," she said, voice husky with tiredness. "To be known. Only we're too scared to show our real selves."

"I want to see all of you, Libby."

"Um, mission accomplished?" Laughing, she rolled away before he could administer the tickling that remark deserved.

"You know what I mean."

"I do." She settled back against him, head resting on his shoulder. Her hand covered his heart. "I couldn't help showing myself to you. It slipped out."

Maybe that was how it worked. Some people fit each other like a lock and key. Hadn't he sensed from the minute he met Libby that she could get under his skin? The unraveling was a steady progression from that point to this.

It didn't mean it would be easy, or that they'd figured out how or where they'd see each other next. For now, it was enough for Jefferson to know they both wanted to try. That was a hope you could build on, one day at a time.

Morning light filtered through the blinds. A whole new day with Libby. He felt like his pockets were filled with gold. Or would have been, if he were wearing pants.

She fed him another bite of malasada. "What are you thinking about, Pensive McPenserson?"

He considered not telling her, in case it ruined the mood, but Jefferson had forgotten how to hold back when it came to Libby. "I was thinking this would be my Me-mas."

"Here? In this apartment?" She lowered her voice like the building might resent her incredulous tone.

"You're happy. I'm happy. We're together." Three ways of saying the same thing, but it was worth repeating.

"And we have donuts."

"What more could you want out of life?"

Libby thought it over. "I don't know."

"See?"

"I do see." She ran a finger down the center of his chest. "You're covered in sugar. Again." Shaking her head in mock-disappointment, Libby shifted so she was kneeling above him.

He closed his eyes as her tongue flicked over his skin. Cheek and then jaw, the hollow beneath his collarbone, a little lower.

"Right there?" he asked. "Are you sure?"

"This nipple is practically glazed," she assured him. "Oops, missed a spot."

Jefferson slowly returned to earth, watching Libby sit up and reach for her donut.

"You know you're ruining my brand," she said.

"I don't see how. Unless your brand is not licking people?"

"I'm supposed to be tragic. A hot mess."

"One out of three isn't bad." Jefferson's hand moved over her hip in a light caress. How was her skin this soft? Maybe it was the air here. "You'll have to spin it."

She took a bite of the pastry before pulling off another piece for him. "How about this? *After a wild night with my hot out-doorsy boyfriend who is super-fit from hiking through the woods, I like to refuel with fried carbs and sugar.*"

"Nice. You could throw in a fashion tip."

"Such as?"

He touched the pearl at her throat. "Jewelry looks better with bare skin."

"Maybe not super-practical in all climates."

"I didn't realize practical was the goal."

"Yes. The new me tries to deal in very realistic advice. And then I wrap it all up with a pithy saying."

"It's a marathon, not a sprint?" he suggested.

"If you want to make an omelet, you have to break some eggs."

"You win some, you lose some."

"But then you win again."

Jefferson rolled to the side, pulling Libby on top of him.

"I was going to get you coffee." It was a mild protest, especially when she undercut it by settling herself more fully against him.

"I'm feeling plenty awake," he assured her.

"Maybe that's what I should tell everyone. Some things are better than caffeine."

"Don't tell everyone." He kissed her lower lip, and then the upper. "Just me."

"Just you," she agreed. "Love, Libby."

Acknowledgments

If I close my eyes, I can almost conjure sand underfoot, a salt-tinged breeze, and tickling tendrils of the Pacific washing against the shore—but it's a lot harder to see the screen of my computer, so I'd better stop. Sitting in this cluttered office, thousands of miles from any coastline, I'm grateful for the memory of beautiful places, and the family who were there with me: in the waves, at the food trucks, trekking to waterfalls, standing in line for shave ice, staying up late to talk story. Special thanks to Auntie Margo, Uncle Hank, Kalanikau, Pohai, Sean, Micah, Evan, and Kyla for hosting.

While writing this book, I had the privilege of reading my aunt Margo's collected stories from her years as a kupuna in Oahu public schools, about 'aumakua and Night Marchers and why you should never drive through the Pali tunnel with pork in your car. Her kid-friendly take on the tale of Malaekahana directly inspired the revisionist version Tutu Lua tells Hildy's uncle.

A solid third of my adolescent scrapbook is devoted to the trip I took to Hawaii with my aunt Kathy when I was twelve, which opened my eyes to the glamour of travel, and discovering new places through food, as well as the specific magic of the North Shore. More recently, she talked me through the ups and downs of goat ownership and supplied a steady stream of articles about island life to keep me inspired during a drab midwestern winter. Thank you for broadening my horizons, and being a constant source of aunt-spiration.

The other spark for this book came from old movies, specifically of the screwball comedy variety. I inherited my love of Hollywood's golden age directly from my mother. (Inheritance, indoctrination; it's a fine line.) Mom, thanks for introducing me to the fast-talking romance of all those black-and-white classics, which for me remain the epitome of wit and style. I took most of the F-bombs out of this book for you. You're welcome.

Thanks also to Bridget Smith, for immediately saying "yes, that one!" when I pitched the idea of retelling my favorite old movies as modern-day rom-coms, even though it required leaping into a whole new genre.

Everything I write depends on the encouragement and insight of my genius critique partners, Miranda Asebedo and Megan Bannen. I couldn't do this job/life/calling without you, and your sustaining text threads and group calls. Hail to the NDC!

My sister Claire interrupts important lawyering to talk through each step on the writing journey with me. I feel a teensy bit guilty about taking up so much of her time, but mostly incredibly lucky.

Thank you to my friend and fellow romance reader/writer Laura Huffman, for early feedback that filled me with hope, and to the writer friends who helped with advice and camaraderie at every stage, including Natalie Parker, Sierra Simone, Maggie Light, Julie Tollefson, and Sarah Henning.

Things that make me feel gloriously alive: buttercream frosting, and the incredible blurbs I received from authors I'm used to admiring through the narrow end of a telescope. To Sarah Hogle, Alicia Thompson, Lily Chu, Megan Bannen, and Suzanne Park, please know that you could not have bestowed your kindness on a more grateful object.

I am profoundly indebted to my wonderful editor, Lisa Bonvissuto, for opening the door to Romancelandia. Thank you for your faith in me and these stories, for laughing at my jokes, and for gently guiding me onto the right path with your insightful notes. It's been a joy working with you and the team at St. Martin's, including Meryl Levavi, Olga Grlic, Kejana Ayala, Zoe Miller, Ken Silver, Chrisinda Lynch, Janna Dokos, and Eileen Rothschild. I can't wait to collaborate on Jean's even more madcap adventures! Special thanks to copy editor Dave Cole, for curbing my chaotic tendencies and saving Lillibet from the unfortunate hashtag Layer Snot Lies, and to artist Vi-An Nguyen for a cover that manages to be both gorgeously evocative (the light! The colors!) and still make room for those misbehaving goats to crash the party.

Pithy acknowledgments are clearly not my strong suit, but I'll try to wrap things up with a big blanket hug for my family, who are so awesomely supportive of this book writing gig. Brothers, nieces, nephews, in-laws, my personal hype squad (aka Dad), the whole extended Henry/Howlett clan, my belle-fille Lucile, future podcast cohost and in-house creative consultant Gillian, and my husband Fred, who will turn straight to this page after checking to see if I dedicated this one to him. (Be patient! I have a plan.) You are all as essential to me as snacks are to Libby.

And finally, to every reader who picks up this book, thank you so much! I hope it goes down as easy as a bowl of Matsumoto's shave ice on a sunny afternoon.

About the Author

Frédéric Sellet

Amanda Sellet is a former journalist and the author of rom-coms for teens and adults, including *By the Book,* which *Booklist* described in a starred review as "impossible to read without laughing out loud." She loves old movies, baked goods, and embarrassing her teen daughter. *Hate to Fake It to You* is her adult debut.